The Affairs of Sherlock Holmes

By

Sax Rohmer

Volume II

THE AFFAIR OF THE

VOODOO MENACE

• • •

Edited by

Alan Lance Andersen

INTRODUCTION

Sax Rohmer, the pen name of Arthur Sarsfield Ward, is best known today for his blood-and-thunder mysteries involving the insidious Chinese criminal mastermind — Fu Manchu. These stories, first published in magazines, were subsequently made into movies, radio dramas, theatre dramas, television shows, and published books.

Less known (but perhaps better written) were Rohmer's stories of Bazarada — who was based on Rohmer's friend Harry Houdini, as evidenced by this quotation from *The Jade Serpent:* "Locks meant less than nothing to Bazarada; no prison bars could cage him. Men of first-class intelligence credited him with occult powers. And those who were present when, handcuffed and leg-ironed in a sealed wine cask, he was lowered into the Rhine at Duesseldorf, will remember the moment when he swam to the surface. My own seal, amongst others, was intact on the cask when we hauled it up. Inside, we found the manacles and leg-irons ..."

And then there were Rohmer's tales of Chinatown from 1916. These were set in the London Limehouse district near the Thames docks, as opposed to the better-known San Francisco Chinatown or the ones in New York City, Los Angeles, Vancouver, Chicago, Toronto, Boston, Philadelphia, Detroit, and Montreal; as well as international Chinatowns in Manila, Nagasaki, and elsewhere. Unlike San Francisco's Chinatown, London's is NOT a tourist destination. In Rohmer's day, it was an unwholesome slum with a warren of dark narrow streets and shadowy alleyways, derelict warehouses, dangerous taverns, and opium dens. Limehouse before the first World War housed an Asian community, largely criminal, which lived by foreign laws more ancient than the laws of England.

It was an area in which Rohmer loved to go "slumming" — and he made lifelong friends of many of the Chinese who lived there. It was on a dark and foggy night in Limehouse, in an alley off a dingy street near the canal, that Sax Rohmer had a *very brief glimpse* of the Chinese crime lord that ruled London's Chinatown in 1911, and it nearly scared him to death. He said the man was the living embodiment of Satan. It was this "King of Chinatown," master of gambling houses, cocaine, and opium who served as Rohmer's model for the character Fu Manchu.

In the late 1800s and early 1900s, at the peak of Sherlock Holmes' popularity, a number of writers wrote their own mystery stories that were in many ways similar to Holmes. Many of Sax Rohmer's little-known stories read, but for the names and places, almost exactly like Arthur Conan Doyle's original Sherlock Holmes stories — in fact, much of the language is more like the original Holmes canon than most stories written by modern authors. Rohmer was also a much better writer than many of the other "Rivals of Sherlock Holmes" authors.

The editor of this volume has carefully edited some of Rohmer's best Chinatown tales into Sherlock Holmes pastiches.

PREFACE

Rivals of Conan Doyle:

Inherent Problems for Modern Authors Writing Sherlock Holmes Pastiches

By Alan Lance Andersen

Modern authors from John Dickson Carr to Nicholas Meyer have attempted to recapture the mood of gaslit London and the mystique of Sir Arthur Conan Doyle's adventures of Sherlock Holmes by writing "new" Holmes novels and short stories. Such authors usually seize upon certain elements of the Holmes canon — the tobacco in the slipper, the violin, the use of cocaine — to lend an air of verisimilitude to their "Victorian" stories. Yet these attempts invariably fail to capture the original flavor of the Conan Doyle tales.

On the other hand, Conan Doyle's contemporaries — such mystery authors as Robert Eustace, L.T. Meade, Clifford Halifax, Richard Harding Davis, and Sax Rohmer (whose stories are featured in this volume) — were writing about characters of their own invention; nevertheless they sound more like Conan Doyle than do any of his modern deliberate imitators. It is my belief that this results from the Victorians sharing a common linguistic and rhetorical background, world view, and social mind-set which later writers can never fully understand. Writers of "new" Victorian mysteries would do well to focus on the language and societal culture of the period rather than on furniture and dress; and they should avoid having characters behave in ways which, clever though they may be in terms of plot, are nevertheless out-of-character for a 19th Century writer to include in a story.

• • •

Most mystery writers acknowledge Edgar Allan Poe and Sir Arthur Conan Doyle for their roles in the development of the mystery story as we know it today. Throughout the history of detective literature, there have been outstanding writers whose works have helped to shape the mystery genre. Beginning in 1891, the *Strand Magazine* began featuring a Sherlock Holmes short story in each issue, which assured instant success for the new publication. Prior to that time, there had been only two Holmes tales, both novels. The first, *A Study in Scarlet*, was published in *Beeton's Christmas Annual* in 1887 and the second, *The Sign of the Four*, was published in *Lippincott's Magazine* in 1890.

It was with the publication of "A Scandal in Bohemia" in *The Strand Magazine* in July 1991 that stories really caught on. They made Conan Doyle's career and catapulted *The Strand Magazine* to the position of premier periodical of its day. It was not long before other writers of short mystery fiction began to appear in *Pearson's Magazine, Cassell's Magazine, The Harmsworth Magazine, The Royal Magazine, The Windsor Magazine, The Ludgate Monthly,* and *The London Magazine* — as well as in *The Strand Magazine*. Such authors included L. T. Meade, Robert Eustace, Clifford Halifax, Jacques Futrelle, Baroness Orczy, Brett Harte, Jack London, Guy Boothby, Arthur Morrison, E. W. Hornung, William McHarg, Edwin Balmer, Samuel Hopkins Adams, Francis Lynde, Catherine Louisa Pirkis, William Hope Hodgson, Ernest Bramah, Richard Harding Davis, Robert Barr, Cutcliffe Hyne, Grant Allen, and Sarsfield Ward (before *and* after he took the pen name of Sax Rohmer). These authors created their own characters — detectives and master criminals — and the first golden age of mystery writing began.

A number of modern writers have undertaken to write their own Sherlock Holmes mysteries, yet none of these recent stories has ever fully captured the quality and flavor of the original. Eric Zorn writes in the Chicago *Tribune*, "One can scarcely turn around in a bookstore without seeing (Holmes) rocketing into space, solving President Kennedy's assassination, or consorting with clones and vampires ... Modern writers, using all the gimmicks at their disposal, seem determined to cash in on the late Arthur Conan Doyle's work."

Even if we discount the science fiction and fantasy writers of Sherlock Holmes stories and focus on those honestly trying to recreate the style and tone of the original canon, we find that modern authors invariably fail to capture the flavor of the Conan Doyle stories. They use the "trappings" of Sherlock Holmes — the tobacco in the slipper, the violin, the use of cocaine — to lend an air of verisimilitude to their "Victorian" stories. But these imitators often attempt to introduce ideas of their own which are not consistent with late Victorian times, language, or literary conventions.

Other modern writers have written period mysteries set in 19th Century England using their own characters or fictionalized versions of historical figures. Some of these stories are quite successful in recreating Victorian-seeming prose, while others fall into the same traps as the Conan Doyle imitators.

Among the better known of the latter-day Sherlock Holmes novels are Nicholas Meyer's *The Seven-Per-Cent Solution* and *The West End Horror*. Meyer's stories are intriguing, his knowledge of Holmes is thorough, and his attention to detail is excellent. The main problem with these stories is that Meyer is an inveterate name-dropper. He insists on peopling his stories with such famous figures as Sigmund Freud, Oscar Wilde, and George Bernard Shaw.

While Holmes would certainly have had dealings with celebrities like Wilde and Shaw, Conan Doyle would never have actually named them in a story; he would have used euphemisms like "a notorious poet" or "a celebrated playwright." In *The West End Horror*, Holmes is called in to help capture Jack the Ripper. Perhaps the worst example of this is a scene in *The Seven-Per-Cent Solution* with a cameo appearance by a character from Anthony Hope's *The Prisoner of Zenda*. This plays no part whatsoever in the story; it simply gives Meyer the opportunity to footnote, "Here is one of the great accidental meetings in recent English history, pregnant with all sorts of irony."

The fact is that Conan Doyle never mentions real people by name in his stories. It was a matter of Victorian reserve to be subtle about such things. Conan Doyle features the King of Bohemia in one of his tales, at about the same time that Robert Louis Stevenson was writing stories in the *New Arabian Nights* about Prince Florizel of Bohemia — who in turn was helped in solving a mystery by "a celebrated London detective." Conan Doyle and Stevenson were correspondents at this time, and "borrowed" each others characters. But it would have been in poor taste to name them. Good taste was everything to a Victorian gentleman.

Conan Doyle might have had Dr. Watson come home to find Holmes taking cocaine, but he would never have been so indiscreet as to *quote* Holmes' unfortunate language while under the influence. But in Michael Hardwick's *Revenge of the Hound,* an entire chapter is devoted to describing Holmes' aberrant behavior and his berating of Watson during a cocaine session. This so shatters the familiar image of Holmes' and Watson's domestic scene that it ruins the rest of the book. One of the things that makes the Sherlock Holmes stories so endearing to readers are the glimpses of domestic life at 221B Baker Street, and Hardwick totally failed to capture that mood.

The biggest problem with many modern Sherlock Holmes stories is that the author comes up with his own pet notions about Holmes and tries to be cute in his portrayal. For example, in *The Private Life of Sherlock Holmes,* Holmes asserts that he and Watson were homosexual lovers. Even if that were true — which it is NOT — Holmes would never say anything about it. If one is going to write stories using someone else's characters, the least one can do is be faithful to the original.

Another problem for the modern writer is that the English language has changed considerably since Victorian times. While we can read and easily understand Victorian prose, we tend not to *think* in that style, which makes writing it difficult. Furthermore, phrases that sound perfectly normal to us may not have even been used back then. In the recent television production of *Jack the Ripper,* which is set in 1888, Michael Caine starring as Detective Inspector Frederick Abberline says to another character, "Shut your face." According to Wenworth and Flexner's *Dictionary of American Slang,* this figure of speech was not used until after 1915, and it is an American expression — not British.

Such anachronisms, while subtle, can create an overall effect in which the story simply does not "ring true."

Zorn writes, "Revival pastiches typically have been greeted with hoots of derision from true Sherlockians, a righteous bunch who do not suffer gladly transgressions upon the sacred memory of Holmes and Dr. Watson."

A good way to get a feel for authentic Victorian language is to read Castle Books' *Rivals of Sherlock Holmes*, a two-volume facsimile edition of original mystery stories from *Strand Magazine, Windsor Magazine, The Royal Magazine,* and other publications from the era of gaslight and hansom cabs. These stories, written by the 19th century writers listed above, read very much like those of Sir Arthur Conan Doyle. One sees numerous similarities in style — and these are the hallmarks of late Victorian prose. One will also be able to pick out the elements of Conan Doyle's personal writing style, for they stand out distinctly once one is steeped in the language of the period. The original illustrations reproduced in these facsimile editions also help create a feeling for the Victorian era.

One of the best of the "rivals" is Richard Harding Davis' "In the Fog," a trilogy of short stories originally published in *The Windsor Magazine*. A group of gentlemen at a private London club regale each other with tales of a convoluted mystery that so engages the interest of Sir Andrew, an elderly gentleman and devoted Sherlock Holmes fan, that he fails to depart for the House of Lords to make a speech on the Navy Increase Bill. The surprise ending of this story is a true Victorian masterpiece.

The prolific L.T. Meade, one of the foremost women mystery writers of the time, collaborated with Dr. Edgar

Beaumont to write a series of stories in which Dr. Clifford Hallifax (Beaumont's pseudonym) solves a number of insidious crimes. With Robert Eustace, she penned a trilogy of stories about Madame Sarah, "The Sorceress of the Strand" — a villainess to rival Conan Doyle's Professor Moriarty.

Some late Victorian mysteries featured the villain as a protagonist who habitually outwitted the police. E. W. Hornung's cricketer and notorious master thief A. J. Raffles was so popular that the series was continued by other writers after Hornung's death.

Baroness Orczy — better known, perhaps, for her tales of the adventurous and heroic Scarlet Pimpernel — penned a series of stories about Patrick "Skin O' My Tooth" Mulligan, a lawyer with a reputation for winning particularly close criminal court cases.

All of these mystery stories — and those found in other anthologies — illustrate the style of writing, the social attitudes, and the literary conventions of the late Victorian and Edwardian period. There is a naive freshness to these stories and a mystique not easily captured by modern writers.

The most "successful" of Conan Doyle's plagiarists was a contemporary unemployed architect by the name of Arthur Whitaker, whose story, *The Man Who Was Wanted,* was subsequently believed by Adrian and Denis Conan Doyle to have been written by their father. The story of literary feuding and fiascoes that surrounded the publication of Arthur Whitaker's story is presented in its entirety in Jon L. Lellenberg's *Nova 57 Minor.*

Unlike Sir Arthur's modern imitators, Whitaker wrote his Holmes story at the same time that Conan Doyle was at the peak of his popularity; and there is a ring of authenticity in the narrative that modern imitators are lacking. Still, Whitaker's story might never have seen the light of day were it not for a series of misadventures which led to his manuscript being discovered among Sir Arthur's papers after his death — *with no mention of the typescript's origin!*

Although Whitaker's attempt to imitate Conan Doyle's literary style was more successful than those of modern imitators, it did not feel quite right to Holmes aficionados. Whitaker wrote the story in the *style of the period* and included *all the traditional trappings* of a Sherlock Holmes story, but his *personal writing style* differed from Sir Arthur's! This was lost on sons Adrian Conan Doyle and Denis Conan Doyle (who not only deified their father's memory but who had also reportedly been paid $15,000 for the story) — but it was not lost on daughter Jean Conan Doyle. Lellenberg says Jean was certain *The Man Who Was Wanted* was not written by her father when she first read the story in the *Sunday Dispatch*, and that she was put out with her brother Adrian for not telling her of it's impending publication.

Lellenberg writes "Adrian lacked the special knowledge, or insight, or prescience (or whatever it is) of the dyed-in-the-wool enthusiast ... for whom the story did not 'ring true.' Some have that sensitivity, while others do not. Only one of Conan Doyle's children had it, and she had not been consulted."

Adrian Conan Doyle was adamant in his denunciation of writers who "plagiarized" his father's characters. Lellenberg describes Adrian preventing Ellery Queen from publishing an anthology of Sherlockian parodies and pastiches. A promising series of Holmes pastiches by mystery writer Stuart Palmer was "nipped in the bud" when "the legal heirs of the late Sir Arthur Conan Doyle set up shrill wails of agony at the very idea of the continuance of the series."

Adrian described his views on plagiarism and the Whitaker story in a letter to Vincent Starrett:

"Is it not infuriating that one can be put to so much trouble and inconvenience, after 40 years, thanks directly to the abominable habit of a would-be writer in making use of characters invented by an established Author."

Considering his attitude, it is amusing to note that Adrian Conan Doyle himself subsequently wrote a series of Sherlock Holmes stories in collaboration with John Dickson Carr in the 1940s. These stories have interesting mystery plots and are fairly constrained in their adherence to the original format, yet they are flawed. John Dickson Carr's writing style is so forceful that his personality comes through in spite of his efforts to imitate Sir Arthur.

In a review of Edward B. Hanna's *The Whitechapel Horrors,* another book in which Holmes is called in to help capture Jack the Ripper, Bruce Southworth points out that book's shortcomings (*Once Upon a Crime,* Vol. 1, No. 4). At one point early in *The Whitechapel Horrors*, Watson espouses the out-of-character sentiment that "the poor are poor because they're deserving of nothing better. They could rise above their station if they wished ... Those who choose to live like animals do so because they are animals." Southworth point out that this quote colors the rest of the book.

11

In another passage, Holmes mutters a celebrated modern obscenity. According to Southworth, this is "Not an uncommon word nowadays, but (one) which, in my almost 25 years of involvement with the adventures of Holmes, and the 'writings about the writings,' is a first."

It is very doubtful whether the word in question was used in that fashion in Victorian England. It was never used in print when I was a boy; Watson would certainly never have quoted Holmes — even if he *had* said it.

Southworth writes, "It is an extensively researched and well-written Ripper novel. As for Hanna's efforts to write a Holmes novel, this must be judged a failure. If you ... pretend that the characters of Holmes, Watson, Mycroft, *et al.* are other than those created by Doyle, you will enjoy *The Whitechapel Horrors*. If you are a Holmesian purist, this is not the book for you." By this standard, *The Man Who Was Wanted* is a success, for the characters are very true to the canon. Southworth further points out, "Sir Arthur Conan Doyle advised would-be pastiche writers to invent their own characters rather than use his. Hanna should have heeded the sage advice from the man who knew Holmes best, his creator."

This final statement refers to Conan Doyle's letter to Whitaker (reproduced in *Nova 57 Minor)*, wherein Sir Arthur writes of *The Man Who Was Wanted,* "You should ... change the names and try to get published yourself. Of course you could not use the names of my characters."

It is the modern authors who take Sir Arthur's advice that are most successful. Victorian mystery stories were very much formula writing, and were sometimes rather stuffy and naive.

By combining the Victorian style with modern plot and characterization, it is possible to come up with stories that are even better than some of the originals.

A particularly successful period novel is Peter Lovesey's *Bertie and the Tinman*, which actually reads as though it were written by a gentleman of the 1880s, but which has more excitement and humor than is usually found in the writing of that period. In this case, the detective is Albert Edward, the Prince of Wales and future King of England. Since Lovesey is not attempting to imitate another writer's style of writing, the use of a historical figure as the hero is appropriate.

Another noteworthy period novel is *The Detective and Mr. Dickens*, by modern author W. J. Palmer, in which Charles Dickens and Wilkie Collins are enlisted to help Inspector Field — a Bow Street policeman found in Dickens' sketches in *Household Words* — to solve a murder committed by a group of "gentlemen." Dickens and Collins are able to enter London's private clubs to gather information where Inspector Field would never be accepted. The tale is presented as "a secret journal" supposedly penned by Wilkie Collins after Dickens' death.

While quite successful at recreating the world of gaslit London, both *Bertie and the Tinman* and *The Detective and Mr. Dickens* suffer from a problem common to many modern writers of Victorian and Edwardian novels. They are much more explicit in describing sexual details than any 19th Century writer would have been. This is a matter of propriety. We know that there were rakes and libertines in the 19th Century, but writers of that period would have used euphemisms, vagueness, or pretended innocence rather than offend public sensibilities. This matter of propriety and taste were so codified in Victorian times that the euphemisms and phraseology actually became part of the literary style.

Historical novels with flaws in fact or style are painful to the knowledgeable reader, but well-crafted period mysteries that pay attention to style and detail are often among the very best writing in the mystery genre.

A very young A. Sarsfield Ward wrote the science fiction murder mystery "The Green Spider" in 1904, years before creating the most infamous villain of mystery fiction, Fu Manchu, under the pen name of Sax Rohmer. He was also the creator of Bazarada — a mystery solving magician based on Harry Houdini. Many of his later detective mysteries were so like Sherlock Holmes that — with the names and locations changed — they read more like late Victorian Holmes pastiches than those penned by modern writers who try so hard to write like Conan Doyle.

The stories in this book are mystery tales by Sax Rohmer carefully edited to turn them into Sherlock Holmes pastiches.

CONTENTS

THE AFFAIR OF THE VOODOO MENACE

THE AFFAIR OF THE

VOODOO MENACE

1.

SHERLOCK HOLMES OF BAKER STREET

Toward the hour of six on a hot summer's evening,
Mr. Sherlock Holmes was seated in his private lodgings in
Baker Street reading through a number of letters which Mrs.
Hudson, his landlady, had brought him that afternoon. Only
one more remained to be perused, but it was a long,
confidential report upon a certain matter which Holmes had
prepared for His Majesty's Principal Secretary of State for
the Home Department. He glanced with a sigh of weariness
at the little clock upon his table before commencing to read.

"Shall detain you for only a few minutes now, Watson,"
Holmes said.

I nodded, smiling. I was quite content to sit and watch my
friend at work.

Sherlock Holmes occupied a unique place in the maelstrom
of vice and ambition which is sometimes called London life.
Whilst at present he held no official post, some of the most
momentous problems of British policy during the past five
years, problems imperiling inter-state relationships (and not
infrequently threatening a world war), had recalled my friend
from bee-keeping on the Sussex Downs. These dilemmas
owed their solution to the peculiar genius of Holmes.

And so he had taken up rooms once more with Mrs. Hudson in Baker Street.

No clue to his profession appeared upon a plain brass plate attached to his door, and little did those who regarded Sherlock Holmes merely as a successful private detective suspect that he was in the confidence of some who guided the destinies of the Empire. Sherlock Holmes's work in Constantinople during the feverish months preceding hostilities with Turkey, although unknown to the general public, had been of a most extraordinary nature. His recommendations were never adopted, unfortunately. Otherwise, the tragedy of the Dardanelles might have been averted.

His surroundings as he sat there, gaze bent upon the typewritten pages, were those of any other professional man. So it would have seemed to the casual observer. But perhaps there was a quality in the atmosphere of the receiving room which would have told a more sensitive visitor that it was the apartment of no ordinary man of business. Whilst there were filing cabinets and bookshelves laden with works of reference, many of them legal, a large and handsome Burmese cabinet struck an unexpected note.

On closer inspection, other splashes of significant colour must have been detected in the scheme, notably a very fine engraving of Edgar Allan Poe, from the daguerreotype of 1848; and upon the man himself lay the indelible mark of time recently spend in the tropics. His clean-cut aquiline features had that hint of underlying bronze which tells of moths spent beneath a merciless sun, and the touch of gray at his temples only added to the eager, almost fierce vitality of the man's face. Sherlock Holmes was notable because of that intellectual strength which does not strike one immediately, since it is purely temperamental, but which, nevertheless, invests its possessor with an aura of distinction.

Writing his name at the bottom of the report, Holmes enclosed the pages in a long envelope and dropped the envelope into a basket which contained a number of other letters. His work for the day was ended and, glancing at me with a triumphant smile, he stood up. The receiving room was a part of a residential flat, but although, like some old-time burgher of the city, he lived on the premises, he now had a stoutly-built oak door which separated the receiving room which he used for business dealings from his private rooms. The locking of this door marked the close of his business day. Pressing a bell which connected with the rooms below, occupied by his landlady, Sherlock Holmes stood up as Mrs. Hudson entered.

"There's nothing further, is there, Mrs. Hudson?" he asked.

"Nothing, Mr. Holmes, if you have read the Home Office report?"

Sherlock Holmes laughed shortly.

"There it is," he replied, pointing to the basket; "a tedious and thankless job, Mrs. Hudson. It is the fifth draft I have prepared and it will have to do."

He took up a letter which lay unsealed upon the table. "This is the Rokeby affair," he said. "I have decided to hold it over, after all, until my return."

"Ah!" said Mrs. Hudson, quietly glancing at each envelope as he took it from the basket. "I see you have turned down the little job offered by the Marquis."

"I have," replied Holmes, smiling grimly, "and a fee of five hundred guineas with it. I have also intimated to that distressed nobleman that my work here is a business and that a laundry is the proper place to take his dirty linen. No, there's nothing further to-night, Mrs. Hudson. You can get along now. Has Miss Smithson gone?"

But as if in answer to his enquiry, Miss Smithson, the typist who worked afternoons for Holmes came in at that moment, a card in her hand. Holmes glanced across in my direction and then at the card, with a wry expression.

"Colonel Juan Menendez," he read aloud, "Cavendish Club," and glanced reflectively at me. "Do we know the Colonel?"

"I think not," I answered, "the name is unfamiliar to me."

"I wonder," murmured Holmes. "It's an awful nuisance, Watson, just as I thought the decks were clear. Is it something really interesting, or does he want a woman watched? However, his name sounds piquant, so perhaps I had better see him. Ask him to come in, Miss Smithson."

Mrs. Hudson and Miss Smithson then retiring, there presently entered a man of most striking and unusual presence. In the first place, Colonel Menendez must have stood fully six feet in his boots, and he carried himself like a grandee of the golden days of Spain. His complexion was extraordinarily dusky, whilst his hair, which was close cropped, was iron gray. His heavy eyebrows and curling moustache with its little points were equally black, so that his large teeth gleamed very fiercely when he smiled. His eyes were large, dark, and brilliant, and although he wore an admirably cut tweed suit, for some reason I pictured him as habitually wearing riding kit. Indeed I almost seemed to hear the jingle of his spurs.

He carried an ebony cane for which I mentally substituted a crop, and his black derby hat I thought hardly as suitable as a sombrero. His age might have been anything between fifty and fifty-five.

Standing in the doorway he bowed and, if his smile was Mephistophelean, there was much about Colonel Juan Menendez which commanded respect.

"Mr. Holmes," he began, and his high, thin voice afforded yet another surprise, "I feel somewhat ill at ease to — how do you say it? — appropriate your time, as I am by no means sure that what I have to say justifies my doing so."

He spoke most fluent, indeed florid, English. But his sentences were at times oddly constructed; yet, save for a faint accent, and his frequent interpolation of such expressions as "how do you say?" — a sort of nervous mannerism — one might have supposed him to be a Britisher who had lived much abroad. I formed the opinion that he had read extensively, and this, as I learned later, was indeed the case.

"Sit down, Colonel Menendez," said Holmes with quiet geniality. "Officially, my working day is ended, I admit, but if you have no objection to the presence of my friend, Dr. Watson, I shall be most happy to chat with you."

He smiled in a way all his own.

"If your business is of a painfully professional nature," he added, "I must beg you to excuse me for fourteen days, as I am taking a badly needed holiday with my friend."

"Ah, is it so?" replied the Colonel, placing his hat and cane upon the table and sitting down rather wearily in a big leathern armchair which Holmes had pushed forward. "If I intrude I am sorry, but indeed my business is most urgent, and I come to you on the recommendation of my friend, Señor Don Merry del Val, the Spanish Ambassador."

He raised his eyes to Holmes's face with an expression of peculiar appeal. I rose to depart, but:

"Sit down, Watson," said Holmes, and turned again to the visitor. "Please proceed," he requested. "Dr. Watson has been with me in some of the most delicate cases which I have ever handled, and you may rely upon his discretion as you may rely upon mine." He pushed forward a box of cigars. "Will you smoke?"

"Thanks, no," was the answer; "you see, I rarely smoke anything but my own cigarettes."

Colonel Menendez extracted a slip of rice paper from a little packet which he carried, next, dipping two long, yellow fingers into his coat pocket, he brought out a portion of tobacco, laid it in the paper, and almost in the twinkling of an eye had made, rolled, and lighted a very creditable cigarette. His dexterity was astonishing and, seeing my surprise he raised his heavy eyebrows:

"Practice makes perfect, is it not said?" he remarked.

He shrugged his shoulders and dropped the extinguished match in an ash tray, whilst I studied him with increasing interest. Some dread, real or imaginary, was oppressing the man's mind, I mused. I felt my presence to be unwelcome, but:

"Very well," he began, suddenly. "I expect, Mr. Holmes, that you will be disposed to regard what I have to tell you rather as a symptom of what you call nerves than as evidence of any agency directed against me."

Sherlock Holmes stared curiously at the speaker. "Do I understand you to suspect that someone is desirous of harming you?" he enquired.

Colonel Menendez slowly nodded his head.

"Such is my meaning," he replied.

"You refer to bodily harm?"

"But yes, emphatically."

"Hmm," said Holmes; and taking out a tin of tobacco from a cabinet beside him he began in leisurely manner to load a briar. "No doubt you have good reasons for this suspicion?"

"If I had not good reasons, Mr. Holmes, nothing could have induced me to trouble you. Yet, even now that I have compelled myself to come here, I find it difficult, almost impossible, to explain those reasons to you."

An expression of embarrassment appeared upon the brown face, and now Colonel Menendez paused and was plainly at a loss for words with which to continue.

Holmes replaced the tin in the cupboard and struck a match. Lighting his pipe he nodded good humouredly as if to say, "I quite understand." As a matter of fact, he probably thought, as I did, that this was a familiar case of a man of possibly blameless life who had become subject to that delusion which leads people to believe themselves threatened by mysterious and unnamable danger.

Our visitor inhaled deeply.

"You, of course, are waiting for the facts," he presently resumed, speaking with a slowness which told of a mind labouring for the right mode of expression. "These are so scanty, I fear, of so, shall I say, phantom a kind, that even when they are in your possession you will consider me to be merely the victim of a delusion. In the first place, then, I have reason to believe that someone followed me from my home to your lodgings."

"Indeed," said Sherlock Holmes, sympathetically, for this I perceived was exactly what he had anticipated, and merely tended to confirm his suspicion. "Some member of your household?"

"Certainly not."

"Did you actually see this follower?"

"My dear sir," cried Colonel Menendez, excitement emphasizing his accent, "if I had seen him, so much would have been made clear, so much! I have never seen him, but I have heard him and felt him — felt his presence, I mean."

"In what way?" asked Holmes, leaning back in his chair and studying the fierce face.

"On several occasions on turning out the light in my bedroom and looking across the lawn from my window I have observed the shadow of someone — how do you say? — lurking in the garden."

"The shadow?"

"Precisely. The person himself was concealed beneath a tree. When he moved his shadow was visible on the ground."

"You were not deceived by a waving branch?"

"Certainly not. I speak of a still, moonlight night."

"Possibly, then, it was the shadow of a tramp," suggested Holmes. "I gather that you refer to a house in the country?"

"It was not," declared Colonel Menendez, emphatically; "it was not. I wish to God I could believe it had been. Then there was, a month ago, an attempt to enter my house."

Sherlock Holmes exhibited evidence of a quickening curiosity. He had perceived, as I had perceived, that the manner of the speaker differed from that of the ordinary victim of delusion, with whom he had become professionally familiar.

"You had actual evidence of this?" he suggested.

"It was due to insomnia, sleeplessness, brought about, yes, I will admit it, by apprehension, that I heard the footsteps of this intruder."

"But you did not see him?"

"Only his shadow"

"What!"

"You can obtain the evidence of all my household that someone had actually entered," declared Colonel Menendez, eagerly. "Of this, at least, I can give you the certain facts. Whoever it was had obtained access through a kitchen window, had forced two locks, and was coming stealthily along the hallway when the sound of his footsteps attracted my attention."

"What did you do?"

"I came out on to the landing and looked down the stairs. But even the slight sound which I made had been sufficient to alarm the midnight visitor, for I had never a glimpse of him. Only, as he went swiftly back in the direction from which he had come, the moonlight shining in through a window in the hall cast his shadow on the carpet."

"Strange," murmured Holmes. "Very strange, indeed. The shadow told you nothing?"

"Nothing at all."

Colonel Menendez hesitated momentarily, and glanced swiftly across at Holmes.

"It was just a vague — do you say blur? — and then it was gone. But — "

"Yes," said Holmes. "But?"

"Ah," Colonel Menendez blew a cloud of smoke into the air, "I come now to the matter which I find so hard to explain."

He inhaled again deeply and was silent for a while.

"Nothing was stolen?" asked Holmes.

"Nothing whatever."

"And no clue was left behind?"

"No clue except the filed fastening of a window and two open doors which had been locked as usual when the household retired."

"Hmm," mused Holmes again; "this incident, of course, may have been an isolated one and in no way connected with the surveillance of which you complain. I mean that this person who undoubtedly entered your house might prove to be an ordinary burglar."

"On a table in the hallway of Cray's Folly," replied Colonel Menendez, impressively — "so my house is named — stands a case containing presentation gold plate. The moonlight of which I have spoken was shining fully upon this case, and does the burglar live who will pass such a prize and leave it untouched?"

"I quite agree," said Holmes, quietly, "that this is a very big point."

"You are beginning at last," suggested the Colonel, "to believe that my suspicions are not quite groundless?"

"There is a distinct possibility that they are more than suspicions," agreed Holmes; "but may I suggest that there is something else? Have you an enemy?"

"Who that has ever held public office is without enemies?"

"Ah, quite so. Then I suggest again that there is something else."

He gazed keenly at his visitor, and the latter, whilst meeting the look unflinchingly with his large dark eyes, was unable to conceal the fact that he had received a home thrust.

"There are two points, Mr. Holmes," he finally confessed, "almost certainly associated one with the other, if you understand, but both these so — shall I say remote? — from my life, that I hesitate to mention them. It seems fantastic to suppose that they contain a clue."

"I beg of you," said Holmes, "to keep nothing back, however remote it may appear to be. It is sometimes the seemingly remote things which prove upon investigation to be the most intimate."

"Very well," resumed Colonel Menendez, beginning to roll a second cigarette whilst continuing to smoke the first, "I know that you are right, of course, but it is nevertheless very difficult for me to explain. I mentioned the attempted burglary, if so I may term it, in order to clear your mind of the idea that my fears were a myth. The next point which I have concerns a man, a neighbour of mine in Surrey. Before I proceed, I should like to make it clear that I do not believe for a moment that he is responsible for this unpleasant business."

Holmes stared at him curiously. "Nevertheless," he said, "there must be some data in your possession which suggest to your mind that he has some connection with it."

"There are, Mr. Holmes, but they belong to things so mystic and far away from ordinary crime that I fear you will think me," he shrugged his great shoulders, "a man haunted by strange superstitions. Do you say 'haunted?' Good. You understand. I should tell you, then, that although of pure Spanish blood, I was born in Cuba. The greater part of my life has been spent in the West Indies, where prior to '98 I held an appointment under the Spanish Government. I have property, not only in Cuba, but in some of the smaller islands which formerly were Spanish, and I shall not conceal from you that during the latter years of my administration I incurred the enmity of a section of the population. Do I make myself clear?"

Sherlock Holmes nodded and exchanged a swift glance with me. I formed a rapid mental picture of native life under the governorship of Colonel Juan Menendez and I began to consider his story from a new viewpoint. Seemingly rendered restless by his reflections, he stood up and began to pace the floor, a tall but curiously graceful figure. I noticed the bulldog tenacity of his chin, the intense pride in his bearing, and I wondered what kind of menace had induced him to seek the aid of Sherlock Holmes; for whatever his failings might be, and I could guess at the nature of several of them, that this thin-lipped Spanish soldier knew the meaning of fear I was not prepared to believe.

"Before you proceed further, Colonel Menendez," said Holmes, "might I ask when you left Cuba?"

"It was some three years ago," was his reply. "Because — " he hesitated curiously — "of health motives, I leased a property in England, believing that here I should find peace."

"In other words, you were afraid of something or someone in Cuba?"

Colonel Menendez turned in a flash, glaring down at the speaker.

"I never feared any man in my life, Mr. Holmes," he said, coldly.

"Then why are you here?"

The Colonel placed the stump of his first cigarette in an ash tray and lighted that which he had newly made.

"It is true," he admitted. "Forgive me. Yet what I said was that I never feared any man."

He stood squarely in front of the Burmese cabinet, resting one hand upon his hip. Then he added a remark which surprised me.

"Do you know anything of Voodoo?" he asked.

Sherlock Holmes took his pipe from between his teeth and stared at the speaker silently for a moment. "Voodoo?" he echoed. "You mean African native magic?"

"Exactly."

"My studies have certainly not embraced it," replied Holmes, quietly, "nor has a definitive case of Voodoo hitherto come within my experience. But since I have traveled in the East, I am prepared to learn that Voodoo may not be a negligible quantity. There are forces at work in India which we in England improperly understand. The same may be true of Cuba."

"The same *is* true of Cuba."

Colonel Menendez glared almost fiercely across the room at Sherlock Holmes.

"And do I understand," asked the latter, "that the danger which you believe to threaten you is associated with Cuba?"

"That, Mr. Holmes, is for you to decide when all the facts shall be in your possession. Do you wish that I proceed?"

"By all means. I must confess that I am intensely interested."

"Very well, Mr. Holmes. I have something to show you."

From an inside breast pocket, Colonel Menendez drew out a gold-mounted case. From the case, he took some flat, irregularly-shaped object wrapped in a piece of tissue paper. Unfolding the paper, he strode across and laid the object which it had contained upon the blotting pad in front of my friend.

Impelled by curiosity, I stood up and advanced to inspect it. It was of a dirty brown colour, some five or six inches long, and appeared to consist of a kind of membrane. Holmes, his elbow on the table, was staring down at it questioningly.

"What is it?" I said; "some kind of leaf?"

"No," replied Holmes, looking up into the dark face of the Spanish colonel; "I think I know what it is."

"I, also, know what it is." declared Colonel Menendez, grimly. "But tell me what to you it seems like, Mr. Holmes?"

Sherlock Holmes's expression was compounded of incredulity, wonder, and something else, as, continuing to stare at the speaker, he replied:

"It is the wing of a bat."

2.

THE VOODOO SWAMP

Often enough, my memory has recaptured that moment in Sherlock Holmes's receiving room, when Holmes, myself, and the tall Spaniard stood looking down at the bat wing lying upon the blotting pad.

My brilliant friend at times displayed a sort of prescience, of which I may have occasion to speak later, but I, together with the rest of pure-blind humanity, am commonly immune from the prophetic instinct. Therefore I chronicle the fact for what it may be worth, that as I gazed with a sort of disgust at the exhibit lying upon the table, I became possessed of a conviction, which had no logical basis, that a door had been opened through which I should step into a new avenue of being; I felt myself to stand upon the threshold of things strange and terrible, but withal alluring. Perhaps it is true that in the great crises of life the inner eye becomes momentarily opened.

With intense curiosity, I awaited the Colonel's next words; but, a cigarette held nervously between his fingers, he stood staring at Holmes, and it was the latter who broke that peculiar silence which had fallen upon us.

"The wing of a bat," he murmured, then touched it gingerly. "Of what kind of bat, Colonel Menendez? Surely not a British species?"

"But emphatically not a British species," replied the Spaniard. "Yet even so the matter would be strange."

"I am all anxiety to learn the remainder of your story, Colonel Menendez."

"Good. Your interest comforts me very greatly, Mr. Holmes. But when first I came, you led me to suppose that you were departing from London?"

"Such, at the time, was my intention, sir." Sherlock Holmes smiled slightly. "Accompanied by my friend, Dr. Watson, I had proposed to indulge in a fortnight's fishing upon the Norfolk Broads."

"Fishing?"

"Yes."

"A peaceful occupation, Mr. Holmes, and a great rest-cure for one who like yourself moves much amid the fiercer passions of life. You were about to make holiday?"

Sherlock Holmes nodded.

"It is cruel of me to intrude upon such plans," continued Colonel Menendez, dexterously rolling his cigarette around between his fingers. "Yet because of my urgent need I dare to do so. Would yourself and your friend honour me with your company at Cray's Folly for a few days? I can promise you good entertainment, although I regret that there is no fishing; but it may chance that there will be other and more exciting sport."

Holmes glanced at me significantly.

"Do I understand you to mean, Colonel Menendez," Holmes asked, "that you have reason to believe that this conspiracy directed against you is about to come to a head?"

Colonel Menendez nodded, at the same time bringing his hand down sharply upon the table.

"Mr. Holmes," he replied, his high, thin voice sunken almost to a whisper, "Wednesday night is the night of the full moon."

"The full moon?"

"It is at the full moon that the danger comes."

Sherlock Holmes stood up and, watched by the Spanish colonel, paced slowly across the receiving room. At the outer door he paused and turned.

"Colonel Menendez," he said, "that you would willingly waste the time of a busy man I do not for a moment believe, therefore I shall ask you as briefly as possible to state your case in detail. When I have heard it, if it appears to me that any good purpose can be served by my friend and myself coming to Cray's Folly I feel sure that he will be happy to accept your proffered hospitality."

"If I am likely to be of the slightest use I shall be delighted," said I, which indeed was perfectly true.

Whilst I had willingly agreed to accompany Holmes to Norfolk I had none of his passion for the piscatorial art, and the promise of novel excitement held out by Colonel Menendez appealed to me more keenly than the lazy days upon the roads which Holmes loved.

"Gentlemen" — the Colonel bowed profoundly — "I am honoured and delighted. When you shall have heard my story I know what your decision will be."

He resumed his seat and began, it seemed almost automatically, to roll a fresh cigarette.

"I am all attention," declared Holmes, and his glance strayed again in a wondering fashion to the bat wing lying on his table.

"I will speak briefly," resumed our visitor, "and any details which may seem to you to be important can be discussed later when you are my guests. You must know then that I first became acquainted with the significance belonging to the term 'Bat Wing' and to the object itself some twenty years ago."

"But surely," interrupted Holmes, incredulously, "you are not going to tell me that the menace of which you complain is of twenty years' standing?"

"At your express request, Mr. Holmes," returned the Colonel a trifle brusquely, "I am dealing with possibilities which are remote, because in your own words it is sometimes the remote which proves to be the intimate. It was then rather more than twenty years ago, at a time when great political changes were taking place in the West Indies, that my business interests, which are mainly concerned with sugar, carried me to one of the smaller islands which had formerly been under — my jurisdiction, do you say? Here I had a house and estate, and here in the past I had experienced much trouble with the natives.

"I do not disguise from you that I was unpopular, and on my return I met with unmistakable signs of hostility. My native workmen were insubordinate. In fact, it was the reports from my overseers which had led me to visit the island. I made a tour of the place, believing it to be necessary to my interests that I should get once more in touch with native feeling, since I had returned to my home in Cuba after the upheavals in '98. Very well.

"The manager of my estate, a capable man, was of opinion that there existed a secret organization amongst the native labourers operating — you understand? — against my interests. He produced certain evidences of this. They were not convincing; and all my enquiries and examinations of certain inhabitants led to no definite results. Yet I grew more and more to feel that enemies surrounded me."

He paused to light his third cigarette; and whilst he did so, I conjured up a mental picture of his "examinations of certain inhabitants." I recalled hazily those stories of Spanish mismanagement and cruelty which had directly led to United States interferences in the islands. But whilst I could well believe that this man's life had not been safe in those bad old days in the West Indies, I found it difficult to suppose that a native plot against his safety could have survived for more than twenty years and have come to a climax in England. However, I realized that there was more to follow, and presently, having lighted his cigarette, the Colonel resumed:

"In the neighbourhood of the *haçienda* which had once been my official residence there was a belt of low-lying pest country — you understand pest country? — which was a hot-bed of poisonous diseases. It followed the winding course of a nearly stagnant creek. From the earliest times the Black Belt — it was so called — had been avoided by European inhabitants, and indeed by the coloured population as well. Apart from the malaria of the swampy ground, it was infested with reptiles and with poisonous insects of a greater variety and of a more venomous character than I have ever known in any part of the world.

"I must explain that what I regarded as a weak point in my manager's theory was this: Whilst he held that the native labourers to a man were linked together under some head, or guiding influence, he had never succeeded in surprising anything in the nature of a native meeting. Indeed, he had prohibited all gatherings of this kind. His answer to my criticism was a curious one. He declared that the members of this mysterious society met and received their instructions at some place within the poison area to which I have referred, believing themselves there to be safe from European interference.

"For a long time I disputed this with poor Valera — for such was my manager's name; when one night as I was dismounting from my horse before the veranda, having returned from a long ride around the estate, a shot was fired from the border of the Black Belt which at one point crept up dangerously close to the *haçienda*.

"The shot was a good one. I had caught my spur in the stirrup in dismounting, and stumbled. Otherwise I must have been a dead man. The bullet pierced the crown of my hat, only missing my skull by an inch or less. The alarm was given. But no search-party could be mustered, do you see? — which was prepared to explore the poison swamp — or so declared my native servants. Valera, however, seized upon this incident to illustrate his theory that there were those in the island who did not hesitate to enter the Black Belt popularly supposed to cast up noxious vapours at dusk of a sort fatal to any traveller.

"That night over our wine, we discussed the situation, and he pointed out to me that now was the hour to test his theory. Orders had evidently been given for my assassination, and the attempt had failed.

" 'There will be a meeting,' said Valera, 'to discuss the next move. And it will take place to-morrow night!'

"I challenged him with a glance and I replied:

" 'To-morrow night is a full moon and, if you are agreeable, we will make a secret expedition into the swamp and endeavour to find the clearing which you say is there, and which you believe to be the rendezvous of the conspirators.'

"Even in the light of the lamp I saw Valera turn pale, but he was a Spaniard and a man of courage.

" 'I agree, Señor,' he replied. 'If my information is correct we shall find the way.'

"I must explain that the information to which he referred had been supplied by a native girl who loved him. That this clearing was a meeting-place she had denied. But she had admitted that it was possible to obtain access to it, and had even described the path." He paused. "She died of a lingering sickness."

Colonel Menendez spoke these last words with great deliberation and treated each of us to a long and significant stare.

"Presently," he added, "I will tell you what was nailed to the wall of her hut on the night that she fell ill. But to continue my narrative: On the following evening, suitably equipped, Valera and myself set out, leaving by a side door and striking into the woods at a point east of the *haçienda,* where, according to his information, a footpath existed, which would lead us to the clearing we desired to visit. Of that journey, gentlemen, I have most terrible memories.

"Imagine a dense and poisonous jungle, carpeted by rotten vegetation in which one's feet sank deeply and from which arose a visible and stenching vapour. Imagine living things, slimy things, moving beneath the tread, sometimes coiling about our riding boots, sometimes making hissing sounds. Imagine places where the path was overgrown, and we must thrust our way through bushes where great bloated spiders weaved their webs, where clammy night things touched us as we passed, where unfamiliar and venomous insects clung to our garments.

"We proceeded onward for more than half an hour guided by the moonlight, but this, although tropically brilliant, at some places scarcely penetrated the thick vapour which arose from the jungle. In those days, I was a young and vigorous man;

my companion was several years my senior; and his sufferings were far greater than my own. But if the jungle was horrible, worse was yet to come.

"Presently, we stumbled upon an open space almost quite bare of vegetation, a poisonous green carpet spread in the heart of the woods. Here the vapour was more dense than ever, but I welcomed the sight of open ground after the reptile-infested thicket. Alas! It was a snare, a death-trap, a sort of morass, in which we sank up to our knees. *Pah !* It was filthy — vile! And I became aware of great — lassitude, do you say? — whilst Valera's panting breath told that he had almost reached the end of his resources.

"A faint breeze moved through the clearing, and for a few moments we were enabled to perceive one another more distinctly. I uttered an exclamation of horror.

"My companion's garments were a mass of strange-looking patches.

"Even as I noticed them, I glanced rapidly down — and found myself in similar condition. As I did so, one of these patches upon the sleeve of my tunic intruded coldly upon my bare wrist. At that I cried out aloud in fear. Valera and I commenced what was literally a fight for life.

"Gentlemen, we were attacked by some kind of blood-red leeches which came out of the slime! In detaching them, one detached patches of skin, and they swarmed over our bodies like ants upon carrion.

"They penetrated beneath our garments, these swollen, lustful, unclean things; and it was whilst we staggered on through the swamp in agony of mind and body that we saw the light of many torches amid the trees ahead of us, and in their smoky glare witnessed the flight of hundreds of bats. The moonlight creeping dimly through the mist, and the torchlight — how do you say? — enflaming the vegetation, created a scene like that of Inferno, in which naked figures danced wildly, uttering animal cries.

"Above the shrieking and howling, which rose and fell in a sort of unholy chorus, I heard one long, wailing sound, repeated and repeated. It was an African word. But I knew its meaning.

"It was *'Bat Wing !'*

"My doubts were dispersed. This was a meeting-place of Devil-worshippers, or devotees of the cult of Voodoo! One man only could I see clearly enough so as to remember him, a big black man employed upon one of my estates. He seemed to be a sort of high priest or president of the orgies. Attached to his arms were giant imitations of bat wings, which he moved grotesquely as if in flight. There were many women in the throng, which numbered fully I should think a hundred people. But the final collapse of my brave, unhappy Valera at this point brought home to me the nature of the peril in which I stood.

"He lay at my feet, moving convulsively, and sinking ever deeper in the swamp, red leeches moving slowly, slowly over his fast-disappearing body."

Colonel Menendez paused in his appalling narrative and wiped his moist forehead with a silk handkerchief. Neither Holmes nor I spoke. I knew not if my friend believed the Spaniard's story. For my own part I found it difficult to do so. But that the narrator was deeply moved was a fact beyond dispute.

He suddenly commenced again:

"My next recollection is of awakening in my own bed at the *haçienda*. I had staggered back as far as the veranda, in raving delirium, and in the grip of a strange fever which prostrated me for many months, and which defied the knowledge of all the specialists who could be procured from Cuba and the United States. My survival was due to an iron constitution; but I have never been the same man. I was ordered to leave the West Indies directly it became possible for me to be moved. I arranged my affairs accordingly, and did not return for many years.

"Finally, however, I again took up my residence in Cuba, and for a time all went well, and might have continued to do so, but for the following incident. One night, being troubled by insomnia — sleeplessness — and the heat, I walked out on to the balcony in front of my bedroom window. As I did so, a figure which had been — you say lurking? — somewhere under the veranda ran swiftly off; but not so swiftly that I failed to obtain a glimpse of the uplifted face.

"It was the big black man! Although many years had elapsed since I had seen him wearing the bat wings at those unholy rites, I knew him instantly.

"On a little table close behind me where I stood lay a loaded revolver. I snatched it in a flash and fired shot after shot at the retreating figure."

Colonel Menendez shrugged his shoulders and selected a fresh cigarette paper.

"Gentlemen," he continued, "from that moment until this I have gone in hourly peril of my life. Whether I hit my man or missed him, I have never known to this day. If he lives or is dead I cannot say. But — " he paused impressively — "I have told you of something that was nailed to the hut of a certain native girl? Before she died I knew that it was a death-token.

"On the morning after the episode which I have just related attached to the main door of the *haçienda* was found that same token."

"And it was??" said Holmes, eagerly.

"It was the wing of a bat!

"I am perhaps a hasty man. It is in my blood. I tore the unclean thing from the panel and stamped it under my feet. No one of the servants who had drawn my attention to its presence would consent to touch it. Indeed, they all shrank from me as though I, too, were unclean. I endeavoured to forget it. Who was I to be influenced by the threats of natives?

"That night, just at the hour of sunset, a shot was fired at me from a neighbouring clump of trees, only missing me I think by the fraction of an inch. I realized that the peril was real, and was one against which I could not fight.

"Permit me to be brief, gentlemen. Six attempts of various kinds were made upon my life in Cuba. I crossed to the United States. In Washington, the political capital of the country, an assassin gained access to my hotel apartment and but for the fact that a friend chanced to call me up on the telephone at that late hour of the night, thereby awakening me, I should have received a knife in my heart. I saw the knife in the dim light; I saw the shadowy figure. I leapt out on the opposite side of the bed, seized a table-lamp which stood there, and hurled it at my assailant.

"There was a crash, a stifled exclamation, shuffling, the door opened, and my would-be assassin was gone. But I had learned something, and to my old fears a new one was added."

"What had you learned?" asked Holmes, whose interest in the narrative was displayed by the fact that his pipe had long since gone out.

"Vaguely, vaguely, you understand, for there was little light, I had seen the face of the man. He wore some kind of black cloak doubtless to conceal his movements. His silhouette resembled that of a bat. But, gentlemen, he was neither a black man nor even a half-caste; he was of the white races, to that I could swear."

Colonel Menendez lighted the cigarette which he had been busily rolling, and fixed his dark eyes upon Holmes.

"You puzzle me, sir," said the latter. "Do you wish me to believe that this cult of Voodoo claims European or American devotees?"

"I wish you to believe," returned the Colonel, "that although as the result of the alarm which I gave the hotel was searched and the Washington police exerted themselves to the utmost, no trace was ever found of the man who had tried to murder me, except" — he extended a long, yellow forefinger and

pointed to the wing of the bat lying upon Holmes's table —
"a bat wing was found pinned to my bedroom door."

Silence fell for a while; an impressive silence. Truly this was
the strangest story to which I had ever listened.

"How long ago was that?" asked Holmes.

"Only two years ago. At about the time that the Great War
terminated. I came to Europe and believed that at last I had
found security. I lived for a time in London amidst a
refreshing peace that was new to me. Then, chancing to hear
of a property in Surrey which was available, I leased it for a
period of years, installing — is it correct? — my cousin,
Madame de Stämer, as housekeeper. Madame, alas, is an
invalid, but" — he kissed his fingers — "a genius. She has
with her, as companion, a very charming English girl,
Miss Valeria Beverley, the orphaned daughter of a
distinguished surgeon of Edinburg. Miss Beverley was with
my cousin in the hospital which she established in France
during the war. If you will honour me with your presence at
Cray's Folly to-morrow, gentlemen, you will not lack
congenial company, I can assure you."

He raised his heavy eyebrows, looking interrogatively from
Holmes to myself.

"For my own part," said my friend, slowly, "I shall be
delighted. What do you say, Watson?"

"I also."

"But," continued Holmes, "your presence here today,
Colonel Menendez, suggests to my mind that England has
not proved so safe a haven as you had anticipated?"

Colonel Menendez crossed the room and stood once more before the Burmese cabinet, one hand resting upon his hip; a massive yet graceful figure.

"Mr. Holmes," he replied, "four days ago my butler, who is a Spaniard, brought me that — " He pointed to the bat wing lying upon the blotting pad. "He had found it pinned to an oaken panel of the main entrance door."

"Was it prior to this discovery, or after it," asked Holmes, "that you detected the presence of someone lurking in the neighbourhood of the house?"

"Before it."

"And the burglarious entrance?"

"That took place rather less than a month ago. On the eve of the full moon."

Sherlock Holmes stood up and relighted his pipe.

"There are quite a number of other details, Colonel," he said, "which I shall require you to place in my possession. Since I have determined to visit Cray's Folly, these can wait until my arrival. I particularly refer to a remark concerning a neighbour of yours in Surrey."

Colonel Menendez nodded, twirling his cigarette between his long, yellow fingers.

"It is a delicate matter, gentlemen," he confessed.

"I must take time to consider how I shall place it before you. But I may count upon your arrival tomorrow?"

"Certainly. I am looking forward to the visit with keen interest."

"It is important," declared our visitor; "for on Wednesday is the full moon, and the full moon is in some way associated with the sacrificial rites of Voodoo."

3.

THE VAMPIRE BAT

An hour had elapsed since the departure of our visitor, and Sherlock Holmes and I sat in his cozy, book-lined sitting room discussing the strange narrative which had been related to us. Holmes, who had a friend attached to the Spanish Embassy, had succeeded in getting in touch with him at his chambers, and had obtained some few particulars of interest concerning Colonel Don Juan Sarmiento Menendez, for such were the full names and titles of our late caller.

He was apparently the last representative of a once-great Spanish family, established for many generations in Cuba. His wealth was incalculable, although the value of his numerous estates had depreciated in recent years. His family had produced many men of subtle intellect and powerful administrative qualities; but allied to this they had all possessed traits of cruelty and debauchery which at one time had made the name of Menendez a by-word in the West Indies. That there were many people in that part of the world who would gladly have assassinated the Colonel, Sherlock Holmes's informant did not deny. But although this information somewhat enlarged our knowledge of my friend's newest client, it threw no fresh light upon that side of his story which related to Voodoo and the extraordinary bat wing episodes.

"Of course," said Holmes, after a long silence, "there is one possibility of which we must not lose sight."

"What possibility is that?" I asked.

"That Menendez may be mad. Remorse for crimes of cruelty committed in his youth, and beyond doubt he has been guilty of many, may have led to a sort of obsession. I have known such cases."

"That was my first impression," I confessed, "but it faded somewhat as the Colonel's story proceeded. I don't think any such explanation would cover the facts."

"Neither do I," agreed my friend; "but it is distinctly possible that such an obsession exists, and that someone is deliberately playing upon it for his own ends."

"You mean that someone who knows of these episodes in the earlier life of Menendez is employing them now for a secret purpose of his own?"

"Exactly."

"It renders the case none the less interesting."

"I quite agree, Watson. With you, I believe, that even if the Colonel is not quite sane, at the same time his fears are by no means imaginary."

He gingerly took up the bat wing from the arm of his chair where he had placed it after a detailed examination.

"It seems to be pretty certain," he said, "that this thing is the wing of a Desmodus or Vampire Bat. Now, according to our authority" — he touched a work which lay open on the other arm of his chair — "these are natives of tropical America, therefore the presence of a living vampire bat in Surrey is not to be anticipated. I am personally satisfied, however, that this unpleasant fragment has been preserved in some way."

"You mean that it is part of a specimen from someone's collection?"

"Quite possibly. But even a collection of such bats would be quite a novelty. I don't know that I can recollect one outside the Museums. To follow this bat wing business further: there was one very curious point in the Colonel's narrative. You recollect his reference to a native girl who had betrayed certain information to the manager of the estate?"

I nodded rapidly.

"A bat wing was affixed to the wall of her hut and she died, according to our informant, of a lingering sickness. Now this lingering sickness might have been anæmia, and anæmia may be induced, either in man or beast, by frequent but unsuspected visits of a Vampire Bat."

"Good Heavens, Holmes!" I exclaimed, "what a horrible idea."

"It *is* a horrible idea, but in countries infested by these creatures such things happen occasionally. I distinctly recollect a story which I once heard, of a little girl in some district of tropical America falling into such a decline, from which she was only rescued in the nick of time by the discovery that one of these Vampire Bats, a particularly large one, had formed the habit of flying into her room at night and attaching itself to her bare arm which lay outside the coverlet."

"How did it penetrate the mosquito curtains?" I enquired, incredulously.

"The very point, Watson, which led to the discovery of the truth. The thing, exhibiting a sort of uncanny intelligence, used to work its way up under the edge of the netting. This disturbance of the curtains was noticed on several occasions by the nurse who occupied an adjoining room, and finally led to the detection of the bat!"

"But surely," I said, "such a visitation would awaken any sleeper?"

"On the contrary, it induces deeper sleep. But I have not yet come to my point, Watson. The vengeance of the High Priest of Voodoo, who figured in the Colonel's narrative, was characteristic in the case of the native woman, since her symptoms at least simulated those which would result from the visits of a Vampire Bat, although of course they may have been due to a slow poison. But you will not have failed to note that the several attacks upon the Colonel personally were made with more ordinary weapons. On two occasions at least a rifle was employed."

"Yes," I replied, slowly. "You are wondering why the lingering sickness did not visit him?"

"I am, Watson. I can only suppose that he proved to be immune. You recall his statement that he made an almost miraculous recovery from the fever which attacked him after his visit to the Black Belt? This would seem to point to the fact that he possesses that rare type of constitution which almost defies organisms deadly to ordinary men."

"I see. Hence the dagger and the rifle?"

"So it would appear."

"But, Holmes," I cried, "what appalling crime can the man have committed to call down upon his head a vengeance which has survived for so many years?"

Sherlock Holmes shrugged his shoulders in a whimsical imitation of the Spaniard.

"I doubt if the feud dates any earlier," he replied, "than the time of Menendez's last return to Cuba. On that occasion he evidently killed the High Priest of Voodoo."

I uttered an exclamation of scorn.

"My dear Holmes," I said, "the whole thing is too utterly fantastic. I begin to believe again that we are dealing with a madman."

Holmes glanced down at the wing of the bat.

"We shall see," he murmured. "Even if the only result of our visit is to make the acquaintance of the Colonel's household, our time will not have been wasted."

"No," said I, "that is true enough. I am looking forward to meeting Madame de Stämer — "

"The Colonel's invalid cousin," added Holmes, tonelessly.

"And her companion, Miss Beverley."

"Quite so. Nor must we forget the Spanish butler, and the Colonel himself, whose acquaintance I am extremely anxious to renew."

"The whole thing is wildly bizarre, Holmes."

"My dear Watson," he replied, stretching himself luxuriously in the long lounge chair, "the most commonplace life hovers on the edge of the bizarre. But those of us who overstep the border become preposterous in the eyes of those who have never done so. This is not because the unusual is necessarily the untrue, but because writers of fiction have claimed the unusual as their particular province, and in doing so have divorced it from fact in the public eye. Thus I, myself, am a myth, and so are you, Watson!"

He raised his hand and pointed to the doorway communicating with the receiving room.

"We owe our mythological existence to that American genius whose portrait hangs beside the Burmese cabinet and who indiscreetly created the character of C. Auguste Dupin. The doings of this amateur investigator were chronicled by an admirer, you may remember; and since then, no private detective has been allowed to exist outside the pages of fiction. My most trivial habits confirm my unreality.

"For instance, I have a friend who is good enough sometimes to record my movements. So had Dupin. I smoke a pipe. So did Dupin. I investigate crime, and I am sometimes successful. Here I differ from Dupin. Dupin was always successful. But my argument is this — you complain that the life of Colonel Don Juan Sarmiento Menendez, on his own showing, has been at least as romantic as his name. It would not be accounted romantic by the adventurous, Watson; it is only romantic to the prosaic mind. In the same way his name is only unusual to our English ears. In Spain it would pass unnoticed."

"I see your point," I said, grudgingly; "but think of Voodoo in the Surrey Hills."

"I am thinking of it, Watson, and it affords me much delight to think of it. You have placed your finger I upon the very point I was endeavouring to make. Voodoo in the Surrey Hills! Quite so. Voodoo in some island of the Caribbean Seas, yes, but Voodoo in the Surrey Hills, no. Yet, my dear fellow, there is a regular steamer service between South America and England. Or one may embark at Liverpool and disembark in the Spanish Main. Why, then, may not one embark in the West Indies and disembark at Liverpool? This granted, you will also grant that from Liverpool to Surrey is a feasible journey. Why, then, should you exclaim, 'but Voodoo in the Surrey Hills!' You would be surprised to meet an Esquimaux in the Strand, but there is no reason why an Esquimaux should not visit the Strand. In short, the most annoying thing about fact is its resemblance to fiction. I am looking forward to the day, Watson, when I can retire from my present fictitious profession to become a recognized member of the community; to return to my beekeeping in Sussex!"

He burst out laughing, and reaching over to a side-table refilled my glass and his own.

"There lies the wing of a Vampire Bat," he said, pointing, "in Baker Street. It is impossible. Yet," he raised his glass,

" 'Pussyfoot' Johnson has visited Scotland, the home of Whisky!"

We were silent for a while, whilst I considered his remarks.

"The conclusion to which I have come," declared Holmes, "is that nothing is so strange as the commonplace. A rod and line, a boat, a luncheon hamper, a jar of good ale, and the peculiar peace of a Norfolk river — these joys I willingly curtail in favour of the unknown things which await us at Cray's Folly. Remember, Watson," he stared at me queerly, "Wednesday is the night of the full moon.

4.

CRAY'S FOLLY

Sherlock Holmes lay back upon the cushions and glanced at me with a quizzical smile. The big, up-to-date motorcar which Colonel Menendez had placed at our disposal was surmounting a steep Surrey lane as though no gradient had existed.

"Some engine!" he said, approvingly.

I nodded in agreement, but felt disinclined for conversation, being absorbed in watching the characteristically English scenery. This, indeed, was very beautiful. The lane along which we were speeding was narrow, winding, and over-arched by trees. Here and there sunlight penetrated to spread a golden carpet before us, but for the most part the way lay in cool and grateful shadow.

On one side, a wooded slope hemmed us in blackly, on the other lay dell after dell down into the cradle of the valley. It was a poetic corner of England, and I thought it almost unbelievable that London was only some twenty miles behind. A fit place this for elves and fairies to survive, a spot in which the presence of a modern automobile seemed a desecration. Higher we mounted and higher, the engine running strongly and smoothly; then, presently, we were out upon a narrow open road with the crescent of the hills sweeping away on the right and dense woods dipping valleyward to the left and behind us.

The chauffeur turned, and meeting my glance:

"Cray's Folly, sir," he said.

He jerked his hand in the direction of a square, gray-stone tower somewhat resembling a campanile, which rose from a distant clump of woods cresting a greater eminence.

"Ah," murmured Holmes, "the famous tower."

Following the departure of the Colonel on the previous evening, Holmes had looked up Cray's Folly and had found it to be one of a series of houses erected by the eccentric and wealthy man whose name it bore. He had had a mania for building houses with towers, in which his rival — and contemporary — had been William Beckford, the author of "Vathek," a work which for some obscure reason has survived as well as two of the three towers erected by its writer.

I became conscious of a keen sense of anticipation. In this, I think the figure of Miss Valeria Beverley played a leading part. There was something pathetic in the presence of this lonely English girl in so singular a household; for if the menage at Cray's Folly should prove half so strange as Colonel Menendez had led us to believe, then truly we were about to find ourselves amid unusual people.

Presently the road inclined southward somewhat and we entered the fringe of the trees. I noticed one or two very ancient cottages, but no trace of the modern builder. This was a fragment of real Old England, and I was not sorry when presently we lost sight of the square tower; for amidst such scenery it was an anomaly and a rebuke.

What Sherlock Holmes's thoughts may have been I cannot say, but he preserved an unbroken silence up to the very moment that we came to the gate lodge.

The gates were monstrosities of elaborate iron scrollwork, craftsmanship clever enough in its way, but of an ornate style more in keeping with the orange trees of the South than with this wooded Surrey countryside.

A very surly-looking girl, quite obviously un-English (a daughter of Pedro, the butler, I learned later), opened the gates, and we entered upon a winding drive literally tunnelled through the trees. Of the house we never a glimpse until we were right under its walls, nor should I have known that we were come to the main entrance if the car had not stopped.

"Looks like a monastery," muttered Holmes.

Indeed that part of the building — the north front — which was visible from this point had a strangely monastic appearance, being built of solid gray blocks and boasting only a few small, heavily-barred windows. The eccentricity of the Victorian gentleman who had expended thousands of pounds upon erecting this house was only equalled, I thought, by that of Colonel Menendez, who had chosen it for a home. An out-jutting wing shut us in on the west, and to the east, the prospect was closed by the tallest and most densely grown box hedge I had ever seen, trimmed most perfectly and having an arched opening in the centre. Thus, the entrance to Cray's Folly lay in a sort of bay.

But even as we stepped from the car, the great church-like oaken doors were thrown open; and there, framed in the monkish porch, stood the tall, elegant figure of the Colonel.

"Gentlemen," he cried, "welcome to Cray's Folly."

He advanced smiling, and in the bright sunlight seemed even more Mephistophelean than he had seemed in Holmes's receiving room.

"Pedro," he called, and a strange-looking Spanish butler who wore his side-whiskers like a bull fighter appeared behind his master; a sallow, furtive fellow with whom I determined I should never feel at ease.

However, the Colonel greeted us heartily enough, and then conducted us through a kind of paved, covered courtyard into a great lofty hall. Indeed, it more closely resembled a studio, being partly lighted by a most curious dome. It was furnished in a manner quite un-English, but very luxuriously. A magnificent oaken staircase communicated with a gallery on the left, and at the foot of this staircase, in a mechanical chair which she managed with astonishing dexterity, sat Madame de Stämer.

She had snow-white hair crowning the face of a comparatively young woman, and large, dark-brown eyes which reminded me strangely of the eyes of some animal although in the first moment of meeting I could not identify the resemblance. Her hands were very slender and beautiful, and when, as the Colonel presented us, she extended her fingers, I was not surprised to see Holmes stoop and kiss them in Continental fashion; which Madame evidently expected. I followed suit; but truth to tell, after that first glance at the masterful figure in the invalid chair I had had no eyes for Madame de Stämer, being fully employed in gazing at someone who stood beside her.

This was an evasively pretty girl, or such was my first impression. That is to say, that whilst her attractiveness was beyond dispute, analysis of her small features failed to detect from which particular quality this charm was derived. The contour of her face certainly formed a delightful oval, and there was a wistful look in her eyes which was half appealing and half impish. Her demure expression was not convincing, and there rested a vague smile, or promise of a smile, upon lips which were perfectly moulded, and indeed the only strictly regular feature of a nevertheless bewitching face. She had slightly curling hair and the line of her neck and shoulder was most graceful and charming. Of one thing I was sure: She was glad to see visitors at Cray's Folly.

"And now, gentlemen," said Colonel Menendez, "having presented you to Madame, my cousin, permit me to present you to Miss Val Beverley, my cousin's companion, and our very dear friend."

The girl bowed in a formal English fashion, which contrasted sharply with the Continental manner of Madame. Her face flushed slightly, and as I met her glance she demurely lowered her eyes.

"Now Monsieur Holmes and Monsieur Watson," said Madame, vivaciously, "you are quite at home. Pedro will show you to your rooms and lunch will be ready in half an hour."

She waved her white hand coquettishly, and ignoring the proffered aid of Miss Beverley, wheeled her chair away at a great rate under a sort of arch on the right of the hall, which communicated with the domestic offices of the establishment.

"Is she not wonderful?" exclaimed Colonel Menendez, taking Holmes's left arm and my right and guiding us upstairs followed by Pedro and the chauffeur, the latter carrying our grips. "Many women would be prostrated by such an affliction, but she — " he shrugged his shoulders.

Holmes and I had been placed in adjoining rooms. I had never seen such rooms as those in Cray's Folly. The place contained enough oak to have driven a modern builder crazy. Oak had simply been lavished upon it. My own room, which was almost directly above the box hedge to which I have referred, had a beautiful carved ceiling and a floor as highly polished as that of a ballroom. It was tastefully furnished, but the foreign note was perceptible everywhere.

"We have here some grand prospects," said the Colonel, and truly enough the view from the great, high, wide window was a very fine one.

I perceived that the grounds of Cray's Folly were extensive and carefully cultivated. I had a glimpse of a Tudor sunken garden, but the best view of this was from the window of Holmes's room, which because it was the end room on the north front overlooked another part of the grounds, and offered a prospect of the east lawns and distant park land.

When presently Colonel Menendez and I accompanied my friend there I was charmed by the picturesque scene below. Here was a real old herbal garden, bright with flowers and intersected by tiled moss-grown paths. There were bushes exhibiting fantastic examples of the topiary art, and here, too, was a sun-dial. My first impression of this beautiful spot was one of delight. Later, I was to regard that enchanted demesne with something akin to horror; but as we stood there watching a gardener clipping the bushes I thought that, although Cray's Folly might be adjudged ugly, its grounds were delightful.

Suddenly Holmes turned to our host. "Where is the famous tower?" he enquired. "It is not visible from the front of the house, nor from the drive."

"No, no," replied the Colonel, "it is right out at the end of the east wing, which is disused. I keep it locked up. There are four rooms in the tower and a staircase, of course, but it is inconvenient. I cannot imagine why it was built."

"The architect may have had some definite object in view," said Holmes, "or it may have been merely a freak of his client. Is there anything characteristic about the topmost room, for instance?"

Colonel Menendez shrugged his massive shoulders. "Nothing," he replied. "It is the same as the others below, except that there is a stair leading to a gallery on the roof. Presently I will take you up, if you wish."

"I should be interested," murmured Holmes, and tactfully changed the subject, which evidently was not altogether pleasing to our host. I concluded that he had found the east wing of the house something of a white elephant, and was accordingly sensitive upon the point.

Presently the Colonel left us and I returned to my own room, but before long I rejoined Holmes. I did not knock but entered unceremoniously.

"Halloa!" I exclaimed. "What have you seen?"

He was standing staring out of the window, nor did he turn as I entered.

"What is it?" I said, joining him.

He glanced at me oddly.

"An impression," he replied; "but it has gone now."

"I understand," I said, quietly.

Familiarity with crime in many guises and under many skies had developed in Sherlock Holmes a sort of sixth sense. It was a fugitive, fickle thing, as are all the powers which belong to the realm of genius or inspiration. Often enough, it failed him entirely, he had assured me, that odd, sudden chill as of an abrupt lowering of the temperature, which, I understood, often advised him of the nearness of enmity actively malignant.

Now, standing at the window, looking down into that old-world garden, he was "sensing" the atmosphere keenly, seeking for the note of danger. It was sheer intuition, perhaps, but whilst he could never rely upon its answering his summons, once active it never misled him.

"You think some real menace overhangs Colonel Menendez?"

"I am sure of it." He stared into my face. "There is something very, very strange about this bat wing business."

"Do you still incline to the idea that he has been followed to England?"

Sherlock Holmes reflected for a moment, then:

"That explanation would be almost too simple," he said. "There is something bizarre, something unclean — I had almost said unholy — at work in this house, Watson."

"He has foreign servants."

Holmes shook his head.

"I shall make it my business to become acquainted with all of them," he replied, "but the danger does not come from there. Let us go down to lunch."

5.

VAL BEVERLEY

The luncheon was so good as to be almost ostentatious. One could not have lunched better at the Carlton. Yet, since this luxurious living was evidently customary in the colonel's household, a charge of ostentation would not have been deserved. The sinister-looking Pedro proved to be an excellent servant; and because of the excitement of feeling myself to stand upon the edge of unusual things, the enjoyment of a perfectly served repast, and the sheer delight which I experienced in watching the play of expression upon the face of Miss Beverley, I count that luncheon at Cray's Folly a memorable hour of my life.

Frankly, Val Beverley puzzled me. It may or may not have been curious, that amidst such singular company, I selected for my especial study a girl so freshly and typically English. I had thought at the moment of meeting her that she was provokingly pretty; I determined, as the lunch proceeded, that she was beautiful. Once I caught Holmes smiling at me in his quizzical fashion, and I wondered guiltily if I were displaying an undue interest in the companion of Madame.

Many topics were discussed, I remember, and beyond doubt the colonel's cousin-housekeeper dominated the debate. She possessed extraordinary force of personality. Her English was not nearly so fluent as that spoken by the colonel, but this handicap only served to emphasize the masculine strength of her intellect. Truly she was a remarkable woman. With her blanched hair and her young face, and those fine, velvety eyes which possessed a quality almost hypnotic, she might have posed for the figure of a sorceress. She had unfamiliar gestures and employed her long white hands in a manner that was new to me and utterly strange.

I could detect no family resemblance between the cousins, and I wondered if their kinship were very distant. One thing was evident enough: Madame de Stämer was devoted to the Colonel. Her expression when she looked at him changed entirely. For a woman of such intense vitality, her eyes were uncannily still; that is to say that whilst she frequently moved her head, she rarely moved her eyes. Again and again I found myself wondering where I had seen such eyes before. I lived to identify that memory, as I shall presently relate.

In vain I endeavoured to define the relationship between these three people, so incongruously set beneath one roof. Of the fact that Miss Beverly was not happy I became assured. But respecting her exact position in the household, I was reduced to surmises.

The Colonel improved on acquaintance. I decided that he belonged to an order of Spanish grandees now almost extinct. I believed he would have made a very staunch friend; I felt sure he would have proved a most implacable enemy. Altogether, it was a memorable meal; and one notable result of that brief companionship was a kind of link of understanding between myself and Miss Beverley.

Once, when I had been studying Madame de Stämer, and again, as I removed my glance from the dark face of Colonel Menendez, I detected the girl watching me; and her eyes said, "You understand; so do I."

Some things perhaps I did understand, but how few the near future was to show.

The signal for our departure from table was given by Madame de Stämer. She whisked her wheelchair back with extraordinary rapidity, the contrast between her swift, nervous movements and those still, basilisk eyes being almost uncanny.

"Off you go, Juan," she said; "your visitors would like to see the garden, no doubt. I must be away for my afternoon siesta. Come, my dear" — to the girl — "smoke one little cigarette with me, then I will let you go."

She retired, wheeling herself rapidly out of the room, and my glance lingered upon the graceful figure of Val Beverley until both she and Madame were out of sight.

"Now, gentlemen," said the Colonel, resuming his seat and pushing the decanter toward Sherlock Holmes, "I am at your service either for business or amusement. I think" — to Holmes — "you expressed a desire to see the tower?"

"I did," my friend replied, lighting his cigar, "but only if it would amuse you to show me."

"Decidedly. Dr. Watson will join us?"

Holmes, unseen by the Colonel, glanced at me in a way which I knew.

"Thanks all the same," I said, smiling, "but following a perfect luncheon, I should much prefer to loll upon the lawn, if you don't mind."

"But certainly I do not mind," cried the Colonel. "I wish you to be happy."

"Join you in a few minutes, Watson," said Holmes as he went out with our host.

"All right," I replied, "I should like to take a stroll around the gardens. You will join me there later, no doubt."

As I walked out into the bright sunshine, I wondered why Sherlock Holmes had wished to be left alone with Colonel Menendez; but knowing that I should learn his motive later, I strolled on through the gardens, my mind filled with speculations respecting these unusual people with whom Fate had brought me in contact. I felt that Miss Beverley needed protection of some kind, and I was conscious of a keen desire to afford her that protection. In her glance I had read, or thought I had read, an appeal for sympathy.

Not the least mystery of Cray's Folly was the presence of this girl. Only toward the end of luncheon had I made up my mind upon a point which had been puzzling me. Val Beverley's gaiety was a cloak. Once I had detected her watching Madame de Stämer with a look strangely like that of fear.

Puffing contentedly at my cigar I proceeded to make a tour of the house. It was constructed irregularly. Practically the entire building was of gray stone, which created a depressing effect even in the blazing sunlight, lending Cray's Folly something of an austere aspect. There were fine lofty windows, however, to most of the ground-floor rooms overlooking the lawns, and some of those above had balconies of the same gray stone. Quite an extensive kitchen garden and a line of glasshouses adjoined the west wing, and here were outbuildings, coach-houses, and a garage, all connected by a covered passage with the servants' quarters.

Pursuing my enquiries, I proceeded to the north front of the building, which was closely hemmed in by trees, and which as we had observed on our arrival resembled the entrance to a monastery.

Passing the massive oaken door by which we had entered and which was now closed again, I walked on through the opening in the box hedge into a part of the grounds which was not so sprucely groomed as the rest. On one side were the yews flanking the Tudor garden and before me uprose the famous tower. As I stared up at the square structure, with its uncurtained windows, I wondered, as others had wondered before me, what could have ever possessed any man to build it.

Visible at points for many miles around, it undoubtedly disfigured an otherwise beautiful landscape.

I pressed on, noting that the windows of the rooms in the east wing were shuttered and the apartments evidently disused. I came to the base of the tower, To the south, the country rose up to the highest point in the crescent of hills and, peeping above the trees at no great distance away, I detected the red brick chimneys of some old house in the woods. North and east, velvet sward swept down to the park.

As I stood there admiring the prospect and telling myself that no Voodoo devilry could find a home in this peaceful English countryside, I detected a faint sound of voices far above. Someone had evidently come out upon the gallery of the tower. I looked upward, but I could not see the speakers. I pursued my stroll, until, near the eastern base of the tower, I encountered a perfect thicket of rhododendrons. Finding no path through this shrubbery, I retraced my steps, presently entering the Tudor garden; and there strolling toward me, a book in her hand, was Miss Beverley.

"Holloa, Dr. Watson," she called; "I thought you had gone up the tower?"

"No," I replied, laughing, "I lack the energy."

"Do you?" she said, softly, "then sit down and talk to me."

She dropped down upon a grassy bank, looking up at me invitingly, and I accepted the invitation without demur.

"I love this old garden," she declared, "although of course it is really no older than the rest of the place. I always think there should be peacocks, though."

"Yes," I agreed, "peacocks would be appropriate."

"And little pages dressed in yellow velvet."

She met my glance soberly for a moment and then burst into a peal of merry laughter.

"Do you know, Miss Beverley," I said, watching her, "I find it hard to place you in the household of the Colonel."

"Yes?" she said simply; "you must."

"Oh, then you realize that you are — "

"Out of place here?"

"Quite."

"Of course I am."

She smiled, shook her head, and changed the subject.

"I am so glad Mr. Sherlock Holmes has come down," she confessed.

"You know my friend by name, then?"

"Yes," she replied, "someone I met in Nice spoke of him, and I know he is very clever."

"In Nice? Did you live in Nice before you came here?"

Val Beverley nodded slowly, and her glance grew oddly retrospective.

"I lived for over a year with Madame de Stämer in a little villa on the Promenade des Anglaise," she replied. "That was after Madame was injured."

"She sustained her injuries during the war, I understand?"

"Yes. Poor Madame. The hospital of which she was in charge was bombed and the shock left her as you see her. I was there, too, but I luckily escaped without injury."

"What, you were there?"

"Yes. That was where I first met Madame de Stämer. She used to be very wealthy, you see, and she established this hospital in France at her own expense, and I was one of her assistants for a time. She lost both her husband and her fortune in the war, and as if that were not bad enough, lost the use of her limbs, too."

"Poor woman," I said. "I had no idea her life had been so tragic. She has wonderful courage."

"Courage!" exclaimed the girl, "if you knew all that I know about her."

Her face grew sweetly animated as she bent toward me excitedly and confidentially.

"Really, she is simply wonderful. I learned to respect her in those days as I have never respected any other woman in the world; and when, after all her splendid work, she, so vital and active, was stricken down like that, I felt that I simply could not leave her, especially as she asked me to stay."

"So you went with her to Nice?"

"Yes. Then the Colonel took this house, and we came here, but — "

She hesitated and glanced at me curiously.

"Perhaps you are not quite happy?"

"No," she said, "I am not. You see it was different in France. I knew so many people. But here at Cray's Folly it is so lonely, and Madame is — "

Again she hesitated.

"Yes?"

"Well," she laughed in an embarrassed fashion, "I am afraid of her at times."

"In what way?"

"Oh, in a silly, womanish sort of way. Of course she is a wonderful manager; she rules the house with a rod of iron. But really I haven't anything to do here, and I feel frightfully out of place sometimes. Then the Colonel — Oh, but what am I talking about?"

"Won't you tell me what it is that the Colonel fears?"

"You know that he fears something, then?"

"Of course. That is why Sherlock Holmes is here."

A change came over the girl's face; a look almost of dread.

"I wish I knew what it all meant."

"You are aware, then, that there is something wrong?"

"Naturally I am. Sometimes I have been so frightened that I have made up my mind to leave the very next day."

"You mean that you have been frightened at night?" I asked with curiosity.

"Dreadfully frightened."

"Won't you tell me in what way?"

She looked up at me swiftly, then turned her head aside, and bit her lip.

"No, not now," she replied. "I can't very well."

"Then at least tell me why you stayed?"

"Well," she smiled at me rather pathetically, "for one thing, I haven't anywhere else to go."

"Have you no friends in England?"

She shook her head.

"No. There was only poor daddy, and he died over two years ago. That was when I went to Nice."

"Poor little girl," I said; and the words were spoken before I realized their undue familiarity.

An apology was on the tip of my tongue, but Miss Beverley did not seem to have noticed the indiscretion. Indeed my sympathy was sincere, and I think she had appreciated the fact.

She looked up again with a bright smile.

"Why are we talking about such depressing things on this simply heavenly day?" she exclaimed.

"Goodness knows," said I. "Will you show me round these lovely gardens?"

"Delighted, sir!" replied the girl, rising and sweeping me a mocking curtsey.

Thereupon we set out, and at every step I found a new delight in some wayward curl, in a gesture, in the sweet voice of my companion. Her merry laugh was music, but in wistful mood I think she was even more alluring.

The menace, if menace there were, which overhung Cray's Folly, ceased to exist — for me, at least, and I blessed the lucky chance which had led to my presence there.

We were presently rejoined by Colonel Menendez and Sherlock Holmes, and I gathered that my surmise that it had been their voices which I had heard proceeding from the top of the tower to have been only partly accurate.

"I know you will excuse me, Mr. Holmes," said the Colonel, "for detailing the duty to Pedro, but my wind is not good enough for the stairs."

He used idiomatic English at times with that facility which some foreigners acquire, but always smiled in a self-satisfied way when he had employed a slang term.

"I quite understand, Colonel," replied Holmes. "The view from the top was very fine."

"And now, gentlemen," continued the Colonel, "if Miss Beverley will excuse us, we will retire to the library and discuss business."

"As you wish," said Holmes; "but I have an idea that it is your custom to rest in the afternoon."

Colonel Menendez shrugged his shoulders. "It used to be," he admitted, "but I have too much to think about in these days."

"I can see that you have much to tell me," admitted Holmes; "and therefore I am entirely at your service."

Val Beverley smiled and walked away swinging her book, at the same time treating me to a glance which puzzled me considerably. I wondered if I had mistaken its significance, for it had seemed to imply that she had accepted me as an ally. Certainly it served to awaken me to the fact that I had discovered a keen personal interest in the mystery which hung over this queerly assorted household.

I glanced at Sherlock Holmes as the Colonel led the way into the house. I saw him staring upward with a peculiar expression upon his face and, following the direction of his glance, I could see an awning spread over one of the gray-stone balconies. Beneath it, reclining in a long cane chair, lay Madame de Stämer. I think she was asleep; at any rate, she gave no sign, but lay there motionless, as Holmes and I walked in through the open French window followed by Colonel Menendez.

Odd and unimportant details sometimes linger long in the memory. And I remember noticing that a needle of sunlight, piercing a crack in the gaily-striped awning rested upon a ring which Madame wore, so that the diamonds glittered like sparks of white-hot fire.

6.

THE BARRIER

Colonel Menendez conducted us to a long, lofty library in which might be detected the same note of un-English luxury manifested in the other appointments of the house. The room, in common with every other which I had visited in Cray's Folly, was carried out in oak: doors, window frames, mantelpiece, and ceiling representing fine examples of this massive woodwork. Indeed, if the eccentricity of the designer of Cray's Folly were not sufficiently demonstrated by the peculiar plan of the building, its construction wholly of granite and oak must have remarked him a man of unusual if substantial ideas.

There were four long windows opening on to a veranda which commanded a view of part of the rose garden and of three terraced lawns descending to a lake upon which I perceived a number of swans. Beyond, in the valley, lay verdant pastures where cattle grazed. A lark hung carolling blithely far above, and the sky was almost cloudless. I could hear a steam reaper at work somewhere in the distance. This, with the more intimate rattle of a lawn-mower wielded by a gardener who was not visible from where I stood, alone disturbed the serene silence; except that presently I detected the droning of many bees among the roses. Sunlight flooded the prospect; but the veranda lay in shadow; and that long, oaken room was refreshingly cool and laden with the heavy perfume of the flowers.

From the windows, then, one beheld a typical English summer-scape, but the library itself struck an altogether more exotic note. There were many glazed bookcases of a garish design in ebony and gilt, and these were laden with a vast collection of works in almost every European language, reflecting perhaps the cosmopolitan character of the colonel's household. There was strange Spanish furniture upholstered in perforated leather and again displaying much gilt. There were suits of black armour and a great number of Moorish ornaments. The pictures were fine but sombre, and all of the Spanish school.

One Velasquez in particular I noted with surprise, reflecting that, assuming it to be an authentic work of the master, my entire worldly possessions could not have enabled me to buy it. It was the portrait of a typical Spanish cavalier and beyond doubt a Menendez. In fact, the resemblance between the haughty Spanish grandee, who seemed about to step out of the canvas and pick a quarrel with the spectator, and Colonel Don Juan himself was almost startling. Evidently, our host had imported most of his belongings from Cuba.

"Gentlemen," he said, as we entered, "make yourselves quite at home, I beg. All my poor establishment contains is for your entertainment and service."

He drew up two long, low lounge chairs, the arms provided with receptacles to contain cooling drinks; and the mere sight of these chairs mentally translated me to the Spanish Main, where I pictured them set upon the veranda of that *haçienda* which had formerly been our host's residence.

Holmes and I became seated and Colonel Menendez disposed himself upon a leather-covered couch, nodding apologetically as he did so.

"My health requires that I should recline for a certain number of hours every day," he explained. "So you will please forgive me."

"My dear Colonel Menendez," said Holmes, "I feel sure that you are interrupting your siesta in order to discuss the unpleasant business which finds us in such pleasant surroundings. Allow me once again to suggest that we postpone this matter until, shall we say, after dinner?"

"No, no! No, no," protested the Colonel, waving his hand deprecatingly. "Here is Pedro with coffee and some *curaçao* of a kind which I can really recommend, although you may be unfamiliar with it."

I was certainly unfamiliar with the liqueur which he insisted we must taste, and which was contained in a sort of square, opaque bottle unknown, I think, to English wine merchants. Beyond doubt it was potent stuff; and some cigars which the Spaniard produced on this occasion and which were enclosed in little glass cylinders resembling test-tubes and elaborately sealed, I recognized to be priceless. They convinced me, if conviction had not visited me already, that Colonel Don Juan Sarmiento Menendez belonged to that old school of West Indian planters by whom the tradition of the Golden Americas had been for long preserved in the Spanish Main.

We discussed indifferent matters for a while, sipping this wonderful curaçao of our host's. The effect created by the Colonel's story faded entirely; and when, the latter being unable to conceal his drowsiness, Holmes stood up, I took the hint with gratitude; for at that moment I did not feel in the mood to discuss serious business or indeed business of any kind.

"Gentlemen," said the Colonel, also rising, in spite of our protests, "I will observe your wishes. My guests' wishes are mine. We will meet the ladies for tea on the terrace."

Holmes and I walked out into the garden together, our courteous host standing in the open window, and bowing in that exaggerated fashion which in another might have been ridiculous but which was possible in Colonel Menendez, because of the peculiar grace of deportment which was his.

As we descended the steps, I turned and glanced back, I know not why. But the impression which I derived of the Colonel's face as he stood there in the shadow of the veranda was one I can never forget.

His expression had changed utterly, or so it seemed to me. He no longer resembled Velasquez' haughty cavalier; gone, too, was the *debonnaire* bearing, I turned my head aside swiftly, hoping that he had not detected my backward glance.

I felt that I had violated hospitality. I felt that I had seen what I should not have seen. And the result was to bring about that which no story of West Indian magic could ever have wrought in my mind.

A dreadful, cold premonition claimed me, a premonition that this was a doomed man.

The look which I had detected upon his face was an indefinable, an indescribable look; but I had seen it in the eyes of one who had been bitten by a poisonous reptile and who knew his hours to be numbered. It was uncanny, unnerving; and whereas at first the atmosphere of Colonel Menendez's home had seemed to be laden with prosperous security, now that sense of ease and restfulness was gone — and gone forever.

"Holmes," I said, speaking almost at random, "this promises to be the strangest case you have ever handled."

"Promises?" Sherlock Holmes laughed shortly. "It *is* the strangest case, Watson. It is a case of wheels-within-wheels, of mystery crowning mystery. Have you studied our host?"

"Closely."

"And what conclusion have you formed?"

"None at the moment; but I think one is slowly crystallizing."

"Hmm," muttered Holmes, as we paced slowly on amid the rose trees. "Of one thing I am satisfied."

"What is that?"

"That Colonel Menendez is not afraid of Bat Wing, whoever or whatever Bat Wing may be."

"Not afraid?"

"Certainly he is not afraid, Watson. He has possibly been afraid in the past, but now he is resigned."

"Resigned to what?"

"Resigned to death!"

"Good God, Holmes, you are right!" I cried. "You are right! I saw it in his eyes as we left the library."

Holmes stopped and turned to me sharply.

"You saw this in the Colonel's eyes?" he challenged.

"I did."

"Which corroborates my theory," he said, softly; "for *I* had seen it elsewhere."

"Where do you mean, Holmes?"

"In the face of Madame de Stämer."

"What?"

"Watson" — Holmes rested his hand upon my arm and looked about him cautiously — *"she knows."*

"But knows what?"

"That is the question which we are here to answer, but I am as sure as it is humanly possible to be sure of anything, that whatever Colonel Menendez may tell us to-night, one point at least he will withhold."

"What do you expect him to withhold?"

"The meaning of the sign of the Bat Wing."

"Then you think he knows its meaning?"

"He has told us that it is the death-token of Voodoo."

I stared at Holmes in perplexity.

"Then you believe his explanation to be false?"

"Not necessarily, Watson. It may be what he claims for it. But he is keeping something back. He speaks all the time from behind a barrier which he, himself, has deliberately erected against me."

"I cannot understand why he should do so," I declared, as he looked at me steadily. "Within the last few moments I have become definitely convinced that his appeal to you was no idle one. Therefore, why should he not offer you every aid in his power?"

"Why, indeed?" muttered Holmes.

"The same thing," I continued, "applies to Madame de Stämer. If ever I have seen love-light in a woman's eyes, I have seen it in hers to-day, whenever her glance has rested upon Colonel Menendez. Holmes, I believe she literally worships the ground he walks upon."

"She does, she does!" cried my companion, and emphasized the words with beats of his clenched fist. "It is utterly, damnably mystifying. But I tell you, she knows, Watson, she knows!"

"You mean she knows that he is a doomed man?"

Holmes nodded rapidly.

"They both know," he replied; "but there is something which they dare not divulge."

He glanced at me swiftly, and his aquiline face wore a peculiar expression.

"Have you had an opportunity of any private conversation with Miss Val Beverley?" he enquired.

"Yes," I said. "Surely you remember that you found me chatting with her when you returned from your inspection of the tower."

"I remember perfectly well, but I thought you might have just met. Now it appears to me, Watson, that you have quickly established yourself in the good books of a very charming girl. My only reason for visiting the tower was to afford you just this opportunity! Don't frown. Beyond reminding you of the fact that she has been on intimate terms with Madame de Stämer for some years, I will not intrude in any way upon your private plans in that direction."

I stared at him, and I suppose my expression was an angry one.

"Surely you don't misunderstand me?" he said. "A cultured English girl of that type cannot possibly have lived with these people without learning something of the matters which are puzzling us so badly. Am I asking too much?"

"I see what you mean," I said, slowly. "No, I suppose you are right, Holmes."

"Good," he muttered. "I will leave that side of the enquiry in your very capable hands, Watson."

He paused and began to stare about him.

"From this point," said he, "we have an unobstructed view of the tower."

We turned and stood looking up at the unsightly gray structure, with its geometrical rows of windows and the minaret-like gallery at the top.

"Of course" — I broke a silence of some moments duration — "the entire scheme of Cray's Folly is peculiar, but the rooms, except for a uniformity which is monotonous, and an unimaginative scheme of decoration which makes them all seem alike, are airy and well lighted, eminently sane and substantial. The tower, however, is quite inexcusable, unless the idea was to enable the occupant to look over the tops of the trees in all directions."

"Yes," agreed Holmes, "it is an ugly landmark. But yonder up the slope I can see the corner of what seems to be a very picturesque house of some kind."

"I caught a glimpse of it earlier to-day," I replied. "Yes, from this point a little more of it is visible. Apparently quite an old place."

I paused, staring up the hillside, but Holmes, hands locked behind him and chin lowered reflectively, was pacing on. I joined him and we proceeded for some little distance in silence, passing a gardener who touched his cap respectfully and to whom I thought at first my companion was about to address some remark. Holmes passed on, however, still occupied, it seemed, with his reflections, and coming to a gravel path which, bordering one side of the lawns, led down from terrace to terrace into the valley, turned, and began to descend.

"Let us go and interview the swans," he murmured absently.

7.

AT THE LAVENDER ARMS

In certain moods, Sherlock Holmes was impossible as a companion, and I (who knew him well) had learned to leave him to his own devices at such times. These moods invariably corresponded with his meeting some problem to the heart of which the lance of his keen wit failed to penetrate. His humour might not display itself in the spoken word, he merely became oblivious of everything and everybody around him. People might talk to him and he scarcely noted their presence; familiar faces would appear and he would see them not. Outwardly, he remained the observant Holmes who could see further into a mystery than any other in England, but his observation was entirely introspective; although he moved amid the hustle of life, he was spiritually alone, communing with the solitude which dwells in every man's heart.

Presently, then, as we came to the lake at the foot of the sloping lawns where water lilies were growing and quite a number of swans had their habitation, I detected the fact that I had ceased to exist so far as Holmes was concerned. Knowing this mood of old, I pursued my way alone, pressing on across the valley and making for a swinging gate which seemed to open upon a public footpath. Coming to this gate, I turned and looked back.

Sherlock Holmes was standing where I had left him by the edge of the lake, staring as if hypnotized at the slowly moving swans. But I would have been prepared to wager that he saw neither swans nor lake, but mentally was far from the spot, deep in some complex maze of reflection through which no ordinary mind could hope to follow him.

I glanced at my watch and found that it was but little after two o'clock. Luncheon at Cray's Folly was early. I therefore had some time upon my hands, so I determined to employ it in exploring part of the neighbourhood. Accordingly, I filled and lighted my pipe and strolled leisurely along the footpath, enjoying the beauty of the afternoon, and admiring the magnificent timber which grew upon the southerly slopes of the valley.

Larks sang high above me and the air was fragrant with those wonderful earthy scents which belong to an English countryside. A herd of very fine Jersey cattle presently claimed inspection, and a little farther on, I found myself upon a high road where a brown-faced fellow seated aloft upon a hay-cart cheerily gave me good-day as I passed.

Quite at random, I turned to the left and followed the road, so that presently I found myself in a very small village, the principal building of which was a very small inn called the "Lavender Arms."

Colonel Menendez's curaçao, combined with the heat of the day, had made me thirsty; for which reason I stepped into the bar-parlour determined to sample the local ale. I was served by the landlady, a neat, round, red little person, and as she retired, having placed a foam-capped mug upon the counter, her glance rested for a moment upon the only other occupant of the room, a man seated in an armchair immediately to the right of the door. A glass of whisky stood on the window ledge at his elbow, and that it was by no means the first which he had imbibed, his appearance seemed to indicate.

Having tasted the cool contents of my mug, I leaned back against the counter and looked at this person curiously.

He was apparently of about medium height, but of a somewhat fragile appearance. He was dressed like a country gentleman, and a stick and soft hat lay upon the ledge near his glass. But the thing about him which had immediately arrested my attention was his really extraordinary resemblance to Sherlock Holmes's engraving of Edgar Allan Poe.

I wondered at first if Holmes's frequent references to the eccentric American genius were responsible for my imagining a close resemblance where only a slight one existed. But inspection of that strange, dark face convinced me of the fact that my first impression had been a true one. Perhaps, in my curiosity, I stared rather rudely.

"You will pardon me, sir," said the stranger, and I was startled to note that he spoke with a faint American accent, "but are you a literary man?"

As I had judged to be the case, he was slightly bemused, but by no means drunk, and although his question was abrupt it was spoken civilly enough.

"Journalism is one of the several occupations in which I have failed," I replied, lightly.

"You are not a fiction writer?"

"I lack the imagination necessary for that craft, sir."

The other wagged his head slowly and took a drink of whisky. "Nevertheless," he said, and raised his finger solemnly, "you were thinking that I resembled Edgar Allan Poe!"

"Good Heavens!" I exclaimed, for the man had really amazed me. "You clearly resemble him in more ways than one. I must really ask you to inform me how you deduced such a fact from a mere glance of mine."

"I will tell you, sir," he replied. "But, first, I must replenish my glass, and I should be honoured if you would permit me to replenish yours."

"Thanks very much," I said, "but I would rather you excused me."

"As you wish, sir," replied the American with grave courtesy, "as you wish."

He stepped up to the counter and rapped upon it with half a crown, until the landlady appeared. She treated me to a pathetic glance, but refilled the empty glass.

My American acquaintance having returned to his seat and, having added a very little water to the whisky, he went on:

"Now, sir," said he, "my name is Colin Camber, formerly of Richmond, Virginia, United States of America, but now of the Guest House, Surrey, England, at your service."

Taking my cue from Mr. Camber's gloomy but lofty manner, I bowed formally and mentioned my name.

"I am delighted to make your acquaintance, Dr. Watson," he assured me; "and now, sir, to answer your question. When you came in a few moments ago you glanced at me. Your eyes did not open widely as is the case when one recognizes, or thinks one recognizes, an acquaintance. Your eyes narrowed. This indicated retrospection. For a moment they turned aside. You were focussing a fugitive idea, a memory. You captured it. You looked at me again, and your successive glances read as follows: The hair worn uncommonly long, the mathematical brow, the eyes of a poet, the slight moustache, small mouth, weak chin; the glass at his elbow. The resemblance is complete. Knowing how complete it is myself, sir, I ventured to test my theory, and it proved to be sound."

Now, as Mr. Colin Camber had thus spoken in the serious manner of a slightly drunken man, I had formed the opinion that I stood in the presence of a very singular character. Here was that seeming *mésalliance* which not infrequently begets genius: a powerful and original mind allied to a weak will. I wondered what Mr. Colin Camber's occupation might be, and somewhat, too, I wondered why his name was unfamiliar to me. For that the possessor of that brow and those eyes could fail to make his mark in any profession which he might take up I was unwilling to believe.

"Your exposition has been very interesting, Mr. Camber," I said. "You are a singularly close observer, I perceive."

"Yes," he replied, "I have passed my life in observing the ways of my fellowmen, a study which I have pursued in various parts of the world without appreciable benefit to myself. I refer to financial benefit."

He contemplated me with a look which had grown suddenly pathetic.

"I would not have you think, sir," he added, "that I am an habitual toper. I have latterly been much upset by — domestic worries, and — er — " He emptied his glass at a draught. "Surely, Dr. Watson, you are going to replenish? Whilst you are doing so, would you kindly request Mrs. Wootton to extend the same favour to myself?"

But at that moment Mrs. Wootton in person appeared behind the counter. "Time, please, gentlemen," she said; "it is gone half-past two."

"What!" exclaimed Mr. Camber, rising. "What is that? You decline to serve me, Mrs. Wootton?"

"Why, not at all, Mr. Camber," answered the landlady, "but I can serve no one now; it's after time."

"You decline to serve me," he muttered, his speech becoming slurred. "Am I, then, to be insulted?"

I caught a glance of entreaty from the landlady. "My dear sir," I said, genially, "we must bow to the law, I suppose. At least we are better off here than in America."

"Ah, that is true," agreed Mr. Camber, throwing his head back and speaking the words as though they possessed some deep dramatic significance. "Yes, but such laws are an insult to every intelligent man."

He sat down again rather heavily, and I stood looking from him to the landlady, and wondering what I should do. The matter was decided for me, however, in a way which I could never have foreseen. For, hearing a light footfall upon the step which led up to the bar-parlour, I turned — and there almost beside me stood a wrinkled little Chinaman!

He wore a blue suit and a tweed cap, he wore queer, thick-soled slippers, and his face was like a smiling mask hewn out of very old ivory. I could scarcely credit the evidence of my senses, since the Lavender Arms was one of the last places in which I should have looked for a native of China.

Mr. Colin Camber rose again, and fixing his melancholy eyes upon the newcomer:

"Ah Tsong," he said in a tone of cold anger, "what are you doing here?"

Quite unmoved the Chinaman replied:

"Blingee you chit, sir, vellee soon go back."

"What do you mean?" demanded Mr. Camber. "Answer me, Ah Tsong: who sent you?"

"Lilly missee," crooned the Chinaman, smiling up into the other's face with a sort of childish entreaty. "Lilly missee."

"Oh," said Mr. Camber in a changed voice. "Oh."

He stood very upright for a moment, his gaze set upon the wrinkled Chinese face. Then he looked at Mrs. Wootton and bowed, and looked at me and bowed, very stiffly.

"I must excuse myself, sir," he announced. "My wife desires my presence at home."

I returned his bow, and as he walked quite steadily toward the door, followed by Ah Tsong, he paused, turned, and said: "Dr. Watson, I should esteem it a friendly action if you would spare me an hour of your company before you leave Surrey. My visitors are few. Anyone, anyone, will direct you to the Guest House. I am persuaded that we have much in common. Good-day, sir."

He went down the steps, disappearing in company with the Chinaman, and having watched them go, I turned to Mrs. Wootton, the landlady, in silent astonishment.

She nodded her head and sighed.

"The same every day and every evening for months past," she said. "I am afraid it's going to be the death of him."

92

"Do you mean that Mr. Camber comes here every day and is always fetched by the Chinaman?"

"Twice every day," corrected the landlady, "and his poor wife sends here regularly."

"What a tragedy," I muttered, "and such a brilliant man."

"Ah," said she, busily removing jugs and glasses from the counter, "it does seem a terrible thing."

"Has Mr. Camber lived for long in this neighbourhood?" I ventured to inquire.

"It was about three years ago, sir, that he took the old Guest House at Mid-Hatton. I remember the time well enough because of all the trouble there was about him bringing a Chinaman down here."

"I can imagine it must have created something of a sensation," I murmured. "Is the Guest House a large property?"

"Oh, no, sir, only ten rooms and a garden, and it had been vacant for a long time. It belongs to what is called the Crayland Park Estate."

"Mr. Camber, I take it, is a literary man?"

"So I believe, sir."

Mrs. Wootton, having cleared the counter, glanced up at the clock and then at me with a cheery but significant smile.

"I see that it is after time," I said, returning the smile, "but the queer people who seem to live hereabouts interest me very much."

"I can't wonder at that, sir!" said the landlady, laughing outright. "Chinamen and Spanish men and what-not. If some of the old gentry that lived here before the war could see it, they wouldn't recognize the place, of that I am sure."

"Ah, well," said I, pausing at the step, "I shall hope to see more of Mr. Camber, and of yourself too, madam, for your ale is excellent."

"Thank you, sir, I'm sure," said the landlady much gratified, "but as to Mr. Camber, I really doubt if he would know you if you met him again. Not if he was sober, I mean."

"Really?"

"Oh, it's a fact, believe me. Just in the last six months or so he has started on the rampage like, but some of the people he has met in here and asked to call upon him have done it, thinking he meant it."

"And they have not been well received?" said I, lingering.

"They have had the door shut in their faces!" declared Mrs. Wootton with a certain indignation. "He either does not remember what he says or does when he is in drink, or he pretends he doesn't. Oh, dear, it's a funny world. Well, good-day, sir."

"Good-day," said I, and came out of the Lavender Arms full of sympathy with the views of the "old gentry," as outlined by Mrs. Wootton; for certainly it would seem that this quiet spot in the Surrey Hills had become a rallying ground for peculiar people.

8.

THE CALL OF M'KOMBO

Of tea upon the veranda of Cray's Folly that afternoon I retain several notable memories. I got into closer touch with my host and hostess, without achieving anything like a proper understanding of either of them, and I procured a new viewpoint of Miss Val Beverley. Her repose was misleading. She deliberately subjugated her own vital personality to that of Madame de Stämer, why, I knew not, unless she felt herself under an obligation to do so. That her blue-gray eyes could be wistful was true enough, they could also twinkle; and once I detected in them a look of sadness which dispelled the butterfly illusion belonging to her dainty slenderness, to her mobile lips, to the vagabond curling hair of russet brown.

Sherlock Holmes's manner remained absent, but I who knew his moods so well recognized that this abstraction was no longer real. It was a pose which he often adopted when in reality he was keenly interested in his surroundings. It baffled me, however, as effectively as it baffled others, and whilst at one moment I decided that he was studying Colonel Menendez, in the next I became convinced that Madame de Stämer was the subject upon his mental dissecting table.

That he should find in Madame a fascinating problem did not surprise me. She must have afforded tempting study for any psychologist. I could not fathom the nature of the kinship existing between herself and the Spanish colonel, for Madame de Stämer was exquisitely French to her fingertips. Her expressions, her gestures, her whole outlook on life proclaimed the fashionable *Parisienne*.

She possessed a vigorous masculine intelligence and was the most entertaining companion imaginable. She was daringly outspoken, and it was hard to believe that her gaiety was forced. Yet, as the afternoon wore on, I became more and more convinced that such was the case.

I thought that before affliction visited her, Madame de Stämer must have been a vivacious and a beautiful woman. Her vivacity remained and much of her beauty, so that it was difficult to believe her snow-white hair to be a product of nature. Again and again I found myself regarding it as a powdered coiffure of the Pompadour period and wondering why Madame wore no patches.

That a deep and sympathetic understanding existed between herself and Colonel Menendez was unmistakable. More than once I intercepted glances from the dark eyes of Madame which were lover-like, yet laden with a profound sorrow. She was playing a rôle, and I was convinced that Holmes knew this. It was not merely a courageous fight against affliction on the part of a woman of the world, versed in masking her real self from the prying eyes of society, it was a studied performance prompted by some deeper motive.

She dressed with exquisite taste, and to see her seated there amid her cushions, gesticulating vivaciously, one would never have supposed that she was crippled. My admiration for her momentarily increased, the more so since I could see that she was sincerely fond of Val Beverley, whose every movement she followed with looks of almost motherly affection. This was all the more strange as Madame de Stämer whose age, I supposed, lay somewhere on the sunny side of forty, was of a type which expects and wins admiration long after the average woman has ceased to be attractive.

One endowed with such a temperament is as a rule unreasonably jealous of youth and good looks in another. I could not determine if Madame's attitude were to be ascribed to complacent self-satisfaction or to a nobler motive. It sufficed for me that she took an unfeigned joy in the youthful sweetness of her companion.

"Val, dear," she said, presently, addressing the girl, "you should make those sleeves shorter, my dear."

She had a rapid way of speaking, and possessed a slightly husky but fascinatingly vibrant voice.

"Your arms are very pretty. You should not hide them."

Val Beverley blushed, and laughed to conceal her embarrassment.

"Oh, my dear," exclaimed Madame, "why be ashamed of arms? All women have arms, but some do well to hide them."

"Quite right, Marie," agreed the Colonel, his thin voice affording an odd contrast to the deeper tones of his cousin. "But it is the scraggy ones who seem to delight in displaying their angles."

"The English, yes," Madame admitted, "but the French, no. They are too clever, Juan."

"Frenchwomen think too much about their looks," said Val Beverley, quietly. "Oh, you know they do, Madame. They would rather die than be without admiration."

Madame shrugged her shoulders.

"So would I, my dear," she confessed, "although I cannot walk. Without admiration there is" — she snapped her fingers — "nothing. And who would notice a linnet when a bird of paradise was about, however sweet her voice? Tell me that, my dear?"

Sherlock Holmes aroused himself and laughed heartily.

"Yet," he said, "I think with Miss Beverley, that this love of elegance does not always make for happiness. Surely it is the cause of half the domestic tragedies in France?"

"Ah, the French love elegance," cried Madame, shrugging, "they cannot help it. To secure what is elegant a Frenchwoman will sometimes forget her husband, yes, but never forget herself."

"Really, Marie," protested the Colonel, "you say most strange things!"

"Is that so, Juan?" she replied, casting one of her queer glances in his direction; "but how would you like to be surrounded by a lot of drabs, eh? That man, Dr. Watson," she extended one white hand in the direction of Colonel Menendez, the fingers half closed, in a gesture which curiously reminded me of Sarah Bernhardt, "that man would notice if a parlourmaid came into the room with a shoe unbuttoned. *Poof !* If we love elegance it is because without it the men would never love *us.* "

Colonel Menendez bent across the table and kissed the white fingers in his courtier-like fashion.

"My sweet cousin," he said, "I should love you in rags."

Madame smiled and flushed like a girl, but withdrawing her hand she shrugged.

"They would have to be *pretty* rags!" she added.

During this little scene I detected Val Beverley looking at me in a vaguely troubled way, and it was easy to guess that she was wondering what construction I should place upon it. However:

"I am going into the town," declared Madame de Stämer, energetically. "Half the things ordered from Hartley's have never been sent."

"Oh, Madame, please let *me* go," cried Val Beverley.

"My dear," pronounced Madame, "I will not let you go, but I will let you come with me if you wish."

She rang a little bell which stood upon the tea-table beside the urn, and Pedro came out through the drawing room.

"Pedro," she said, "is the car ready?"

The Spanish butler bowed.

"Tell Carter to bring it round. Hurry, dear," to the girl, "if you are coming with me. I shall not be a minute."

Thereupon she whisked her mechanical chair about, waved her hand to dismiss Pedro, and went steering through the drawing room at a great rate, with Val Beverley walking beside her.

As we resumed our seats, Colonel Menendez lay back with half-closed eyes, his glance following the chair and its occupant until both were swallowed up in the shadows of the big drawing room.

"Madame de Stämer is a very remarkable woman," said Sherlock Holmes.

"Remarkable?" replied the Colonel. "The spirit of all the old chivalry of France is imprisoned within her, I think."

He passed cigarettes around, of a long kind resembling cheroots and wrapped in tobacco leaf. I thought it strange that, having thus emphasized Madame's nationality, he did not feel it incumbent upon him to explain the mystery of their kinship. However, he made no attempt to do so, and almost before we had lighted up, a racy little two-seater was driven around the gravel path by Carter, the chauffeur who had brought us to Cray's Folly from London.

The man descended and began to arrange wraps and cushions, and a few moments later back came Madame again, dressed for driving. Carter was about to lift her into the car when Colonel Menendez stood up and advanced.

"Sit down, Juan, sit down!" said Madame, sharply.

A look of keen anxiety, I had almost said of pain, leapt into her eyes, and the Colonel hesitated.

"How often must I tell you," continued the throbbing voice, "that you must not exert yourself."

Colonel Menendez accepted the rebuke humbly, but the incident struck me as grotesque; for it was difficult to associate delicacy with such a fine specimen of well-preserved manhood as the Colonel.

However, Carter performed the duty of assisting Madame into her little car, and when for a moment he supported her upright, before placing her among the cushions, I noted that she was a tall woman, slender and elegant.

All smiles and light, sparkling conversation, she settled herself comfortably at the wheel and Val Beverley got in beside her. Madame nodded to Carter in dismissal, waved her hand to Colonel Menendez, cried *"Au revoir !"* and then away went the little car, swinging around the angle of the house and out of sight.

Our host stood bare-headed upon the veranda listening to the sound of the engine dying away among the trees. He seemed to be lost in reflection from which he only aroused himself when the purr of the motor became inaudible.

"And now, gentlemen," he said, and suppressed a sigh, "we have much to talk about. This spot is cool, but is it sufficiently private? Perhaps, Mr. Holmes, you would prefer to talk in the library?"

Sherlock Holmes flicked ash from the end of his cigarette.

"Better still in your own study, Colonel Menendez," he replied.

"What, do you suspect eavesdroppers?" asked the Colonel, his manner becoming momentarily agitated.

He looked at Holmes as though he suspected the latter of possessing private information.

"We should neglect no possible precaution," answered my friend. "That agencies inimical to your safety are focussed upon the house your own statement amply demonstrates."

Colonel Menendez seemed to be on the point of speaking again, but he checked himself and in silence led the way through the ornate library to a smaller room which opened out of it, and which was furnished as a study.

Here the motif was distinctly one of officialdom. Although the Southern element was not lacking, it was not so marked as in the library or in the hall. The place was appointed for utility rather than ornament. Everything was in perfect order. In the library, with the blinds drawn, one might have supposed oneself in Trinidad; in the study, under similar conditions, one might equally well have imagined Downing Street to lie outside the windows. Essentially, this was the workroom of a man of affairs.

Having settled ourselves comfortably, Sherlock Holmes opened the conversation.

"In several particulars," said he, "I find my information to be incomplete."

He consulted the back of an envelope, upon which, I presumed during the afternoon, he had made a number of pencilled notes.

"For instance," he continued, "your detection of someone watching the house, and subsequently of someone forcing an entrance, had no visible association with the presence of the bat wing attached to your front door?"

"No," replied the Colonel, slowly, "these episodes took place a month ago."

"Exactly a month ago?"

"They took place immediately before the last full moon."

"Ah, before the full moon. And because you associate the activities of Voodoo with the full moon, you believe that the old menace has again become active?"

The Colonel nodded emphatically. He was busily engaged in rolling one of his eternal cigarettes.

"This belief of yours was recently confirmed by the discovery of the bat wing?"

"I no longer doubted," said Colonel Menendez, shrugging his shoulders. "How could I?"

"Quite so," murmured Holmes, absently, and evidently pursuing some private train of thought. "And now, I take it that your suspicions, if expressed in words would amount to this: During your last visit to Cuba you *(a)* either killed some high priest of Voodoo, or *(b)* seriously injured him? Assuming the first theory to be the correct one, your death was determined upon by the sect over which the high priest had formerly presided. Assuming the second to be accurate, however, it is presumably the man himself for whom we must look. Now, Colonel Menendez, kindly inform me if you recall the name of this man?"

"I recall it very well," replied the Colonel. "His name was M'Kombo, and he was a Benin native."

"Assuming that he is still alive, what, roughly, would his age be to-day?"

The Colonel seemed to meditate, pushing a box of long Martinique cigars across the table in my direction.

"He would be an old man," he pronounced. "I, myself, am fifty-two, and I should say that M'Kombo if alive to-day would be nearer to seventy than sixty."

"Ah," murmured Holmes, "and did he speak English?"

"A few words, I believe."

Sherlock Holmes fixed his gaze upon the dark, aquiline face.

"In short," he said, "do you really suspect that it was M'Kombo whose shadow you saw upon the lawn, who a month ago made a midnight entrance into Cray's Folly, and who recently pinned a bat wing to the door?"

Colonel Menendez seemed somewhat taken aback by this direct question. "I cannot believe it," he confessed.

"Do you believe that this order or religion of Voodooism has any existence outside those places where African natives or descendents of natives are settled?"

"I should not have been prepared to believe it, Mr. Holmes, prior to my experiences in Washington and elsewhere."

"Then you do believe that there are representatives of this cult to be met with in Europe and America?"

"I should have been prepared to believe it possible in America, for in America there are many black people, but in England — "

Again he shrugged his shoulders.

"I would remind you," said Holmes, quietly, "that there are also quite a number of blacks in England. If you seriously believe Voodoo to follow native migration, I can see no objection to assuming it to be a universal cult."

"Such an idea is incredible."

"Yet by what other hypothesis," asked Holmes, "are we to cover the facts of your own case as stated by yourself? Now," he consulted his pencilled notes, "there is another point. I gather that these African sorcerers rely largely upon what I may term intimidation. In other words, they claim the power of wishing an enemy to death."

He raised his eyes and stared grimly at the Colonel.

"I should not like to suppose that a man of your courage and culture could subscribe to such a belief."

"I do not, sir," declared the Colonel, warmly. "No Obeah man could ever exercise his will upon *me* !"

"Yet, if I may say so," murmured Holmes, "your will to live seems to have become somewhat weakened."

"What do you mean?"

Colonel Menendez stood up, his delicate nostrils dilated. He glared angrily at Holmes.

"I mean that I perceive a certain resignation in your manner of which I do not approve."

"You do not *approve?*" said Colonel Menendez, softly; and I thought as he stood looking down upon my friend that I had rarely seen a more formidable figure.

Sherlock Holmes had roused him most unaccountably, and knowing my friend for a master of tact, I knew also that this had been deliberate, although I could not even dimly perceive his object.

"I occupy the position of a specialist," Holmes continued, "and you occupy that of my patient. Now, you cannot disguise from me that your mental opposition to this danger which threatens has become slackened. Allow me to remind you that the strongest defense is counter-attack. You are angry, Colonel Menendez, but I would rather see you angry than apathetic. To come to my last point. You spoke of a neighbour in terms which led me to suppose that you suspected him of some association with your enemies. May I ask for the name of this person?"

Colonel Menendez sat down again, puffing furiously at his cigarette, whilst beginning to roll another. He was much disturbed, was fighting to regain mastery of himself.

"I apologize from the bottom of my heart," he said, "for a breach of good behaviour which really was unforgivable. I was angry when I should have been grateful. Much that you have said is true. Because it is true, I despise myself."

He flashed a glance at Sherlock Holmes.

"Awake," he continued, "I care for no man breathing, black or white; but *asleep*" — he shrugged his shoulders. "It is in sleep that these dealers in unclean things obtain their advantage."

"You excite my curiosity," declared Holmes.

"Listen," Colonel Menendez bent forward, resting his elbows upon his knees. Between the yellow fingers of his left hand he held the newly-completed cigarette whilst he continued to puff vigorously at the old one. "You recollect my speaking of the death of a certain native girl?"

Sherlock Holmes nodded.

"The real cause of her death was never known, but I obtained evidence to show that on the night after the wing of a bat had been attached to her hut, she wandered out in her sleep and visited the Black Belt. Can you doubt that someone was calling her?"

"Calling her?"

"Mr. Holmes, she was obeying the call of M'Kombo!"

"The *call* of M'Kombo? You refer to some kind of hypnotic suggestions?"

"I illustrate," replied the Colonel, "to help to make clear something which I have to tell you. On the night when last the moon was full — on the night after someone had entered the house — I had retired early to bed. Suddenly I awoke, feeling very cold. I awoke, I say, and where do you suppose I found myself?"

"I am all anxiety to hear."

"On the point of entering the Tudor garden — you call it Tudor garden? — which is visible from the window of your room!"

"Most extraordinary," murmured Holmes; "and you were in your night attire?"

"I was."

"And what had awakened you?"

"An accident. I believe a lucky accident. I had cut my bare foot upon the gravel and the pain awakened me."

"You had no recollection of any dream which had prompted you to go down into the garden?"

"None whatever."

"Does your room face in that direction?"

"It does not. It faces the lake on the south of the house. I had descended to a side door, unbarred it, and walked entirely around the east wing before I awakened."

"Your room faces the lake," murmured Holmes.

"Yes."

Their glances met, and in Sherlock Holmes's expression there seemed to be a challenge.

"You have not yet told me," said he, "the name of your neighbour."

Colonel Menendez lighted his new cigarette.

"Mr. Holmes," he confessed, "I regret that I ever referred to this suspicion of mine. Indeed it is hardly a suspicion, it is what I may call a desperate doubt. Do you say that, a most desperate doubt?"

"I think I follow you," said Holmes.

"The fact is this, I only know of one person within ten miles of Cray's Folly who has ever visited Cuba."

"Ah."

"I have no other scrap of evidence to associate him I with my shadowy enemy. This being so, you will pardon me if I ask you to forget that I ever referred to his existence."

He spoke the words with a sort of lofty finality, and accompanied them with a gesture of the hands which really left Holmes no alternative but to drop the subject.

Again their glances met, and it was patent to me that underlying all this conversation was something beyond my ken. What it was that Holmes suspected I could not imagine, nor what it was that Colonel Menendez desired to conceal; but tension was in the very air. The Spaniard was on the defensive, and Sherlock Holmes was puzzled, irritated.

It was a strange interview, and one which in the light of after events I recognized to possess extraordinary significance. That sixth sense of Holmes's was awake, was prompting him, but to what extent he understood its promptings at that hour I did not know, and have never known to this day. Intuitively, I believe, as he sat there staring at Colonel Menendez, he began to perceive the shadow within a shadow which was the secret of Cray's Folly, which was the thing called Bat Wing, which was the devilish force at that very hour alive and potent in our midst.

9.

OBEAH

This conversation in Colonel Menendez's study produced a very unpleasant impression upon my mind. The atmosphere of Cray's Folly seemed to become charged with unrest. Of Madame de Stämer and Miss Beverley I saw nothing up to the time that I retired to dress. Having dressed, I walked into Holmes's room, anxious to learn if he had formed any theory to account for the singular business which had brought us to Surrey.

Holmes had excused himself directly we had left the study, stating that he wished to get to the village post-office in time to send a telegram to London. Our host had suggested a messenger, but this, as well as the offer of a car, Holmes had declined, saying that the exercise would aid reflection. Nevertheless, I was surprised to find his room empty, for I could not imagine why the sending of a telegram should have detained him so long.

Dusk was falling and, viewed from the open window, the Tudor garden below looked very beautiful, part of it lying in a sort of purplish shadow and the rest being mystically lighted as though viewed through a golden veil. To the whole picture a sort of magic quality was added by a speck of high-light which rested upon the face of the old sun-dial.

I thought that here was a fit illustration for a fairy tale; then I remembered the Colonel's account of how he had awakened in the act of entering this romantic *plaisance*, and I was touched anew by an unrestfulness, by a sense of the uncanny.

I observed a book lying upon the dressing table, and concluding that it was one which Holmes had brought with him, I took it up, glancing at the title. It was "African Magic," and switching on the light, for there was a private electric plant in Cray's Folly, I opened the book at random and began to read.

"The religion of the African native," said this authority, "is emotional, and more often than not associated with beliefs in witchcraft and in the rites known as Voodoo or Obi Mysteries. It has been endeavoured by some students to show that these are relics of the Fetish worship of equatorial Africa, but such a genealogy has never been satisfactorily demonstrated. The cannibalistic rituals, human sacrifices, and obscene ceremonies resembling those of the

Black Sabbath of the Middle Ages, reported to prevail in Haiti and other of the islands, and by some among the blacks of the Southern States of America, may be said to rest on doubtful authority. Nevertheless, it is a fact beyond doubt that among the natives both of the West Indies and the United States there is a widespread belief in the powers of the Obeah man. A native who believes himself to have come under the spell of such a sorcerer will sink into a kind of decline and sometimes die."

At this point I discovered several paragraphs underlined in pencil, and concluding that the underlining had been done by Sherlock Holmes, I read them with particular care. They were as follows:

> "According to Hesketh J. Bell, the term Obeah is most probably derived from the substantive Obi, a word used on the East coast of Africa to denote witchcraft, sorcery, and fetishism in general. The etymology of Obi has been traced to a very antique source, stretching far back into Egyptian mythology. A serpent in the Egyptian language was called Ob or Aub. Obion is still the Egyptian name for a serpent. Moses, in the name of God, forbade the Israelites ever to enquire of the demon, Ob, which is translated in our Bible: Charmer or wizard, divinator or sorcerer. The Witch of Endor is called Oub or Ob, translated Pythonissa; and Oubois was the name of the basilisk or royal serpent, emblem of the Sun and an ancient oracular deity of Africa."

A paragraph followed which was doubly underlined, and pursuing my reading I made a discovery which literally caused me to hold my breath. This is what I read:

> "In a recent contribution to the *Occult Review*, Mr. Colin Camber, the American authority, offered some very curious particulars in support of a theory to show that, whereas snakes and scorpions have always been recognized as sacred by Voodoo worshippers, the real emblem of their unclean religion is the bat, especially *the Vampire Bat of South America.*
>
> "He pointed out that the symptoms of one dying beneath the spell of an Obeah man are closely paralleled in the cases of men and animals who have suffered from nocturnal attacks of blood-sucking bats."

I laid the open book down upon the bed. My brain was in a tumult. The several theories, or outlines of theories which hitherto I had entertained, were, by these simple paragraphs, cast into the utmost disorder. I thought of the Colonel's covert references to a neighbour whom he feared, of his guarded statement that the devotees of Voodoo were not confined to the West Indies, of the attack upon him in Washington, of the ominous bat wing pinned to the door of Cray's Folly.

Incredulously, I thought of my acquaintance of the Lavender Arms, with his bemused expression and his magnificent brow; and a great doubt and wonder grew up in my mind.

I became increasingly impatient for the return of Sherlock Holmes. I felt that a clue of the first importance had fallen into my possession; so that when, presently, as I walked impatiently up and down the room, the door opened and Holmes entered, I greeted him excitedly.

"Holmes!" I cried, "Holmes! I have learned a most extraordinary thing!"

Even as I spoke and looked into the keen, eager face, the expression in Holmes's eyes struck me. I recognized that in him, too, intense excitement was pent up. Furthermore, he was in one of his irritable moods. But, full of my own discoveries:

"I chanced to glance at this book," I continued, "whilst I was waiting for you. You have underlined certain passages."

He stared at me queerly.

"I discovered the book in my own library after you had gone last night, Watson, and it was then that I marked the passages which struck me as significant."

"But, Holmes," I cried, "the man who is quoted here, Colin Camber, lives in this very neighbourhood!"

"I know."

"What! You know?"

"I learned it from Inspector Aylesbury of the County Police half an hour ago."

Holmes frowned perplexedly. "Why, in Heaven's name didn't you tell me earlier?" he exclaimed. "It would have saved me a most disagreeable journey into Market Hilton."

"Market Hilton! What, have you been into the town?"

"That is exactly where I have been, Watson. I 'phoned through to Mrs. Hudson from the village post-office after lunch to have the car sent down. There is a convenient garage by the Lavender Arms."

"But the Colonel has three cars," I exclaimed.

"The horse has four legs," replied Sherlock Holmes, irritably, "but although I have only two, there are times when I prefer to use them. I am still wondering why you failed to mention this piece of information when you had obtained it."

"My dear Holmes," said I, patiently, "how could I possibly be expected to attach any importance to the matter? You must remember that at the time I had never seen this work on Voodoo sorcery."

"No," said Holmes, dropping down upon the bed, "that is perfectly true, Watson. I am afraid I have a liver at times; a distinct Indian liver. Excuse me, old man, but to tell you the truth I feel strangely inclined to pack my bag and leave for London without a moment's delay."

"What!" I cried.

"Oh, I know you would be sorry to go, Watson," said Holmes, smiling, "and so, for many reasons, should I. But I have the strongest possible objection to being trifled with."

"I am afraid I don't quite understand you, Holmes."

"Well, just consider the matter for a moment. Do you suppose that Colonel Menendez is ignorant of the fact that his nearest neighbour is a recognized authority upon Voodoo and allied subjects?"

"You are speaking, of course, of Colin Camber?"

"Of none other."

"No," I replied, thoughtfully, "the Colonel must know, of course, that Camber resides in the neighbourhood."

"And that he knows something of the nature of Camber's studies his remarks sufficiently indicate," added Holmes. "The whole theory to account for these attacks upon his life rests on the premise that agents of these Obeah people are established in England and America. Then, in spite of my direct questions, he leaves me to find out for myself that Colin Camber's property practically adjoins his own!"

"Really! Does he reside so near as that?"

"My dear fellow," cried Holmes, "he lives at a place called the Guest House. You can see it from part of the grounds of Cray's Folly. We were looking at it to-day."

"What! The house on the hillside?"

"That's the Guest House! What do you make of it, Watson? That Menendez suspects this man is beyond doubt. Why should he hesitate to mention his name?"

"Well," I replied, slowly, "probably because to associate practical sorcery and assassination with such a character would be preposterous."

"But the man is admittedly a student of these things, Watson."

"He may be, and that he is a genius of some kind I am quite prepared to believe. But having had the pleasure of meeting Mr. Colin Camber, I am not prepared to believe him capable of murder."

I suppose I spoke with a certain air of triumph, for Sherlock Holmes regarded me silently for a while.

"You seem to be taking this case out of my hands, Watson," he said. "Whilst I have been systematically at work racing about the county in quest of information, you would appear to have blundered further into the labyrinth than all my industry has enabled me to do."

He remained in a very disgruntled humour, and now the cause of this suddenly came to light.

"I have spent a thoroughly unpleasant afternoon," Holmes continued, "interviewing an impossible country policeman who had never heard of my existence!"

This display of human resentment honestly delighted me. It was refreshing to know that the omniscient Sherlock Holmes was capable of pique.

"One, Inspector Aylesbury," he went on, bitterly, "a large person bearing a really interesting resemblance to a walrus, but lacking that creature's intelligence. It was not until

Superintendent East had spoken to him from Scotland Yard that he ceased to treat me as a suspect. But his new attitude was almost more provoking than the old one. He adopted the manner of a regimental sergeant-major reluctantly interviewing a private with a grievance. If matters should so develop that we are compelled to deal with that fish-faced idiot, God help us all!"

Holmes burst out laughing, his good humour suddenly quite restored; and taking out his pipe, began industriously to load it.

"I can smoke while I am changing," he said, "and you can sit there and tell me all about Colin Camber."

I did as he requested, and Holmes, who could change quicker than any man I had ever known, had just finished tying his bow as I completed my story of the encounter at the Lavender Arms.

"Hmm," he muttered, as I ceased speaking. "At every turn I realize that without you I should have been lost, Watson. I am afraid I shall have to change your duties to-morrow."

"Change my duties? What do you mean?"

"I warn you that the new ones will be less pleasant than the old! In other words, I must ask you to tear yourself away from Miss Val Beverley for an hour in the morning, and take advantage of Mr. Camber's invitation to call upon him."

"Frankly, I doubt if he would acknowledge me."

"Nevertheless, you have a better excuse than I. In the circumstances, it is most important that we should get in touch with this man."

"Very well," I said, ruefully. "I will do my best. But you don't seriously think, Holmes, that the danger comes from there?"

Sherlock Holmes took his dinner jacket from the chair upon which the man had laid it out, and turned to me.

"My dear Watson," he said, "you may remember that I spoke, recently, of once again retiring from this profession?"

"You did."

"My next retirement will not be voluntary, Watson. I shall be kicked out as an incompetent ass; for, respecting the connection, if any, between the narrative of Colonel Menendez, the bat wing nailed to the door of the house, and Mr. Colin Camber, I have not the foggiest notion. In this, at last, I have triumphed over Auguste Dupin.

Auguste Dupin never confessed defeat."

10.

THE NIGHT WALKER

If luncheon had seemed extravagant, dinner at Cray's Folly proved to be a veritable Roman banquet. To associate ideas of selfishness with Miss Beverley was hateful, but the more I learned of the luxurious life of this queer household hidden away in the Surrey Hills, the less I wondered at anyone's consenting to share such exile. I had hitherto counted an American freak dinner, organized by a lucky plunger and held at the Café de Paris, as the last word in extravagant feasting. But I learned now that what was *caviare* in Monte Carlo was ordinary fare at Cray's Folly.

Colonel Menendez was an epicure with an endless purse. The excellence of one of the courses upon which I had commented led to a curious incident.

"You approve of the efforts of my chef?" said the Colonel.

"He is worthy of his employer," I replied.

Colonel Menendez bowed in his cavalierly fashion and Madame de Stämer positively beamed upon me.

"You shall speak for him," said the Spaniard. "He was with me in Cuba, but has no reputation in London. There are hotels that would snap him up."

I looked at the speaker in surprise.

"Surely he is not leaving you?" I asked.

The Colonel exhibited a momentary embarrassment.

"No, no. No, no," he replied, waving his hand gracefully, "I was only thinking that he — " there was a scarcely perceptible pause — "might wish to better himself. Do you understand?"

I understood only too well; and recollecting the words spoken by Sherlock Holmes that afternoon, respecting the

Colonel's will to live, I became conscious of an uncomfortable sense of chill.

If I had doubted that in so speaking he had been contemplating his own death, the behaviour of Madame de Stämer must have convinced me. Her complexion was slightly but cleverly made up, with all the exquisite art of the Parisienne, but even through the artificial bloom, I saw her cheeks blanch. Her face grew haggard and her eyes burned unnaturally. She turned quickly aside to address Sherlock Holmes, but I knew that the significance of this slight episode had not escaped him.

He was by no means at ease. In the first place, he was badly puzzled; in the second place, he was angry. He felt it incumbent upon him to save this man from a menace which he, Sherlock Holmes, evidently recognized to be real, although to me it appeared wildly chimerical, and the very person upon whose active coöperation he naturally counted not only seemed resigned to his fate, but by deliberate omission of important data added to Holmes's difficulties.

How much of this secret drama proceeding in Cray's Folly was appreciated by Val Beverley I could not determine. On this occasion, I remember, she was simply but perfectly dressed and, in my eyes, seemed the most sweetly desirable woman I had ever known save for my dear departed Mary. Realizing that I had already revealed my interest in the girl, I was oddly self-conscious, and a hundred times during the progress of dinner I glanced across at Holmes, expecting to detect his quizzical smile. He was very stern, however, and seemed more reserved than usual. He was uncertain of his ground, I could see. He resented the understanding which evidently existed between Colonel Menendez and Madame de Stämer, and to which, although his aid had been sought, he was not admitted.

It seemed to me, personally, that an almost palpable shadow lay upon the room. Although, save for this one lapse, our host throughout talked gaily and entertainingly, I was obsessed by a memory of the expression which I had detected upon his face that morning, the expression of a doomed man.

What, in Heaven's name, I asked myself, did it all mean? If ever I saw the fighting spirit looking out of any man's eyes, it looked out of the eyes of Don Juan Sarmiento Menendez. Why, then, did he lie down to the menace of this mysterious Bat Wing, and if he counted opposition futile, why had he summoned Sherlock Holmes to Cray's Folly?

With the passing of every moment, I sympathized more fully with the perplexity of my friend, and no longer wondered that even his highly specialized faculties had failed to detect an explanation.

Remembering Colin Camber as I had seen him at the Lavender Arms, it was simply impossible to suppose that such a man as Menendez could fear such a man as Camber. True, I had seen the latter at a disadvantage, and I knew well enough that many a genius has been also a drunkard. But although I was prepared to find that Colin Camber possessed genius, I found it hard to believe that this was of a criminal type. That such a character could be the representative of some remote cult society was an idea too grotesque to be entertained for a moment.

I was tempted to believe that his presence in the neighbourhood of this haunted Cuban was one of those strange coincidences which in criminal history have sometimes proved so tragic for their victims.

Madame de Stämer, avoiding the Colonel's glances, which were pathetically apologetic, gradually recovered herself, and:

"My dear," she said to Val Beverley, "you look perfectly sweet to-night. Don't you think she looks perfectly sweet, Dr. Watson?"

Ignoring a look of entreaty from the blue-gray eyes:

"Perfectly," I replied.

"Oh, Dr. Watson," cried the girl, "why do you encourage her? She says embarrassing things like that every time I put on a new dress."

Her reference to a new dress set me speculating again upon the apparent anomaly of her presence at Cray's Folly. That she was not a professional "companion" was clear enough. I assumed that her father had left her suitably provided for, since she wore such expensively simple gowns. She had a delightful trick of blushing when attention was focussed upon her, and said Madame de Stämer:

"To be able to blush like that I would give my string of pearls — no, half of it."

"My dear Marie," declared Colonel Menendez, "I have seen you blush perfectly."

"No, no," Madame disclaimed the suggestion with one of those Bernhardt gestures, "I blushed my last blush when my second husband introduced me to my first husband's wife."

"Madame!" exclaimed Val Beverley, "how can you say such things?" She turned to me. "Really, Dr. Watson, they are all fables."

"In fables we renew our youth," said Madame.

"Ah," sighed Colonel Menendez; "our youth, our youth ..."

"Why sigh, Juan, why regret?" cried Madame, immediately. "Old age is tragic only to those who have never been young."

She directed a glance toward him as she spoke those words, and as I had felt when I had seen his tragic face on the veranda that morning I felt again in detecting this look of Madame de Stämer's. The yearning yet selfless love which it expressed was not for my eyes to witness.

"Thank God, Marie," replied the Colonel, and gallantly kissed his hand to her, "we have both been young, gloriously young."

When, at the termination of this truly historic dinner, the two ladies left us:

"Remember, Juan," said Madame, raising her white, jewelled hand, and holding the fingers characteristically curled, "no excitement, no billiards, no cards."

Colonel Menendez bowed deeply, as the invalid wheeled herself from the room, followed by Miss Beverley. My heart

124

was beating delightfully, for in the moment of departure the latter had favoured me with a significant glance, which seemed to say, "I am looking forward to a chat with you presently."

"Ah," said Colonel Menendez, when we three men found ourselves alone, "truly I am blessed in the autumn of my life with such charming companionship. Beauty and wit, youth and discretion. Is he not a happy man who possesses all these?"

"He should be," said Holmes, gravely.

The saturnine Pedro entered with some wonderful crusted port, and Colonel Menendez offered cigars.

"I believe you are a pipe-smoker," said our courteous host to Holmes, "and if this is so, I know that you will prefer your favourite mixture to any cigar that ever was rolled."

"Many thanks," said Holmes, to whom no more delicate compliment could have been paid.

Holmes was indeed an inveterate pipe-smoker, and only rarely did he truly enjoy a cigar, however choice its pedigree. With a sigh of content he began to fill his briar. His mood was more restful, and covertly I watched him studying our host. The night remained very warm and one of the two windows of the dining room, which was the most homely apartment in Cray's Folly, was wide open, offering a prospect of sweeping velvet lawns touched by the magic of the moonlight.

A short silence fell, to be broken by the Colonel.

"Gentlemen," he said, "I trust you do not regret your fishing excursion?"

"I could cheerfully pass the rest of my days in such ideal surroundings," replied Sherlock Holmes.

I nodded in agreement.

"But," continued my friend, speaking very deliberately, "I have to remember that I am here upon business, and that my professional reputation is perhaps at stake."

He stared very hard at Colonel Menendez.

"I have spoken with your butler, known as Pedro, and with some of the other servants, and have learned all that there is to be learned about the person unknown who gained admittance to the house a month ago, and concerning the wing of a bat, found attached to the door more recently."

"And to what conclusion have you come?" asked Colonel Menendez, eagerly.

The Colonel bent forward, resting his elbows upon his knees, a pose which he frequently adopted. He was smoking a cigar, but his total absorption in the topic under discussion was revealed by the fact that from a pocket in his dinner jacket he had taken out a portion of tobacco, had laid it in a slip of rice paper, and was busily rolling one of his eternal cigarettes.

"I might be enabled to come to one," replied Holmes, "if you would answer a very simple question."

"What is this question?"

"It is this — Have you any idea who nailed the bat's wing to your door?"

Colonel Menendez's eyes opened very widely, and his face became more aquiline than ever.

"You have heard my story, Mr. Holmes," he replied, softly. "If I know the explanation, why do I come to you?"

Sherlock Holmes puffed at his pipe. His expression did not alter in the slightest.

"I merely wondered if your suspicions tended in the direction of Mr. Colin Camber," he said.

"Colin Camber!"

As the Colonel spoke, the name either I became victim of a strange delusion or his face was momentarily convulsed. If my senses served me aright then his pronouncing of the words "Colin Camber" occasioned him positive agony. He clutched the arms of his chair, striving, I thought, to retain composure, and in this he succeeded, for when he spoke again his voice was quite normal.

"Do you have any particular reason for your remark, Mr. Holmes?"

"I have a reason," replied Sherlock Holmes, "but don't misunderstand me. I suggest nothing against Mr. Camber. I should be glad, however, to know if you are acquainted with him?"

"We have never met."

"You possibly know him by reputation?"

"I have heard of him, Mr. Holmes. But to be perfectly frank, I have little in common with citizens of the United States."

A note of arrogance, which at times crept into his high, thin voice, became perceptible now, and the aristocratic, aquiline face looked very supercilious.

How the conversation would have developed I know not, but at this moment Pedro entered and delivered a message in Spanish to the Colonel, whereupon the latter arose and with very profuse apologies begged permission to leave us for a few moments.

When he had retired:

"I am going upstairs to write a letter, Watson," said Sherlock Holmes. "Carry on with your old duties to-day, your new ones do not commence until to-morrow."

With that he laughed and walked out of the dining room, leaving me wondering whether to be grateful or annoyed. However, it did not take me long to find my way to the drawing room where the two ladies were seated side by side upon a *settée*, Madame's chair having been wheeled into a corner.

"Ah, Dr. Watson," exclaimed Madame as I entered, "have the others deserted, then?"

"Scarcely deserted, I think. They are merely straggling."

"Absent without leave," murmured Val Beverley.

I laughed and drew up a chair. Madame de Stämer was smoking, but Miss Beverley was not. Accordingly, I offered her a cigarette, which she accepted; and as I was lighting it with elaborate care, every moment finding a new beauty in her charming face, Pedro again appeared and addressed some remark in Spanish to Madame.

"My chair, Pedro," she said; "I will come at once."

The Spanish butler wheeled the chair across to the *settée*, and lifting her with an ease which spoke of long practice, placed her amidst the cushions where she spent so many hours of her life.

"I know you will excuse me, dear," she said to Val Beverley, "because I feel sure that Dr. Watson will do his very best to make up for my absence. Presently, I shall be back."

Pedro holding the door open, she went wheeling out, and I found myself alone with Val Beverley.

At the time I was much too delighted to question the circumstances which had led to this *tête-à-tête,* but had I cared to give the matter any consideration, it must have presented rather curious features. The call first of host and then of hostess was inconsistent with the courtesy of the master of Cray's Folly, which, like the appointments of his home and his mode of life, was elaborate. But these ideas did not trouble me at the moment.

Suddenly, however, indeed before I had time to speak, the girl started and laid her hand upon my arm.

"Did you hear something?" she whispered, "a queer sort of sound?"

"No," I replied, "what kind of sound?"

"An odd sort of sound, almost like — the flapping of wings."

I saw that she had turned pale, I saw the confirmation of something which I had only partly realised before: that her life at Cray's Folly was a constant fight against some haunting shadow. Her gaiety, her lightness, were but a mask. For now, in those wide-open eyes, I read absolute horror.

"Miss Beverley," I said, grasping her hand reassuringly, "you alarm me. What has made you so nervous to-night?"

"To-night!" she echoed, "to-night? It is every night. If you had not come — " she corrected herself — "if someone had not come, I don't think I could have stayed. I am sure I could not have stayed."

"Doubtless the recent attempted burglary alarmed you?" I suggested, intending to sooth her fears.

"Burglary?" She smiled unmirthfully. "It was no burglary."

"Why do you say so, Miss Beverley?"

"Do you think I don't know why Mr. Holmes is here?" she challenged. "Oh, believe me, I know — I know. I, too, saw the bat's wing nailed to the door, Dr. Watson. You are surely not going to suggest that this was the work of a burglar?"

I seated myself beside her on the *settée*.

"You have great courage," I said. "Believe me, I quite understand all that you have suffered."

"Is my acting so poor?" she asked, with a pathetic smile.

"No, it is wonderful, but to a sympathetic observer, only acting, nevertheless."

I noted that my presence reassured her, and was much comforted by this fact.

"Would you like to tell me all about it," I continued; "or would this merely renew your fears?"

"I should like to tell you," she replied in a low voice, glancing about her as if to make sure that we were alone. "Except for odd people, friends, I suppose, of the Colonel's, we have had so few visitors since we have been at Cray's Folly. Apart from all sorts of queer happenings which really" — she laughed nervously — "may have no significance whatever, the crowning mystery to my mind is why Colonel Menendez should have leased this huge house."

"He does not entertain very much, then?"

"Scarcely at all. The 'County' — do you know what I mean by the 'County?' — began by receiving him with open arms and ended by sending him to Coventry. His lavish style of entertainment they labelled 'swank' — a horrible word, but very expressive! They concluded that they did not understand him, and of everything they don't understand they disapprove. So after the first month or so, it became very lonely at Cray's Folly. Our foreign servants — there are five of them altogether — got us a dreadfully bad name. Then, little by little, a sort of cloud seemed to settle on everything. The Colonel made two visits abroad. I don't know exactly where he went, but on his return from the first visit Madame de Stämer changed."

"Changed? — in what way?"

"I am afraid it would be hopeless to try to make you understand, Dr. Watson, but in some subtle way she changed. Underneath all her vivacity, she is a tragic woman, and — oh, how can I explain?" Val Beverley made a little gesture of despair.

"Perhaps you mean," I suggested, "that she seemed to become even less happy than before?"

"Yes," she replied, looking at me eagerly. "Has Colonel Menendez told you anything to account for it?"

"Nothing," I said, "He has left us strangely in the dark. But you say he went abroad on a second and more recent occasion?"

"Yes, not much more than a month ago. And after that, somehow or other, matters seemed to come to a head. I confess I became horribly frightened, but to have left would have seemed like desertion, and Madame de Stämer has been so good to me."

"Did you actually witness any of the episodes which took place about a month ago?"

Val Beverley shook her head.

"I never saw anything really definite," she replied.

"Yet, evidently you either saw or heard something which alarmed you."

"Yes, that is true, but it is so difficult to explain."

"Could you try to explain?"

"I will try if you wish, for really I am longing to talk to someone about it. For instance, on several occasions I have heard footsteps in the corridor outside my room."

"At night?"

"Yes, at night."

"Strange footsteps?"

She nodded.

"That is the uncanny part of it. You know how familiar one grows with the footsteps of persons living in the same house? Well, these footsteps were quite unfamiliar to me."

"And you say they passed your door?"

"Yes. My rooms are almost directly overhead. And right at the end of the corridor, that is on the southeast corner of the building, is Colonel Menendez's bedroom, and facing it a sort of little smoke-room. It was in this direction that the footsteps went."

"To Colonel Menendez's room?"

"Yes. They were light, furtive footsteps."

"This took place late at night?"

"Quite late, long after everyone had retired."

She paused, staring at me with a sort of embarrassment, and presently:

"Were the footsteps those of a man or a woman?" I asked.

"Of a woman. Someone, Dr. Watson," she bent forward, and that look of fear began to creep into her eyes again, "with whose footsteps I was quite unfamiliar."

"You mean a stranger to the house?"

"Yes. Oh, it was uncanny." She shuddered. "The first time I heard it, I had been lying awake listening. I was nervous. Madame de Stämer had told me that morning that the Colonel had seen someone lurking about the lawns on the previous night. Then, as I lay awake listening for the slightest sound, I suddenly detected these footsteps; and they paused — right outside my door."

"Good Heavens!" I exclaimed. "What did you do?"

"Frankly, I was too frightened to do anything. I just lay still with my heart beating horribly, and presently they passed on, and I heard them no more."

"Was your door locked?"

"No." She laughed nervously. "But it has been locked every night since then!"

"And these sounds were repeated on other nights?"

"Yes, I have often heard them, Dr. Watson. What makes it so strange is that all the servants sleep out in the west wing, as you know, and Pedro locks the communicating door every night before retiring."

"It is certainly strange," I muttered.

"It is horrible," declared the girl, almost in a whisper. "For what can it mean except that there is someone in Cray's Folly who is never seen during the daytime?"

"But that is incredible."

"It is not so incredible in a big house like this. Besides, what other explanation can there be?"

"There must be one," I said, reassuringly. "Have you spoken of this to Madame de Stämer?"

"Yes."

Val Beverley's expression grew troubled.

"Had she any explanation to offer?"

"None. Her attitude mystified me very much. Indeed, instead of reassuring me, she frightened me more than ever by her very silence. I grew to dread the coming of each night. Then — " she hesitated again, looking at me pathetically — "twice I have been awakened by a loud cry."

"What kind of cry?"

"I could not tell you, Dr. Watson. You see I have always been asleep when it has come, but I have sat up trembling and dimly aware that what had awakened me was a cry of some kind."

"You have no idea from whence it proceeded?"

"None whatever. Of course, all these things may seem trivial to you, and possibly they can be explained in quite a simple way. But this feeling of something pending has grown almost unendurable. Then, I don't understand Madame and the Colonel at all."

She suddenly stopped speaking and flushed with embarrassment.

"If you mean that Madame de Stämer is in love with her cousin, I agree with you," I said, quietly.

"Oh, is it so evident as that?" murmured Val Beverley. She laughed to cover her confusion. "I wish I could understand what it all means."

At this point our *tête-à-tête* was interrupted by the return of Madame de Stämer.

"Ooh, la la !" she cried, "the Colonel must have allowed himself to become too animated this evening. He is threatened with one of his attacks and I have insisted upon his immediate retirement. He makes his apologies, but knows you will understand."

I expressed my concern, and:

"I was unaware that Colonel Menendez's health was impaired," I said.

"Ah," Madame shrugged characteristically. "Juan has travelled too much of the road of life on top speed,

Dr. Watson." She snapped her white fingers and grimaced significantly. "Excitement is bad for him."

She wheeled her chair up beside Val Beverley, and taking the girl's hand patted it affectionately.

"You look pale to-night, my dear," she said. "All this bogey business is getting on your nerves, eh?"

"Oh, not at all," declared the girl. "It is very mysterious and annoying, of course."

"But Monsieur Sherlock Holmes will presently tell us what it is all about," concluded Madame. "Yes, I trust so. We want no Cuban devils here at Cray's Folly."

I had hoped that she would speak further of the matter, but having thus apologized for our host's absence, she plunged into an amusing account of Parisian society, and of the changes which five years of war had brought about. Her comments, although brilliant, were superficial, the only point I recollect being her reference to a certain Baron Bergmann, a Swedish diplomat, who, according to Madame, had the longest nose and the shortest memory in Paris, so that in the cold weather, "he even sometimes forgot to blow his nose."

Her brightness, I thought, was almost feverish. She chattered and laughed and gesticulated, but on this occasion she was overacting. Underneath all her vivacity lay something cold and grim.

Holmes rejoined us in half an hour or so, but I could see that he was as conscious of the air of tension as I was. All Madame's high spirits could not enable her to conceal the fact that she was anxious to retire. But Holmes's evident desire to do likewise surprised me very greatly; for from the point of view of the investigation the day had been an unsatisfactory one. I knew that there must be a hundred and one things which my friend desired to know, questions which Madame de Stämer could have answered. Nevertheless, at about ten o'clock we separated for the night, and although I was intensely anxious to talk to Holmes, his reticent mood had descended upon him again, and:

"Sleep well, Watson," he said, as he paused at my door. "I may be awakening you early."

With which cryptic remark and not another word he passed on and entered his own room.

11.

THE SHADOW ON THE BLIND

Perhaps it was childish on my part, but I accepted this curt dismissal very ill-humouredly. That Holmes, for some reason of his own, wished to be alone, was evident enough, but I resented being excluded from his confidence, even temporarily. It would seem that he had formed a theory in the prosecution of which my coöperation was not needed. And what with profitless conjectures concerning its nature, and memories of Val Beverley's pathetic parting glance as we had bade one another good-night, sleep seemed to be out of the question, and I stood for a long time staring out of the open window.

The weather remained almost tropically hot, and the moon floated in a cloudless sky. I looked down upon the closely-matted leaves of the box hedge which rose to within a few feet of my window, and to the left I could obtain a view of the close-hemmed courtyard before the doors of Cray's Folly. On the right, the yews obstructed my view of the Tudor garden; but the night air was fragrant, and the outlook one of peace.

After a time, then, as no sound came from the adjoining room, I turned in, and despite all things was soon fast asleep.

Almost immediately, it seemed, I was awakened. In point of fact, nearly four hours had elapsed. A hand grasped my shoulder and I sprang up in bed with a stifled cry, but:

"It's all right, Watson," came Holmes's voice. "Don't make a noise."

"Holmes!" I said. "Holmes! What has happened?"

"Nothing, nothing. I am sorry to have to disturb your beauty sleep, but in the absence of Mrs. Hudson, I am compelled to use you as a dictaphone, Watson. I like to record impressions while they are fresh, hence my having awakened you."

"But what has happened?" I asked again, for my brain was not yet fully alert.

"No, don't light up!" said Holmes, grasping my wrist as I reached out toward the table-lamp.

His figure showed as a black silhouette against the dim square of the window.

"Why not?"

"Well, it's nearly two o'clock. The light might be observed."

"Two o'clock?" I exclaimed.

"Yes. I think we might smoke, though. Have you any cigarettes? I have left my pipe behind."

I managed to find my case, and in the dim light of the match which I presently struck, I saw that Sherlock Holmes's face was very fixed and grim. He seated himself on the edge of my bed, and:

"I have been guilty of a breach of hospitality, Watson," he began. "Not only have I secretly had my own car sent down here, but I have had something else sent as well. I brought it in under my coat this evening."

"To what do you refer, Holmes?"

"You remember the silken rope-ladder with bamboo rungs which I ordered from Hong Kong on one occasion?"

"Yes — "

"Well, I have it in my bag now."

"But, my dear fellow, what possible use can it be to you at Cray's Folly?"

"It has been of great use," he returned, shortly. "It enabled me to descend from my window a couple of hours ago and to return again quite recently without disturbing the household.

Don't reproach me, Watson. I know it is a breach of confidence, but so is the behaviour of Colonel Menendez."

"You refer to his reticence on certain points?"

"I do. I have a reputation to lose, Watson, and if an ingenious piece of Chinese workmanship can save it, it shall be saved."

"But, my dear Holmes, why should you want to leave the house secretly at night?"

Sherlock Holmes's cigarette glowed in the dark, then:

"My original object," he replied, "was to endeavour to learn if anyone were really watching the place. For instance, I wanted to see if all lights were out at the Guest House."

"And were they?" I asked, eagerly.

"They were. Secondly," he continued, "I wanted to convince myself that there were no nocturnal prowlers from within or without."

"What do you mean by within or without?"

"Listen, Watson." He bent toward me in the dark, grasping my shoulder firmly. "One window in Cray's Folly was lighted up."

"At what hour?"

"The light is there yet."

That he was about to make some strange revelation I divined. I detected the fact, too, that he believed this revelation would be unpleasant to me; and in this I found an explanation of his earlier behaviour. He had seemed distraught and ill at ease when he had joined Madame de Stämer, Miss Beverley, and myself in the drawing room. I could only suppose that this and the abrupt parting with me outside my door had been due to his holding a theory which he had proposed to put to the test before confiding it to me. I remember that I spoke very slowly as I asked him the question:

"Whose is the lighted window, Holmes?"

"Has Colonel Menendez taken you into a little snuggery or smoke-room which faces his bedroom in the southeast corner of the house?"

"No, but Miss Beverley has mentioned the room."

"Ah. Well, there is a light in that room, Watson."

"Possibly the Colonel has not retired?"

"According to Madame de Stämer, he went to bed several hours ago, you may remember."

"True," I murmured, fumbling for the significance of his words.

"The next point is this," he resumed. "You saw Madame retire to her own room, which, as you know, is on the ground floor, and I have satisfied myself that the door communicating with the servants' wing is locked."

"I see. But to what is all this leading, Holmes?"

"To a very curious fact, and the fact is this: The Colonel is not alone."

I sat bolt upright.

"What?" I cried.

"Not so loud," warned Holmes.

"But, Holmes — "

"My dear fellow, we must face facts. I repeat, the Colonel is not alone."

"Why do you say so?"

"Twice I have seen a shadow on the blind of the smoke-room."

"His own shadow, probably."

Again Sherlock Holmes's cigarette glowed in the darkness.

"I am prepared to swear," he replied, "that it was the shadow of a woman."

"Holmes — "

"Don't get excited, Watson. I am dealing with the strangest case of my career, and I am jumping to no conclusions. But just let us now look at the circumstances judicially. The whole of the domestic staff we may dismiss, with the one exception of Mrs. Fisher, who, so far as I can make out, occupies the position of a sort of working housekeeper, and whose rooms are in the corner of the west wing immediately facing the kitchen garden. Possibly you have not met Mrs. Fisher, Watson, but I have made it my business to interview the whole of the staff; and I may say that Mrs. Fisher is a short, stout old lady, a native of Kent, I believe, whose outline in no way corresponds to that which I saw upon the blind. Therefore, unless the door which communicates with the servants' quarters was unlocked again to-night — to what are we reduced in seeking to explain the presence of a woman in Colonel Menendez's room? Madame de Stämer, unassisted, could not possibly have mounted the stairs."

"Stop, Holmes!" I said, sternly. "Stop."

He ceased speaking, and I watched the steady glow of his cigarette in the darkness. It lighted up his aquiline face and showed me the steely gleam of his eyes.

"You are counting too much on the locking of the door by Pedro," I continued, speaking very deliberately. "He is a man I would trust no farther than I could see him, and if there is anything dark underlying this matter, you depend that he is involved in it. But the most natural explanation, and also the most simple, is this — Colonel Menendez has been taken seriously ill, and someone is in his room in the capacity of a nurse."

"Her behaviour was scarcely that of a nurse in a sick-room," murmured Holmes.

"For God's sake tell me the truth," I said. "Tell me all you saw."

"I am quite prepared to do so, Watson. On three occasions, then, I saw the figure of a woman, who wore some kind of loose robe, quite clearly silhouetted upon the linen blind. Her gestures strongly resembled those of despair."

"Of despair?"

"Exactly. I gathered that she was addressing someone, presumably Colonel Menendez, and I derived a strong impression that she was in a condition of abject despair."

"Holmes," I said, "on your word of honour did you recognize anything in the movements, or in the outline of the figure, by which you could identify the woman?"

"I did not," he replied, shortly. "It was a woman who wore some kind of loose robe, possibly a kimono. Beyond that I could swear to nothing, except that it was not Mrs. Fisher."

We fell silent for a while. What Sherlock Holmes's thoughts may have been I know not, but my own were strange and troubled. Presently I found my voice again, and:

"I think, Holmes," I said, "that I should report to you something which Miss Beverley told me this evening."

"Yes?" said he, eagerly. "I am anxious to hear anything which may be of the slightest assistance. You are no doubt wondering why I retired so abruptly to-night. My reason was this: I could see that you were full of some story which you had learned from Miss Beverley, and I was anxious to perform my tour of inspection with a perfectly unprejudiced mind."

"You mean that your suspicions rested upon an inmate of Cray's Folly?"

"Not upon any particular inmate, but I had early perceived a distinct possibility that these manifestations of which the Colonel complained might be due to the agency of someone inside the house. That this person might be no more than an accomplice of the prime mover I also recognized, of course. But what did you learn to-night, Watson?"

I repeated Val Beverley's story of the mysterious footsteps and of the cries which had twice awakened her in the night.

"Hmm," muttered Holmes, when I had ceased speaking. "Assuming her account to be true — "

"Why should you doubt it?" I interrupted, hotly.

"My dear Watson, it is my business to doubt everything until I have indisputable evidence of its truth. I say, assuming her story to be true, we find ourselves face-to-face with the fantastic theory that some woman unknown is living secretly in Cray's Folly."

"Perhaps in one of the tower rooms," I suggested, eagerly. "Why, Holmes, that would account for the Colonel's marked unwillingness to talk about this part of the house."

My sight was now becoming used to the dusk, and I saw Holmes vigorously shake his head.

"No, no," he replied; "I have seen all the tower rooms. I can swear that no one inhabits them. Besides, is it feasible?"

"Then whose were the footsteps that Miss Beverley heard?"

"Obviously, those of the woman who, at this present moment, so far as I know, is in the smoking-room with Colonel Menendez."

I sighed wearily.

"This is a strange business, Holmes. I begin to think that the mystery is darker than I ever supposed."

We fell silent again. The weird cry of a night hawk came from somewhere in the valley, but otherwise everything within and without the great house seemed strangely still. This stillness presently imposed its influence upon me, for when I spoke again, I spoke in a low voice.

"Holmes," I said, "my imagination is playing me tricks. I thought I heard the fluttering of wings at that moment."

"Fortunately, my imagination remains under control," he replied, grimly; "therefore I am in a position to inform you that you did indeed hear the fluttering of wings. An owl has just flown into one of the trees immediately outside the window."

"Oh," said I, and uttered a sigh of relief.

"It is extremely fortunate that my imagination is so carefully trained," continued Holmes; "otherwise, when the woman whose shadow I saw upon the blind to-night raised her arms in a peculiar fashion, I could not well have failed to attach undue importance to the shape of the shadow thus created."

"What was the shape of the shadow, then?"

"Remarkably like that of a bat."

He spoke the words quietly, but in that still darkness, with dawn yet a long way off, they possessed the power which belongs to certain chords in music, and to certain lines in poetry. I was chilled unaccountably, and I peopled the empty corridors of Cray's Folly with I know not what uncanny creatures; nightmare fancies conjured up from memories of haunted manors.

Such was my mood, then, when suddenly Sherlock Holmes stood up. My eyes were growing more and more used to the darkness; and from something strained in his attitude, I detected the fact that he was listening intently.

He placed his cigarette on the table beside the bed and quietly crossed the room. I knew from his silent tread that he wore shoes with rubber soles. Very quietly he turned the handle and opened the door.

"What is it, Holmes?" I whispered.

Dimly I saw him raise his hand. Inch-by-inch he opened the door. My nerves in a state of tension, I sat there watching him, when without a sound, he slipped out of the room and was gone. Thereupon I arose and followed as far as the doorway.

Holmes was standing immediately outside in the corridor. Seeing me, he stepped back, and:

"Don't move, Watson," he said, speaking very close to my ear. "There is someone downstairs in the hall. Wait for me here."

With that he moved stealthily off, and I stood there, my heart beating with unusual rapidity, listening — listening for a challenge, a cry, a scuffle — I knew not what to expect.

Cavernous and dimly lighted, the corridor stretched away to my left. On the right it branched sharply in the direction of the gallery overlooking the hall.

The seconds passed, but no sound rewarded my alert listening — until, very faintly, but echoing in a muffled, church-like fashion around that peculiar building, came a slight, almost sibilant sound, which I took to be the gentle closing of a distant door.

Whilst I was still wondering if I had really heard this sound or merely imagined it:

"Who goes there?" came sharply in Holmes's voice.

I heard a faint click and knew that he had shone the light of an electric torch down into the hall.

I hesitated no longer, but ran along to join him. As I came to the head of the main staircase, however, I saw him crossing the hall below. He was making in the direction of the door which shut off the servants' quarters. Here he paused, and I saw him trying the handle. Evidently the door was locked, for he turned and swept the white ray all about the place. He tried several other doors, but found them all to be locked, for presently he came upstairs again, smiling grimly when he saw me there awaiting him.

"Did you hear it, Watson?" he said.

"A sound like the closing of a door?"

Sherlock Holmes nodded.

"It *was* the closing of a door," he replied; "but before that, I had distinctly heard a stair creak. Someone crossed the hall then, Watson. Yet, as you perceive for yourself, it affords no hiding-place."

His glance met and challenged mine.

"The Colonel's visitor has left him," he murmured. "Unless something quite unforeseen occurs, I shall throw up the case to-morrow."

12.

MORNING MISTS

The man known as Manoel awakened me in the morning. Although characteristically Spanish, he belonged to a more sanguine type than the butler and spoke much better English than Pedro. He placed upon the table beside me a tray containing a small pot of China tea, an apple, a peach, and three slices of toast.

"How soon would you like your bath, sir?" he enquired.

"In about half an hour," I replied.

"Breakfast is served at 9:30 if you wish, sir," continued Manoel, "but the ladies rarely come down. Would you prefer breakfast in your room?"

"What is Mr. Holmes doing?"

"He tells me that he does not take breakfast, sir. Colonel Don Juan Menendez will be unable to ride with you this morning, but a groom will accompany you to the heath if you wish, which is the best place for a gallop. Breakfast on the south veranda is very pleasant, sir, if you are riding first."

"Good," I replied, for indeed I felt strangely heavy; "it shall be the heath, then, and breakfast on the veranda."

Having drunk a cup of tea and dressed I went into Holmes's room, to find him propped up in bed reading the *Daily Telegraph* and smoking a cigarette.

"I am off for a ride," I said. "Won't you join me?"

He fixed his pillows more comfortably, and slowly shook his head.

"Not a bit of it, Watson," he replied, "At my age, I find exercise to be fatal to concentration."

"I know you have weird theories on the subject, but this is a beautiful morning."

"I grant you the beautiful morning, Watson, but you will find me here when you return."

I knew him too well to debate the point, and accordingly I left him to his newspaper and cigarette, and made my way downstairs. A housemaid was busy in the hall, and in the courtyard before the monastic porch, a groom of African ancestry awaited me with two fine mounts. He touched his hat and grinned expansively as I appeared. A spirited young chestnut was saddled for my use, and the groom, who informed me that his name was Jim, rode a smaller, Spanish horse, a beautiful but rather wicked-looking creature.

We proceeded down the drive. Pedro was standing at the door of the lodge, talking to his surly-looking daughter. He saluted me very ceremoniously as I passed.

Pursuing an easterly route for a quarter of a mile or so, we came to a narrow lane which branched off to the left in a tremendous declivity. Indeed, it presented the appearance of the dry bed of a mountain torrent, and in wet weather a torrent this lane became, so I was informed by Jim. It was very rugged and dangerous, and here we dismounted, the groom leading the horses.

Then we were upon a well-laid main road, and along this we trotted on to a tempting stretch of heath-land. There was a heavy mist, but the scent of the heather in the early morning was delightful, and there was something exhilarating in the dull thud of the hoofs upon the springy turf. The black man was a natural horseman, and he seemed to enjoy the ride every bit as much as I did. For my own part, I was sorry to return. But the vapours of the night had been effectively cleared from my mind, and when presently we headed again for the hills, I could think more coolly of those problems which overnight had seemed well-nigh insoluble.

We returned by a less direct route, but only at one point was the path so steep as that by which we had descended. This brought us out on a road above and about a mile to the south of Cray's Folly. At one point, through a gap in the trees, I found myself looking down at the gray stone building in its setting of velvet lawns and gaily patterned gardens. A faint mist hovered like smoke over the grass.

Five minutes later, we passed a queer old Jacobean house, so deeply hidden amidst trees that the early morning sun had not yet penetrated to it, except for one upstanding gable which was bathed in golden light. I should never have recognized the place from that aspect, but because of its situation I knew that this must be the Guest House. It seemed very gloomy and dark, and remembering how I was pledged to call upon Mr. Colin Camber that day, I apprehended that my reception might be a cold one.

Presently we left the road and cantered across the valley meadows, in which I had walked on the previous day, reentering Cray's Folly on the south, although we had left it on the north. We dismounted in the stable-yard, and I noted two other saddle horses in the stalls, a pair of very clean-looking hunters, as well as two perfectly matched ponies, which, Jim informed me, Madame de Stämer sometimes drove in a chaise.

Feeling vastly improved by the exercise, I walked around to the veranda, and through the drawing room to the hall. Manoel was standing there, and:

"Your bath is ready, sir," he said.

I nodded and went upstairs. It seemed to me that life at Cray's Folly was quite agreeable, and such was my mood that the shadowy Bat Wing menace found no place in, it save as the chimera of a sick man's imagination. One thing only troubled me: the identity of the woman who had been with Colonel Menendez on the previous night.

However, such unconscious sun worshippers are we all that in the glory of that summer morning, I realized that life was good, and I resolutely put behind me the dark suspicions of the night.

I looked into Holmes's room ere descending and, as he had assured me would be the case, there he was, propped up in bed, the *Daily Telegraph* upon the floor beside him and the *Times* now open upon the coverlet.

"I am ravenously hungry," I said, maliciously, "and am going down to eat a hearty breakfast."

"Good," he returned, treating me to one of his quizzical smiles. "It is delightful to know that someone is happy."

Manoel had removed my unopened newspapers from the bedroom, placing them on the breakfast table on the south veranda; and I had propped the *Mail* up before me and had commenced to explore a juicy grapefruit when something, perhaps a faint breath of perfume, a slight rustle of draperies, or merely that indefinable aura which belongs to the presence of a woman, drew my glance upward and to the left. And there was Val Beverley smiling down at me.

"Good morning, Dr. Watson," she said. "Oh, please don't interrupt your breakfast. May I sit down and talk to you?"

"I should be most annoyed if you refused."

She was dressed in a simple summery frock which left her round, sun-browned arms bare above the elbow, and she laid a huge bunch of roses upon the table beside my tray.

"I am the florist of the establishment," she explained. "These will delight your eyes at luncheon. Don't you think we are a lot of barbarians here, Dr. Watson?"

"Why?"

"Well, if I had not taken pity upon you, here you would have bat over a lonely breakfast just as though you were staying at a hotel."

"Delightful," I replied, "now that you are here."

"Ah," said she, and smiled roguishly, "that afterthought just saved you."

"But honestly," I continued, "the hospitality of Colonel Menendez is true hospitality. To expect one's guests to perform their parlour tricks around a breakfast table in the morning is, on the other hand, true barbarism."

"I quite agree with you," she said, quietly. "There is a perfectly delightful freedom about the Colonel's way of living. Only some horrid old Victorian prude could possibly take exception to it. Did you enjoy your ride?"

"Immensely," I replied, watching her delightedly as she arranged the roses in carefully blended groups.

Her fingers were very delicate and tactile, and such is the character which resides in the human hand, that whereas the gestures of Madame de Stämer were curiously stimulating, there was something in the movement of Val Beverley's pretty fingers amidst the blooms which I found most soothing.

"I passed the Guest House on my return," I continued. "Do you know Mr. Camber?"

She looked at me in a startled way.

"No," she replied, "I don't. Do you?"

"I met him by chance yesterday."

"Really? I thought he was quite unapproachable; a sort of ogre."

"On the contrary, he is a man of great charm."

"Oh," said Val Beverley, "well, since you have said so, I might as well admit that he has always seemed a charming man to me. I have never spoken to him, but he looks as though he could be very fascinating. Have you met his wife?"

"No. Is she also American?"

My companion shook her head.

"I have no idea," she replied. "I have seen her several times, of course, and she is one of the daintiest creatures imaginable, but I know nothing about her nationality."

"She is young, then?"

"Very young, I should say. She looks quite a child."

"The reason of my interest," I replied, "is that Mr. Camber asked me to call upon him, and I propose to do so later this morning."

"Really?"

Again I detected the startled expression upon Val Beverley's face.

"That is rather curious, since you are staying here."

"Why?"

"Well," she looked about her nervously, "I don't know the reason, but the name of Mr. Camber is anathema in Cray's Folly."

"Colonel Menendez told me last night that he had never met Mr. Camber."

Val Beverley shrugged her shoulders, a habit which it was easy to see she had acquired from Madame de Stämer.

"Perhaps not," she replied, "but I am certain he hates him."

"Hates Mr. Camber?"

"Yes." Her expression grew troubled. "It is another of those mysteries which seem to be part of Colonel Menendez's normal existence."

"And is this dislike mutual?"

"That I cannot say, since I have never met Mr. Camber."

"And Madame de Stämer, does she share it?"

"Fully, I think. But don't ask me what it means, because I don't know."

She dismissed the subject with a light gesture and poured me out a second cup of coffee.

"I am going to leave you now," she said. "I have to justify my existence in my own eyes."

"Must you really go?"

"I must really."

"Then tell me something before you go."

She gathered up the bunches of roses and looked down at me with a wistful expression.

"Yes, what is it?"

"Did you detect those mysterious footsteps again last night?"

The look of wistfulness changed to another which I hated to see in her eyes, an expression of repressed fear.

"No," she replied in a very low voice, "but why do you ask the question?"

Doubt of her had been far enough from my mind, but that something in the tone of my voice had put her on her guard I could see.

"I am naturally curious," I replied, gravely.

"No," she repeated, "I have not heard the sound for some time now. Perhaps, after all, my fears were imaginary."

There was a constraint in her manner which was all too obvious, and when presently, laden with the spoil of the rose garden, she gave me a parting smile and hurried into the house, I sat there very still for a while, and something of the brightness had faded from the coming, nor did life seem so glad a business as I had thought it quite recently.

13.

AT THE GUEST HOUSE

I presented myself at the Guest House at half-past eleven. My mental state was troubled and indescribably complex. Perhaps my own uneasy thoughts were responsible for the idea, but it seemed to me that the atmosphere of Cray's Folly had changed yet again. Never before had I experienced a sense of foreboding like that which had possessed me throughout the hours of this bright summer's morning.

Colonel Menendez had appeared about nine o'clock. He exhibiting no traces of illness that were perceptible to me. But this subtle change which I had detected, or thought I had detected, was more marked in Madame Stämer than in anyone. In her strange, still eyes I had read what I can only describe as a stricken look. It had none of the heroic resignation and acceptance of the inevitable which had so startled me in the face of the Colonel on the previous day. There was a bitterness in it, as of one who has made a great but unwilling sacrifice, and again I found myself questing that faint but fugitive memory, conjured up by the eyes of Madame de Stämer.

Never had the shadow lain so darkly upon the house as it lay this morning with the Sun blazing gladly out of a serene sky. The birds, the flowers, and Mother Earth herself bespoke the joy of summer. But beneath the roof of Cray's Folly dwelt a spirit of unrest, of apprehension. I thought of that queer lull which comes before a tropical storm, and I thought I read a knowledge of pending evil even in the glances of the servants.

I had spoken to Holmes of this fear. He had smiled and nodded grimly, saying:

"Evidently, Watson, you have forgotten that to-night is the night of the full moon."

It was in no easy state of mind, then, that I opened the gate and walked up to the porch of the Guest House. That the solution of the grand mystery of Cray's Folly would automatically resolve these lesser mysteries I felt assured, and I was supported by the idea that a clue might lie here.

The house, which from the roadway had an air of neglect, proved on close inspection to be well tended, but of an unprosperous aspect. The brass knocker, door knob, and letter box were brilliantly polished, whilst the windows and the window curtains were spotlessly clean. But the place cried aloud for the service of the decorator, and it did not need the deductive powers of a Sherlock Holmes to determine that Mr. Colin Camber was in straitened circumstances.

In response to my ringing, the door was presently opened by Ah Tsong. His yellow face exhibited no trace of emotion whatever. He merely opened the door and stood there looking at me.

"Is Mr. Camber at home?" I enquired.

"Master no got," crooned Ah Tsong.

He proceeded quietly to close the door again.

"One moment," I said, "one moment. I wish, at any rate, to leave my card."

Ah Tsong allowed the door to remain open, but:

"No usee palaber so fashion," he said. "No feller comee here. Sabby?"

"I savvy, right enough," said I, "but all the same you have got to take my card in to Mr. Camber."

I handed him a card as I spoke and, suddenly addressing him in "pidgin" (of which, fortunately, I had a smattering):

"Belong very quick, Ah Tsong," I said, sharply, "or plenty big trouble, savvy?"

"Sabby, sabby," he muttered, nodding his head; and leaving me standing in the porch he retired along the sparsely carpeted hall.

This hall was very gloomily lighted, but I could see several pieces of massive old furniture and a number of bookcases, all looking incredibly untidy.

Rather less than a minute elapsed, I suppose, when from some place at the farther end of the hallway Mr. Camber appeared in person. He wore a threadbare dressing gown, the silken collar and cuffs of which were very badly frayed. His hair was dishevelled, and palpably he had not shaved this morning.

He was smoking a corncob pipe as he slowly approached, glancing from the card which he held in his hand in my direction, and then back again at the card, with a curious sort of hesitancy. In spite of his untidy appearance, I could not fail to mark the dignity of his bearing, and the almost arrogant angle at which he held his head.

"Mr. — er — John Watson?" he began, fixing his large eyes upon me with a look in which I could detect no sign of recognition. "I am advised that you desire to see me?"

"That is so, Mr. Camber," I replied, cheerily. "I fear I have interrupted your work, but as no other opportunity may occur of renewing an acquaintance which for my part I found extremely pleasant — "

"Of renewing an acquaintance, you say, Dr. Watson?"

"Yes."

"Quite." He looked me up and down critically. "To be sure, we have met before, I understand?"

"We met yesterday, Mr. Camber, you may recall. Having chanced to come across a contribution of yours of the *Occult Review*, I have availed myself of your invitation to drop in for a chat."

His expression changed immediately and the sombre eyes lighted up.

"Ah, of course," he cried, "you are a student of the transcendental. Forgive my seeming rudeness, Dr. Watson, but indeed my memory is of the poorest. Pray come in, sir; your visit is very welcome."

He held the door wide open, and inclined his head in a gesture of curious old-world courtesy which was strange in so young a man. And congratulating myself upon the happy thought which had enabled me to win such instant favour, I presently found myself in a study which I despair of describing.

In some respects it resembled the lumber room of an antiquary, whilst in many particulars it corresponded to the interior of one of those second-hand bookshops which abound in the neighbourhood of Charing Cross Road. The shelves with which it was lined literally bulged with books, and there were books on the floor, books on the mantelpiece, and books, some open and some shut, some handsomely bound, and some having the covers torn off, upon every table and nearly every chair in the place.

Volume seven of Burton's monumental *A Thousand Nights and One Arabian Nights* lay upon a littered desk before which I presumed Mr. Camber had been seated at the time of my arrival. Some wet vessel, probably a cup of tea or coffee, had at some time been set down upon the page at which this volume was open, for it was marked with a dark brown ring. A volume of Fraser's *Golden Bough* had been used as an ash tray, apparently, since the binding was burned in several places where cigarettes had been laid upon it.

In this interesting, indeed unique apartment, East met West, unabashed by Kipling's dictum. Roman tear-vases and Egyptian tomb-offerings stood upon the same shelf as empty Bass bottles; and a hideous wooden idol from the South Sea Islands leered on eternally, unmoved by the presence upon his distorted head of a soft felt hat made, I believe, in Philadelphia.

Strange implements from early British barrows found themselves in the company of *Thugee* daggers. There were carved mammals' tusks and snake emblems from Yucatan; against a Chinese ivory model of the Temple of Ten Thousand Buddhas rested a Coptic crucifix made from a twig of the Holy Rose Tree. Across an ancient Spanish coffer was thrown a Persian rug into which had been woven the monogram of Shah-Jehan and a text from the Koran. It was easy to see that Mr. Colin Camber's studies must have imposed a severe strain upon his purse.

"Sit down, Dr. Watson, sit down," he said, sweeping a vellum-bound volume of *Eliphas Levi* from a chair, and pushing the chair forward. "The visit of a fellow-student is a rare pleasure for me. And you find me, sir," he seated himself in a curious, carved chair which stood before the desk, "you find me engaged upon enquiries, the result of which will constitute chapter forty-two of my present book. Pray glance at the contents of this little box."

He placed in my hands a small box of dark wood, evidently of great age. It contained what looked like a number of shrivelled beans.

Having glanced at it curiously I returned it to him, shaking my head blankly.

"You are puzzled?" he said, with a kind of boyish triumph, which lighted up his face, which rejuvenated him and gave me a glimpse of another man. "These, sir," he touched the shrivelled objects with a long, delicate forefinger "are seeds of the sacred lotus of Ancient Egypt. They were found in the tomb of a priest."

"And in what way do they bear upon the enquiry to which you referred, Mr. Camber?"

"In this way," he replied, drawing toward him a piece of newspaper upon which rested a mound of coarse shag. "I maintain that the vital principle survives within them. Now, I propose to cultivate these seeds, Dr. Watson. Do you grasp the significance of this experiment?"

He knocked out the corn-cob upon the heel of his slipper and began to refill the hot bowl with shag from the newspaper at his elbow.

"From a physical point of view, yes," I replied, slowly. "But I should not have supposed such an experiment to come within the scope of your own particular activities, Mr. Camber."

"Ah," he returned, triumphantly, at the same time stuffing tobacco into the bowl of the corn-cob, "it is for this very reason that chapter forty-two of my book must prove to be the hub of the whole, and the whole, Dr. Watson, I am egotist enough to believe, shall establish a new focus for thought, an intellectual Rome bestriding and uniting the Seven Hills of Unbelief."

He lighted his pipe and stared at me complacently.

Whilst I had greatly revised my first estimate of the man, my revisions had been all in his favour. Respecting his genius, my first impression was confirmed. That he was ahead of his generation, perhaps a new Galileo, I was prepared to believe. He had a pride of bearing which I think was partly racial, but which in part, too, was the insignia of intellectual superiority. He stood above the commonplace, caring little for the views of those around and beneath him. From vanity he was utterly free. His was strangely like the egotism of true genius.

"Now, sir," he continued, puffing furiously at his corn-cob, "I observed you glancing a moment ago at this volume of the *Golden Bough.*" He pointed to the scarred book which I have already mentioned. "It is a work of profound scholarship. But having perused its hundreds of pages, what has the student learned? Does he know why the twenty-sixth chapter of the 'Book of the Dead' was written upon lapis-lazuli, the twenty-seventh upon green felspar, the twenty-ninth upon cornelian, and the thirtieth upon serpentine? He does not. Having studied Part Four, has he learned the secret of why Osiris was a black god, although he typified the Sun? Has he learned why modern Christianity is losing its hold upon the nations, whilst Buddhism, so called, counts its disciples by millions? He has not. This is because the scholar is rarely the seer."

"I quite agree with you," I said, thinking that I detected the drift of his argument.

"Very well," said Mr. Camber. "I am an American citizen, Dr. Watson, which is tantamount to stating that I belong to the greatest community of traders which has appeared since the Phoenicians overran the then known world. America has not produced the mystic, yet Judæa produced the founder of Christianity, and Gautama Buddha, born of a royal line, established the creed of human equity. In what way did these magicians, for a miracle-worker is nothing but a magician, differ from ordinary men? In one respect only: They had learned to control that force which we have to-day termed Will."

As he spoke those words, Colin Camber directed upon me a glance from his luminous eyes which frankly thrilled me. The bemused figure of the Lavender Arms was forgotten. I perceived before me a man of power, a man of extraordinary knowledge and intellectual daring. His voice, which was very beautiful, together with his glance, held me enthralled.

"What we call Will," he continued, "is what the Ancient Egyptians called *Khu*. It is not mental: it is a property of the soul. At this point, Dr. Watson, I depart from the laws generally accepted by my contemporaries. I shall presently propose to you that the eye of the Divine Architect literally watches every creature upon the earth."

"Literally?"

"Literally, Dr. Watson. We need no images, no idols, no paintings. All power, all light comes from one source. That source is the Sun! The Sun controls Will, and the Will is the soul. If there were a cavern in the earth so deep that the Sun could never reach it, and if it were possible for a child to be born in that cavern, do you know what that child would be?"

"Almost certainly blind," I replied; "beyond which my imagination fails me."

"Then I will inform you, Dr. Watson. It would be a demon."

"What!" I cried, and was momentarily touched with the fear that this was a brilliant madman.

"Listen," he said, and pointed with the stem of his pipe. "Why, in all ancient creeds, is Hades depicted as below?

For the simple reason that could such a spot exist and be inhabited, it must be *sunless*, when it could only be inhabited by devils; and what are devils but creatures without souls?"

"You mean that a child born beyond reach of the Sun's influence would have no soul?"

"Such is my meaning, Dr. Watson. Do you begin to see the importance of my experiment with the lotus seeds?"

I shook my head slowly. Whereupon, laying his corn-cob upon the desk, Colin Camber burst into a fit of boyish laughter, which seemed to rejuvenate him again, which wiped out the image of the magus completely, and only left before me a very human student of strange subjects, and withal a fascinating companion.

"I fear, sir," he said, presently, "that my steps have led me farther into the wilderness than it has been your fate to penetrate. The whole secret of the universe is contained in the words Day and Night, Darkness and Light. I have studied both the light and the darkness, deliberately and without fear. A new age is about to dawn, sir, and a new age requires new beliefs, new truths. Were you ever in the country of the Hill Dyaks?"

This abrupt question rather startled me, but:

"You refer to the Borneo hill-country?"

"Precisely."

"No, I was never there."

"Then this little magical implement will be new to you," said he.

Standing up, he crossed to a cabinet littered untidily with all sorts of strange-looking objects, carved bones, queer little inlaid boxes, images, untidy manuscripts, and what-not.

He took up what looked like a very ungainly tobacco-pipe, made of some rich brown wood, and, handing it to me:

"Examine this, Dr. Watson," he said, the boyish smile of triumph returning again to his face.

I did as he requested, and made no discovery of note. The thing clearly was not intended for a pipe. The stem was soiled and, moreover, there was carving inside the bowl. So that presently I returned it to him, shaking my head.

"Unless one should be informed of the properties of this little instrument," he declared, "discovery by experiment is improbable. Now, note."

He struck the hollow of the bowl upon the palm of his hand, and it delivered a high, bell-like note which lingered curiously. Then:

"Note again."

He made a short striking motion with the thing, similar to that which one would employ who had designed to jerk something out of the bowl. And at the very spot on the floor where any object contained in the bowl would have fallen, came a reprise of the bell note! Clearly, from almost at my feet, it sounded, a high, metallic ring.

He struck upward, and the bell-note sounded on the ceiling; to the right, and it came from the window; in my direction, and the tiny bell seemed to ring beside my ear! I will honestly admit that I was startled, but:

"Dyak magic," said Colin Camber; "one of nature's secrets not yet discovered by conventional Western science. It was known to the Egyptian priesthood, of course; hence the Vocal Memnon. It was known to Madame Blavatsky, who employed an 'astral bell'; and it is known to me."

He returned the little instrument to its place upon the cabinet.

"I wonder if the fact will strike you as significant," said he, "that the note which you have just heard can only be produced between sunrise and sunset?"

Without giving me time to reply:

"The most notable survival of black magic — that is, the scientific employment of darkness against light — is to be met with in Haiti and other islands of the West Indies."

"You are referring to Voodooism?" I said, slowly.

He nodded, replacing his pipe between his teeth.

"A subject, Dr. Watson, which I investigated exhaustively some years ago."

I was watching him closely as he spoke, and a shadow, a strange shadow, crept over his face, a look almost of exaltation — of mingled sorrow and gladness which I find myself quite unable to describe.

"In the West Indies, Dr. Watson," Mr. Camber continued, in a strangely altered voice, "I lost all and found all. Have you ever realized, sir, that sorrow is the price we must pay for joy?"

I did not understand his question, and was still wondering about it when I heard a gentle knock, the door opened, and a woman came in.

14.

YSOLA CAMBER

I find it difficult, now, to recapture my first impression of that meeting. About the woman, hesitating before me, there was something unexpected, something wholly unfamiliar. She belonged to a type with which I was not acquainted. Nor was it wonderful that she should strike me in this fashion, since my wanderings, although fairly extensive, had never included the West Indies, nor had I been to Spain; and this girl — I could have sworn that she was under twenty — was one of those rare beauties, a golden Spaniard.

That she was not purely Spanish I learned later.

She was small, and girlishly slight, with slender ankles and exquisite little feet; indeed I think she had the tiniest feet of any woman I had ever met. She wore a sort of white pinafore over her dress, and her arms, which were bare because of the short sleeves of her frock, were of a child-like roundness, whilst her creamy skin was touched with a faint tinge of bronze, as though, I remember thinking, it had absorbed and retained something of the Southern sunshine. She had the swaying carriage which usually belongs to a tall woman, and her head and neck were Grecian in poise.

Her hair, which was of a curious dull gold colour, presented a mass of thick, tight curls, and her beauty was of that unusual character which makes a Cleopatra a subject of deathless debate. What I mean to say is this: whilst no man could have denied, for instance, that Val Beverley was a charmingly pretty woman, nine critics out of ten must have failed to classify this golden Spaniard correctly or justly. Her complexion was peach-like in the Oriental sense, that strange hint of gold underlying the delicate skin, and her dark blue eyes were shaded by really wonderful silken lashes.

Emotion had the effect of enlarging the pupils, a pheno-menon rarely met with, so that now as she entered the room and found a stranger present, they seemed to be rather black than blue.

Her embarrassment was acute, and I think she would have retired without speaking, but:

"Ysola," said Colin Camber, regarding her with a look curiously compounded of sorrow and pride, "allow me to present Mr. John Watson, who has honoured us with a visit."

He turned to me.

"Dr. Watson," he said, "it gives me great pleasure that you should meet my wife."

Perhaps I had expected this, indeed, subconsciously, I think I had. Nevertheless, at the words "my wife" I felt that I started. The analogy with Edgar Allan Poe was complete.

As Mrs. Camber extended her hand with a sort of appealing timidity, it appeared to me that she felt herself to be intruding. The expression in her beautiful eyes when she glanced at her husband could only be described as one of adoration; and whilst it was impossible to doubt his love for her, I wondered if his colossal egotism were capable of stooping to affection. I wondered if he knew how to tend and protect this delicate Southern girl wife of his.

Remembering the episode of the Lavender Arms, I felt justified in doubting her happiness, and in this I saw an explanation of the mingled sorrow and pride with which Colin Camber regarded her. It might betoken recognition of his own shortcomings as a husband.

"How nice of you to come and see us, Dr. Watson," she said.

She spoke in a faintly husky manner which was curiously attractive, although lacking the deep, vibrant tones of Madame de Stämer's memorable voice. Her English was imperfect, but her accent good.

"Your husband has been carrying me to enchanted lands, Mrs. Camber," I replied. "I have never known a morning to pass so quickly."

"Oh," she replied, and laughed with a childish glee which I was glad to witness. "Did he tell you all about the book which is going to make the world good? Did he tell you it will make us rich as well?"

"Rich?" said Camber, frowning slightly. "Nature's riches are health and love. If we hold these, the rest will come. Now that you have joined us, Ysola, I shall beg Dr. Watson, in honour of this occasion, to drink a glass of wine and break a biscuit as a pledge of future meetings."

I watched him as he spoke, a lean, unkempt figure invested with a curious dignity, and I found it almost impossible to believe that this was the same man who had sat in the bar of the Lavender Arms sipping whisky and water. The resemblance to the portrait in Holmes's study became more marked than ever. There was an air of high breeding about the delicate features which, curiously enough, was accentuated by the unshaven chin. I recognized that refusal would be regarded as a rebuff, and therefore:

"You are very kind," I said.

Colin Camber inclined his head gravely and courteously.

"We are very glad to have you with us, Dr. Watson," he replied.

He clapped his hands and, silent as a shadow, Ah Tsong appeared. I noted that although it was Camber who had summoned him, it was to Mrs. Camber that the Chinaman turned for orders. I had thought his yellow face incapable of expression, but as his oblique eyes turned in the direction of the girl, I read in them a sort of dumb worship such as one sees in the eyes of a dog.

She spoke to him rapidly in Chinese.

"Hoi, hoi," Ah Tsong muttered, *"hoi, hoi."* He nodded his head, and went out.

I saw that Colin Camber had detected my interest, for:

"Ah Tsong is really my wife's servant," he explained.

"Oh," she said in a low voice and looked at me earnestly, "Ah Tsong nursed me when I was a little baby so high." She held her hand about four feet from the floor and laughed gleefully. "Can you imagine what a funny little thing I was?"

"You must have been a wonder-child, Mrs. Camber," I replied with sincerity; "and Ah Tsong has remained with you ever since?"

"Ever since," she echoed, shaking her head in a vaguely pathetic way. "He will never leave me, do you think, Colin?"

"Never," replied her husband; "you are all he loves in the world. A case, Dr. Watson," he turned to me, "of deathless fidelity rarely met with nowadays and only possible, perhaps, in its true form, in an Oriental."

Mrs. Camber having seated herself upon one of the few chairs which was not piled with books, her husband had resumed his place by the writing desk, and I sought in vain to interpret the glances which passed between them.

The fact that these two were lovers, none could have mistaken. But here again, as at Cray's Folly, I detected a shadow. I felt that something had struck at the very root of their happiness; in fact, I wondered if they had been parted, and were but newly reunited, for there was a sort of constraint between them, the more marked on the woman's side than on the man's. I wondered how long they had been married, but felt that it would have been indiscreet to ask.

Even as the idea occurred to me, however, an opportunity arose of learning what I wished to know. I heard a bell ring, and:

"There is someone at the door, Colin," said Mrs. Camber.

"I will go," he replied. "Ah Tsong has enough to do."

Without another word he stood up and walked out of the room.

"You see," said Mrs. Camber, smiling in her naive way, "we only have one servant, except Ah Tsong, her name is Mrs. Powis. She is visiting her daughter who is married. We made the poor old lady take a holiday."

"It is difficult to imagine you burdened with household responsibilities, Mrs. Camber," I replied. "Please forgive me, but I cannot help wondering how long you have been married?"

"For nearly four years."

"Really?" I exclaimed. "You must have been married very young?"

"I was twenty. Do I look so young?"

I gazed at her in amazement.

"You astonish me," I declared, which was quite true and no mere compliment. "I had guessed your age to be eighteen."

"Oh," she laughed and, resting her hands upon the *settée*, leaned forward with sparkling eyes, "how funny. Sometimes

I wish I looked older. It is dreadful in this place, although we have been so happy here. At all the shops they look at me so funny, so I always send Mrs. Powis now."

"You are really quite wonderful," I said. "You are Spanish, are you not, Mrs. Camber?"

She slightly shook her head and I saw the pupils begin to dilate.

"Not really Spanish," she replied, haltingly. "I was born in Cuba."

"In Cuba?"

She nodded.

"Then it was in Cuba that you met Mr. Camber?"

She nodded again, watching me intently.

"It is strange that a Virginian should settle in Surrey."

"Yes?" she murmured, "you think so? But really it is not strange at all. Colin's people are so proud, so proud. Do you know what they are like, those Virginians? Oh! I hate them."

"You hate them?"

"No, I cannot hate them, for he is one. But he will never go back."

"Why should he never go back, Mrs. Camber?"

"Because of me."

"You mean that you do not wish to settle in America?"

"I could not — not where he comes from. They would not have me."

Her eyes grew misty and she quickly lowered her lashes.

"Would not have you?" I exclaimed. "I don't understand."

"No?" she said, and smiled up at me very gravely. "It is simple. I am a Cuban, one, as they say, of an inferior race — and of mixed blood."

She shook her golden head as if to dismiss the subject, and stood up as Camber entered, followed by Ah Tsong bearing a tray of refreshments.

Of the ensuing conversation I remember nothing. My mind was focussed upon the one vital fact, that Mrs. Camber was a Cuban Creole. Dimly I felt that here was the missing link for which Sherlock Holmes was groping. For it was in Cuba that Colin Camber had met his wife, and it was from Cuba that the menace of Bat Wing came.

What could it mean? Surely it was more than a coincidence that these two families, both associated with the West Indies, should reside within sight of one another in the Surrey Hills. Yet, if it were the result of design, the design must be on the part of Colonel Menendez, since the Cambers had occupied the Guest House before he leased Cray's Folly.

I know not if I betrayed my absentmindedness during the time that I was struggling vainly with these maddening problems, but presently, Mrs. Camber having departed about her household duties, I found myself walking down the garden with her husband.

"This is the summer house of which I was speaking, Dr. Watson," he said, and I regret to state that I retained no impression of his having previously mentioned the subject. "During the time that Sir James Appleton resided at Cray's Folly, I worked here regularly in the summer months. It was Sir James, of course, who laid out the greater part of the gardens and who rescued the property from the state of decay into which it had fallen."

I aroused myself from the profitless reverie in which I had become lost. We were standing before a sort of arbour that marked the end of the grounds of the Guest House. It overhung the edge of a miniature ravine in which, over a pebbly course, a little stream pursued its way down the valley to feed the lake in the grounds of Cray's Folly.

From this point of vantage I could see the greater part of Colonel Menendez's residence. I had an unobstructed view of the tower and of the Tudor garden.

"I abandoned my work-shop," pursued Colin Camber, "when the — er — the new tenant took up his residence. I work now in the room in which you found me this morning."

He sighed and, turning abruptly, led the way back to the house, holding himself very erect, and presenting a queer figure in his threadbare dressing gown.

It was now a perfect summer's day, and I commented upon the beauty of the old garden, which in places was bordered by a crumbling wall.

"Yes, a quaint old spot," said Camber. "I thought at one time, because of the name of the house, that it might have been part of a monastery or convent. This was not the case, however. It derives its name from a certain Sir Jaspar Guest, who flourished, I believe, under King Charles of merry memory."

"Nevertheless," I added, "the Guest House is a charming survival of more spacious days."

"True," returned Colin Camber, gravely. "Here it is possible to lead one's own life, away from the noisy world," he sighed again wearily. "Yes, I shall regret leaving the Guest House."

"What! You are leaving?"

"I am leaving as soon as I can find another residence, suited both to my requirements and to my slender purse. But these domestic affairs can be of no possible interest to you. I take it, Dr. Watson, that you will grant my wife and myself the pleasure of your company at lunch?"

"Many thanks," I replied, "but really I must return to Cray's Folly."

As I spoke the words, I had moved a little ahead at a point where the path was overgrown by a rose bush, for the garden was somewhat neglected.

"You will quite understand," I said, and turned.

Never can I forget the spectacle which I beheld.

Colin Camber's peculiarly pale complexion had assumed a truly ghastly pallor, and he stood with tightly clenched hands, glaring at me almost insanely.

"Mr. Camber," I cried, with concern, "are you unwell?"

He moistened his dry lips, and:

"You are returning — to Cray's Folly?" he said, speaking, it seemed, with difficulty.

"I am, sir. I am staying with Colonel Menendez."

"Ah!"

He clutched the collar of his pyjama jacket and wrenched so strongly that the button was torn off. His passion was incredible, insane. The power of speech had almost left him.

"You are a guest of — of Devil Menendez," he whispered, and the speaking of the name seemed almost to choke him. "Of — Devil Menendez. You — you — are a spy. You have stolen my hospitality — you have obtained access to my house under false pretences. God! if I had known!"

"Mr. Camber," I said, sternly, and realized that I, too, had clenched my fists, for the man's language was grossly insulting, "you forget yourself."

"Perhaps I do," he muttered, thickly; "and therefore" — Mr. Camber raised a quivering forefinger — "go! If you have any spark of compassion in your breast, go! Leave my house."

Nostrils dilated, he stood with that quivering finger outstretched, and now having become as speechless as he, I turned and walked rapidly up to the house.

"Ah Tsong! Ah Tsong!" came a cry from behind me in tones which I can only describe as hysterical — "Dr. Watson's hat and stick. Quickly."

As I walked in past the study door, the Chinaman came to meet me, holding my hat and cane. I took them from him without a word and, the door being held open by Ah Tsong, I walked out on to the road.

My heart was beating rapidly. I did not know what to think nor what to do. This ignominious dismissal afforded an experience new to me. I was humiliated, mortified, but above all, wildly angry.

How far I had gone on my homeward journey I cannot say, when the sound of quickly pattering footsteps intruded upon my wild reverie. I stopped, turned, and there was Ah Tsong almost at my heels.

"Blinga chit flom lilly missee," he said, and held the note toward me.

I hesitated, glaring at him in a way that must have been very unpleasant; but recovering myself, I tore open the envelope, and read the following note, written in pencil and very shakily:

DR. WATSON.
Please forgive him. If you knew what we
have suffered from Señor Don Juan

Menendez, I know you would forgive him. Please, for my sake.

YSOLA CAMBER.

The Chinaman was watching me, that strangely pathetic expression in his eyes, and:

"Tell your mistress that I quite understand and will write to her," I said.

"Hoi, hoi."

Ah Tsong turned and ran swiftly off as I pursued my way back to Cray's Folly in a mood which I shall not attempt to describe.

15.

UNREST

I sat in Sherlock Holmes's room. Luncheon was over, and although, as on the previous day, it had been a perfect repast, perfectly served, the sense of tension which I had experienced throughout the meal had made me horribly ill at ease.

That shadow of which I have spoken elsewhere seemed to have become almost palpable. In vain I had ascribed it to a morbid imagination: persistently it lingered.

Madame de Stämer's gaiety rang more false than ever. She twirled the rings upon her slender fingers and shot little enquiring glances all around the table. This spirit of unrest, from wherever it arose, had communicated itself to everybody. Madame's several *bon mots* one and all were failures. She delivered them without conviction like an amateur repeating lines learned by heart. The Colonel was unusually silent, eating little but drinking much. There was something unreal, almost ghastly, about the whole affair; and when at last Madame de Stämer retired, bearing Val Beverley with her, I felt certain that the Colonel would make some communication to us. If ever knowledge of portentous evil were written upon a man's face it, was written upon his as he sat there at the head of the table, staring straightly before him. However:

"Gentlemen," he said, "if your enquiries here have led to no result of, shall I say, a tangible character, at least I feel sure that you must have realized one thing."

Holmes stared at him sternly.

"I have realized, Colonel Menendez," Holmes replied, "that something is pending."

"Ah!" murmured the Colonel, and he clutched the edge of the table with his strong brown hands.

"But," continued my friend, "I have realized something more. You have asked for my aid, and I am here. Now you have deliberately tied my hands."

"What do you mean, sir?" asked the other, softly.

"I will speak plainly. I mean that you know more about the nature of this danger than you have ever communicated to me. Allow me to proceed, if you please, Colonel Menendez. For your delightful hospitality, I thank you. As your guest,

I could be happy; but as a professional investigator whose services have been called upon under most unusual circumstances, I cannot be happy and I do not thank you."

Their glances met. Both were angry, willful, and self-confident. Following a few moments of silence:

"Perhaps, Mr. Holmes," said the Colonel, "you have something further to say?"

"I have this to say," was the answer: "I esteem your friendship, but I fear I must return to town without delay."

The Colonel's jaws were clenched so tightly that I could see the muscles protruding. He was fighting an inward battle; then:

"What!" he said, "you would desert me?"

"I never deserted any man who sought my aid."

"I have sought your aid."

"Then accept it!" cried Holmes. "This, or allow me to retire from the case. You ask me to find an enemy who threatens you, and you withhold every clue which could aid me in my search."

"What clue have I withheld?"

Sherlock Holmes stood up.

"It is useless to discuss the matter further, Colonel Menendez," he said, coldly.

The Colonel rose also, and:

"Mr. Holmes," he replied, and his high voice was ill-controlled, "if I give you my word of honour that I dare not tell you more, and if, having done so, I beg of you to remain at least another night, can you refuse me?"

Holmes stood at the end of the table watching him.

"Colonel Menendez," he said, "this would appear to be a game in which my handicap rests on the fact that I do not know against whom I am pitted. Very well. You leave me no alternative but to reply that I will stay."

"I thank you, Mr. Holmes. As I fear I am far from well, dare I hope to be excused if I retire to my room for an hour's rest?"

Holmes and I bowed; and the Colonel, returning our salutations, walked slowly out, his bearing one of grace and dignity. So that memorable luncheon terminated, and now we found ourselves alone and faced with a problem which, from whatever point one viewed it, offered no single opening whereby one might hope to penetrate to the truth.

Sherlock Holmes was pacing up and down the room in a state of such nervous irritability as I never remembered to have witnessed in him before.

I had just finished an account of my visit to the Guest House and of the indignity which had been put upon me, when:

"Conundrums! Conundrums!" my friend exclaimed. "This Quest of the Bat Wing is like the quest of Heaven, Watson. A hundred open doors invite us, each one promising to lead us to the light, and if we enter where do they lead? — to mystification. For instance, Colonel Menendez has broadly hinted that he looks upon Colin Camber as an enemy. Judging from your reception at the Guest House to-day, such an enmity, and a deadly enmity, actually exists. But whereas Camber has resided here for three years, the Colonel is a newcomer. We are, therefore, offered the spectacle of a trembling victim seeking the sacrifice. Bah! It is preposterous."

"If you had seen Colin Camber's face to-day, you might not have thought it so preposterous."

"But I should, Watson! I should! It is impossible to suppose that Colonel Menendez was unaware when he leased Cray's Folly that Camber occupied the Guest House."

"And Mrs. Camber is a Cuban," I murmured.

"Don't, Watson!" my friend implored. "This case is driving me mad. I have a conviction that it is going to prove my Waterloo."

"My dear fellow," I said, "this mood is new to you."

"Why don't you advise me to remember Auguste Dupin?" asked Holmes, bitterly. "That great man, preserving his philosophical calm, doubtless by this time would have pieced together these disjointed clues, and have produced an elegant pattern ready to be framed and exhibited to the admiring public."

He dropped down upon the bed and, taking his briar pipe from his pocket, began to load it in a manner which was almost vicious. I stood watching him and offered no remark, until, having lighted the pipe, he began to smoke. I knew that these "Indian moods" were of short duration, and, sure enough, presently:

"God bless us all, Watson," he said, breaking into an amused smile, "how we bristle when someone tries to prove that we are not infallible! How human we are, Watson, but how fortunate that we can laugh at ourselves."

I sighed with relief, for Holmes at these times imposed a severe strain even upon my easy-going disposition.

"Let us go down to the billiard room," he continued. "I will play you a hundred up. I have arrived at a point where my ideas persistently work in circles. The best cure is golf; failing golf, billiards."

The billiard room was immediately beneath us, adjoining the last apartment in the east wing, and there we made our way. Holmes played keenly, deliberately, concentrating upon the game. I was less successful, for I found myself alternately glancing toward the door and the open window, in the hope that Val Beverley would join us. I was disappointed, however. We saw no more of the ladies until tea-time, and if a spirit of constraint had prevailed throughout luncheon, then a veritable demon of unrest presided upon the terrace during tea.

Madame de Stämer made apologies on behalf of the Colonel. He was prolonging his siesta, but he hoped to join us at dinner.

"Is the Colonel's heart affected?" Holmes asked.

Madame de Stämer shrugged her shoulders and shook her head, blankly.

"It is mysterious, the state of his health," she replied. "An old trouble, which began years and years ago in Cuba."

Holmes nodded sympathetically, but I could see that he was not satisfied. Yet, although he might doubt her explanation, he had noted, and so had I, that Madame de Stämer's concern was very real. Her slender hands were strangely unsteady; indeed her condition bordered on one of distraction.

Holmes concealed his thoughts, whatever they may have been, beneath that mask of reserve which I knew so well, whilst I endeavoured in vain to draw Val Beverley into conversation with me.

I gathered that Madame de Stämer had been to visit the invalid, and that she was all anxiety to return was a fact she was wholly unable to conceal. There was a tired look in her still eyes, as though she had undertaken a task beyond her powers to perform and, so unnatural a quartette were we, that when presently she withdrew, I was glad, even though she took Val Beverley with her.

Sherlock Holmes resumed his seat, staring at me with unseeing eyes. A sound reached us through the drawing room which told us that Madame de Stämer's chair was being taken upstairs, a task always performed when Madame desired to visit the upper floors, by Manoel and Pedro's daughter, Nita, who acted as Madame's maid. These sounds died away, and I thought how silent everything had become. Even the birds were still, and presently, my eye being attracted to a black speck in the sky above, I learned why the feathered choir was mute. A hawk was hovering loftily overhead.

Noting my upward glance, Sherlock Holmes also raised his eyes.

"Ah," he murmured, "a hawk. All the birds are cowering in their nests. Nature is a cruel mistress, Watson."

16.

RED EVE

Over the remainder of that afternoon I will pass in silence. Indeed, looking backward now, I cannot recollect that it afforded one incident worthy of record. But because great things overshadow small, so it may be that, whereas my recollections of quite trivial episodes are sharp enough up to a point, my memories from this point onward to the horrible and tragic happening which I have set myself to relate are hazy and indistinct. I was troubled by the continued absence of Val Beverley. I thought that she was avoiding me by design, and in Holmes's gloomy reticence I could find no shadow of comfort.

We wandered aimlessly about the grounds, Holmes staring up in a vague fashion at the windows of Cray's Folly; and presently, when I stopped to inspect a very perfect rose bush, he left me without a word, and I found myself alone.

Later, as I sauntered toward the Tudor garden, where I had hoped to encounter Miss Beverley, I heard the clicking of billiard balls; and there was Holmes at the table, practising fancy shots.

He glanced up at me as I paused by the open window, stopped to relight his pipe, and then bent over the table again.

"Leave me alone, Watson," he muttered; "I am not fit for human society."

Understanding his moods as well as I did, I merely laughed and withdrew.

I strolled around into the library and inspected scores of books without forming any definite impression of the contents of any of them. Manoel came in whilst I was there, and I was strongly tempted to send a message to Miss Beverley; but common sense overcame the inclination.

When at last my watch told me that the hour for dressing was arrived, I heaved a sigh of relief. I cannot say that I was bored, my ill-temper sprang from a deeper source than this. The mysterious disappearance of the inmates of Cray's Folly, and a sort of brooding stillness which lay over the great house, had utterly oppressed me.

As I passed along the terrace, I paused to admire the spectacle afforded by the setting sun. The horizon was on fire from north to south, and the countryside was stained with that mystic radiance which is sometimes called the Blood of Apollo. Turning, I saw the disk of the moon coldly rising in the heavens. I thought of the silent birds and the hovering hawk, and I began my preparations for dinner mechanically, dressing as an automaton might dress.

Sherlock Holmes's personality was never more marked than in his evil moods. His power to fascinate was only equalled by his power to repel. Thus, although there was a light in his room and I could hear him moving about, I did not join him when I had finished dressing, but lighting a cigarette, I walked downstairs.

The beauty of the night called to me, although as I stepped out upon the terrace I realized with a sort of shock that the gathering dusk held a menace, so that I found myself questioning the shadows and doubting the rustle of every leaf. Something invisible, intangible yet potent, brooded over Cray's Folly. I began to think more kindly of the disappearance of Val Beverley during the afternoon. Doubtless she, too, had been touched by this spirit of unrest, and in solitude had sought to dispel it.

So thinking, I walked on in the direction of the Tudor garden. The place was bathed in a sort of purple half-light, lending it a fairy air of unreality, as though banished sun and rising moon yet disputed for mastery over earth. This idea set me thinking of Colin Camber, of Osiris, whom he had described as a black god, and of Isis, whose silver disk now held undisputed sovereignty of the evening sky.

Resentment of the treatment which I had received at the Guest House still burned hotly within me, but the mystery of it all had taken the keen edge off my wrath, and I think a sort of melancholy was the keynote of my reflections as, descending the steps to the sunken garden, I saw Val Beverley, in a delicate blue gown, coming toward me. She was the spirit of my dreams, and the embodiment of my mood. When she lowered her eyes at my approach, I knew by virtue of a sort of inspiration that the girl had been avoiding me.

"Miss Beverley," I said, "I have been looking for you all the afternoon."

"Have you? I have been in my room writing letters."

I paced slowly along beside her.

"I wish you would be very frank with me," I said.

She glanced up swiftly, and as swiftly lowered her lashes again.

"Do you think I am not frank?"

"I do think so. I understand why."

"Do you really understand?"

"I think I do. Your woman's intuition has told you that there is something wrong."

"In what way?"

"You are afraid of your thoughts. You can see that Madame de Stämer and Colonel Menendez are deliberately concealing something from Sherlock Holmes, and you don't know where your duty lies. Am I right?"

She met my glance for a moment in a startled way, then: "Yes," she said, softly; "you are quite right. How have you guessed?"

"I have tried very hard to understand you," I replied, "and so perhaps up to a point I have succeeded."

"Oh, Dr. Watson." She suddenly laid her hand upon my arm. "I am oppressed with such a dreadful foreboding, yet I don't know how to explain it to you."

"I understand. I, too, have felt it."

"You have?" She paused and looked at me eagerly. "Then it is not just morbid imagination on my part. If only I knew what to do, what to believe. Really, I am bewildered. I have just left Madame de Stämer — "

"Yes?" I said, for she had paused in evident doubt.

"Well, she has utterly broken down."

"Broken down?"

"She came to my room and sobbed hysterically for nearly an hour this afternoon."

"But what was the cause of her grief?"

"I simply cannot understand."

"Is it possible that Colonel Menendez is dangerously ill?"

"It may be so, Dr. Watson, but in that event why have they not sent for a physician?"

"True," I murmured; "and no one has been sent for?"

"No one."

"Have you seen Colonel Menendez?"

"Not since lunch-time."

"Have you ever known him to suffer in this way before?"

"Never. It is utterly unaccountable. Certainly during the last few months, he has given up riding practically altogether, and in other ways has changed his former habits; but I have never known him to exhibit traces of any real illness."

"Has any medical man attended him?"

"Not that I know of. Oh, there is something uncanny about it all. Whatever should I do if you were not here?"

She had spoken on impulse and, seeing her swift embarrassment:

"Miss Beverley," I said, "I am delighted to know that my company cheers you."

Truth to tell, my heart was beating rapidly, and so selfish is the nature of man, I was more glad to learn that my company was acceptable to Val Beverley than I should have been to have had the riddle of Cray's Folly laid bare before me.

Those sweetly indiscreet words, however, had raised a momentary barrier between us, and we walked on silently to the house, and entered the brightly lighted hall.

The silver peal of a Chinese tubular gong rang out just when we reached the veranda, and as Val Beverley and I walked in from the garden, Madame de Stämer came wheeling through the doorway, closely followed by Sherlock Holmes. In her, the art of the *toilette* amounted almost to genius, and she had so successfully concealed all traces of her recent grief that I wondered if this could have been real.

"My dear Dr. Watson," she cried, "I seem to be fated always to apologize for other people. The Colonel is truly desolate, but he cannot join us for dinner. I have already explained to Mr. Holmes."

Holmes inclined his head sympathetically, and assisted to arrange Madame in her place.

"The Colonel requests us to smoke a cigar with him after dinner, Watson," he said, glancing across to me. "It would seem that troubles never come singly."

"Ah," Madame shrugged her shoulders, which her low gown left daringly bare, "they come in flocks, or not at all. But I suppose we should feel lonely in the world without a few little sorrows, eh, Mr. Holmes?"

I loved her unquenchable spirit, and I have wondered often enough what I should have thought of her if I had known the truth. France has bred some wonderful women, both good and bad, but none I think more wonderful than Marie de Stämer.

If such a thing were possible, we dined more extravagantly than on the previous night. Madame's wit was at its keenest; she was truly brilliant. Pedro, from the big *bouffet* at the end of the room, supervised this feast of Lucullus; and except for odd moments of silence in which Madame seemed to be listening for some distant sound, there was nothing, I think, which could have told a casual observer that a black cloud rested upon the house.

Once, interrupting a *tête-à-tête* between Val Beverley and Sherlock Holmes:

"Do not encourage her, Mr. Holmes," said Madame, "she is a desperate flirt."

"Oh, Madame," cried Val Beverley and blushed deeply.

"You know you are, my dear, and you are very wise. Flirt all your life, but never fall in love. It is fatal, don't you think so, Dr. Watson?" — turning to me in her rapid manner.

I looked into her still eyes, which concealed so much.

"Say, rather, that it is Fate," I murmured.

"Yes, that is more pretty, but not so true. If I could live my life again, Monsieur Watson," she said, for she sometimes used the French and sometimes the English mode of address, "I should build a stone wall around my heart. It could peep over, but no one could ever reach it."

Oddly enough, then, as it seems to me now, the spirit of unrest seemed almost to depart for awhile, and in the company of the vivacious Frenchwoman, time passed very quickly up to the moment when Holmes and I walked slowly upstairs to join the Colonel.

During the latter part of dinner, an idea had presented itself to me which I was anxious to mention to Holmes, and:

"Holmes," I said, "an explanation of the Colonel's absence has occurred to me."

"Really!" he replied; "possibly the same one that has occurred to me."

"What is that?"

Sherlock Holmes paused on the stairs, turning to me.

"You are thinking that he has taken cover from the danger which he believes particularly to threaten him to-night?"

"Exactly."

"You may be right," he murmured, proceeding upstairs.

He led the way to a little smoke-room which hitherto I had never visited, and in response to his knock:

"Come in," cried the high voice of Colonel Menendez.

We entered to find ourselves in a small and very cozy room. There was a handsome oak bureau against one wall which was littered with papers of various kinds, and there was also a large bookcase occupied almost exclusively by French novels. It occurred to me that the Colonel spent a greater part of his time in this little snuggery than in the more formal study below. At the moment of our arrival, he was stretched upon a *settée* near which stood a little table; and on this table I observed the remains of what appeared to me to have been a fairly substantial repast. For some reason which I did not pause to analyze at the moment, I noted with disfavour the presence of a bowl of roses upon the silver tray.

Colonel Menendez was smoking a cigarette, and Manoel was in the act of removing the tray.

"Gentlemen," said the Colonel, "I have no words in which to express my sorrow. Manoel, pull up those armchairs. Help yourself to port, Mr. Holmes, and fill Dr. Watson's glass. I can recommend the cigars in the long box."

As we seated ourselves:

"I am extremely sorry to find you indisposed, sir," said Holmes.

He was watching the dark face keenly, and probably thinking, as I was thinking, that it exhibited no trace of illness.

Colonel Menendez waved his cigarette gracefully, settling himself amid the cushions.

"An old trouble, Mr. Holmes," he replied, lightly; "a legacy from ancestors who drank too deep of the wine of life."

"You are surely taking medical advice?"

Colonel Menendez shrugged slightly.

"There is no doctor in England who would understand the case," he replied. "Besides, there is nothing for it but rest and avoidance of excitement."

"In that event, Colonel," said Holmes, "we will not disturb you for long. Indeed, I should not have consented to disturb you at all, if I had not thought that you might have some request to make upon this important night."

"Ah!" Colonel Menendez shot a swift glance in his direction. "You have remembered about to-night?"

199

"Naturally."

"Your interest comforts me very greatly, gentlemen, and I am only sorry that my uncertain health has made me so poor a host. Nothing has occurred since your arrival to help you, I am aware. Not that I am anxious for any new activity on the part of my enemies. But almost anything which should end this deathly suspense would be welcome."

He spoke the final words with a peculiar intonation. I saw Holmes watching him closely.

"However," he continued, "everything is in the hands of Fate, and if your visit should prove futile, I can only apologize for having interrupted your original plans. Respecting to-night" — he shrugged — "what can I say?"

"Nothing has occurred," asked Holmes, slowly, "nothing fresh, I mean, to indicate that the danger which you apprehend may really culminate to-night?"

"Nothing fresh, Mr. Holmes, unless you yourself have observed anything."

"Ah," murmured Sherlock Holmes, "let us hope that the threat will never be fulfilled."

Colonel Menendez inclined his head gravely.

"Let us hope so," he said.

On the whole, he was curiously subdued. He was most solicitous for our comfort, and his exquisite courtesy had never been more marked. I often think of him now — his big but graceful figure reclining upon the *settée*, whilst he skillfully rolled his eternal cigarettes and chatted in that peculiar, light voice. Before the memory of Colonel Don Juan Sarmiento Menendez, I sometimes stand appalled. If his Maker had but endowed him with other qualities of mind and heart equal to his magnificent courage, then truly he had been a great man.

17.

NIGHT OF THE FULL MOON

I stood at Holmes's open window — looking down in the Tudor garden. The moon, like a silver mirror, hung in a cloudless sky. Over an hour had elapsed since I had heard Pedro making his nightly rounds. Nothing whatever of an unusual nature had occurred and, although Holmes and I had listened for any sound of nocturnal footsteps, our vigilance had passed unrewarded. Holmes, unrolling the Chinese ladder, had set out upon a secret tour of the grounds, warning me that it must be a long business, since the brilliance of the moonlight rendered it necessary that he should make a wide detour, in order to avoid possible observation from the windows. I had wished to join him, but:

"I count it most important that one of us should remain in the house," Holmes had replied.

As a result, here was I at the open window, questioning the shadows to right and left of me, and every moment expecting to see Holmes reappear. I wondered what discoveries he would make. It would not have surprised me to learn that there were lights in many windows of Cray's Folly to-night.

Although, when we had rejoined the ladies for half an hour after leaving Colonel Menendez's room, there had been no overt reference to the menace overhanging the house; yet, as we separated for the night, I had detected again in Val Beverley's eyes that look of repressed fear. Indeed, she was palpably disinclined to retire, but was carried off by the masterful Madame, who declared that she looked tired.

I wondered now, as I gazed down into the moon-bathed gardens, if Holmes and I were the only wakeful members of the household at that hour. I should have been prepared to wager that there were others. I thought of the strange footsteps which so often passed Miss Beverley's room, and I discovered this thought to be an uncomfortable one.

Normally, I was sceptical enough, but on this night of the full moon as I stood there at the window, the horrors which Colonel Menendez had related to us grew very real in my eyes, and I thought that the mysteries of Voodoo might conceal strange and ghastly truths. "The scientific employment of darkness against light." Colin Camber's words leapt unbidden to my mind; and, such is the magic of moonlight, they became invested with a new and a deeper significance. Strange that theories which one rejects whilst the Sun is shining should assume a spectral shape in the light of the moon.

Such were my musings, when suddenly I heard a faint sound as of footsteps crunching upon gravel. I leaned farther out of the window, listening intently. I could not believe that Holmes would be guilty of such an indiscretion as this, yet who else could be walking upon the path below?

As I watched, craning from the window, a tall figure appeared; and, slowly crossing the gravel path, it descended the moss-grown steps to the Tudor garden.

It was Colonel Menendez!

He was bare-headed, but fully dressed as I had seen him in the smoking-room; and not yet grasping the portent of his appearance at that hour, but merely wondering why he had not yet retired, I continued to watch him. As I did so, something in his gait, something unnatural in his movements, caught hold of my mind with a sudden great conviction. He had reached the path that led to the sun-dial; and with short, queer, ataxic steps, he was proceeding in its direction, a striking figure in the brilliant moonlight which touched his gray hair with a silvery sheen.

His unnatural, automatic movements told their own story. He was walking in his sleep! Could it be in obedience to the call of M'Kombo?

My throat grew dry and I knew not how to act. Unwillingly it seemed, with ever-halting steps, the figure moved onward. I could see that his fists were tightly clenched and that he held his head rigidly upright. All horrors, real and imaginary, which I had ever experienced culminated in the moment when I saw this man of inflexible character, I could have sworn of indomitable will, moving like a puppet under the influence of some unnameable force.

He was almost come to the sun-dial when I determined to cry out. Then, remembering the shock experienced by a suddenly awakened somnambulist, and remembering that the Chinese ladder hung from the window at my feet, I changed my mind. Checking the cry upon my lips, I got astride of the window ledge, and began to grope for the bamboo rungs beneath me. I had found the first of these, and, turning, had begun to descend, when:

"Watson! Watson!" came softly from the opening in the box hedge, "what the devil are you about?"

It was Sherlock Holmes returned from his tour of the building.

"Holmes!" I whispered, descending. "Quick! The Colonel has just gone into the Tudor garden!"

"What!" There was a note of absolute horror in the exclamation. "You should have stopped him, Watson, you should have stopped him!" cried Holmes, and with that he ran off in the same direction.

Disentangling my foot from the rungs of the ladder which lay upon the ground, I was about to follow, *when it happened !* — that strange and ghastly thing toward which, secretly, darkly, events had been tending.

The crack of a rifle sounded sharply in the stillness, echoing and re-echoing from wing-to-wing of Cray's Folly and then, more dimly, up the wooded slopes beyond! Somewhere ahead of me I heard Holmes cry out:

"My God, I am too late! They have got him!"

Then, hotfoot, I was making for the entrance to the garden. Just as I came to it and raced down the steps, I heard another sound the memory of which haunts me to this day.

Where it came from I had no idea. Perhaps I was too confused to judge accurately. It might have come from the house, or from the slopes beyond the house. But it was a sort of shrill, choking laugh, and it set the ultimate touch of horror upon a *scène macabre* which, even as I write of it, seems unreal to me.

I ran up the path to where Holmes was kneeling beside the sun-dial. Analysis of my emotions at this moment were futile; I can only say that I had come to a state of stupefaction. Face downward on the grass, arms outstretched and fists clenched, lay Colonel Menendez. I think I saw him move convulsively, but as I gained his side Holmes looked up at me, and beneath the tan which he never lost his face had grown pale. He spoke through clenched teeth.

"Merciful God," he said, "he is shot through the head."

One glance I gave at the ghastly wound in the base of the Colonel's skull, and then swayed backward. I had seen many men die in Afghanistan, in fact I had been shot in the leg myself while serving in that far-off country; but to see a man die in so *macabre* a setting, a man one has known and called friend, is strange and terrible. Here in this moon-bathed Tudor garden, it was a horror almost beyond my powers to endure.

Sherlock Holmes, without touching the prone figure, stood up. Indeed no examination of the victim was necessary. A rifle bullet had pierced his brain, and he lay there dead with his head toward the hills.

I clutched at Holmes's shoulder, but he stood rigidly, staring up the slope past the angle of the tower, to where a gable of the Guest House jutted out from the trees.

"Did you hear — that cry?" I whispered, "immediately after the shot?"

"I heard it."

A moment longer he stood fixedly watching, and then:

"Not a wisp of smoke," he said. "You note the direction in which he was facing when he fell?"

He spoke in a stern and unnatural voice.

"I do. He must have turned half-right when he came to the sun-dial."

"Where were you when the shot was fired?"

"Running in this direction."

"You saw no flash?"

"None."

"Neither did I," groaned Holmes; "neither did I. And short of throwing a cordon around the hills, what can be done? How can I move?"

He had somewhat relaxed, but now as I continued to clutch his arm, I felt the muscles grow rigid again.

"Look, Watson!" he whispered — "Look!"

I followed the direction of his fixed stare, and through the trees on the hillside a dim light shone out. Someone had lighted a lamp in the Guest House.

A faint, sibilant sound drew my glance upward, and there overhead a large bat circled — circled — dipped — and flew off toward the distant woods. So still was the night that I could distinguish the babble of the little stream which ran down into the lake. Then, suddenly, came a loud flapping of wings. The swans had been awakened by the sound of the shot. Others had been awakened, too, for now distant voices became audible, and then a muffled scream from somewhere within Cray's Folly.

"Get back to the house, Watson," said Holmes, hoarsely. "For God's sake keep the women away. Get Pedro and send Manoel for the nearest doctor. It's useless but usual. Let no one deface his footprints. My worst anticipations have come true. The local police must be informed."

Throughout the time that he spoke, Holmes continued to search the moon-bathed landscape with feverish eagerness; but except for a faint movement of birds in the trees, for they, like the swans on the lake, had been alarmed by the shot, nothing stirred.

"It came from the hillside," he muttered. "Off you go, Watson."

And even as I started on my unpleasant errand, he had set out running toward the gate in the southern corner of the garden.

For my part, I scrambled unceremoniously up the bank and emerged where the yews stood sentinel beside the path. I ran through the gap in the box hedge just as the main doors were thrown open by Pedro.

He started back as he saw me.

"Pedro! Pedro!" I cried, "have the ladies been awakened?"

"Yes, yes! There is terrible trouble, sir. What has happened? What has happened?"

"A tragedy," I said, shortly. "Pull yourself together. Where is Madame de Stämer?"

Pedro uttered some exclamation in Spanish and stood, pale-faced, swaying before me, a dishevelled figure in a dressing gown. And now in the background, Mrs. Fisher appeared. One frightened glance she cast in my direction, and would have hurried across the hall but I intercepted her.

"Where are you going, Mrs. Fisher?" I demanded. "What has happened here?"

"To Madame, to Madame," she sobbed, pointing toward the corridor which communicated with Madame de Stämer's bedchamber.

I heard a frightened cry proceeding from that direction, and recognized the voice of Nita, the girl who acted as Madame's maid. Then I heard Val Beverley.

"Go and fetch Mrs. Fisher, Nita, at once — and try to behave yourself. I have trouble enough."

I entered the corridor and pulled up short. Valeria Beverley, fully dressed, was kneeling beside Madame de Stämer, who wore a kimono over her night-robe, and who lay huddled on the floor immediately outside the door of her room!

"Oh, Dr. Watson!" cried the girl pitifully as she raised frightened eyes to me. "For God's sake, tell me what has happened?"

Nita, the Spanish girl, who was sobbing hysterically, ran along to join Mrs. Fisher.

"I will tell you in a moment," I said, quietly, rendered cool, as one always is, by the need of others. "But first tell me — how did Madame de Stämer get here?"

"I don't know, I don't know! I was startled by the shot. It has awakened everybody. And just as I opened my door to listen, I heard Madame cry out in the hall below. I ran down, turned on the light, and found her lying here. She, too, had been awakened, I suppose, and was endeavouring to drag herself from her room when her strength failed her and she swooned. She is too heavy for me to lift," added the girl, pathetically, "and Pedro is out of his senses, and Nita, who was the first of the servants to come, is simply hysterical, as you can see."

I nodded reassuringly and stooping, lifted the swooning woman. She was much heavier than I should have supposed, but, Val Beverley leading the way, I carried her into her apartment and placed her upon the bed.

"I will leave her to you," I said. "You have courage, and so I will tell you what has happened."

"Yes, tell me; oh, tell me!"

Val laid her hands upon my shoulders appealingly and looked up into my eyes in a way that made me long to ignore the differences in our ages and take her in my arms to comfort her; an insane longing which I only crushed with difficulty.

"Someone has shot Colonel Menendez," I said, in a low voice, for Mrs. Fisher had just entered.

"You mean — "

I nodded.

"Oh!"

Val Beverley opened and closed her eyes, clutching at me dizzily for a moment, then:

"I think," she whispered, "she must have known, and that was why she swooned. Oh, my God! How horrible."

I made her sit down in an armchair and watched her anxiously; but although every speck of colour had faded from her cheeks, she was splendidly courageous, and almost immediately Val Beverley smiled up at me, very wanly, but confidently.

"I will look after her," she said. "Mr. Holmes will need your assistance."

When I returned to the hall, I found it already filled with a number of servants incongruously attired. Carter the chauffeur, who lived at the lodge, was just coming in at the door, and:

"Carter," I said, "get a car out quickly, and bring the nearest doctor. If there is another man who can drive, send him for the police. Your master has been shot."

18.

INSPECTOR AYLESBURY OF MARKET HILTON

"Now, gentlemen," said Inspector Aylesbury, "I will take evidence."

Dawn was creeping grayly over the hills, and the view from the library windows resembled a study by Bastien-Lepage. The lamps burned yellowly, and the exotic appointments of the library viewed in that cold light for some reason reminded me of a stage set seen in daylight. The Velasquez portrait mentally translated me to the billiard room where something lay upon the *settée* with a white sheet drawn over it; and I wondered if my own face looked as wan and comfortless as did the faces of my companions; that is, of two of them, for I must except Inspector Aylesbury's

Squarely before the oaken mantel he stood: a large, pompous man; but in this hour, I could find no humour in Sherlock Holmes's description of him as resembling a walrus. He had a large auburn moustache tinged with gray and prominent brown eyes, but the lower part of his face, which terminated in a big double chin, was ill-balanced by his small forehead. He was bulkily built, and I had conceived an unreasonable distaste for his puffy hands. His official air and oratorical manner were provoking.

Holmes sat in the chair which he had occupied during our last interview with Colonel Menendez in the library, and I realized — a realization which made me uncomfortable — that I was seated upon the couch on which the Colonel had reclined. Only one other person was present, Dr. Rolleston of Mid-Hatton, a slight, fair man with a brisk, military manner, acquired perhaps during six years of war service. He was standing beside me smoking a cigarette.

"I have taken all the necessary particulars concerning the position of the body," continued the Inspector, "the nature of the wound, contents of pockets, etc., and I now turn to you, Mr. Holmes, as the first person to discover the murdered man."

Sherlock Holmes lay back in the armchair watching the speaker.

"Before we come to what happened here to-night I should like to be quite clear about your own position in the matter, Mr. Holmes. Now" — Inspector Aylesbury raised one finger in forensic manner — "now, you visited me yesterday afternoon, Mr. Holmes, and asked for certain information regarding the neighbourhood."

"I did," said Holmes, shortly.

"The questions which you asked me were," continued the Inspector, slowly and impressively, "did I know of any coloured people living in, or about, Mid-Hatton, and could I give you a list of the residents within a two-mile radius of Cray's Folly. I gave you the information which you required, and now it is your turn to give me some. Why did you ask those questions?"

"For this reason," was the reply — "I had been requested by Colonel Menendez to visit Cray's Folly, accompanied by my friend Dr. Watson, in order that I might investigate certain occurrences which had taken place here."

"Oh," said the Inspector, raising his eyebrows, "I see. You were here to make investigations?"

"Yes."

"And these occurrences: will you tell me what they were?"

"Simple enough in themselves," replied Holmes. "Someone broke into the house one night."

"Broke into the house?"

"Undoubtedly."

"But this was never reported to us."

"Possibly not, but someone broke in nevertheless. Secondly, Colonel Menendez had detected someone lurking about the lawns; and thirdly, the wing of a bat was nailed to the main door."

Inspector Aylesbury lowered his eyebrows and concentrated a frowning glance upon the speaker.

"Of course, sir," he said, "I don't want to jump to conclusions, but you are not by any chance trying to be funny at a time like this?"

"My sense of humour has failed me entirely," replied Holmes. "I am merely stating bald facts in reply to your questions."

"Oh, I see."

The Inspector cleared his throat.

"Someone broke into Cray's Folly, then, a fact which was not reported to me; a suspicious loiterer was seen in the grounds, again not reported; and someone played a silly practical joke by nailing the wing of a bat, you say, to the door. Might I ask, Mr. Holmes, why you mention this matter? The other things are serious, but why you should mention the trick of some mischievous boy at a time like this I can't imagine."

"No," said Holmes, wearily, "it does sound absurd, Inspector; I quite appreciate the fact. But, you see, Colonel Menendez regarded it as the most significant episode of them all."

"What! The bat wing nailed on the door?"

"The bat wing, decidedly. He believed it to be the token of a Voodoo secret society which had determined upon his death, hence my enquiries regarding coloured men in the neighbourhood. Do you understand, Inspector?"

Inspector Aylesbury took a large handkerchief from his pocket and blew his nose. Replacing the handkerchief he cleared his throat, and:

"Am I to understand," he enquired, "that the late Colonel Menendez had expected to be attacked?"

"You may understand that," replied Holmes. "It explains my presence in the house."

"Oh," said the Inspector, "I see. It looks as though he might have done better if he had applied to me."

Sherlock Holmes glanced across in my direction and smiled grimly.

"As I had predicted, Watson," he murmured, "my Waterloo."

"What's that you say about Waterloo, Mr. Holmes?" demanded the Inspector.

"Nothing germane to the case," replied Holmes. "It was a reference to a battle, not to a railway station."

Inspector Aylesbury stared at him dully.

"You quite understand, sir, that you are giving evidence?" he said.

"It were impossible not to appreciate the fact."

"Very well, then. The late Colonel Menendez thought he was in danger from Voodoo cultists. Why did he think that?"

"He was a retired West Indian planter," replied Holmes, patiently, "and he was under the impression that he had offended a powerful native society, and that for many years their vengeance had pursued him. Attempts to assassinate him had already taken place in Cuba and in the United States."

"What sort of attempts?"

"He was shot at several times, and once, in Washington, was attacked by a man with a knife. He maintained in my presence and in the presence of my friend, Dr. Watson, here, that these various attempts were due to members of a sect or religion known as Voodoo."

"Voodoo?"

"Voodoo, Inspector, also known as Obeah, a cult which has spread from the West Coast of Africa throughout the West Indies and to parts of the United States. The bat wing is said to be a sign used by these people."

Inspector Aylesbury scratched his chin.

"Now let me get this thing clear," said he: "Colonel Menendez believed that people called Voodoos wanted to kill him? Before we go any farther, why?"

"Twenty years ago in the West Indies, he had shot an important member of this sect."

"Twenty years ago?"

"According to a statement which he made to me, yes."

"I see. Then for twenty years, these *Voodoos* have been trying to kill him? Then he comes and settles here in Surrey and someone nails a bat wing to his door? Did you see this bat wing?"

"I did. I have it upstairs in my bag if you would care to examine it."

"Oh," said the Inspector, "I see. And thinking he had been followed to England, he came to you to see if you could save him?"

Sherlock Holmes nodded grimly.

"Why did he go to you in preference to the local police, the proper authorities?" demanded the Inspector.

"He was advised to do so by the Spanish ambassador, or so he informed me."

"Is that so? Well, I suppose it had to be. Coming from foreign parts, I expect he didn't know what our police are for." He cleared his throat. "Very well, I understand now what you were doing here, Mr. Holmes. The next thing is, what were you doing tonight, as I see that both you and Dr. Watson are still in evening dress?"

"We were keeping watch," I replied.

Inspector Aylesbury turned to me ponderously, raising a fat hand. "One moment, Dr. Watson, one moment," he protested. "The evidence of one witness at a time."

"We were keeping watch," said Holmes, deliberately echoing my words.

"Why?"

"More or less because we were here for that purpose. You see, on the night of the full moon, according to Colonel Menendez, Obeah people become particularly active."

"Why on the night of the full moon?"

"This I cannot tell you."

"Oh, I see. You were keeping watch. Where were you keeping watch?"

"In my room."

"In which part of the house is your room?"

"Northeast. It overlooks the Tudor garden."

"At what time did you retire?"

"About half-past ten."

"Did you leave the Colonel well?"

"No, he had been unwell all day. He had remained in his room."

"Had he asked you to sit up?"

"Not at all; our vigil was quite voluntary."

"Very well, then. You were in your room when the shot was fired?"

"On the contrary, I was on the path in front of the house."

"Oh, I see. The front door was open, then?"

"Not at all. Pedro had locked up for the night."

"And locked you out?"

"No; I descended from my window by means of a ladder which I had brought with me for the purpose."

"With a ladder? That's rather extraordinary, Mr. Holmes."

"It is extraordinary. I have strange habits."

Inspector Aylesbury cleared his throat again and looked frowningly across at my friend.

"What part of the grounds were you in when the shot was fired?" he demanded.

"Halfway along the north side."

"What were you doing?"

"I was running."

"Running?"

"You see, Inspector, I regarded it as my duty to patrol the grounds of the house after nightfall since, for all I knew to the contrary, some of the servants might be responsible for the attempts of which the Colonel complained. I had descended from the window of my room, passed entirely around the house east to west, and returned to my starting-point when Dr. Watson, who was looking out of the window, observed Colonel Menendez entering the Tudor garden."

"Oh. Colonel Menendez was not visible to you?"

"Not from my position below; but being informed by my friend, who was hurriedly descending the ladder, that the Colonel had entered the garden, I set off running to intercept him."

"Why?"

"He had acquired a habit of walking in his sleep, and I presumed that he was doing so on this occasion."

"Oh, I see. So being told by the gentleman at the window that Colonel Menendez was in the garden, you started to run toward him. While you were running you heard a shot?"

"I did."

"Where do you think it came from?"

"Nothing is more difficult to judge, Inspector, especially when one is near to a large building surrounded by trees."

"Nevertheless," said the Inspector, again raising his finger and frowning at Holmes, "you cannot tell me that you formed no impression on the point. For instance, was it near, or a long way off?"

"It was fairly near."

"Ten yards, twenty yards, a hundred yards, a mile?"

"Within a hundred yards. I cannot be more exact."

"Within a hundred yards, and you have no idea from which direction the shot was fired?"

"From the sound I could form none."

"Oh, I see. And what did you do?"

"I ran on and down into the sunken garden. I saw Colonel Menendez lying upon his face near the sun-dial. He was moving convulsively. Running up to him, I saw that he had been shot through the head."

"What steps did you take?"

"My friend, Dr. Watson, had joined me, and I sent him for assistance."

"But what steps did you take to apprehend the murderer?"

Sherlock Holmes looked at him quietly.

"What steps should you have taken?" he asked.

Inspector Aylesbury cleared his throat again, and:

"I don't think I should have let my man slip through my fingers like that," he replied. "Why! By now he may be out of the county."

"Your theory is quite feasible," said Holmes, tonelessly.

"You were actually on the spot when the shot was fired, you admit that it was fired within a hundred yards, yet you did nothing to apprehend the murderer."

"No," replied Holmes, "I was ridiculously inactive. You see, I am a mere amateur, Inspector. For my future guidance, I should be glad to know what the correct procedure would have been."

Inspector Aylesbury blew his nose.

"I know my job," he said. "If I had been called in there might have been a different tale to tell. But he was a foreigner, and he paid for his ignorance, poor fellow."

Sherlock Holmes took out his pipe and began to load it in a deliberate and lazy manner.

Inspector Aylesbury turned his prominent eyes in my direction.

19.

COMPLICATIONS

"I am afraid of this man Aylesbury," said Sherlock Holmes. We sat in the deserted dining room. I had contributed my account of the evening's happenings, Dr. Rolleston had made his report, and Inspector Aylesbury was now examining the servants in the library. Holmes and I had obtained his official permission to withdraw, and the physician was visiting Madame de Stämer, who lay in a state of utter prostration.

"What do you mean, Holmes?"

"I mean that he will presently make some tragic blunder. Good God, Watson, to think that this man had sought my aid, and that I stood by idly whilst he walked out to his death. I shall never forgive myself." He banged the table with his fist. "Even now that these unknown fiends have achieved their object, I am helpless, helpless. There was not a wisp of smoke to guide me, Watson, and one man cannot search a county."

I sighed wearily.

"Do you know, Holmes," I said, "I am thinking of a verse of Kipling's."

"I know!" he interrupted, almost savagely.

"A Snider squibbed in the jungle. Somebody laughed and fled — "

"Oh, I know, Watson. I heard that damnable laughter, too."

"My God," I whispered, "who was it? What was it? Where did it come from?"

"As well to ask where the shot came from, Watson. Out amongst all those trees, with a house that might have been built for a sounding-board, who could presume to say where either came from? One thing we know: that the shot came from the south."

He leaned upon a corner of the table, staring at me intently.

"From the south?" I echoed.

Holmes glanced in the direction of the open door.

"Presently," he said, "we shall have to tell Aylesbury everything that we know. After all, he represents the law; but unless we can get Inspector Lestrade down from Scotland Yard, I foresee a miscarriage of justice. Colonel Menendez lay on his face, and the line made by his recumbent body pointed almost directly toward — "

I nodded, watching him.

"I know, Holmes — toward the Guest House."

Sherlock Holmes inclined his head, grimly.

"The first light which we saw," he continued, "was in a window of the Guest House. It may have had no significance. Awakened by the sound of a rifle-shot near by, anyone would naturally get up."

"And having decided to come downstairs and investigate," I continued, "would naturally light a lamp."

"Quite so." He stared at me very hard. "Yet," he said, "unless Mr. Colin Camber can produce an alibi, I foresee a very stormy time for him."

"So do I, Holmes. A deadly hatred existed between these two men, and probably this horrible deed was done on the spur of the moment. It is of his poor little girl-wife that I am thinking. As though her troubles were not heavy enough already."

"Yes," he agreed. "I am almost tempted to hold my tongue, Watson, until I have personally interviewed these people. But of course, if our blundering friend directly questions me, I shall have no alternative. I shall have to answer him. His talent for examination, however, scarcely amounts to genius, so that we may not be called upon for further details at the moment. I wonder how I can induce him to requisition Scotland Yard?"

He rested his chin in his hand and stared down reflectively at the carpet. I thought that he looked very haggard as he sat there in the early morning light, dressed as for dinner. There was something pathetic in the pose of his bowed head.

Leaning across, I placed my hand on his shoulder.

"Don't get despondent, old chap," I said. "You have not failed yet."

"Oh, but I have, Watson!" he cried, fiercely, "I have! He came to me for protection. Now he lies dead in his own house. Failed? I have failed utterly, miserably."

I turned aside as the door opened and Dr. Rolleston came in.

"Ah, gentlemen," he said, "I wanted to see you before leaving. I have just been to visit Madame de Stämer again."

"Yes," said Holmes, eagerly; "how is she?"

Dr. Rolleston carefully lighted a cigarette, frowning perplexedly the while.

"To be honest," he replied, "her condition puzzles me."

He walked across to the fireplace and dropped the match, staring at Holmes with a curious expression.

"Has anyone told her the truth?" he asked.

"You mean that Colonel Menendez is dead?"

"Yes," replied Dr. Rolleston. "I understood that no one had told her?"

"No one has done so to my knowledge," said Holmes.

"Then the sympathy between them must have been very acute," murmured the physician, "for she certainly knows!"

"Do you really think she knows?" I asked.

"I am certain of it. She must have had knowledge of a danger to be apprehended, and being awakened by the sound of the rifle shot, have realized by a sort of intuition that the expected tragedy had happened. I should say, from the presence of a small bruise which I found upon her forehead, that she had actually walked out into the corridor."

"Walked?" I cried.

"Yes," said the physician. "She is a shell-shock case, of course, and we sometimes find that a second shock counteracts the effect of the first. This, temporarily at any rate, seems to have happened to-night. She is now in a very curious state: a form of hysteria, no doubt, but very curious all the same."

"Miss Beverley is with her?" I asked.

Dr. Rolleston nodded affirmatively.

"Yes, a very capable nurse. I am glad to know that Madame de Stämer is in such good hands. I am calling again early in the morning, and I have told Mrs. Fisher to see that nothing is said within hearing of the room which could enable Madame de Stämer to obtain confirmation of the idea, which she evidently entertains, that Colonel Menendez is dead."

"Does she actually assert that he is dead?" asked Holmes.

"My dear sir," replied Dr. Rolleston, "she asserts nothing. She sits there like Niobe changed to stone, staring straight before her. She seems to be unaware of the presence of everyone except Miss Beverley. The only words she has spoken since recovering consciousness have been, 'Don't leave me!' "

"Hmm," muttered Holmes. "You have not attended Madame de Stämer before, doctor?"

"No," was the reply, "this is the first time I have entered Cray's Folly since it was occupied by Sir James Appleton."

He was about to take his departure when the door opened and Inspector Aylesbury walked in.

"Ah," said he, "I have two more witnesses to interview: Madame de Stämer and Miss Beverley. From these witnesses I hope to get particulars of the dead man's life which may throw some light upon the identity of his murderer."

"But it is impossible to see either of them at present," replied Dr. Rolleston briskly.

"What's that, doctor?" asked the Inspector. "Are they hysterical, or something?"

"As a result of the shock, Madame de Stämer is dangerously ill," replied the physician, "and Miss Beverley is remaining with her."

"Oh, I see. But Miss Beverley could come out for a few minutes?"

"She could," admitted the physician, sharply, "but I don't wish her to do so."

"Oh, but the law must be served, doctor."

"Quite so, but not at the expense of my patient's reason."

He was a resolute man, this country practitioner, and I saw Holmes smiling in grim approval.

"I have expressed my opinion," he said, finally, walking out of the room; "I shall leave the responsibility to you, Inspector Aylesbury. Good morning, gentlemen."

Inspector Aylesbury scratched his chin.

"That's awkward," he muttered. "The evidence of this woman is highly important."

He turned toward us, doubtingly, whereupon Holmes stood up, yawning.

"If I can be of any further assistance to you, Inspector," said my friend, "command me. Otherwise, I feel sure you will appreciate the fact that both Dr. Watson and myself are extremely tired, and have passed through a very trying ordeal."

"Yes," replied Inspector Aylesbury, "that's all very well, but I find myself at a deadlock."

"You surprise me," declared Holmes.

"I can see nothing to be surprised about," cried the Inspector. "When I was called in, it was already too late."

"Most unfortunate," murmured Holmes, disagreeably. "Come along, Watson, you look tired to death."

"One moment, gentlemen," the Inspector insisted, as I stood up. "One moment. There is a little point which you may be able to clear up."

Holmes paused, his hand on the door knob, and turned.

"The point is this," continued the Inspector, frowning portentously and lowering his chin so that it almost disappeared into the folds of his neck, "I have now interviewed all the inmates of Cray's Folly except the ladies. It appears to me that four people had not gone to bed. There are you two gentlemen, who have explained why I found you in evening dress, Colonel Menendez, who can never explain, and there is one other."

He paused, looking from Holmes to myself.

It had come, the question which I had dreaded, the question which I had been asking myself ever since I had seen Val Beverley kneeling in the corridor, dressed as she had been when we had parted for the night.

"I refer to Miss Val Beverley," the police-court voice proceeded. "This lady had evidently not retired, and neither, it would appear, had the Colonel."

"Neither had I," murmured Sherlock Holmes, "and neither had Dr. Watson."

"Your reason I understand," said the Inspector, "or at least your explanation is a possible one. But if the party broke up as you say it did, somewhere about half-past ten o'clock, and if Madame de Stämer had gone to bed, why should Miss Beverley have remained up?" He paused significantly. "As well as Colonel Menendez?" he added.

"Look here, Inspector Aylesbury," I interrupted, I speaking in a very quiet tone, I remember, "your insinuations annoy me."

"Oh," said he, turning his prominent eyes in my direction, "I see. They annoy you? If they annoy you, sir, perhaps you can explain this point which is puzzling me?"

"I cannot explain it, but doubtless Miss Beverley can do so when you ask her."

"I should like to have asked her now, and I can't make out why she refuses to see me."

"She has not refused to see you," replied Holmes, smoothly. "She is probably unaware of the fact that you wish to see her."

"I don't know so much," muttered the Inspector. "In my opinion I am being deliberately baffled on all sides. You can throw no light on this matter, then?"

"None," I answered, shortly, and Sherlock Holmes shook his head.

"But you must remember, Inspector," he explained, "that the entire household was in a state of unrest."

"In other words, everybody was waiting for this very thing to happen?"

"Consciously, or subconsciously, everybody was."

"What do you mean by consciously or subconsciously?"

"I mean that those of us who were aware of the previous attempts on the life of the Colonel apprehended this danger. And I believe that something of this apprehension had extended even to the servants."

"Oh, to the servants? Now, I have seen all the servants, except the chef, who lives at a house on the outskirts of Mid-Hatton, as you may know. Can you give me any information about this man?"

"I have seen him," replied Holmes, "and have congratulated him upon his culinary art. His name, I believe, is Deronne. He is a Spaniard, and a little fat man. Quite an amiable creature," he added.

"Hmm." The Inspector cleared his throat noisily.

"If that is all," said Holmes, "I should welcome an opportunity of a few hours' sleep."

"Oh," said the Inspector. "Well, I suppose that is quite natural, but I shall probably have a lot more questions to ask you later."

"Quite," muttered Holmes. "Quite. Come on, Watson. Good-night, Inspector Aylesbury."

"Good-night."

Holmes walked out of the dining room and across the deserted hall. He slowly mounted the stairs and I followed him into his room. It was now quite light, and as my friend dropped down upon the bed, I thought that he looked very tired and haggard.

"Watson," he said, "shut the door."

I closed the door and turned to him.

"You heard that question about Miss Beverley?" I began.

"I heard it, and I am wondering what her answer will be when the Inspector puts it to her personally."

"Surely it is obvious?" I cried. "A cloud of apprehension had settled on the house last night, Holmes, which was like the darkness of Egypt. The poor girl was afraid to go to bed. She was probably sitting up reading."

"Hmm," said Holmes, drumming his feet upon the carpet. "Of course you realize that there is one person in Cray's Folly who holds the clue to the heart of the mystery?"

"Madame de Stämer?"

He nodded grimly.

"When the rifle cracked out, Watson, she knew! Remember, no one had told her the truth. Yet can you doubt that she knows?"

"I don't doubt it."

"Neither do I." He clenched his teeth tightly and beat his fists upon the coverlet. "I was dreading that our friend the

Inspector would ask a question which to my mind was very obvious."

"You mean? — "

"Well, what investigator whose skull contained anything more useful than bubbles would have failed to ask if Colonel Menendez had an enemy in the neighbourhood?"

"No one," I admitted; "but I fear the poor man is sadly out of his depth."

"He is wading hopelessly, Watson, but even he cannot fail to learn about Camber to-morrow."

He stared at me in a curiously significant manner.

"Do you mean, Holmes," I began, "that you really think — "

"My dear Watson," he interrupted, "forgetting, if you like, all that preceded the tragedy, with what facts are we left? That Colonel Menendez, at the moment when the bullet entered his brain, must have been standing facing directly toward the Guest House. Now, you have seen the direction of the wound?"

"He was shot squarely between the eyes. A piece of wonderful marksmanship."

"Quite," Holmes nodded his head. "But the bullet came out just at the vertex of the spine."

He paused, as if waiting for some comment, and:

"You mean that the shot came from above?" I said, slowly.

"Obviously it came from above, Watson. Keep these two points in your mind, and then consider the fact that someone lighted a lamp in the Guest House only a few moments after the shot had been fired."

"I remember. I saw it."

"So did I," said Holmes, grimly, "and I saw something else."

"What was that?"

"When you went off to summon assistance, I ran across the lawn, scrambled through the bushes, and succeeded in climbing down into the little gully in which the stream runs, and up on the other side. I had proceeded practically in a straight line from the sun-dial, and do you know where I found myself?"

"I can guess," I replied.

"Of course you can. You have visited the place. I came out immediately beside a little hut, Watson, which stands at the end of the garden of the Guest House. Ahead of me, visible through a tangle of bushes in the neglected garden, a lamp was burning. I crept cautiously forward, and presently obtained a view of the interior of a kitchen. Just as I arrived at this point of vantage, the lamp was extinguished, but not before I had had a glimpse of the only occupant of the room — the man who had extinguished the lamp."

"Who was it?" I asked, in a low voice.

"It was a Chinaman."

"Ah Tsong!" I cried.

"Doubtless."

"Good Heavens, Holmes, do you think — "

"I don't know what to think, Watson. A possible explanation is that the household had been aroused by the sound of the shot, and that Ah Tsong had been directed to go out and see if he could learn what had happened. At any rate, I waited no longer, but returned by the same route I had come. If our portly friend from Market Hilton had possessed the eyes of an Auguste Dupin, he could not have failed to note that my dress boots were caked with light yellow clay; which also, by the way, besmears my trousers."

He stooped and examined the garments as he spoke.

"A number of thorns are also present," he continued. "In short, from the point of view of an investigation, I am a most provoking object."

He sighed wearily and stared out of the window in the direction of the Tudor garden. There was a slight chilliness in the air, which, or perhaps a sudden memory of that which lay in the billiard room beneath us, may have accounted for the fact that I shivered violently.

Holmes glanced up with a rather sad smile.

"The morning after Waterloo," he said. "Sleep well, Watson."

20.

A SPANISH CIGARETTE

Sleep was not for me, despite Holmes's injunction; and although I was early afoot, the big house was already astir with significant movements which set the imagination on fire, to conjure up again the moonlight scene in the garden, making mock of the song of the birds and of the glory of the morning.

Manoel replied to my ring and prepared my bath, but it was easy to see that he had not slept.

No sound came from Holmes's room, therefore I did not disturb him, but proceeded downstairs in the hope of finding Miss Beverley about. Pedro was in the front hall, talking to Mrs. Fisher, and:

"Is Inspector Aylesbury here?" I asked.

"No, sir, but he will be returning at about half-past eight, so he said."

"How is Madame de Stämer, Mrs. Fisher?" I enquired.

"Oh, poor, poor Madame," said the old lady, "she is asleep, thank God. But I am dreading her awakening."

"The blow is a dreadful one," I admitted; "and Miss Beverley?"

"She didn't go to her room until after four o'clock, sir, but Nita tells me that she will be down any moment now."

"Ah," said I, and lighting a cigarette, I walked out of the open doors into the courtyard.

I dreaded all the ghastly official formalities which the day would bring, since I realized that the brunt of the trouble must fall upon the shoulders of Miss Beverley in the absence of Madame de Stämer.

I wandered about restlessly, awaiting the girl's appearance. A little two seater was drawn up in the courtyard, but I had not paid much attention to it, until, wandering through the opening in the box hedge and on along the gravel path, I saw unfamiliar figures moving in the billiard room. I turned hastily and retraced my steps. Officialdom was at work already, and I knew that there would be no rest for any of us from that hour onward.

As I reëntered the hall, I saw Val Beverley coming down the staircase. She looked pale, but seemed to be in better spirits than I could have hoped for, although there were dark shadows under her eyes.

"Good morning, Miss Beverley," I said.

"Good morning, Dr. Watson. It was good of you to come down so early."

"I had hoped for a chat with you before Inspector Aylesbury returned," I explained.

She looked at me pathetically.

"I suppose he will want me to give evidence?"

"He will. We had great difficulty in persuading him not to demand your presence last night."

"It was impossible," she protested. "It would have been cruel to make me leave Madame in the circumstances."

"We realized this, Miss Beverley, but you will have to face the ordeal this morning."

We walked through into the library, where a maid white-faced and frightened-looking, was dusting in a desultory fashion. She went out as we entered, and Val Beverley stood looking from the open window out into the rose garden bathed in the morning sunlight.

"Oh, Heavens," she said, clenching her hands desperately, "even now I cannot realize that the horrible thing is true." She turned to me. "Who can possibly have committed this cold-blooded crime?" she said in a low voice. "What does Mr. Holmes think? Has he any idea, any idea whatever?"

"Not that he has confided to me," I said, watching her intently. "But tell me, does Madame de Stämer know yet?"

"What do you mean?"

"I mean has she been told the truth?"

The girl shook her head.

"No," she replied; "I am positive that no one has told her. I was with her all the time, up to the very moment that she fell asleep. Yet — "

She hesitated.

"Yes?"

"She knows! Oh, Dr. Watson! To me, that is the most horrible thing of all: that she knows, that she must have known all along — that the mere sound of the shot told her everything!"

"You realize, now," I said, quietly, "that she had anticipated the end?"

"Yes, yes. This was the meaning of the sorrow which I had seen so often in her eyes, the meaning of so much that puzzled me in her words, the explanation of lots of little things which have made me wonder in the past."

I was silent for a while, then:

"If she was so certain that no one could save him," I said, "she must have had information which neither he nor she ever imparted to us."

"I am sure she had," declared Val Beverley.

"But can you think of any reason why she should not have confided in Sherlock Holmes?"

"I cannot, I cannot — unless — "

"Yes?"

"Unless, Dr. Watson," she looked at me strangely, "they were both under some vow of silence. Oh! It sounds ridiculous, wildly ridiculous, but what other explanation can there be?"

"What other, indeed? And now, Miss Beverley, I know one of the questions Inspector Aylesbury will ask you."

"What is it?"

"He has learned, from one of the servants I presume, as he did not see you, that you had not retired last night at the time of the tragedy."

"I had not," said Val Beverley, quietly. "Is that so singular?"

"To me it is no more than natural."

"I have never been so frightened in all my life as I was last night. Sleep was utterly out of the question. There was mystery in the very air. I knew, oh, Dr. Watson, in some way I knew that a tragedy was going to happen."

"I believe I knew, too," I said. "Good God, to think that we might have saved him!"

"Do you think — "began Val Beverley, and then paused.

"Yes?" I prompted.

"Oh, I was going to say a strange thing that suddenly occurred to me, but it is utterly foolish, I suppose. Inspector Aylesbury is coming back at nine o'clock, is he not?"

"At half-past eight, so I understand."

"I am afraid I have very little to tell him. I was sitting in my room in an appalling state of nerves when the shot was fired. I was not even reading; I was just waiting, waiting, for something to happen."

"I understand. My own experience was nearly identical."

"Then," continued the girl, "as I unlocked my door and peeped out, feeling too frightened to venture farther in the darkness, I heard Madame's voice in the hall below."

"Crying for help?"

"No," replied the girl, a puzzled frown appearing between her brows. "She cried out something in French. The intonation told me that it was French, although I could not detect a single word. Then I thought I heard a moan."

"And you ran down?"

"Yes. I summoned up enough courage to turn on the light in the corridor and to run down to the hall. And there she was, lying just outside the door of her room."

"Was her room in darkness?"

"Yes. I turned on the light and succeeded in partly raising her, but she was too heavy for me to lift. I was still trying to revive her when Pedro opened the door of the servants' quarters. Oh," she closed her eyes wearily, "I shall never forget it."

I took her hand and pressed it reassuringly.

"Your courage has been wonderful throughout," I declared, "and I hope it will remain so to the end."

She smiled and flushed slightly, as I released her hand again.

"I must go and take a peep at Madame now," she said, "but of course I shall not disturb her if she is still sleeping."

We turned and walked slowly back to the hall, and there just entering from the courtyard was Inspector Aylesbury.

"Ah!" he exclaimed, "Good morning, Dr. Watson. This is Miss Beverley, I presume?"

"Yes, Inspector," replied the girl. "I understand that you wish to speak to me?"

"I do, Miss, but I shall not detain you for many minutes."

"Very well," she said, and as she turned and retraced her steps, he followed her back into the library.

I walked out to the courtyard and, avoiding the Tudor garden and the billiard room, turned in the other direction, passing the stables where Jim, the black groom, saluted me very sadly, and proceeded round to the south side of the house.

Inspector Aylesbury, I perceived, had wasted no time. I counted no fewer than four men, two of them in uniform, searching the lawns and the slopes beyond, although what they were looking for I could not imagine.

Giving the library a wide berth, I walked along the second terrace, and presently came in sight of the east wing and the tower. There, apparently engaged in studying the rhododendrons, I saw Sherlock Holmes.

He signalled to me, and, crossing the lawn, I joined him where he stood.

Without any word of greeting:

"You see, Watson," he said, speaking in the eager manner which betokened a rapidly working brain, "this is the path which the Colonel must have followed last night. Yonder is the door by which, according to his own account, he came out on a previous occasion, walking in his sleep. Do you remember?"

"I remember," I replied.

"Well, Pedro found it unlocked this morning. You see, it faces practically due south; and the Colonel's bedroom is immediately above us where we stand." He stared at me queerly. "I must have passed this door last night only a few moments before the Colonel came out, for I was just crossing the courtyard and could see you at my window at the moment when you saw poor Menendez enter the Tudor garden. He must have actually been walking around the east wing at the same time that I was walking around the west. Now, I am going to show you something, Watson, something which I have just discovered."

From his waistcoat pocket he took out a half-smoked cigarette. I stared at it uncomprehendingly.

"Of course," he continued, "the weather has been bone dry for more than a week now, and it may have lain there for a long time; but to me, Watson, to me it looks suspiciously fresh."

"What is the point?" I asked, perplexedly.

"The point is that it is a hand-made cigarette, one of the Colonel's. Don't you recognize it?"

"Good Heavens!" I said; "yes, of course it is."

He returned it to his pocket without another word.

"It may mean nothing," he murmured, "or it may mean everything. And now, Watson, we are going to escape."

"To escape?" I cried.

"Precisely. We are going to anticipate the probable movements of our blundering Aylesbury. In short, I wish you to present me to Mr. Colin Camber."

"What?" I exclaimed, staring at him incredulously.

"I am going to ask you," he began, and then, breaking off: "Quick, Watson, run!" he said.

And thereupon, to my amazement, he set off through the rhododendron bushes in the direction of the tower!

Utterly unable to grasp the meaning of his behaviour, I followed, nevertheless, and as we rounded the corner of the tower Holmes pulled up short, and:

"I am not mad," he explained rather breathlessly, "but I wanted to avoid being seen by that constable who is prowling about at the bottom of the lawn making signals in the direction of the library. Presumably he is replying to Inspector Aylesbury, who wants to talk to us. I am determined to interview Camber before submitting to further official interrogation. It must be a cross-country journey, Watson. I am afraid we shall be a very muddy pair, but great issues may hang upon the success of our expedition."

He set off briskly toward a belt of shrubbery that marked the edge of the little stream. Appreciating something of his intentions, I followed his lead unquestioningly; and, scrambling through the bushes:

"This was the point at which I descended last night," he said. "You will have to wade, Watson, but the water is hardly above one's ankles."

He dropped into the brook, waded across, and began to climb up the opposite bank. I imitated his movements, and presently, having scrambled up on the farther side, we found ourselves standing on a narrow bank immediately under that summer house which Colin Camber had told me he had formerly used as a study.

"We can scarcely present ourselves at the kitchen door," murmured Holmes; "therefore we must try to find a way round to the front. There is barbed wire here. Be careful."

I had now entered with zest into the business, and so the pair of us waded through rank grass which in places was waist high, and on through a perfect wilderness of weeds in which nettles dominated. Presently we came to a dry ditch, which we negotiated successfully, to find ourselves upon the high road some hundred yards to the west of the Guest House.

"I predict an unfriendly reception," I said, panting from my exertions, and surveying my friend, who was a mockery of his ordinarily spruce self.

"We must face it," he replied, grimly. "He has everything to gain by being civil to us."

We proceeded along the dusty high road, almost overarched by trees.

"Holmes," I said, "this is going to be a highly unpleasant ordeal for me."

Holmes stopped short, staring at me sternly.

"I know, Watson," he replied; "but I suppose you realize that a man's life is at stake."

"You mean — ?"

"I mean that when we are both compelled to tell all we know, I doubt if there is a counsel in the land who would undertake the defense of Mr. Colin Camber."

"Good God! Then you think he is guilty?"

"Did I say so?" asked Holmes, continuing on his way. "I don't recollect saying so, Watson; but I do say that it will be a giant's task to prove him innocent."

"Then you believe him to be innocent?" I cried, eagerly.

"My dear fellow," he replied, somewhat irritably, "I have not yet met Mr. Colin Camber. I will answer your question at the conclusion of the interview."

21.

THE WING OF A BAT

For a long time, our knocking and ringing elicited no response. The brilliant state of the door-brass afforded evidence of the fact that Ah Tsong had arisen, even if the other members of the household were still sleeping; and Holmes, growing irritable, executed a loud tattoo upon the knocker. This had its desired effect. The door opened and Ah Tsong looked out.

"Tell your master that Mr. Sherlock Holmes has called to see him upon urgent business."

"Master no got," replied Ah Tsong, and proceeded to close the door.

Sherlock Holmes thrust his hand against it and addressed the man rapidly in Chinese. I could not have supposed the face of Ah Tsong capable of expressing so much animation. At the sound of his native tongue his eyes lighted up, and:

"*Tchée, tchée,*" he said, turned, and disappeared.

Although the man had studiously avoided looking at me, that Ah Tsong would inform his master of the identity of his second visitor I did not doubt. If I had doubted, I should promptly have been disillusioned, for:

"Tell them to go away!" came a muffled cry from somewhere within. "No spy of Devil Menendez shall ever pass my doors again!"

The Chinaman, on retiring, had left the door wide open, and I could see right to the end of the gloomy hall. Ah Tsong presently re-appeared, shuffling along in our direction. Unemotionally:

"Master no got," he repeated.

Sherlock Holmes stamped his foot irritably.

"Good God, Watson," he said, "this unreasonable fool almost exhausts my patience."

Again he addressed Ah Tsong in Chinese, and although the man's wrinkled ivory face exhibited no trace of emotion, a deep understanding was to be read in those oblique eyes; and a second time Ah Tsong turned and trotted back to the study. I could hear a muttered colloquy in progress, and suddenly the gaunt figure of Colin Camber burst into view.

He was shaved this morning, but arrayed as I had last seen him. Whilst he was not in that state of incoherent anger which I remembered and still resented, he was nevertheless in an evil temper.

He strode along the hallway, his large eyes widely opened, and fixing a cold stare upon the face of Holmes.

"I learn that your name is Mr. Sherlock Holmes," he said, entirely ignoring my presence, "and you send me a very strange message. I am used to the ways of Señor Menendez, therefore your message does not deceive me. The gateway, sir, is directly behind you."

Holmes clenched his teeth, then:

"The scaffold, Mr. Camber," he replied, "is directly in front of you."

"What do you mean, sir?" demanded the other, and despite my resentment of the treatment which I had received at his hands, I could only admire the lofty disdain of his manner.

"I mean, Mr. Camber, that the police are close upon my heels."

"The police? Of what interest can this be to me?"

Holmes's keen eyes were searching the pale face of the man before him.

"Mr. Camber," he said, "the shot was a good one."

Not a muscle of Colin Camber's face moved, but slowly he looked Sherlock Holmes up and down, then:

"I have been called a hasty man," he replied, coldly, "but I can scarcely be accused of leaping to a conclusion when I say that I believe you to be quite mad. You have interrupted me, sir. Good morning."

He stepped back, and would have closed the door, but:

"Mr. Camber," said Sherlock Holmes, and the tone of his voice was arresting.

Colin Camber paused.

"My name is evidently unfamiliar to you," Holmes continued. "You regard myself and Dr. Watson as friends of the late Colonel Menendez — "

At that Colin Camber started forward.

"The *late* Colonel Menendez?" he echoed, speaking almost in a whisper.

But as if he had not heard him Holmes continued:

"As a matter of fact, I am a criminal investigator, and Dr. Watson is assisting me in my present case."

Colin Camber clenched his hands and seemed to be fighting with some emotion which possessed him, then:

"Do you mean," he said, hoarsely — "do you mean that Menendez is — dead?"

"I do," replied Holmes. "May I request the privilege of ten minutes' private conversation with you?"

Colin Camber stood aside, holding the door open, and inclining his head in that grave salutation which I knew; but on this occasion, I think, principally with intent to hide his emotion.

Not another word did he speak until the three of us stood in the strange study where East grimaced at West, and emblems of remote devil-worship jostled the cross of the Holy Rose. The place was laden with tobacco smoke, and scattered on the carpet about the feet of the writing table lay twenty or more pages of closely written manuscript. Although this was a brilliant summer's morning, an old-fashioned reading lamp, called, I believe, a Victoria, having a nickel receptacle for oil at one side of the standard and a burner with a green glass shade upon the other, still shed its light upon the desk.

It was only reasonable to suppose that Colin Camber had been at work all night.

He placed chairs for us, clearing them of the open volumes which they bore, and, seating himself at the desk:

"Dr. Watson," he began, slowly, paused, and then stood up, "I accused you of something when you last visited my house, something of which I would not lightly accuse any man. If I was wrong, I wish to apologize."

"Only a matter of the utmost urgency could have induced me to cross your threshold again," I replied, coldly. "Your behaviour, sir, was inexcusable."

He rested his long white hands upon the desk, looking across at me.

"Whatever I did and whatever I said," Colin Camber continued, "one insult I laid upon you more deadly than the rest: I accused you of friendship with Juan Menendez. Was I unjust?"

He paused for a moment.

"I had been retained professionally by Colonel Menendez," replied Holmes without hesitation, "and Dr. Watson kindly consented to accompany me."

Colin Camber looked very hard at the speaker, and then equally hard at me.

"Was it at behest of Colonel Menendez that you called upon me, Dr. Watson?"

"It was not," said Holmes, tersely; "it was at mine. And he is here now at my request. Come, sir, we are wasting time. At any moment — "

Colin Camber held up his hand, interrupting him.

"By your leave, Mr. Holmes," he said, and there was something compelling in voice and gesture, "I must first perform my duty as a gentleman."

He stepped forward in my direction.

"Dr. Watson, I have grossly insulted you. Yet if you knew what had inspired my behaviour, I believe you could find it in your heart to forgive me. I do not ask you to do so, however; I accept the humiliation of knowing that I have mortally offended a guest."

He bowed to me formally, and would have returned to his seat, but:

"Pray say no more," I said, standing up and extending my hand. Indeed, so impressive was the man's strange personality that I felt rather as one receiving a royal pardon than as an offended party being offered an apology. "It was a misunderstanding. Let us forget it."

His eyes gleamed, and he seized my hand in a warm grip.

"You are generous, Dr. Watson, you are generous. And now, sir," he inclined his head in Sherlock Holmes's direction, and resumed his seat.

Holmes had suffered this odd little interlude in silence but now:

"Mr. Camber," he said, rapidly, "I sent you a message by your Chinese servant to the effect that the police would be here within ten minutes to arrest you."

"You did, sir," replied Colin Camber, drawing toward him a piece of newspaper upon which rested a dwindling mound of shag. "This is most disturbing, of course. But since I have not rendered myself amenable to the law, it leaves me moderately unmoved. Upon your second point, Mr. Holmes, I shall beg you, to enlarge. You tell me that Don Juan Menendez is dead?"

He had begun to fill his corn-cob as he spoke the words; but from where I sat, I could just see his face, so that although his voice was well controlled, the gleam in his eyes was unmistakable.

"He was shot through the head shortly after midnight."

"What?"

Colin Camber dropped the corn-cob and stood up again, the light of a dawning comprehension in his eyes.

"Do you mean that he was murdered?"

"I do."

"Good God," whispered Camber, "at last I understand."

"That is why we are here, Mr. Camber, and that is why the police will be here at any moment."

Colin Camber stood erect, one hand resting upon the desk.

"So this was the meaning of the shot which we heard in the night," he said, slowly.

Crossing the room, he closed and locked the study door, then, returning, he sat down once more, entirely, master of himself. Frowning slightly he looked from Holmes in my direction, and then back again at Holmes.

"Gentlemen," he resumed, "I appreciate the urgency of my danger. Preposterous though I know it to be, nevertheless it is perhaps no more than natural that suspicion should fall upon me."

He was evidently thinking rapidly. His manner had grown quite cool, and I could see that he had focussed his keen brain upon the abyss which he perceived to lie in his path.

"Before I commit myself to any statements which might be used as evidence," he said, "doubtless, Mr. Holmes, you will inform me of your exact standpoint in this matter. Do you represent the late Colonel Menendez, do you represent the law, or may I regard you as a perfectly impartial enquirer?"

"You may regard me, Mr. Camber, as one to whom nothing but the truth is of the slightest interest. I was requested by the late Colonel Menendez to visit Cray's Folly."

"Professionally?"

"To endeavour to trace the origin of certain occurrences which had led him to believe his life to be in danger."

Holmes paused, staring hard at Colin Camber.

"Since I recognize myself to be standing in the position of a suspect," said the latter, "it is perhaps unfair to request you to acquaint me with the nature of these occurrences?"

"The one, sir," replied Sherlock Holmes, "which most intimately concerns yourself is this: Almost exactly a month ago, the wing of a bat was nailed to the door of Cray's Folly."

"What?" exclaimed Colin Camber, leaning forward eagerly — "the wing of a bat? What kind of bat?"

"Of a South American Vampire Bat."

The effect of those words was curious. If any doubt respecting Camber's innocence had remained with me at this time, I think his expression as he leaned forward across the desk must certainly have removed it. That the man was intellectually unusual, and intensely difficult to understand, must have been apparent to the most superficial observer; but I found it hard to believe that these moods of his were simulated. At the words "A South American Vampire Bat," the enthusiasm of the specialist leapt into his eyes. Personal danger was forgotten. Holmes had trenched upon his particular territory, and I knew that if Colin Camber had actually killed Colonel Menendez, then it had been the act of a maniac. No man newly come from so bloody a deed could have acted as Camber acted now.

"It is the death-sign of Voodoo!" he exclaimed, excitedly.

Yet again he arose and, crossing to one of the many cabinets which were in the room, he pulled open a drawer and took out a shallow tray.

My friend was watching him intently, and from the expression upon his aquiline face I could deduce the fact that in Colin Camber he had met the supreme puzzle of his career. As Camber stood there, holding up an object which he had taken from the tray, whilst Sherlock Holmes sat staring at him, I thought the scene was one transcending the grotesque. Here was the suspected man triumphantly producing evidence to hang himself.

Between his finger and thumb Camber held the wing of a bat!

22.

COLIN CAMBER'S SECRET

"I brought this bat wing from Haiti," he explained, replacing it in the tray. "It was found beneath the pillow of a black missionary who had died mysteriously during the night."

He returned the tray to the drawer, closed the latter, and, standing erect, raised clenched hands above his head.

"With no thought of blasphemy," he said, "but with reverence, I thank God from the bottom of my heart that Juan Menendez is dead."

He reseated himself, whilst Holmes regarded him silently, then:

" 'The evil that men do lives after them,' " he murmured. He rested his chin upon his hand and sighed. "A bat wing," he continued, musingly. "A bat wing was nailed to

Menendez's door." He stared across at Holmes. "Am I to believe, sir, that this was the clue which led you to the Guest House?"

Sherlock Holmes nodded.

"It was."

"I understand. I must therefore take no more excursions into my special subject, but must endeavour to regard the matter from the point of view of the enquiry. Am I to assume that Menendez was acquainted with the significance of this token?"

"He had seen it employed in the West Indies."

"Ah, the black-hearted devil! But I fear I am involving myself more deeply in suspicion. Perhaps, Mr. Holmes, the ends of justice would be better served if you were to question me, and I to confine myself to answering you."

"Very well," Holmes agreed: "when and where did you meet the late Colonel Menendez?"

"I never met him in my life."

"Do you mean that you had never spoken to him?"

"Never."

"Hmm. Tell me, Mr. Camber, where were you at twelve o'clock last night?"

"Here, writing."

"And where was Ah Tsong?"

"Ah Tsong?" Colin Camber stared uncomprehendingly. "Ah Tsong was in bed."

"Did anything disturb you?"

"Yes, the sound of a rifle shot."

"You knew it for a rifle shot?"

"It was unmistakable."

"What did you do?"

"I was in the midst of a most important passage, and I should probably have taken no steps in the matter but that Ah Tsong knocked upon the study door to inform me that my wife had been awakened by the sound of the shot. She is somewhat nervous and had rung for Ah Tsong, asking him to see if all were well with me."

"Do I understand that she imagined the sound to have come from this room?"

"When we are newly awakened from sleep, Mr. Holmes, we retain only an imperfect impression of that which awakened us."

"True," replied Sherlock Holmes. "And did Ah Tsong return to his room?"

"Not immediately. Permit me to say, Mr. Holmes, that the nature of your questions surprises me. At the moment, I fail to see their bearing upon the main issue. He returned and reported to my wife that I was writing, and she then requested him to bring her a glass of milk. Accordingly, he came down again, and going out into the kitchen, executed this order."

"Ah. He would have to light a candle for that purpose, I suppose?"

"A candle, or a lamp," replied Colin Camber, staring at Sherlock Holmes. Then, his expression altering: "Of course!" he cried. "You saw the light from Cray's Folly? I understand at last."

We were silent for a while, until:

"How long a time elapsed between the firing of the shot and Ah Tsong's knocking at the study door?" asked Holmes.

"I could not answer definitely. I was absorbed in my work. But probably only a minute or two."

"Was the sound a loud one?"

"Fairly loud. And very startling, of course, in the silence of the night."

"The shot, then, was fired from somewhere quite near the house?"

"I presume so."

"But you thought no more about the matter?"

"Frankly, I had forgotten it. You see, the neighbourhood is rich with game; it might have been a poacher."

"Quite," murmured Holmes, but his face was very stern. "I wonder if you fully realize the danger of your position, Mr. Camber?"

"Believe me," was the reply, "I can anticipate almost every question which I shall be called upon to answer."

Sherlock Holmes stared at him in a way which told me that he was comparing his features line for line with the etching of Edgar Allen Poe which hung in his study in Baker Street, and:

"I do believe you," he replied, "and I am wondering if you are in a position to clear yourself?"

"On the contrary," Camber assured him, "I am only waiting to hear that Juan Menendez was shot in the grounds of Cray's Folly, and not within the house, to propose to you that unless the real assassin be discovered, I shall quite possibly pay the penalty of his crime."

"He was shot in the Tudor garden," replied Holmes, "within sight of your windows."

"Ah!" Colin Camber resumed the task of stuffing shag into his corn-cob. "Then if it would interest you, Mr. Holmes, I will briefly outline the case against myself. I had never troubled to disguise the fact that I hated Menendez. Many witnesses can be called to testify to this. He was in Cuba when I was in Cuba, and evidence is doubtless obtainable to show that we stayed at the same hotels in various cities of the United States prior to my coming to England and leasing the Guest House. Finally, he became my neighbour in Surrey."

He carefully lighted his pipe, whilst Holmes and I watched him silently, then:

"Menendez had the bat wing nailed to the door of his house," he continued. "He believed himself to be in danger, and associated this sign with the source of his danger. Excepting himself and possibly certain other members of his household, it is improbable that anyone else in Surrey understands the significance of the token save myself. The unholy rites of Voodoo are a closed book to the Western nations. I have opened that book, Mr. Holmes. The powers of the Obeah man, and especially of the arch-sorceror known and dreaded by every *Voodooiene* as 'Bat Wing,' are familiar to me. Since I was alone at the time that the shot was fired, and for some few minutes afterward, and since the Tudor garden of Cray's Folly is within easy range of the Guest House, to fail to place me under arrest would be an act of sheer stupidity."

He spoke the words with a sort of triumph. Like the fakir, he possessed the art of spiritual detachment, which is an attribute of genius. From an intellectual eminence he was surveying his own peril. Colin Camber in the flesh had ceased to exist; he was merely a pawn in a fascinating game.

Sherlock Holmes glanced at his watch.

"Mr. Camber," he said, "I have just sustained the most crushing defeat of my career. The man who had summoned me to his aid was killed almost before my eyes. One thing I must do or accept professional oblivion."

"I understand." Colin Camber nodded. "Apprehend his murderer?"

"Ultimately, yes. But, firstly, I must see that to the assassination of Colonel Menendez a judicial murder is not added."

"You mean — ?" asked Camber, eagerly.

"I mean that if you killed Menendez, you are a madman, and I have formed the opinion during our brief conversation that you are brilliantly sane."

Colin Camber rose and bowed in that old-world fashion which was his.

"I am obliged to you, Mr. Holmes," he replied. "But has Dr. Watson informed you of my bibulous habits?"

Sherlock Holmes nodded.

"They will, of course, be ascribed," continued Camber, "and there are many suitable analogies, to deliberate contemplation of a murderous deed. I would remind you that chronic alcoholism is a recognized form of insanity."

His mood changed again and, sighing wearily, he lay back in the chair. Over his pale face crept an expression which I knew, instinctively, to mean that he was thinking of his wife.

"Mr. Holmes," he said, speaking in a very low tone which scorned to accentuate the beauty of his voice, "I have suffered much in the quest of truth. Suffering is the gate beyond which we find compassion. Perhaps you have thought my foregoing remarks frivolous, in view of the fact that last night a soul was sent to its reckoning almost at my doors. I revere the truth, however, above all lesser laws and above all expediency. I do not, and I cannot, regret the end of the man Menendez. But for three reasons I should regret to pay the penalty of a crime which I did not commit. These reasons are — one," he ticked them off upon his delicate fingers — "It would be bitter to know that Devil Menendez even in death had injured me; two — My work in this world, is unfinished; and, three — My wife."

I watched and listened, almost awed by the strangeness of the man who sat before me. His three reasons were illuminating. A casual observer might have regarded Colin Camber as a monument of selfishness. But it was evident to me, and I knew it must be evident to Sherlock Holmes, that his egotism was quite selfless. To a natural human resentment and a pathetic love for his wife he had added, as an equal clause, the claim of the world upon his genius.

"I have heard you," said Sherlock Holmes, quietly, "and you have led me to the most important point of all."

"What point is that, Mr. Holmes?"

"You have referred to your recent lapse from abstem-iousness. Excuse me if I discuss personal matters. This you ascribed to domestic troubles, or so Dr. Watson has informed me. You have also referred to your undisguised hatred of the late Colonel Juan Menendez. I am going to ask you, Mr. Camber, to tell me quite frankly what was the nature of those domestic troubles, and what had caused this hatred which survives even the death of its object?"

Colin Camber stood up, angular, untidy, but a figure of great dignity.

"Mr. Holmes," he replied, "I cannot answer your questions."

Sherlock Holmes inclined his head gravely.

"May I suggest," he said, "that you will be called upon to do so under circumstances which will brook no denial."

Colin Camber watched him unflinchingly.

" 'The fate of every man is hung around his neck,' " he replied.

"Yet, in this secret history which you refuse to divulge, and which therefore must count against you, the truth may lie which exculpates you."

"It may be so. But my determination remains unaltered."

"Very well," answered Sherlock Holmes, quietly, but I could see that he was exercising a tremendous restraint upon himself. "I respect your decision, but you have given me a giant's task, and for this I cannot thank you, Mr. Camber."

I heard a car pulled up in the road outside the Guest House. Colin Camber clenched his hands and sat down again in the carved chair.

"The opportunity has passed," said Holmes. "The police are here."

23.

INSPECTOR AYLESBURY CROSS-EXAMINES

"Oh, I see," said Inspector Aylesbury, "a little private confab, eh?"

He sank his chin into its enveloping folds, treating Holmes and myself each to a stare of disapproval.

"These gentlemen very kindly called to advise me of the tragic occurrence at Cray's Folly," explained Colin Camber. "Won't you be seated, Inspector?"

"Thanks, but I can conduct my examination better standing."

He turned to Sherlock Holmes.

"Might I ask, Mr. Holmes," he said, "what concern this is of yours?"

"I am naturally interested in anything appertaining to the death of a client, Inspector Aylesbury."

"Oh, so you slip in ahead of me, having deliberately withheld information from the police, and think you are going to get all the credit. Is that it?"

"That is it, Inspector," replied Holmes, smiling. "An instance of professional jealousy."

"Professional jealousy?" cried the Inspector. "Allow me to remind you that you have no official standing in this case whatever. You are merely a member of the public, nothing more, nothing less."

"I am happy to be recognized as a member of that much-misunderstood body."

"Ah, well, we shall see. Now, Mr. Camber, your attention, please."

He raised his finger impressively.

"I am informed by Miss Beverley that the late Colonel Menendez looked upon you as a dangerous enemy."

"Were those her exact words?" I murmured.

"Dr. Watson!"

The inspector turned rapidly, confronting me. "I have already warned your friend. But if I have any interruptions from you, I will have you removed."

He continued to glare at me for some moments, and then, turning again to Colin Camber:

"I say, I have information that Colonel Menendez looked upon you as a dangerous neighbour."

"In that event," replied Colin Camber, "why did he lease an adjoining property?"

"That's an evasion, sir. Answer my first question, if you please."

"You have asked me no question, Inspector."

"Oh, I see. That's your attitude, is it? Very well, then. Were you, or were you not, an enemy of the late Colonel Menendez?"

"I was."

"What's that?"

"I say I was. I hated him, and I hate him no less in death than I hated him living."

I think that I had never seen a man so taken aback, Inspector Aylesbury, drawing out a large handkerchief blew his nose. Replacing the handkerchief, he produced a note-book.

"I am placing that statement on record, sir," he said.

He made an entry in the book, and then:

"Where did you first meet Colonel Menendez?" he asked.

"I never met him in my life."

"What's that?"

Colin Camber merely shrugged his shoulders.

"I will repeat my question," said the Inspector, pompously. "Where did you first meet Colonel Juan Menendez?"

"I have answered you, Inspector."

"Oh, I see. You decline to answer that question. Very well, I will make a note of this." He did so. "And now," said he, "what were you doing at midnight last night?"

"I was writing."

"Where?"

"Here."

"What happened?"

Very succinctly, Colin Camber repeated the statement which he had already made to Sherlock Holmes, and at its conclusion:

"Send for the man, Ah Tsong," directed Inspector Aylesbury.

Colin Camber inclined his head, clapped his bands, and silently Ah Tsong entered.

The Inspector stared at him for several moments as a visitor to the Zoo might stare at some rare animal; then:

"Your name is Ah Tsong?" he began.

"Ah Tsong," murmured the Chinaman.

"I am going to ask you to give an exact account of your movements last night."

"No sabby."

Inspector Aylesbury cleared his throat.

"I say I wish to know exactly what you did last night. Answer me."

Ah Tseng's face remained quite expressionless, and:

"No sabby," he repeated.

"Oh, I see," said the Inspector, "This witness refuses to answer at all."

"You are wrong," explained Colin Camber, quietly. "Ah Tsong is a Chinaman, and his knowledge of English is very limited. He does not understand you."

"He understood my first question. You can't draw wool over my eyes. He knows well enough. Are you going to answer me?" he demanded, angrily, of the Chinaman.

"No sabby, master," he said, glancing aside at Colin Camber. "Numbcr-one p'licee-man gotchee no pidgin."

Sherlock Holmes was leisurely filling his pipe, and:

"If you think the evidence of Ah Tsong important, Inspector," he said, "I will interpret if you wish."

"You will do what?"

"I will act as interpreter."

"Do you want me to believe that you speak Chinese?"

"Your beliefs do not concern me, Inspector. I am merely offering my services."

"Thanks," said the Inspector, dryly, "but I won't trouble you. I should like a few words with Mrs. Camber."

269

"Very good."

Colin Camber bent his head gravely and gave an order to Ah Tsong, who turned and went out.

"And what firearms have you in the house?" asked Inspector Aylesbury.

"An early Dutch *arquebus,* which you see in the corner," was the reply.

"That doesn't interest me. I mean up-to-date weapons."

"And a Colt revolver which I have in a drawer here."

As he spoke, Colin Camber opened a drawer in his desk and took out a heavy revolver of the American Army Service pattern.

"I should like to examine it, if you please."

Camber passed it to the Inspector, and the latter, having satisfied himself that none of the chambers were loaded, peered down the barrel, and smelled at the weapon suspiciously.

"If it has been recently used, it has been well cleaned," he said, and placed it on a cabinet beside him. "Anything else?"

"Nothing."

"No sporting rifles?"

"None. I never shoot."

"Oh, I see."

The door opened and Mrs. Camber came in. She was very simply dressed, and looked even more child-like than she had seemed before. I think Ah Tsong had warned her of the nature of the ordeal which she was to expect, but her wide-eyed timidity was nevertheless pathetic to witness.

She glanced at me with a ghost of a smile, and:

"Ysola," said Colin Camber, inclining his head toward me in a grave gesture of courtesy, "Dr. Watson has generously forgiven me a breach of good manners for which I shall never forgive myself. I beg you to thank him, as I have done."

"It is so good of you," she said, sweetly, and held out her hand. "But I knew you would understand that it was just a great mistake."

"Mr. Sherlock Holmes," Colin Camber continued, "my wife welcomes you; and this, Ysola, is Inspector Aylesbury, who desires a few moments' conversation upon a rather painful matter."

"I have heard, I have heard," she whispered. "Ah Tsong has told me."

The pupils of her eyes dilated, as she fixed an appealing glance upon the Inspector.

In justice to the latter, he was palpably abashed by the delicate beauty of the girl who stood before him, by her naivete, and by that childishness of appearance and manner which must have awakened the latent chivalry in almost any man's heart.

"I am sorry to have to trouble you with this disagreeable business, Mrs. Camber," he began; "but I believe you were awakened last night by the sound of a shot."

"Yes," she replied, watching him intently, "that is so."

"May I ask at what time this was heard?"

"Ah Tsong told me it was after twelve o'clock."

"Was the sound a loud one?"

"Yes. It must have been to have awakened me."

"I see. Did you think it was in the house?"

"Oh, no."

"In the garden?"

"I really could not say, but I think that it was farther away than that."

"And what did you do?"

"I rang the bell for Ah Tsong."

"Did he come immediately?"

"Almost immediately."

"He was dressed, then?"

"No, I don't think he was. He had quickly put on an overcoat. He usually answers at once when I ring for him, you see."

"I see. What did you do then?"

"Well, I was frightened, you understand, and I told him to find out if all was well with my husband. He came back and told me that Colin was writing. But the sound had alarmed me very much."

"Oh, and now perhaps *you* will tell me, Mrs. Camber, when and where your husband first met Colonel Menendez?"

Every vestige of colour fled from the girl's face.

"So far as I know — thcy never met," she replied, haltingly.

"Could you swear to that?"

"Yes."

I think that hitherto she had not fully realized the nature of the situation; but now something in the Inspector's voice, or perhaps in our glances, told her the truth. She moved to where Colin Camber was sitting, looking down at him questioningly, pitifully. He put his arm about her and drew her close.

Inspector Aylesbury cleared his throat and returned his notebook to his pocket.

"I am going to take a look around the garden now," he announced.

My respect for him increased slightly, and Holmes and I followed him out of the study. A police sergeant was sitting in the hall, and Ah Tsong was standing just outside the door.

"Show me the way to the garden," directed the Inspector.

Ah Tsong stared stupidly, whereupon Sherlock Holmes addressed him in his native language, rapidly and in a low voice, in order, as I divined, that the Inspector should not hear him.

"I feel dreadfully guilty, Watson," he confessed, in a murmured aside. "For any Englishman, fictitious characters excepted, to possess a knowledge of Chinese is almost indecent."

Presently, then, I found myself once more in that unkempt garden of which I retained such unpleasant memories.

Inspector Aylesbury stared all about and up at the back of the house, humming to himself and generally behaving as though he were alone. Before the little summer study, he stood still, and:

"Oh, I see," he muttered.

What he had seen was painfully evident. The right-hand window, beneath which there was a permanent wooden seat, commanded an unobstructed view of the Tudor garden in the grounds of Cray's Folly. Clearly I could detect the speck of high-light upon the top of the sun-dial.

The Inspector stepped into the hut. It contained a bookshelf upon which a number of books remained, a table and a chair, with some few other dilapidated appointments. I glanced at

Holmes and saw that he was staring as if hypnotized at the prospect in the valley below. I observed a constable on duty at the top of the steps which led down into the Tudor garden, but I could see nothing to account for Holmes's fixed regard, until:

"Pardon me one moment, Inspector," he muttered, brusquely.

Brushing past the indignant Aylesbury, who was examining the contents of the shelves in the hut, he knelt upon the wooden seat and stared intently through the open window.

"One-two-three-four-five-six-*seven*," he chanted. "Good! That will settle it."

"Oh, I see," said Inspector Aylesbury, standing strictly upright, his prominent eyes turned in the direction of the kneeling Holmes. "One, two, three, four, and so on will settle it, eh? If you don't mind me saying so, it was settled already."

"Yes?" replied Holmes, standing up, and I saw that his eyes were very bright and that his face was slightly flushed. "You think the case is so simple as that?"

"Simple?" exclaimed the Inspector. "It's the most cunning thing that was ever planned, but I flatter myself that I have a good straight eye which can see a fairly long way."

"Excellent," murmured Holmes. "I congratulate you. Myopia is so common in the present generation. You have decided, of course, that the murder was committed by Ah Tsong?"

Inspector Aylesbury's eyes seemed to protrude extraordinarily.

"Ah Tsong!" he exclaimed. "Ah Tsong!"

"Surely it is palpable," continued Holmes, "that of the three people residing in the Guest House, Ah Tsong is the only one who could possibly have done the deed."

"Who could possibly — who could possibly — "stuttered the Inspector, then paused because of sheer lack of words.

"Review the evidence," continued Holmes, coolly. "Mrs. Camber was awakened by the sound of a shot. She immediately rang for Ah Tsong. There was a short interval before Ah Tsong appeared — and when he did appear he was wearing an overcoat. Note this point, Inspector: wearing an overcoat. He descended to the study and found Mr. Camber writing. Now, Ah Tsong sleeps in a room adjoining the kitchen on the ground floor. We passed his quarters on our way to the garden a moment ago. Of course, you had noted this? Mr. Camber is therefore eliminated from our list of suspects."

The Inspector was growing very red, but ere he had time to speak Holmes continued:

"The first of these three persons to have heard a shot fired at the end of the garden would have been Ah Tsong and not Mrs. Camber, whose room is upstairs and in the front of the house. If it had been fired by Mr. Camber from the spot upon which we now stand, he would still have been in the garden at the moment when Mrs. Camber was ringing the bell for Ah Tsong. Mr. Camber must therefore have returned from the end of the garden to the study, and have passed

Ah Tsong's room — unheard by the occupant — between the time that the bell rang and the time that Ah Tsong went upstairs. This I submit to be impossible. There is an alternative: it is that he slipped in whilst Ah Tsong, standing on the landing above, was receiving his mistress's orders. I submit that the alternative is also impossible. We thus eliminate Mr. Camber from the case, as I have already mentioned."

"Eliminate — eliminate!" cried the Inspector, beginning to recover power of speech. "Do you think you can fuddle me with a mass of words, Mr. Holmes? Allow me to point out to you, sir, that you are in no way officially associated with this matter."

"You have already drawn my attention to the fact, Inspector, but it can do no harm to jog my memory."

Holmes spoke entirely without bitterness, and I, who knew his every mood, realized that he was thoroughly enjoying himself. Therefore I knew that at last he had found a clue.

"I may add, Inspector," said he, "that upon further reflection, I have also eliminated Ah Tsong from the case. I forgot to mention that he lacks the first and second fingers of his right hand; and I have yet to meet the marksman who can shoot a man squarely between the eyes, by moonlight, at a hundred yards, employing his third finger as trigger-finger. There are other points, but these will be sufficient to show you that this case is more complicated than you had assumed it to be."

Inspector Aylesbury did not deign to reply, or could not trust himself to do so. He turned and made his way back to the house.

24.

AN OFFICIAL MOVE

We reëntered the study to find Mrs. Camber sitting in a chair very close to her husband. Inspector Aylesbury stood in the open doorway for a moment and then, stepping back into the hall:

"Sergeant Butler," he said, addressing the man who waited there.

"Yes, sir."

"Go out to the gate and get Edson to relieve you. I shall want you to go back to headquarters in a few minutes."

"Very good, sir."

I scented what was coming, and as Inspector Aylesbury reentered the room:

"I should like to make a statement," announced Sherlock Holmes, quietly.

The Inspector frowned, and lowering his chin, regarded him with little favour.

"I have not invited any statement from you, Mr. Holmes," said he.

"Quite," returned Holmes. "I am volunteering it. It is this: I gather that you are about to take an important step officially. Having in view certain steps which I, also, am about to take, I would ask you to defer action, purely in your own interests, for at least twenty-four hours."

"I hear you," said the Inspector, sarcastically.

"Very well, Inspector. You have come newly into this case, and I assure you that its apparent simplicity is illusive. As new facts come into your possession, you will realize that what I say is perfectly true; and if you act now, you will be acting hastily. All that I have learned I am prepared to place at your disposal. But I predict that the intervention of Scotland Yard will be necessary before this enquiry is concluded. Therefore I suggest, since you have rejected my cooperation, that you obtain that of Detective Inspector Lestrade, of the Criminal Investigation Department. In short, this is no one-man job. You will do yourself harm by jumping to conclusions, and cause unnecessary trouble to perfectly innocent people."

"Is your statement concluded?" asked the Inspector.

"For the moment I have nothing to add."

"Oh, I see. Very good. Then we can now get to business. Always with your permission, Mr. Holmes."

Inspector Aylesbury took his stand before the fireplace, very erect, and invested with his most official manner. Mrs. Camber watched him in a way that was pathetic. Camber seemed to be quite composed, although his face was unusually pale.

"Now, Mr. Camber," said the Inspector, "I find your answers to all the questions which I have put to you very unsatisfactory."

"I am sorry," said Colin Camber, quietly.

"One moment, Inspector," interrupted Sherlock Holmes, "you have not warned Mr. Camber."

Thereupon the long-repressed wrath of Inspector Aylesbury burst forth.

"Then I will warn *you*, sir!" he shouted. "One more word and you leave this house."

"Yet I am going to venture on one more word," continued Holmes, unperturbed. He turned to Colin Camber. "Since my return from the Sussex Downs, I took time to study law. I happen to be a member of the Bar, Mr. Camber," he said, "although I rarely accept a brief. Have I your authority to act for you?"

"I am grateful, Mr. Holmes, and I leave this unpleasant affair in your hands with every confidence."

Camber stood up, bowing formally.

The expression upon the inflamed face of Inspector Aylesbury was really indescribable, and recognizing his mental limitations, I was almost tempted to feel sorry for him. However, he did not lack self-confidence, and:

"I suppose you have scored, Mr. Holmes," he said, a certain hoarseness perceptible in his voice, "but I know my duty and I am not afraid to perform it. Now, Mr. Camber, did you, or did you not, at about twelve o'clock last night — "

"Warn the accused," murmured Holmes.

Inspector Aylesbury uttered a choking sound, but:

"I have to warn you," he said, "that your answers may be used as evidence. I will repeat: Did you, or did you not, at about twelve o'clock last night, shoot, with intent to murder, Colonel Juan Menendez?"

Ysola Camber leapt up, clutching at her husband's arm as if to hold him back.

"I did not," he replied, quietly.

"Nevertheless," continued the Inspector, looking aggressively at Sherlock Holmes whilst he spoke, "I am going to detain you pending further enquiries."

Colin Camber inclined his head.

"Very well," he said; "you only do your duty."

The little fingers clutching his sleeve slowly relaxed, and Mrs. Camber, uttering a long sigh, sank in a swoon at his feet.

"Ysola! Ysola!" he muttered. Stooping he raised the child-like figure. "If you will kindly open the door, Dr. Watson," he said, "I will carry my wife to her room."

I sprang to the door and held it widely open.

Colin Camber, deadly pale, but holding his head very erect, walked in the direction of the hallway with his pathetic burden. Mis-reading the purpose written upon the stern white face, Inspector Aylesbury stepped forward.

"Let someone else attend to Mrs. Camber," he cried, sharply. "I wish you to remain here."

His detaining hand was already upon Camber's shoulder when Holmes's arm shot out like a barrier across the Inspector's chest, and Colin Camber proceeded on his way. Momentarily, he glanced aside, and I saw that his eyes were unnaturally bright.

"Thank you, Mr. Holmes," he said, and carried his wife from the room.

Holmes dropped his arm, and crossing, stood staring out of the window. Inspector Aylesbury ran heavily to the door.

"Sergeant!" he called, "Sergeant! Keep that man in sight. He must return here immediately."

I heard the sound of heavy footsteps following Camber's up the stairs, then Inspector Aylesbury turned, a bulky figure in the open doorway, and:

"Now, Mr. Holmes," said he, entering and reclosing the door, "you are a barrister, I understand. Very well, then, I suppose you are aware that you have resisted and obstructed an officer of the law in the execution of his duty."

Sherlock Holmes spun round upon his heel.

"Is that a charge," he inquired, "or merely a warning?"

The two glared at one another for a moment, then:

"From now onward," continued the Inspector, "I am going to have no more trouble with you, Mr. Holmes. In the first place, I'll have you looked up in the Law List; in the second place, I shall ask you to stick to your proper duties, and leave me to look after mine."

"I have endeavoured from the outset," replied Holmes, his good humour quite restored, "to assist you in every way in my power. You have declined all my offers; and finally, upon the most flimsy evidence, you have detained a perfectly innocent man."

"Oh, I see. A perfectly innocent man, eh?"

"Perfectly innocent, Inspector. There are so many points that you have overlooked. For instance, do you seriously suppose that Mr. Camber had been waiting up here night-after-night on the off-chance that Colonel Menendez would appear in the grounds of Cray's Folly?"

"No, I don't. I have got that worked out."

"Indeed? You interest me."

"Mr. Camber has an accomplice at Cray's Folly."

"What?" exclaimed Holmes, and into his keen grey eyes crept a look of real interest.

"He has an accomplice," repeated the Inspector. "A certain witness was strangely reluctant to mention Mr. Camber's name. It was only after very keen examination that I got it at last. Now, Colonel Menendez had not retired last night, neither had a certain other party. That other party, sir, knows *why* Colonel Menendez was wandering about the garden at midnight."

At first, I think, this astonishing innuendo did not fully penetrate to my mind, but when it did so, it seemed to galvanize me. Springing up from the chair in which I had been seated:

"You preposterous fool!" I exclaimed, hotly.

It was the last straw. Inspector Aylesbury strode to the door and throwing it open once more, turned to me:

"Be good enough to leave the house, Dr. Watson," he said. "I am about to have it officially searched, and I will have no strangers present."

I think I could have strangled him with pleasure; but even in my rage, I was not foolhardy enough to lay myself open to that of which the Inspector was quite capable at this moment.

Without another word, I walked out of the study, took up my hat and stick and, opening the front door, quitted the Guest House from which I had thus a second time been dismissed ignominiously.

Appreciation of this fact, which came to me as I stepped into the porch, awakened my sense of humour — a gift truly divine which has saved many a man from desperation or worse. I felt like a schoolboy who had been turned out of a class-room, and I was glad that I could laugh at myself.

A constable was standing in the porch, and he looked at me suspiciously. No doubt he perceived something very sardonic in my merriment.

I walked out of the gate, before which a car was standing and, as I paused to light a cigarette, I heard the door of the

Guest House open and close. I glanced back, and there was Sherlock Holmes coming to join me.

"Now, Watson," he said, briskly, "we have got our hands full."

"My dear Holmes, I am both angry and bewildered. Too angry and too bewildered to think clearly."

"I can quite understand it. I should become homicidal if I were forced to submit for long to the company of Inspector Aylesbury. Of course, I had anticipated the arrest of Colin Camber, and I fear there is worse to come."

"What do you mean, Holmes?"

"I mean that failing the apprehension of the real murderer, I cannot see, at the moment, upon what the case for the defense is to rest."

"But surely you demonstrated out there in the garden that he could not possibly have fired the shot?"

"Words, Watson, words. I could pick a dozen loopholes in my own argument. I had only hoped to defer the inevitable. I tell you, there is worse to come. Two things we must do at once."

"What are they?"

"We must persuade the man on duty to allow us to examine the Tudor garden, and we must see the Chief Constable, whoever he may be, and prevail upon him to requisition the assistance of Scotland Yard. With Lestrade in charge of the case, I might have a chance. Whilst this disastrous man Aylesbury holds the keys, there is none."

"You heard what he said about Miss Beverley?"

We were now walking rapidly along the high road, and Holmes nodded.

"I did," he said. "I had expected it. He was inspired with this brilliant idea last night, and his ideas are too few to be lightly scrapped. If the Chief Constable is anything like the Inspector, what we are going to do Heaven only knows."

"I take it, Holmes, that you are convinced of Colin Camber's innocence?"

Holmes did not answer for a moment, whereupon I glanced at him anxiously, then:

"Colin Camber," he replied, "is of so peculiar a type that I could not presume to say of what he is capable or is not capable. The most significant point in his favour is this: He is a man of unusual intellect. The planning of this cunning crime to such a man would have been child's play — child's play, Watson. But is it possible to believe that his genius would have failed him upon the most essential detail of all, namely, an alibi?"

"It is not."

"Of course it is not. Which, continuing to regard Camber as an assassin, reduces us to the theory that the crime was committed in a moment of passion. This I maintain to be also impossible. It was no deed of impulse."

"I agree with you."

"Now, I believe that the enquiry is going to turn upon a very delicate point. If I am wrong in this, then perhaps I am wrong in my whole conception of the case. But have you considered the mass of evidence against Colin Camber?"

"I have, Holmes," I replied, sadly, "I have."

"Think of all that we know, and which the Inspector does not know. Every single datum points in the same direction. No prosecution could ask for a more perfect case. Upon this fact I pin my hopes. Where an Aylesbury rushes in, I fear to tread. The analogy with an angel was accidental, Watson!" he added, smilingly. "In other words, it is all too obvious. Yet I have failed once, Watson, failed disastrously; and it may be that in my anxiety to justify myself, I am seeking for subtlety where no subtlety exists."

25.

AYLESBURY'S THEORY

There were strangers about Cray's Folly and a sort of furtive activity, horribly suggestive. We had not pursued the circular route by the high road which would have brought us to the lodge, but had turned aside where the swing-gate opened upon a footpath into the meadows. It was the path which I had pursued upon the day of my visit to the Lavender Arms. A second private gate here gave access to the grounds at a point directly opposite the lake; and as we crossed the valley, making for the terraced lawns, I saw unfamiliar figures upon the veranda, and knew that the cumbersome processes of the law were already in motion.

I was longing to speak to Val Beverley and to learn what had taken place during her interview with Inspector Aylesbury, but Holmes led the way toward the tower wing; and by a tortuous path through the rhododendrons, we finally came out on the northeast front and in sight of the Tudor garden.

Holmes crossed to the entrance and was about to descend the steps when the constable on duty there held out his arm.

"Excuse me, sir," he said, "but I have orders to admit no one to this part of the garden."

"Oh," said Holmes, pulling up short, "but I am acting in this case. My name is Sherlock Holmes."

"Sorry, sir," replied the constable, "but you will have to see Inspector Aylesbury."

My friend uttered an impatient exclamation. Then turning aside:

"Very well, constable," he muttered; "I suppose I must submit. Our friend, Aylesbury," he added to me, as we walked away, "would appear to be a martinet as well as a walrus. At every step, Watson, he proves himself a tragic nuisance. This means waste of priceless time."

"What had you hoped to do, Holmes?"

"Prove my theory," he returned. "But since every moment is precious, I must move in another direction."

He hurried on through the opening in the box hedge and into the courtyard. Manoel had just opened the doors to a sepulchral-looking person who proved to be the coroner's officer, and:

"Manoel!" cried Holmes. "Tell Carter to bring a car round at once."

"Yes, sir."

"I haven't time to fetch my own," he explained.

"Where are you off to?"

"I am off to see the Chief Constable, Watson. Aylesbury must be superseded at whatever cost. If the Chief Constable fails, I shall not hesitate to go higher. I will get along to the garage. I don't expect to be more than an hour. Meanwhile, do your best to act as a buffer between Aylesbury and the women. You understand me?"

"Quite," I returned, shortly. "But the task may prove no light one, Holmes."

"It won't," he assured me, smiling grimly. "How you must regret, Watson, that we didn't go fishing!"

With that he was off, eager-eyed and alert, the mood of dreamy abstraction dropped like a cloak discarded. He fully realized, as I did, that his unique reputation was at stake. I wondered, as I had wondered at the Guest House, whether in undertaking to clear Colin Camber, he had acted upon sheer conviction or, embittered by the death of his client, had taken a gambler's chance. It was unlike him to do so. But now beyond reach of that charm of manner which Colin

Camber possessed, and discounting the pathetic sweetness of his girl-wife, I realized how black was the evidence against him.

Occupied with these and even more troubled thoughts, I was making my way toward the library, undetermined how to act, when I saw Val Beverley coming along the corridor which communicated with Madame de Stämer's room.

I read a welcome in her eyes which made my heart beat the faster.

"Oh, Dr. Watson," she cried, "I am so glad you have returned. Tell me all that has happened, for I feel in some way that I am responsible for it."

I nodded gravely.

"You know, then, where Inspector Aylesbury went when he left here, after his interview with you?"

She looked at me pathetically.

"He went to the Guest House, of course."

"Yes," I said. "He was close behind us."

"And" — she hesitated — "Mr. Camber?"

"He has been detained."

"Oh!" she moaned. "I could hate myself! Yet what could I say, what could I do?"

"Just tell me all about it," I urged. "What were the Inspector's questions?"

"Well," explained the girl, "he had evidently learned from someone, presumably one of the servants, that there was enmity between Mr. Camber and Colonel Menendez. He asked me if I knew of this, and of course I had to admit that I did. But when I told him that I had no idea of its cause, he did not seem to believe me."

"No," I murmured. "Any evidence which fails to dove-tail with his preconceived theories he puts down as a lie."

"He seemed to have made up his mind for some reason," she continued, "that I was intimately acquainted with Mr. Camber. Whereas, of course, I have never spoken to him in my life, although whenever he has passed me in the road, he has always saluted me with quite delightful courtesy. Oh, Dr. Watson, it is horrible to think of this great misfortune coming to those poor people." She looked at me pleadingly. "How did his wife take it?"

"Poor little girl," I replied, "it was an awful blow."

"I feel that I want to set out this very minute," declared Val Beverley, "and go to her and try to comfort her. Because I feel in my very soul that her husband is innocent. She is such a sweet little thing. I have wanted to speak to her since the very first time I ever saw her, but on the rare occasions when we have met in the village, she has hurried past as though she were afraid of me. Mr. Holmes surely knows that her husband is not guilty?"

"I think he does," I replied, "but he may have great difficulty in proving it. And what else did Inspector Aylesbury wish to know?"

"How can I tell you?" she said in a low voice; and biting her lip agitatedly she turned her head aside.

"Perhaps I can guess."

"Can you?" she asked, looking at me quickly. "Well, then, he seemed to attach a ridiculous importance to the fact that I had not retired last night at the time of the tragedy."

"I know," said I, grimly. "Another preconceived idea of his."

"I told him the truth of the matter, which is surely quite simple; and at first I was unable to understand the nature of his suspicions. Then, after a time, his questions enlightened me. He finally suggested, quite openly, that I had not come down from my room to the corridor in which Madame de Stämer was lying, but had actually been there at the time!"

"In the corridor outside her room?"

"Yes. He seemed to think that I had just come in from the door near the end of the east wing and beside the tower, which opens into the shrubbery."

"That you had just come in?" I exclaimed. "He thinks, then, that you had been out in the grounds?"

Val Beverley's face had been very pale, but now she flushed indignantly, and glanced away from me as she replied:

"He dared to suggest that I had been to keep an assignation."

"The fool!" I cried. "The ignorant, impudent fool!"

"Oh," she declared, "I felt quite ill with indignation. I am afraid I may regard Inspector Aylesbury as an enemy from now onward; for when I had recovered from the shock, I told him very plainly what I thought about his intellect, or lack of it."

"I am glad you did," I said, warmly. "Before Inspector Aylesbury is through with this business, I fancy he will know more about his limitations than he knows at present. The fact of the matter is that he is badly out of his depth, but he is not man enough to acknowledge the fact even to himself."

She smiled at me pathetically.

"Whatever should I have done if I had been alone?" she said.

I was tempted to direct the conversation into a purely personal channel, but common sense prevailed, and:

"Is Madame de Stämer awake?" I asked.

"Yes." The girl nodded. "Dr. Rolleston is with her now."

"And does she know?"

"Yes. She sent for me directly she awoke, and asked me."

"And you told her?"

"How could I do otherwise? She was quite composed, wonderfully composed; and the way she heard the news was simply heroic. But here is Dr. Rolleston, coming now."

I glanced along the corridor, and there was the physician approaching briskly.

"Good morning, Dr. Watson," he said.

"Good morning, doctor. I hear that your patient is much improved?"

"Wonderfully so," he answered. "She has enough courage for ten men. She wishes to see you, Dr. Watson, and to hear your account of the tragedy."

"Do you think it would be wise?"

"I think it would be best."

"Do you hold any hope of her permanently recovering the use of her limbs?"

Dr. Rolleston shook his head doubtfully.

"It may have only been temporary," he replied. "These obscure nervous affections are very fickle. It is unsafe to make predictions. But mentally, at least, she is quite restored from the effects of last night's shock. You need apprehend no hysteria or anything of that nature, Dr. Watson."

"Oh, I see," exclaimed a loud voice behind us.

We all three turned, and there was Inspector Aylesbury crossing the hall in our direction.

"Good morning, Dr. Rolleston," said the Inspector, deliberately ignoring my presence. "I hear that your patient is quite well again this morning?"

"She is much improved," returned the physician, dryly.

"Then I can get her testimony, which is most important to my case?"

"She is somewhat better. If she cares to see you, I do not forbid the interview."

"Oh, that's good of you, doctor." He bowed to Miss Beverley. "Perhaps, Miss, you would ask Madame de Stämer to see me for a few minutes."

Val Beverley looked at me appealingly, then shrugged her shoulders, turned aside, and walked in the direction of Madame de Stämer's door.

"Well," said Dr. Rolleston, in his brisk way, shaking me by the hand, "I must be getting along. Good morning, Dr. Watson. Good morning, Inspector Aylesbury."

He walked rapidly out to his waiting car. The presence of Inspector Aylesbury exercised upon Dr. Rolleston a similar effect to that which a red rag has upon a bull. As he took his departure, the Inspector drew out his pocket-book and, humming gently to himself, began to consult certain entries therein, with a portentous air of reflection which would have been funny if it had not been so irritating.

Thus we stood when Val Beverley returned, and:

"Madame de Stämer will see you, Inspector Aylesbury," she said, "but wishes Dr. Watson to be present at the interview."

"Oh," said the Inspector, lowering his chin, "I see. Oh, very well."

26.

IN MADAME'S ROOM

Madame de Stämer's apartment was a large and elegant one. From the window-drapings, which were of some light, figured satiny material, to the bed-cover, the lampshades, and the carpet, it was French. Faintly perfumed and decorated with many bowls of roses, it reflected, in its ornaments, its pictures, its slender-legged furniture, the personality of the occupant. In a large, high bed, reclining amidst a number of silken pillows, lay Madame de Stämer. The theme of the room was violet-and-silver, and to this everything conformed. The toilet service was of dull silver-and-violet enamel. The mirrors and some of the pictures had dull silver frames. There was nothing tawdry or glittering. The bed itself, which I thought resembled a bed of state, was of the same dull silver, with a coverlet of delicate violet hue. But Madame's *décolleté* robe was trimmed with white fur, so that her hair, dressed high upon her head, seemed to be of silver, too.

Reclining there upon her pillows, she looked like some grande dame of that France which was swept away by the Revolution. Immediately above the dressing-table, I observed a large portrait of Colonel Menendez dressed as I had imagined he should be dressed when I had first set eyes on him — in tropical riding kit and holding a broad-brimmed hat in his hand. A strikingly handsome, arrogant figure he made, uncannily like the Velasquez in the library.

At the face of Madame de Stämer I looked long and searchingly. She had not neglected the art of the *toilette*. Blinds tempered the sunlight which flooded her room; but that failing the service of rouge, Madame had been pale this morning, I perceived immediately. In some subtle way, the night had changed her. Something was gone out of her face, and something come into it. I thought, and lived to remember the thought, that it was thus Marie Antoinette might have looked when they told her how the drums had rolled in the *Place de la Revolution on* that morning of the twenty-first of January.

"Oh, Monsieur Watson," she said, sadly, "you are here, I see. Come and sit here beside me, my friend. Valeria, dear, please remain. Is this Inspector Aylesbury who wishes to speak to me?"

The Inspector, who had entered with all the confidence in the world, seemed to lose some of it in the presence of this grand lady, who was so little impressed by the dignity of his office.

She waved one slender hand in the direction of a violet brocaded chair.

"Sit down, Monsieur l'Inspecteur," she commanded, for it was rather a command than an invitation.

Inspector Aylesbury cleared his throat and sat down.

"Ah, Monsieur Watson!" exclaimed Madame, turning to me with one of her rapid movements, "Is your friend Monsieur Holmes afraid to face me, then? Does he think that he has failed? Does he think that I condemn him?"

297

"He knows that he has failed, Madame de Stämer," I replied, "but his absence is due to the fact that at this hour he is hot upon the trail of the assassin."

"What!" she exclaimed, "What!" — and bending forward touched my arm. "Tell me again! Tell me again!"

"He is following a clue, Madame de Stämer, which he hopes will lead to the truth."

"Ah! If I could believe it would lead to the truth," she said. "If I dared to believe this."

"Why should it not?"

She shook her head, smiling with such a resigned sadness that I averted my gaze and glanced across at Val Beverley, who was seated on the opposite side of the bed.

"If you knew — if you only knew."

I looked again into the tragic face, and realized that this was an older woman than the brilliant hostess I had known. She sighed, shrugged, and:

"Tell me, Monsieur Watson," she continued, "it was swift and merciful, eh?"

"Instantaneous," I replied, in a low voice.

"A good shot?" she asked, strangely.

"A wonderful shot," I answered, thinking that she imposed unnecessary torture upon herself.

"They say he must be taken away, Monsieur Watson, but I reply: not until I have seen him."

"Madame," began Val Beverley, gently.

"Ah, my dear!" Madame de Stämer, without looking at the speaker, extended one hand in her direction, the fingers characteristically curled. "You do not know me. Perhaps it is a good job. You are a man, Dr. Watson, and men — especially men who write — know more of women than they know of themselves, is it not so? You will understand that I must see him again?"

"Madame de Stämer," I said, "your courage is almost terrifying."

She shrugged her shoulders.

"I am not proud to be brave, my friend. The animals are brave, but many cowards are proud. Listen again. He suffered no pain, you think?"

"None, Madame de Stämer."

"So Dr. Rolleston assures me. He died in his sleep? You do not think he was awake, eh?"

"Most certainly he was not awake."

"It is the best way to die," she said, simply. "Yet he, who was brave and had faced death many times, would have counted it ... " Madame de Stämer snapped her white fingers. She glanced across the room to where Inspector Aylesbury, very subdued, sat upon the brocaded chair twirling his cap between his hands. "And now, Inspector Aylesbury," she asked, "what is it you wish me to tell you?"

"Well, Madame," began the Inspector, and stood up, evidently in an endeavour to recover his dignity, but:

"Sit down, Mr. Inspector! I beg of you be seated," cried Madame. "I will not be questioned by one who stands. And if you were to walk about, I should shriek."

He resumed his seat, clearing his throat nervously.

"Very well, Madame," he continued, "I have come to you particularly for some information respecting a certain Mr. Camber."

"Oh, yes," said Madame.

Her vibrant voice was very low.

"You know him, no doubt?"

"I have never met him."

"What?" exclaimed the Inspector.

Madame shrugged and glanced at me eloquently.

"Well," he continued, "this gets more and more peculiar. I am told by Pedro the butler that Colonel Menendez looked upon Mr. Camber as an enemy, and Miss Beverley here admitted that it was true. Yet although he was an enemy, nobody ever seems to have spoken to him, and he swears that he had never spoken to Colonel Menendez."

"Yes?" said Madame, listlessly, "Is that so?"

"It is so, Madame, and now you tell me that you have never met him."

"I did tell you so, yes."

"His wife, then?"

"I never met his wife," said Madame, rapidly.

"But it is a fact that Colonel Menendez regarded Mr. Camber as an enemy?"

"It is a fact — yes."

"Ah, now we are coming to it. What was the cause of this?"

"I cannot tell you."

"Do you mean that you don't know?"

"I mean that I cannot tell you."

"Oh," said the Inspector, blankly, "I see. That's not helping me very much, is it?"

"No, it is no help," said Madame, twirling a ring upon her finger.

The Inspector cleared his throat again, then:

"There had been other attempts, I believe, at assassination?" he asked.

Madame nodded.

"Several."

"Did you witness any of these?"

"None of them."

"But you know that they took place?"

"Juan — Colonel Menendez — had told me so."

"And he suspected that there was someone lurking about this house?"

"Yes."

"Also, someone broke in?"

"There were doors unfastened, and a great disturbance, so I suppose someone must have done so."

I wondered if he would refer to the bat wing nailed to the door, but he had evidently decided that this clue was without importance, nor did he once refer to the aspect of the case which concerned Voodoo. He possessed a sort of mulish obstinacy, and was evidently determined to use no scrap of information which he had obtained from Sherlock Holmes.

"Now, Madame," said he, "you heard the shot fired last night?"

"I did."

"It woke you up?"

"I was already awake."

"Oh, I see: you were awake?"

"I was awake."

"Where did you think the sound came from?"

"From back yonder, beyond the east wing."

"Beyond the east wing?" muttered Inspector Aylesbury. "Now, let me see." He turned ponderously in his chair, gazing out of the windows. "We look out on the south here? You say the sound of the shot came from the east?"

"So it seemed to me."

"Oh." This piece of information seemed badly to puzzle him. "And what then?"

"I was so startled that I ran to the door before I remembered that I could not walk."

She glanced aside at me with a tired smile and laid her hand upon my arm in an oddly caressing way, as if to say, "He is so stupid; I should not have expressed myself in that way."

Truly enough the Inspector misunderstood, for:

"I don't follow what you mean, Madame," he declared. "You say you forgot that you could not walk?"

"No, no, I expressed myself wrongly," Madame replied in a weary voice. "The fright, the terror, gave me strength to stagger to the door, and there I fell and swooned."

"Oh, I see. You speak of fright and terror. Were these caused by the sound of the shot?"

"For some reason, my cousin believed himself to be in peril," explained Madame. "He went in dread of assassination, you understand? Very well, he caused me to feel this dread also. When I heard the shot, something told me, something told me that — "she paused, and suddenly placing her hands before her face, added in a whisper — "that it had come."

Val Beverley was watching Madame de Stämer anxiously, and the fact that she was unfit to undergo further examination was so obvious that anyone other than an Inspector Aylesbury would have withdrawn. The latter, however, seemed now to be glued to his chair, and:

"Oh, I see," he said; "and now there's another point: Have you any idea what took Colonel Menendez out into the grounds last night?"

Madame de Stämer lowered her hands and gazed across at the speaker.

"What is that, Monsieur l'Inspecteur?"

"Well, you don't think he might have gone out to talk to someone?"

"To someone? To what one?" demanded Madame, scornfully.

"Well, it isn't natural for a man to go walking about the garden at midnight when he's unwell, is it? Not alone. But if there was a lady in the case he might go."

"A lady?" said Madame, softly. "Yes — continue."

"Well," resumed the Inspector, deceived by the soft voice, "the young lady sitting beside you was still wearing her evening dress when I arrived here last night. I found that out, although she didn't give me a chance to see her."

His words had an effect more dramatic than he could have foreseen.

Madame de Stämer threw her arm around Val Beverley and hugged her so closely to her side that the girl's curly brown head was pressed against Madame's shoulder. Thus holding her, she sat rigidly upright, her strange, still eyes glaring across the room at Inspector Aylesbury. Her whole pose was instinct with challenge, with defiance; and in that moment, I identified the illusive memory which the eyes of Madame so often had conjured up in my mind.

Once, years before, I had seen a wounded tigress standing over her cubs: a beautiful, fearless creature, blazing defiance with dying eyes upon those who had destroyed her, the mother-instinct supreme to the last; for as she fell to rise no more, she had thrown her paw around the cowering cubs. It was not in shape, nor in colour, but in expression and in their stillness, that the eyes of Madame de Stämer resembled the eyes of the tigress.

"Oh, Madame, Madame," moaned the girl, "how dare he!"

"Ah!" Madame de Stämer raised her head yet higher, a royal gesture, that unmoving stare set upon the face of the discomfited Inspector Aylesbury. "Leave my apartment." Her left hand shot out dramatically in the direction of the door, but even yet the fingers remained curled. "Stupid, gross fool!"

Inspector Aylesbury stood up, his face very flushed.

"I am only doing my duty, Madame," he said.

"Go, go!" commanded Madame, "I insist that you go!"

Convulsively she held Val Beverley to her side, and although I could not see the girl's face, I knew that she was weeping.

Those implacable flaming eyes followed with their stare the figure of the Inspector right to the doorway; for he essayed no further speech, but retired.

I, also, rose, and:

"Madame de Stämer," I said, speaking, I fear, very unnaturally, "I love your spirit."

She threw back her head, smiling up at me. I shall never forget that look, nor shall I attempt to portray all which it conveyed — for I know I should fail.

"My friend!" she said, and extended her hand to be kissed.

27.

AN INSPIRATION

Inspector Aylesbury had disappeared when I came out of the hall, but Pedro was standing there to remind me of the fact that I had not breakfasted. I realized that despite all tragic happenings, I was ravenously hungry, and accordingly I agreed to his proposal that I should take breakfast on the south veranda, as on the previous morning.

To the south veranda I made my way, rather despising myself because I was capable of hunger at such a time and amidst such horrors. The daily papers were on my table, for Carter drove into Market Hilton every morning to meet the London train which brought them down — but I did not open any of them.

Pedro waited upon me in person. I could see that the man was pathetically anxious to talk. Accordingly, when he presently brought me a fresh supply of hot rolls:

"This has been a dreadful blow to you, Pedro?" I said.

"Dreadful, sir," he returned. "Fearful. I lose a splendid master, I lose my place, and I am far, far from home."

"You are from Cuba?"

"Yes, yes. I was with Señor the Colonel Don Juan in Cuba."

"And do you know anything of the previous attempts which had been made upon his life, Pedro?"

"Nothing, sir. Nothing at all."

"But the bat wing, Pedro?"

He looked at me in a startled way.

"Yes, sir," he replied. "I found it pinned to the door here."

"And what did you think it meant?"

"I thought it was a joke, sir — not a nice joke — by someone who knew Cuba."

"You know the meaning of Bat Wing, then?"

"It is Obeah. I have never seen it before, but I have heard of it."

"And what did you think?" said I, proceeding with my breakfast.

"I thought it was meant to frighten."

"But who did you think had done it?"

"I had heard Señor Don Juan say that Mr. Camber hated him, so I thought perhaps he had sent someone to do it."

"But why should Mr. Camber have hated the Colonel?"

"I cannot say, sir. I wish I could tell."

"Was your master popular in the West Indies?" I asked.

"Well, sir — " Pedro hesitated — "perhaps not so well liked."

"No," I said. "I had gathered as much."

The man withdrew, and I continued my solitary meal, listening to the song of the skylarks and thinking how complex was human existence, compared with any other form of life beneath the Sun.

How to employ my time until Sherlock Holmes should return I knew not. Common delicacy dictated an avoidance of Val Beverley until she should have recovered from the effect of Inspector Aylesbury's gross insinuations, and I was curiously disinclined to become involved in the gloomy formalities which ensue upon a crime of violence. Nevertheless, I felt compelled to remain within call, realizing that there might be unpleasant duties which Pedro could not perform, and which must therefore devolve upon Val Beverley.

I lighted my pipe and walked out on to the sloping lawn. A gardener was at work with a big syringe, destroying a patch of weeds which had appeared in one corner of the velvet turf. He looked up in a sort of startled way as I passed, bidding me good morning, and then resuming his task. I thought that this man's activities were symbolic of the way of the world, in whose eternal progression one poor human life counts as nothing.

Presently, I came in sight of that door which opened into the rhododendron shrubbery, the door by which Colonel Menendez had come out to meet his death. His bedroom was directly above, and as I picked my way through the closely growing bushes, which at an earlier time I had thought to be impassable, I paused in the very shadow of the tower and glanced back and upward. I could see the windows of the little smoke-room in which we had held our last interview with Menendez; and I thought of the shadow which Holmes had seen upon the blind. I was unable to disguise from myself the fact that when Inspector Aylesbury should learn of this occurrence, as presently he must do, it would give new vigour to his ridiculous and unpleasant suspicions.

I passed on, and considering the matter impartially, found myself faced by the questions — Whose was the shadow which Holmes had seen upon the blind? And with what purpose did Colonel Menendez leave the house at midnight?

Somnambulism might solve the second riddle, but to the first I could find no answer acceptable to my reason. And now, pursuing my aimless way, I presently came in sight of a gable of the Guest House. I could obtain a glimpse of the hut which had once been Colin Camber's workroom. The window, through which Sherlock Holmes had stared so intently, possessed sliding panes. These were closed, and a ray of sunlight striking upon the glass produced, because of an over-leaning branch which crossed the top of the window, an effect like that of a giant eye glittering evilly through the trees. I could see a constable moving about in the garden. Ever and anon the Sun shone upon the buttons of his tunic.

By such steps, my thoughts led me on to the pathetic figure of Ysola Camber. Save for the faithful Ah Tsong, she was alone in that house to which tragedy had come unbidden, unforeseen. I doubted if she had a woman friend in all the countryside. Doubtless, I reflected, the old housekeeper, to whom she had referred, would return as speedily as possible, but pending the arrival of someone to whom she could confide all her sorrows, I found it almost impossible to contemplate the loneliness of the tragic little figure.

Such was my mental state, and my thoughts were all of compassion, when suddenly, like a lurid light, an inspiration came to me.

I had passed out from the shadow of the tower and was walking in the direction of the sentinel yews when this idea, dreadfully complete, leapt to my mind. I pulled up short, as though hindered by a palpable barrier. Vague musings, evanescent theories, vanished like smoke, and a ghastly, consistent theory of the crime unrolled itself before me, with all the cold logic of truth.

"My God!" I groaned aloud, "I see it all. *I see it all!*"

28.

MY THEORY OF THE CRIME

The afternoon was well advanced before Sherlock Holmes returned.

So deep was my conviction that I had hit upon the truth, and so well did my theory stand every test which I could apply to it, that I felt disinclined for conversation with anyone concerned in the tragedy until I should have submitted the matter to the keen analysis of Holmes. Upon the sorrow of Madame de Stämer I naturally did not intrude, nor did I seek to learn if she had carried out her project of looking upon the dead man.

About mid-day, the body was removed, after which an oppressive and awesome stillness seemed to descend upon Cray's Folly.

Inspector Aylesbury had not returned from his investigations at the Guest House and, learning that Miss Beverley was remaining with Madame de Stämer, I declined to face the ordeal of a solitary luncheon in the dining room, and merely ate a few sandwiches, walking over to the Lavender Arms for a glass of Mrs. Wootton's excellent ale.

Here I found the bar-parlour full of local customers, and although a heated discussion was in progress as I opened the door, silence fell upon my appearance. Mrs. Wootton greeted me sadly.

"Ah, sir," she said, as she placed a foaming mug before me; "of course you've heard?"

"I have, madam," I replied, perceiving that she did not know me to be a guest at Cray's Folly.

"Well, well!" She shook her head. "It had to come, with all these foreign folk about."

She retired to some sanctum at the rear of the bar, and I drank my beer amid one of those silences which sometimes descend upon such a gathering when a stranger appears in its midst. Not until I moved to depart was this silence broken, then:

"Ah, well," said an old fellow, evidently a farm-hand, "we know now why he was priming of hisself with the drink, we do."

"Aye!" came a growling chorus.

I came out of the Lavender Arms full of a knowledge that so far as Mid-Hatton was concerned, Colin Camber was already found guilty.

I had hoped to see something of Val Beverley on my return, but she remained closeted with Madame de Stämer, and I was left in loneliness to pursue my own reflections; and to perfect that theory which had presented itself to my mind.

In Holmes's absence, I had taken it upon myself to give an order to Pedro to the effect that no reporters were to be admitted; and in this I had done well. So quickly does evil news fly that, between mid-day and the hour of Holmes's return, no fewer than five reporters, I believe, presented themselves at Cray's Folly. Some of the more persistent continued to haunt the neighbourhood, and I had withdrawn to the deserted library in order to avoid observation, when I heard a car draw up in the courtyard, and a moment later heard Holmes asking for me.

I hurried out to meet him, and as I appeared at the door of the library:

"Hullo, Watson," Holmes called, running up the steps. "Any developments?"

"No actual development?" I replied, "except that several members of the Press have been here."

"You told them nothing?" he asked, eagerly.

"No; they were not admitted."

"Good, good," he muttered.

"I had expected you long before this, Holmes."

"Naturally," he said, with a sort of irritation. "I have been all the way to Whitehall and back."

"To Whitehall! What, you have been to London?"

"I had half anticipated it, Watson. The Chief Constable, although quite a decent fellow, is a stickler for routine.

On the strength of those facts which I thought fit to place before him, he could see no reason for superseding Aylesbury. Accordingly, without further waste of time, I headed straight for Whitehall. You may remember a somewhat elaborate report which I completed upon the eve of our departure from Baker Street?"

I nodded.

"A very thankless job for the Home Office, Watson. But I received my reward to-day. Inspector Lestrade has been placed in charge of the case, and I hope he will be down here within the hour. Pending his arrival, I am tied hand and foot."

We had walked into the library, and, stopping, suddenly, Holmes stared me very hard in the face.

"You are bottling something up, Watson," he declared. "Out with it. Has Aylesbury distinguished himself again?"

"No," I replied; "on the contrary. He interviewed Madame de Stämer, and came out with a flea in his ear."

"Good," said Holmes, smiling. "A clever woman, and a woman of spirit, Watson."

"You are right," I replied, "and you are also right in supposing that I have a communication to make to you."

"Ah, I thought so. What is it?"

"It is a theory, Holmes, which appears to me to cover the facts of the case."

"Indeed?" said he, continuing to stare at me. "And what inspired it?"

"I was staring up at the window of the smoke-room to-day, and I remembered the shadow which you had seen upon the blind."

"Yes?" he cried, eagerly; "and does your theory explain that, too?"

"It does, Holmes."

"Then I am all anxiety to hear it."

"Very well, then, I will endeavour to be brief. Do you recollect Miss Beverley's story of the unfamiliar footsteps which passed her door on several occasions?"

"Perfectly."

"You recollect that you, yourself, heard someone crossing the hall, and that both of us heard a door close?"

"We did."

"And finally you saw the shadow of a woman upon the blind of the Colonel's private study. Very well. Excluding the preposterous theory of Inspector Aylesbury, there is no woman in Cray's Folly whose footsteps could possibly have been heard in that corridor, and whose shadow could possibly have been seen upon the blind of Colonel Menendez's room."

"I agree," said Holmes, quietly. "I have definitely eliminated all the servants from the case. Therefore, proceed, Watson, I am all attention."

"I will do so. There is a door on the south side of the house, close to the tower and opening into the rhododendron shrubbery. This was the door used by Colonel Menendez in his somnambulistic rambles, according to his own account. Now, assuming his statement to have been untrue in one particular, that is, assuming he was not walking in his sleep, but was fully awake — "

"Eh?" exclaimed Holmes, his expression undergoing a subtle change. "Do you think his statement was untrue?"

"According to my theory, Holmes, his statement was untrue, in this particular, at least. But to proceed: Might he not have employed this door to admit a nocturnal visitor?"

"It is feasible," muttered Holmes, watching me closely.

"For the Colonel to descend to this side door when the household was sleeping," I continued, "and to admit a woman secretly to Cray's Folly, would have been a simple matter. Indeed, on the occasions of these visits, he might even have unbolted the door himself after Pedro had bolted it in order to enable her to enter without his descending for the purpose of admitting her."

"By Heavens! Watson," said Holmes, "I believe that you have it!"

His eyes were gleaming excitedly, and I proceeded:

"Hence the footsteps which passed Miss Beverley's door, hence the shadow which you saw upon the blind; and the sounds which you detected in the hall were caused, of course, by this woman retiring. It was the door leading into the shrubbery which we heard being closed!"

"Continue," said Holmes; "although I can plainly see to what this is leading."

"You can see, Holmes?" I cried; "of course you can see! The enmity between Camber and Menendez is understandable at last."

"You mean that Menendez was Mrs. Camber's lover?"

"Don't you agree with me?"

"It is feasible, Watson, dreadfully feasible. But go on."

"My theory also explains Colin Camber's lapse from sobriety. It is legitimate to suppose that his wife, who was a Cuban, had been intimate with Menendez before her meeting with Camber. Perhaps she had broken the tie at the time of her marriage, but this is mere supposition. Then, her old lover, his infatuation by no means abated, leases the property adjoining that of his successful rival."

"Watson!" exclaimed Sherlock Holmes, "this is brilliant. I am all impatience for the *dénouement.*"

"That is coming," I said, triumphantly. "Relations are reëstablished clandestinely. Colin Camber learns of this. A passionate quarrel ensues, resulting in a long drinking bout designed to drown his sorrows. His love for his wife is so great that he has forgiven her this infidelity. Accordingly, she has promised to see her lover no more. Hers was the figure which you saw outlined upon the blind on the night before the tragedy, Holmes! The gestures, which you described as those of despair, furnish evidence to confirm my theory. It was a final meeting!"

"Hmm," muttered Holmes. "It would be taking big chances, because we have to suppose, Watson, that these visits to Cray's Folly were made whilst her husband was at work in the study. If he had suddenly decided to turn in, all would have been discovered."

"True," I agreed, "but is it impossible?"

"No, not a bit. Women are dreadful gamblers. But continue, Watson."

"Very well. Colonel Menendez has refused to accept his dismissal, and Mrs. Camber had been compelled to promise, without necessarily intending to carry out the promise, that she would see him again on the following night. She failed to come; whereupon he, growing impatient, walked out into the grounds of Cray's Folly to look for her. She may even have intended to come and have been intercepted by her husband. But in any event, the latter, seeing the man who had wronged him, standing out there in the moonlight, found temptation to be too strong. On the whole, I favour the idea that he had intercepted his wife, and snatching up a rifle, had actually gone out into the garden with the intention of shooting Menendez."

"I see," murmured Holmes in a low voice. "This hypothesis, Watson, does not embrace the Bat Wing episodes."

"If Menendez has lied upon one point," I returned, "it is permissible to suppose that his entire story was merely a tissue of falsehood."

"I see. But why did he bring me to Cray's Folly?"

"Don't you understand, Holmes?" I cried, excitedly. "He really feared for his life, since he knew that Camber had discovered the intrigue."

Sherlock Holmes heaved a long sigh.

"I must congratulate you, Watson," he said, gravely, "upon a really splendid contribution to my case. In several particulars I find myself much nearer to the truth. But the definite establishment or shattering of your theory rests upon one thing."

"What's that?" I asked. "You are surely not thinking of the bat wing nailed upon the door?"

"Not at all," he replied. "I am thinking of the seventh yew tree from the northeast corner of the Tudor garden."

29.

A LEE-ENFIELD RIFLE

What reply I should have offered to this astonishing remark I cannot say; but at that moment, the library door burst open unceremoniously, and outlined against the warmly illuminated hall, where sunlight poured down through the dome, I beheld the figure of Inspector Aylesbury.

"Ah!" he cried, loudly, "so you have come back, Mr. Holmes? I thought you had thrown up the case."

"Did you?" said Holmes, smilingly. "No, I am still persevering in my ineffectual way."

"Oh, I see. And have you quite convinced yourself that Colin Camber is innocent?"

"In one or two particulars my evidence remains incomplete."

"Oh, in one or two particulars, eh? But generally speaking you don't doubt his innocence?"

"I don't doubt it for a moment."

Holmes's words surprised me. I recognized, of course, that he might merely be bluffing the Inspector, but it was totally alien to his character to score a rhetorical success at the expense of what he knew to be the truth; and so sure was I of the accuracy of my deductions that I no longer doubted Colin Camber to be the guilty man.

"At any rate," continued the Inspector, "he is in detention, and likely to remain there. If you are going to defend him at the Assizes, I don't envy you your job, Mr. Holmes."

He was blatantly triumphant, so that the fact was evident enough that he had obtained some further piece of evidence which he regarded as conclusive.

"I have detained the man Ah Tsong as well," he went on. "He was an accomplice of your innocent friend, Mr. Holmes."

"Was he really?" murmured Holmes.

"Finally," continued the Inspector, "I have only to satisfy myself regarding the person who lured Colonel Menendez out into the grounds last night, to have my case complete."

I turned aside, unable to trust myself, but Holmes remarked quite coolly:

"Your industry is admirable, Inspector Aylesbury, but I seem to perceive that you have made a very important discovery of some kind."

"Ah, you have got wind of it, have you?"

"I have no information on the point," replied Holmes, "but your manner urges me to suggest that perhaps success has crowned your efforts?"

"It has," replied the Inspector. "I am a man that doesn't do things by halves. I didn't content myself with just staring out of the window of that little hut in the grounds of the Guest House, like you did, Mr. Holmes, and saying 'twice one are two' — I looked at every book on the shelves, and at every page of those books."

"You must have materially added to your information?"

"Ah, very likely, but my enquiries didn't stop there. I had the floor up."

"The floor of the hut?"

"The floor of the hut, sir. The planks were quite loose. I had satisfied myself that it was a likely hiding place."

"What did you find there, a dead rat?"

Inspector Aylesbury turned, and:

"Sergeant Butler," he called.

The sergeant came forward from the hall, carrying a cricket bag. This Inspector Aylesbury took from him, placing it upon the floor of the library at his feet.

"New, sir," said he, "I borrowed this bag in which to bring the evidence away — the hanging evidence which I discovered beneath the floor of the hut."

I had turned again, when the man had referred to his discovery; and now, glancing at Holmes, I saw that his face had grown suddenly very stern.

"Show me your evidence, Inspector?" he asked, shortly.

"There can be no objection," returned the Inspector.

Opening the bag, he took out a rifle!

Sherlock Holmes's hands were thrust in his coat pockets. By the movement of the cloth, I could see that he had clenched his fists. Here was confirmation of my theory!

"A Service rifle," said the Inspector, triumphantly, holding up the weapon. "A Lee-Enfield charger-loader. It contains four cartridges, three undischarged, and one discharged. He had not even troubled to eject it."

The Inspector dropped the weapon into the bag with a dramatic movement.

"Fancy theories about bat wings and Voodoos," he said, scornfully, "may satisfy you, Mr. Holmes, but I think this rifle will prove more satisfactory to the Coroner."

He picked up the bag and walked out of the library.

Holmes stood posed in a curiously rigid way, looking after him. Even when the door had closed, he did not change his position at once. Then, turning slowly, he walked to an armchair and sat down.

"Holmes," I said, hesitatingly, "has this discovery surprised you?"

"Surprised me?" he returned in a low voice. "It has appalled me."

"Then, although you seemed to regard my theory as sound," I continued rather resentfully, "all the time you continued to believe Colin Camber to be innocent?"

"I believe so still."

"What?"

"I thought we had determined, Watson," he said, wearily, "that a man of Camber's genius, having decided upon murder, must have arranged for an unassailable alibi. Very well. Are we now to leap to the other end of the scale, and to credit him with such utter stupidity as to place hanging evidence where it could not fail to be discovered by the most idiotic policeman? Preserve your balance, Watson. Theories are wild horses. They run away with us. I know that of old, for which very reason I always avoid speculation until I have a solid foundation of fact upon which to erect it."

"But, my dear fellow," I cried, "was Camber to foresee that the floor of the hut would be taken up?"

Holmes sighed, and leaned back in his chair.

"Do you recollect your first meeting with this man, Watson?"

"Perfectly."

"What occurred?"

"He was slightly drunk."

"Yes, but what was the nature of his conversation?"

"He suggested that I had recognized his resemblance to Edgar Allan Poe."

"Quite. What had led him to make this suggestion?"

"The manner in which I had looked at him, I suppose."

"Exactly. Although not quite sober, from a mere glance he was able to detect what you were thinking. Do you wish me to believe, Watson, that this same man had not foreseen what the police would think when Colonel Menendez was found shot within a hundred yards of the garden of the Guest House?"

I was somewhat taken aback, for Holmes's argument was strictly logical, and:

"It is certainly very puzzling," I admitted.

"Puzzling!" he exclaimed. "It is maddening. This case is like a Syrian village-mound. Stratum lies under stratum, and in each we meet with evidence of more refined activity than in the last. It seems we have yet to go deeper."

He took out his pipe and began to fill it.

"Tell me about the interview with Madame de Stämer," he directed.

I took a seat facing him, and he did not once interrupt me throughout my account of Inspector Aylesbury's examination of Madame.

"Good," he commented when I had told how the Inspector was dismissed. "But at least, Watson, he has a working theory to which he sticks like an express to the main line, whereas I find myself constantly called upon to readjust my perspective. Directly I can enjoy freedom of movement, however, I shall know whether my hypothesis is a house of cards or a serviceable structure."

"Your hypothesis?" I said. "Then you really have a theory which is entirely different from mine?"

"Not entirely different, Watson — merely not so comprehensive. I have contented myself thus far with a negative theory, if I may so express it."

"Negative theory?"

"Exactly. We are dealing, my dear fellow, with a case of bewildering intricacies. For the moment I have focussed upon one feature only."

"What is that?"

"Upon proving that Colin Camber did not do the murder."

"Did *not* do it?"

"Precisely, Watson. Respecting the person or persons who did do it, I had preserved a moderately open mind, up to the moment that Inspector Aylesbury entered the library with the Lee-Enfield."

"And then?" I said, eagerly.

"Then," he replied, "I began to think hard. However, since I practise what I preach, or endeavour to do so, I must not permit myself to speculate upon this aspect of the matter until I have tested my theory of Camber's innocence."

"In other words," I said bitterly, "although you encouraged me to unfold my ideas regarding Mrs. Camber, you were merely laughing at me all the time!"

"My dear Watson!" exclaimed Holmes, jumping up impulsively, "please don't be unjust. Is it like me? On the contrary, Watson" — he looked me squarely in the eyes — "you have given me a platform on which already I have begun to erect one corner of a theory of the crime. Without new facts I can go no further. But this much at least you have done."

"Thanks, Holmes," I murmured, and indeed I was gratified; "but where do your other corners rest?"

"They rest," he said, slowly, "they rest, respectively, upon a bat wing, a yew tree, and a Lee-Enfield charger-loader."

30.

THE SEVENTH YEW TREE

Detective-Inspector Lestrade arrived at about five o'clock; a quiet, resourceful man, highly competent, and having the appearance of an ex-soldier. His respect for the attainments of Sherlock Holmes alone marked him a student of character. I knew Lestrade well, and was delighted when Pedro showed him into the library.

"Thank God you are here, Lestrade," said Holmes, when we had exchanged greetings. "At last I can move. Have you seen the local officer in charge?"

"No," replied the Inspector, "but I gather that I have been requisitioned over his head."

"You have," said Holmes, grimly, "and over the head of the Chief Constable, too. But I suppose it is unfair to condemn a man for the shortcoming with which nature endowed him, therefore we must endeavour to let Inspector Aylesbury down as lightly as possible. I have an idea that I heard him return a while ago."

He walked out into the hall to make enquiries, and a few moments later I heard Inspector Aylesbury's voice.

"Ah, there you are, Inspector Aylesbury," said Holmes, cheerily. "Will you please step into the library for a moment?"

The Inspector entered, frowning heavily, followed by my friend.

"There is no earthly reason why we should get at loggerheads over this business," Holmes continued; "but the fact of the matter is, Inspector Aylesbury, that there are depths in this case to which neither you nor I have yet succeeded in penetrating. You have a reputation to consider, and so have I. Therefore, I am sure you will welcome the cooperation of Detective-Inspector Lestrade of Scotland Yard, as I do."

"What's this, what's this?" said Aylesbury. "I have made no application to London."

"Nevertheless, Inspector, it is quite in order," declared Lestrade. "I have my instructions here, and I have reported to Market Hilton already. You see, the man you have detained is an American citizen."

"What of that?"

"Well, he seems to have communicated with his Embassy." Lestrade glanced significantly at Sherlock Holmes. "And the Embassy communicated with the Home Office. You mustn't regard my arrival as any reflection on your ability, Inspector Aylesbury. I am sure we can work together quite agreeably."

"Oh," muttered the other, in evident bewilderment, "I see. Well, if that's the way of it, I suppose we must make the best of things."

"Good," cried Lestrade, heartily. "Now perhaps you would like to state your case against the detained man?"

"A sound idea, Lestrade," said Sherlock Holmes. "But perhaps, Inspector Aylesbury, before you begin, you would be good enough to speak to the constable on duty at the entrance to the Tudor garden. I am anxious to take another look at the spot where the body was found."

Inspector Aylesbury took out his handkerchief and blew his nose loudly, continuing throughout the operation to glare at Sherlock Holmes, and finally:

"You are wasting your time, Mr. Holmes," he declared, "as Detective-Inspector Lestrade will be the first to admit when I have given him the facts of my case. Nevertheless, if you want to examine the garden, do so by all means."

He turned without another word and stamped out of the library across the hall and into the courtyard.

"I will join you again in a few minutes, Lestrade," said Sherlock Holmes, following.

"Very good, Mr. Holmes," Lestrade answered. "I know you wouldn't have had me down if the case had been as simple as he seems to think it is."

I joined Holmes, and we walked together up the gravelled path, meeting Inspector Aylesbury and the constable returning.

"Go ahead, Mr. Holmes!" cried the Inspector. "If you can find any stronger evidence than the rifle, I shall be glad to take a look at it."

Holmes nodded good-humouredly, and together we descended the steps to the sunken garden. I was intensely curious respecting the investigation which Holmes had been so anxious to make here, for I recognized that it was associated with something which he had seen from the window of Camber's hut.

He walked along the moss-grown path to the sun-dial and stood for a moment looking down at the spot where Menendez had lain. Then he stared up the hill toward the Guest House; and finally, directing his attention to the yews which lined the sloping bank:

"One, two, three, four," he counted, checking them with his fingers — "five, six, seven."

He mounted the bank and began to examine the trunk of one of the trees, whilst I watched him in growing astonishment.

Presently he turned and looked down at me.

"Not a trace, Watson," he murmured; "not a trace. Let us try again."

He moved along to the yew adjoining that which he had already inspected, but presently shook his head and passed to the next. Then:

"Ah!" he cried. "Come here, Watson!"

I joined him where he was kneeling, staring at what I took to be a large nail, or bolt, protruding from the bark of the tree.

"You see!" he exclaimed. *"You see !"*

I stooped, in order to examine the thing more closely, and as I did so, I realized what it was. It was the bullet which had killed Colonel Menendez!

Holmes stood upright, his face slightly flushed and his eyes very bright.

"We shall not attempt to remove it, Watson," he said. "The depth of penetration may have a tale to tell. The wood of the yew tree is one of the toughest British varieties."

"But, Holmes," I said blankly as we descended to the path, "this is merely another point for the prosecution of Camber. Unless" — I turned to him in sudden excitement, "the bullet was of different — "

"No, no," he murmured, "nothing so easy as that, Watson. The bullet was fired from a Lee-Enfield, beyond doubt."

I stared at him uncomprehendingly.

"Then I am utterly out of my depth, Holmes. It, appears to me that the case against Camber is finally and fatally complete. Only the motive remains to be discovered, and I flatter myself that I have already detected this."

"I am certainly inclined to think," admitted Holmes, "that there is a good deal in your theory."

"Then, Holmes," I said in bewilderment, "you do believe that Camber committed the murder?"

"On the contrary," he replied, "I am certain that he did not."

I stood quite still.

"You are certain?" I began.

"I told you that the test of my theory, Watson, was to be looked for in the seventh yew from the northeast corner of the Tudor garden, did I not?"

"You did. And it is there. A bullet fired from a Lee-Enfield rifle; beyond any possible shadow of doubt the bullet which killed Colonel Menendez."

"Beyond any possible shadow of doubt, as you say, Watson, the bullet which killed Colonel Menendez."

"Therefore Camber is guilty?"

"On the contrary, therefore Camber is innocent!"

"What!"

"You are persistently overlooking one little point, Watson," said Holmes, mounting the steps on to the gravel path. "I spoke of the seventh yew tree from the northeast corner of the garden."

"Well?"

"Well, my dear fellow, surely you observed that the bullet was embedded in the ninth?"

I was still groping for the significance of this point when, re-crossing the hall, we entered the library again, to find Inspector Aylesbury posed squarely before the mantelpiece stating his case to Lestrade.

"You see," he was saying, in his most oratorical manner, as we entered, "every little detail fits perfectly into place. For instance, I find that a woman, called Mrs. Powis, who for the past two years had acted as housekeeper at the Guest House and never taken a holiday, was sent away recently to her married daughter in London. See what that means?

Her room is at the back of the house, and her evidence would have been fatal. Ah Tsong, of course, is a liar. I made up my mind about that the moment I clapped eyes on him. Mrs. Camber is the only innocent party. She was asleep in the front of the house when the shot was fired, and I believe her when she says that she cannot swear to the matter of distance."

"A very interesting case, Inspector," said Lestrade, glancing at Holmes. "I have not examined the body yet, but I understand that it was a clean wound through the head."

"The bullet entered at the juncture of the nasal and frontal bones," explained Holmes, rapidly, "and it came out between the base of the occipital and first cervical. Without going into unpleasant surgical details, the wound was a perfectly *straight* one. There was no ricochet."

"I understand that a regulation rifle was used?"

"Yes," said Inspector Aylesbury; "we have it."

"And at what range did you say, Inspector?"

"Roughly, a hundred yards."

"Possibly less," murmured Holmes.

"Hundred yards or less," said Lestrade, musingly; "and the obstruction met with in the case of a man shot in that way would be — "He looked towards Sherlock Holmes.

"Less than if the bullet had struck the skull higher up," was the reply. "It passed clean through."

"Therefore," continued Lestrade, "I am waiting to hear, Inspector, where you found the bullet lodged?"

"Eh?" said the Inspector, and he slowly turned his prominent eyes in Holmes's direction. "Oh, I see. That's why you wanted to examine the Tudor garden, is it?"

"Exactly," replied Holmes.

The face of Inspector Aylesbury grew very red.

"I had deferred looking for the bullet," he explained, "as the case was already as clear as daylight. Probably Mr. Holmes has discovered it."

"I have," said Holmes, shortly.

"Is it the regulation bullet?" asked Lestrade.

"It is. I found it embedded in one of the yew trees."

"There you are!" exclaimed Aylesbury. "There isn't the ghost of a doubt."

Lestrade looked at Holmes in undisguised perplexity.

"I must say, Mr. Holmes," he admitted, "that I have never met with a clearer case."

"Neither have I," agreed Holmes, cheerfully. "I am going to ask Inspector Aylesbury to return here after nightfall. There is a little experiment which I should like to make which would definitely establish my case."

"*Your* case?" said Aylesbury.

"My case, yes."

"You are not going to tell me that you still persist in believing Camber to be innocent?"

"Not at all. I am merely going to ask you to return at nightfall to assist me in this minor investigation."

"If you ask my opinion," said the Inspector, "no further evidence is needed."

"I don't agree with you," replied Holmes, quietly. "Whatever your own ideas upon the subject may be, I personally have not yet discovered one single piece of convincing evidence for the prosecution of Camber."

"What!" exclaimed Aylesbury, and even Detective-Inspector Lestrade stared at the speaker incredulously.

"My dear Inspector Aylesbury," concluded Holmes, "when you have witnessed the experiment which I propose to make this evening you will realize, as I have already realized, that we are faced by a tremendous task."

"What tremendous task?"

"The task of discovering who shot Colonel Menendez."

31.

YSOLA CAMBER'S CONFESSION

Sherlock Holmes, with Lestrade and Inspector Aylesbury, presently set out for Market Hilton, where Colin Camber and Ah Tsong were detained and where the body of Colonel Menendez had been conveyed for the purpose of the post-mortem. I had volunteered to remain at Cray's Folly, my motive being not wholly an unselfish one.

"Refer reporters to me, Dr. Watson," said Inspector Lestrade. "Don't let them trouble the ladies. And tell them as little as possible, yourself."

The drone of the engine having died away down the avenue, I presently found myself alone; but as I crossed the hall in the direction of the library, intending to walk out upon the southern lawns, I saw Val Beverley coming toward me from Madame de Stämer's room.

She remained rather pale, but smiled at me courageously.

"Have they all gone, Dr. Watson?" she asked. "I have really been hiding. I suppose you knew?"

"I suspected it," I said, smiling. "Yes, they are all gone. How is Madame de Stämer, now?"

"She is quite calm. Curiously, almost uncannily calm. She is writing. Tell me, please, what does Mr. Holmes think of Inspector Aylesbury's preposterous ideas?"

"He thinks he is a fool," I replied, hotly, "as I do."

"But whatever will happen if he persists in dragging me into this horrible case?"

"He will not drag you into it," I said quietly. "He has been superseded by a cleverer man, and the case is practically under Holmes's direction now."

"Thank Heaven for that," she murmured. "I wonder — " She looked at me hesitatingly.

"Yes?" I prompted.

"I have been thinking about poor Mrs. Camber all alone in that gloomy house, and wondering — "

"Perhaps I know. You are going to visit her?"

Val Beverley nodded, watching me.

"Can you leave Madame de Stämer with safety?"

"Oh, yes, I think so. Nita can attend to her."

"And may I accompany you, Miss Beverley? For more reasons than one, I too should like to call upon Mrs. Camber."

"We might try," she said, hesitatingly. "I really only wanted to be kind. You won't begin to cross-examine her, will you?"

"Certainly not," I answered; "although there are many things I should like her to tell us."

"Well, suppose we go," said the girl, "and let events take their own course."

As a result, I presently found myself, Val Beverley by my side, walking across the meadow path. With the unpleasant hush of Cray's Folly left behind, the day seemed to grow brighter. I thought that the skylarks had never sung more sweetly. Yet in this same instant of sheerly physical enjoyment, I experienced a pang of remorse, remembering the tragic woman we had left behind, and the poor little sorrowful girl we were going to visit. My emotions were very mingled then, and I retain no recollection of our conversation up to the time that we came to the Guest House.

We were admitted by a really charming old lady, who informed us that her name was Mrs. Powis and that she was but an hour returned from London, whither she had been summoned by telegram.

She showed us into a quaint, small drawing room which owed its atmosphere quite clearly to Mrs. Camber, for whereas the study was indescribably untidy, this was a model of neatness without being formal or unhomely. Here, in a few moments, Mrs. Camber joined us, an appealing little figure of wistful, almost elfin, beauty. I was surprised and delighted to find that an instant bond of sympathy sprang up between the two girls. I diplomatically left them together for a while, going into Camber's room to smoke my pipe. And when I returned:

"Oh, Dr. Watson," said Val Beverley, "Mrs. Camber has something to tell you which she thinks you ought to know."

"Concerning Colonel Menendez?" I asked, eagerly.

Mrs. Camber nodded her golden head.

"Yes," she replied, but glancing at Val Beverley as if to gather confidence. "The truth can never hurt Colin. He has nothing to conceal. May I tell you?"

"I am all anxiety to hear," I assured her.

"Would you rather I left the room, Mrs. Camber?" asked Val Beverley.

Mrs. Camber reached across and took her hand.

"Please, no," she replied. "Stay here with me. I am afraid it is rather a long story."

"Never mind," I said. "It will be time well spent if it leads us any nearer to the truth."

"Yes?" she questioned, watching me anxiously. "You think so? I think so, too."

She became silent, sitting looking straight before her, the pupils of her blue eyes widely dilated. Then, at first in a queer, far-away voice, she began to speak again.

"I must tell you," she commenced "that before my — my marriage, my name was Isabella de Valera."

I started.

"Ysola was my baby way of saying it, and so I came to be called Ysola. My father was manager of one of Señor Don Juan's estates, in a small island near the coast of Cuba. My mother" — she raised her little hands eloquently — "was half-caste. Do you know?

"And she and my father — "

She looked pleadingly at Val Beverley.

"I understand," whispered the latter with deep sympathy; "but you don't think it makes any difference, do you?"

"No?" said Mrs. Camber with a quaint little gesture. "To you, perhaps not, but there, where I was born — oh, so much! Well, then, my mother died when I was very little. Ah Tsong was her servant. There are many Chinese in the West Indies, you see, and I can just remember he carried me in to see her. Of course I didn't understand. My father quarrelled bitterly with the priests because they would not bury her in holy ground. I think he no longer believed afterward. I loved him very much. He was good to me; and I was a queen in that little island. All the blacks loved me because of my mother, I think, who was partly descended from slaves, as they were. But I had not begun to understand how hard it was all going to be when my father sent me to a convent in Cuba.

"I hated to go, but while I was there I learned all about myself. I knew that I was outcast. It was" — she raised her hand — "not possible to stay. I was only fifteen when I came home, but all the same I was a woman. I was no more a child, and happy no longer. After a while, perhaps, when I forgot what I had suffered at the convent, I became less miserable. My father did all in his power to make me happy, and I was glad the work-people loved me. But I was very lonely. Ah Tsong understood."

Her eyes filled with tears.

"Can you imagine," she asked, "that when my father was away in distant parts of the island at night, Ah Tsong slept outside my door? Some of them say, 'Do not trust the Chinese.' I say, except my husband and my father, I have never known another one to trust but Ah Tsong. Now they have taken him away from me."

Tears glittered on her lashes, but she brushed them aside angrily, and continued:

"I was still less than twenty and looked, they told me, only fourteen, when Señor Menendez came to inspect his estate. I had never seen him before. There had been an uprising in the island in the year after I was born, and he had only just escaped with his life. He was hated. People called him Devil Menendez. Especially, no woman was safe from him, and in the old days, when his power had been great, he had used it for wickedness.

"My father was afraid when he heard he was coming. He would have sent me away, but before it could be arranged, Señor the Colonel arrived. He had in his company a French lady. I thought her very beautiful and elegant. It was Madame de Stämer. It is only four years ago, a little more, but her hair was dark brown. She was splendidly dressed and such a wonderful horsewoman. The first time I saw her, I felt as they had made me feel at the convent. I wanted to hide from her. She was so grand a lady, and I came from slaves."

She paused hesitatingly and stared down at her own tiny feet.

"Pardon me for interrupting you, Mrs. Camber," I said, "but can you tell me in what way these two are related?"

341

She looked up with her naïve smile.

"I can tell you, yes. A cousin of Señor Menendez married a sister of Madame de Stämer."

"Good Heavens!" I exclaimed, "a very remote kinship."

"It was in this way they met, in Paris, I think, and" — she raised her hands expressively — "she came with him to the West Indies, although it was during the great war. I think she loved him more than her soul, and me — me she hated. As Señor Menendez dismounted from his horse in front of the house, he saw me."

She sighed and ceased speaking again. Then:

"That very night," she continued, "he began. Do you know? I was trying to escape from him when Madame de Stämer found us. She called me a shameful name and my father, who heard it, ordered her out of the house. Señor Menendez spoke sharply, and my father struck him."

She paused once more, biting her lip agitatedly, but presently proceeded:

"Do you know what they are like, the Spanish, when their blood is hot? Señor Menendez had a revolver, but my father knocked it from his grasp. Then they fought with their bare hands. I was too frightened even to cry out. It was all a horrible dream. What Madame de Stämer did, I do not know. I could see nothing but two figures twined together on the floor. At last one of them arose. I saw it was my father, and I remember no more."

She was almost overcome by her tragic recollections; but presently, with a wonderful courage which, together with her daintiness of form, spoke eloquently of good blood, continued to speak:

"My father found he must go to Cuba to make arrangements for the future. Of course, our life there was finished. Ah Tsong stayed with me. You have heard how it used to be in those islands in the old days, but now you think it is so different? I used to think it was different, too. On the first night my father was away, Ah Tsong, who had gone out, was so long returning I became afraid. Then a strange native came with news that Ah Tsong had been taken ill with cholera, and was lying at a place not far from the house. I forgot my fears and hurried off with this man. Ah!"

She laughed wildly.

"I did not know that I would never return, and I did not know I should never see my father again. To you this must seem all wild and strange, because there is a law in England. There is a law in Cuba, too, but in some of those little islands, the only law is the law of the strongest."

She raised her hands to her face and there was silence for a while.

"Of course it was a trap," she presently continued. "I was taken to an island called El Manas which belonged to Señor Menendez, and where he had a house. This he could do, but" — she threw back her head proudly — "my spirit he could not break. Lots and lots of money would be mine, and estates of my own; but one thing about him I must tell: he never showed me violence. For one, two, three weeks I stayed a prisoner in his house. All the servants were faithful to him and I could not find a friend among them. Although quite innocent, I was ruined. Do you know?"

She raised her eyes pathetically to Val Beverley.

"I thought my heart was broken, for something told me my father was dead. This was true."

"What!" I exclaimed. "You don't mean — "

"I don't know, I don't know," she answered, brokenly. "He died on his way to Havana. They said it was an accident. Well — at last, Señor Menendez offered me marriage. I thought if I agreed, it would give me my freedom, and I could run away and find Ah Tsong."

She paused, and a flush coloured her delicate face and faded again, leaving it very pale.

"We were married in the house by a Spanish priest. Oh" — she raised her hands pathetically — "do you know what a woman is like? My spirit was not broken, but crushed. I had now nothing but kindness and gifts. I might never have known, but Señor Menendez, who thought" — she smiled sadly — "I was beautiful, took me to Cuba, where he had a great house. Please remember, please," she pleaded, "before you judge of me, that I was so young and had never known love, except the love of my father. I did not even dream, then, that his death was not an accident.

"I was proud of my jewels and fine dresses. But I began to notice that Juan did not present any of his friends to me. We went about, but to strange places, never to visit people of his own kind; and none came to visit us. Then one night, I heard someone on the balcony of my room. I was so frightened I could not cry out. It was good I was like that, for the curtain was pulled open and Ah Tsong came in."

She clutched convulsively at the arms of her chair.

"He told me!" she said in a very low voice.

Then, looking up pitifully:

"Do you know?" she asked in her quaint way. "It was a mock marriage. He had done it and thought no shame, because it was so with my mother. Oh!"

Her beautiful eyes flashed, and for the first time since I had met Ysola Camber I saw the real Spanish spirit of the woman leap to life.

"He did not know me. Perhaps I did not know myself. That night, with no money, without a ring, a piece of lace, a peseta, anything that had belonged to him, I went with Ah Tsong. We made our way to a half-sister of my father's who lived in Puerto Principe, and at first — she would not have me. I was talked about, she said, in all the islands. She told me of my poor father. She told me I had dragged the name of de Valera in the dirt. At last I made her understand — that what everyone else had known, I had never even dreamed of."

She looked up wistfully, as if thinking that we might doubt her.

"Do you know?" she whispered.

"I know — Oh, I know!" said Val Beverley. I loved her for the sympathy in her voice and in her eyes. "It is very, very brave of you to tell us this, Mrs. Camber."

"Yes? Do you think so?" asked the girl, simply. "What does it matter if it can help Colin?

"This aunt of mine," she presently continued, "was a poor woman, and it was while I was hiding in her house — because spies of Señor Menendez were searching for me — that I met — my husband. He was studying in Cuba the strange things he writes about, you see. And before I knew what had happened — I found I loved him more than all else in the world. It is so wonderful, that feeling," she said, looking across at Val Beverley. "Do you know?"

The girl flushed deeply, and lowered her eyes, but made no reply.

"Because you are a woman, too, you will perhaps understand," she resumed. "I did not tell him. I did not dare to tell him at first. I was so madly happy I had no courage to speak. But when" — her voice sank lower and lower — "he asked me to marry him, I told him. Nothing he could ever do would change my love for him now, because he forgave me and made me his wife."

I feared that at last she was going to break down, for her voice became very tremulous and tears leapt again into her eyes. She conquered her emotion, however, and went on:

"We crossed over to the States, and Colin's family who had heard of his marriage — some friend of Señor Menendez had told them — would not accept us. It meant that Colin, who would have been a rich man, was now very poor.

It made no difference to him or to me. He was splendid. And I was so happy, it was all like a dream. He made me forget that I was to blame for his troubles. Then we were in Washington — and I saw Señor Menendez in the hotel!

"Oh, my heart stopped beating. For me it seemed like the end of everything. I knew, I knew, he was following me. But he had not seen me, and without telling Colin the reason, I made him leave Washington, He was glad to go. Wherever we went, in America, they seemed to find out about my mother. I got to hate them, hate them all. We came to England, and Colin heard about this house, and we took it.

"At last we were really happy. No one knew us. Because we were strange, and because of Ah Tsong, they looked at us very funny and kept away, but we did not care. Then Sir James Appleton sold Cray's Folly."

She looked up quickly.

"How can I tell you? It must have been by Ah Tsong that he traced me to Surrey. Some spy had told him there was a Chinaman living here. Oh, I don't know how he found out, but when I heard who was coming to Cray's Folly I thought I should die!

"Something I must tell you now. When I had told my story to Colin, one thing I had not told him, because I was afraid what he might do. I had not told him the name of the man who had caused me to suffer so much. On the day I first saw Señor Menendez walking in the garden of Cray's Folly, I knew I must tell my husband what he had so often asked me to tell him — the name of the man. I told him — and at first I thought he would go mad. He began to drink — do you know? It is a failing in his family. But because I knew

347

— because I knew — I forgave him, and hoped, always hoped, that he would stop. He promised to do so. He had given up going out each day to drink, and was working again like he used to work — too hard, too hard, but it was better than the other way."

She stopped speaking and suddenly, before I could divine her intention, dropped upon her knees, and raised her clasped hands to me.

"He did not, he did not kill him!" she cried, passionately. "He did not! O God! I who love him tell you he did not! You think he did. You do — you do! I can see it in your eyes!"

"Believe me, Mrs. Camber," I answered, deeply moved, "I don't doubt your word for a moment."

She continued to look at me for a while, and then turned to Val Beverley.

"You don't think he did," she sobbed, "do you?"

She looked such a child — such a pretty, helpless child — as she knelt there on the carpet, that I felt a lump rising in my throat.

Val Beverley dropped down impulsively beside her and put her arms around the slender shoulders.

"Of course I don't," she exclaimed, indignantly. "Of course I don't. It's quite unthinkable."

"I know it is," moaned the other, raising her tearful face. "I love him and know his great soul. But what do these others know, and they will never believe *me.*"

"Have courage," I said. "Your courage has never failed you yet. Mr. Sherlock Holmes has promised to clear him by to-night."

"He has promised?" she whispered, still kneeling and clutching Val Beverley tightly. She looked up at me with hope reborn in her beautiful eyes. "He has promised? Oh, I thank him. May God bless him. I know he will succeed."

I turned aside, and walked out across the hall and into the empty study.

32.

SHERLOCK HOLMES'S EXPERIMENT I

I recognize that whosoever may have taken the trouble to follow my chronicle thus far will be little disposed to suffer any intrusion of my personal affairs at such a point. Therefore, I shall pass lightly over the walk back to Cray's Folly, during which I contrived to learn much about Val Beverley's personal history but little to advance the investigation which I was there to assist.

As I had surmised, Miss Beverley had been amply provided for by her father, and was bound to Madame de Stämer by no other ties than those of friendship and esteem. Very reluctantly, I released her on our returning to the house; for she, perforce, hurried off to Madame's room, leaving me looking after her in a state of delightful bewilderment, the significance of which I could not disguise from myself. The absurd suspicions of Inspector Aylesbury were forgotten, as was the shadow upon the blind of Colonel Menendez's study. I only knew that love had come to me again after so many decades of loss, an unbidden guest, to stay forever.

Manoel informed me that a number of pressmen, not to be denied, had taken photographs of the Tudor garden and of the spot where Colonel Menendez had been found, but Pedro, following my instructions, had referred them all to Market Hilton.

I was standing in the doorway talking to Pedro when I heard the drone of Holmes's motor in the avenue and, a moment later, he and Lestrade stepped out in front of the porch and joined me. I thought that Lestrade looked stern and rather confused, but Holmes was quite his old self, his keen eyes gleaming humorously, and an expression of geniality upon his tanned features.

"Hullo, Watson!" he cried. "Any developments?"

"Yes," I said. "Suppose we go up to your room and talk."

"Good enough."

Inspector Lestrade nodded without speaking, and the three of us mounted the staircase and entered Sherlock Holmes's room. Holmes seated himself upon the bed and began to load his pipe, whilst Lestrade, who seemed very restless, stood staring out of the window. I sat down in the armchair, and:

"I have had an interesting interview with Mrs. Camber," I said.

"What?" exclaimed Holmes. "Good. Tell us all about it."

Lestrade turned, hands clasped behind him, and listened in silence to an account which I gave of my visit to the Guest House. When I had finished:

"It seems to me," said the Inspector, slowly, "that the only doubtful point in the case against Camber is cleared up; namely, his motive."

"It certainly looks like it," agreed Holmes. "But how strangely Mrs. Camber's story differs from that of Menendez, although there are points of contact. I regret, however, that you were unable to settle the most important matter of all."

"You mean whether or not she had visited Cray's Folly?"

"Exactly."

"Then you still consider my theory to be correct?" I asked eagerly.

"Up to a point, it has been proved to be," he returned. "I must congratulate you upon a piece of really brilliant reasoning, Watson. But respecting the most crucial moment of all, we are still without information, unfortunately. However, whilst the presence or otherwise of Mrs. Camber in Cray's Folly on the night preceding the tragedy may prove to bear intimately upon the case, an experiment which I propose to make presently will give the matter an entirely different significance."

"Hmm," said Lestrade, doubtfully, "I am looking forward to this experiment of yours, Mr. Holmes, with great interest. To be perfectly honest, I have no more idea than the man in the moon how you hope to clear Camber."

"No," replied Holmes, musingly, "the weight of evidence against him is crushing. But you are a man of great experience, Lestrade, in criminal investigations. Tell me honestly, have you ever known a murder case in which there was such conclusive material for the prosecution?"

"Never," replied the Inspector, promptly. "In this respect, as in others, the case is unique."

"You have seen Camber," continued Holmes, "and have been enabled to form some sort of judgment respecting his character. You will admit that he is a clever man, brilliantly clever. Keep this fact in mind. Remember his studies, and he does not deny that they have included Voodoo. Remember his enquiries into the significance of Bat Wing. Remember, as we now learn definitely from Mrs. Camber's evidence, that he was in Cuba at the same time as the late Colonel Menendez, and once, at least, actually in the same hotel in the United States. Consider the rifle found under the floor of the hut and, having weighed all these points judicially, Lestrade, tell me frankly, if in the whole course of your experience, you have ever met with a more perfect frame-up?"

"What!" shouted Lestrade, in sudden excitement. "What!"

"I said 'a frame-up,' " repeated Holmes, quietly. "It's an American term, but one which will be familiar to you."

"Good God!" muttered the detective. "You have turned all my ideas upside-down."

"What may be termed the *physical* evidence," continued Holmes, "is complete, I admit: too complete. There lies the weak spot. But what I will call the psychological evidence points in a totally different direction. A man clever enough to have planned this crime, and Camber undoubtedly is such a man, could not — it is humanly impossible — have been fool enough, deliberately to lay such a train of damning facts. It's a frame-up, Lestrade! I had begun to suspect this even before I met Camber. Having met him, I knew that I was right. Then came an inspiration. I saw where there must be a flaw in the plan. It was geographically impossible that this could be otherwise."

"Geographically impossible?" I said, in a hushed voice, for Holmes had truly astounded me.

"Geographical is the term, Watson. I admit that the discovery of the rifle beneath the floor of the hut appalled me."

"I could see that it did."

"It was the crowning piece of evidence, Watson, evidence of such fiendish cleverness on the part of those who had plotted Menendez's death that I began to wonder whether after all it would be possible to defeat them. I realized that Camber's life hung upon a hair. For the production of that rifle before a jury of twelve moderately stupid men and true could not fail to carry enormous weight. Whereas the delicate point upon which my counter case rested might be more difficult to demonstrate in court. To-night, however, we shall put it to the test, and there are means, no doubt, which will occur

353

to me later, of making its significance evident to one not acquainted with the locality. The press photographs, which I understand have been taken, may possibly help us in this."

Bewildered by my friend's revolutionary ideas, which explained the hitherto mysterious nature of his enquiries, I scarcely knew what to say; but:

"If it's a frame-up, Mr. Holmes," said Lestrade, "and the more I think about it, the more it has that look to me. Practically speaking, we have not yet started on the search for the murderer."

"We have not," replied Holmes, grimly. "But I have a dawning idea of a method by which we shall be enabled to narrow down this enquiry."

It must be unnecessary for me to speak of the state of suppressed excitement in which we passed the remainder of that afternoon and evening. Dr. Rolleston called again to see Madame de Stämer, and reported that she was quite calm. In fact, he almost echoed Val Beverley's words spoken earlier in the day.

"She is unnaturally calm, Dr. Watson," Dr. Rolleston said in confidence. "I understand that the dead man was a cousin, but I almost suspect that she was madly in love with him."

I nodded shortly, admiring his acute intelligence.

"I think you are right, doctor," I replied, "and if it is so, her amazing fortitude is all the more admirable."

"Admirable?" he echoed. "As I said before, she has the courage of ten men."

A formal dinner was out of the question, of course; indeed, no one attempted to dress. Val Beverley excused herself, saying that she would dine in Madame's room, while Holmes, Lestrade, and I partook of wine and sandwiches in the library.

Inspector Aylesbury arrived about eight o'clock in a mood of repressed irritation. Pedro showed him in to where the three of us were seated, and:

"Good evening, gentlemen," said the Inspector, "here I am, as arranged; but as I am up to my eyes in work on the case, I will ask you, Mr. Holmes, to carry out this experiment of yours as quickly as possible."

"No time shall be lost," replied my friend quietly. "May I request you to accompany Detective-Inspector Lestrade and Dr. Watson to the Guest House by the high road? Do not needlessly alarm Mrs. Camber. Indeed, I think you might confine your attention to Mrs. Powis. Merely request permission to walk down the garden to the hut, and be good enough to wait there until I join you, which will be in a few minutes after your arrival."

Inspector Aylesbury uttered an inarticulate, grunting sound, but I, who knew Holmes so well, could see that he felt himself to be upon the eve of a signal triumph. What he proposed to do, I had no idea, save that it was designed to clear Colin Camber. I prayed that it might also clear his pathetic girl-wife; and in a sort of gloomy silence, I set out with Lestrade and Aylesbury, down the drive, past the lodge, which seemed to be deserted to-night, and along the tree-lined high road, cool and sweet in the dusk of evening.

Aylesbury was very morose, and Lestrade, who had lighted his pipe, did not seem to be in a talkative mood either. He had the utmost faith in Sherlock Holmes, but it was evident enough that he was oppressed by the weight of evidence against Camber. I divined the fact that he was turning over in his mind the idea of the frame-up, and endeavouring to re-adjust the established facts in accordance with this new point of view.

We were admitted to the Guest House by Mrs. Powis, a cheery old soul; one of those born optimists whose special task in life seems to be that of a friend in need.

As she opened the door, she smiled, shook her head, and raised her finger to her lips.

"Be as quiet as you can, sirs," she said. "I have got her to sleep."

She spoke of Mrs. Camber as one refers to a child, and quite understanding her anxiety:

"There will be no occasion to disturb her, Mrs. Powis," I replied. "We merely wish to walk down to the bottom of the garden to make a few enquiries."

"Yes, gentlemen," she whispered, quietly closing the door as we all entered the hall.

She led us through the rear portion of the house, and past the quarters of Ah Tsong into that neglected garden which I remembered so well.

"There you are, sir, and may Heaven help you to find the truth."

"Rest assured that the truth will be found, Mrs. Powis," I answered.

Inspector Aylesbury cleared his throat; but Lestrade, puffing at his pipe, made no remark whatever until we were all come to the hut overhanging the little ravine.

"This is where I found the rifle, Detective-Inspector," explained Aylesbury.

Lestrade nodded absently.

It was another perfect night, with only a faint tracery of cloud to be seen like lingering smoke over on the western horizon. Everything seemed very still, so that although we were several miles from the railway line, when presently a train sped on its way, one might have supposed from the apparent nearness of the sound that the track was no farther off than the grounds of Cray's Folly.

Toward those grounds, automatically, our glances were drawn; and we stood there staring down at the ghostly map of the gardens, and all wondering, no doubt, what Holmes was doing and when he would be joining us.

Very faintly I could hear the water of the little stream bubbling beneath us. Then, just as this awkward silence was becoming intolerable, there came a scraping and scratching from the shadows of the gully, and:

"Give me a hand, Watson!" cried the voice of Holmes from below. "I want to avoid the barbed wire if possible."

He had come cross-country; and as I scrambled down the slope to meet him, I could not help wondering with what object he had sent us ahead by the high road. Presently, when he came clambering up into the garden, this in a measure was explained:

"You are all wondering," he began, rapidly, "what I am up to, no doubt. Let me endeavour to make it clear. In order that my test should be conclusive, and in no way influenced by pre-knowledge of certain arrangements which I had made, I sent you on ahead of me. Not wishing to waste time, I followed by the shorter route. And now, gentlemen, let us begin."

"Good," muttered Inspector Aylesbury.

"But first of all," continued Holmes, "I wish each one of you in turn to look out of the window of the hut, and down into the Tudor garden of Cray's Folly. Will you begin, Lestrade?"

Lestrade, taking his pipe out of his mouth and staring hard at the speaker, nodded and entered the hut and, kneeling on the wooden seat, looked out of the window.

"Open the panes," said Holmes, "so that you have a perfectly clear view."

Lestrade slid the panes open and stared intently down into the valley.

"Do you see anything unusual in the garden?"

"Nothing," he reported.

"And now, Inspector Aylesbury."

Inspector Aylesbury stamped noisily across the little hut, and peered out, briefly.

"I can see the garden," he said.

"Can you see the sun-dial?"

"Quite clearly."

"Good. And now you, Watson."

I followed, filled with astonishment.

"Do you see the sun-dial?" asked Holmes, again.

"Quite clearly."

"And beyond it?"

"Yes, I can see beyond it. I can even see its shadow lying like a black band on the path."

"And you can see the yew trees?"

"Of course."

"But nothing else? Nothing unusual?"

"Nothing."

"Very well," said Holmes, tersely. "And now, gentlemen, we take to the rough ground, proceeding due east. Will you be good enough to follow?"

Walking around the hut, Holmes found an opening in the hedges and scrambled down into the place where rank grass grew and through which he and I on a previous occasion had made our way to the high road. To-night, however, he did not turn toward the high road, but proceeded along the crest of the hill.

I followed him, excited by the novelty of the proceedings. Lestrade, very silent, came behind me, and Inspector Aylesbury, swearing under his breath, waded through the long grass at the rear.

"Will you all turn your attention to the garden again, please?" cried Holmes.

We all paused, looking to the right.

"Anything unusual?"

We were agreed that there was not.

"Very well," said my friend. "You will kindly note that from this point onward the formation of the ground prevents our obtaining any other view of Cray's Folly or its gardens until we reach the path to the valley, or turn on to the high road. From a point on the latter, the tower may be seen — but that is all. The first part of my experiment is concluded, gentlemen. We will now return."

Giving us no opportunity for comment, he plunged on in the direction of the stream and, at a point which I regarded as unnecessarily difficult, crossed it — to the great discomfiture of the heavy Inspector Aylesbury. A few minutes later, we found ourselves once more again in the grounds of Cray's Folly.

Holmes, evidently with a definite objective in view, led the way up the terraces, through the rhododendrons, and round the base of the tower. He crossed to the sunken garden and paused at the top of the steps.

"Be good enough to regard the sun-dial from this point," he directed.

Even as he spoke, I caught my breath, and I heard Aylesbury utter a sort of gasping sound.

Beyond the sun-dial and slightly to the left of it, viewed from where we stood, a faint, elfin light flickered, at a point apparently some four or five feet above the ground!

"What's this?" muttered Lestrade.

"Follow again, gentlemen," said Holmes quietly.

He led the way down to the garden and along the path to the sun-dial. This he passed, pausing immediately in front of the yew tree in which I knew the bullet to be embedded.

He did not speak, but, extending his finger, pointed.

A piece of candle, some four inches long, was attached by means of a nail to the bark of the tree, so that its flame burned immediately in front of the bullet embedded there!

For perhaps ten seconds no one spoke; indeed I think no one moved. Then:

"Good God!" murmured Lestrade. "You have done some clever things to my knowledge, Mr. Holmes, but this crowns them all."

"Clever things!" said Inspector Aylesbury. "I think it's a lot of damned tomfoolery."

"Do you, Inspector?" asked the Scotland Yard man, quietly. "I don't. I think it has saved the life of an innocent man."

"What's that? *What's that?*" cried Aylesbury.

"This candle was burning here on the yew tree," explained Holmes, "at the time that you looked out of the window of the hut. You could not see it. You could not see it from the crest adjoining the Guest House — the only other spot in the neighbourhood from which this garden is visible. Now, since the course of a bullet is more or less straight, and since the nature of the murdered man's wound proves that it was not deflected in any way, I submit that the one embedded in the yew tree here could not possibly have been fired from the Guest House! The second part of my experiment, gentlemen, will be designed to prove from whence it *was* fired."

33.

SHERLOCK HOLMES'S EXPERIMENT II

Up to the very moment that Sherlock Holmes, who had withdrawn, rejoined us in the garden, Inspector Aylesbury had not grasped the significance of that candle burning upon the yew tree. He continued to stare at it as if hypnotized, and when my friend re-appeared carrying a long ash staff and a sheet of cardboard, I could have laughed to witness the expression upon the Inspector's face, had I not been too deeply impressed with that which underlay this strange business.

Lestrade, on the other hand, was watching my friend eagerly, as an earnest student in the class-room might watch a demonstration by some celebrated lecturer.

"You will notice," said Sherlock Holmes, "that I have had a number of boards laid down upon the ground yonder, near the sun-dial. They cover a spot where the turf has worn very thin. Now, this garden, because of its sunken position, is naturally damp. Perhaps, Lestrade, you would take up these planks for me."

Inspector Lestrade obeyed, and Holmes, laying the ash stick and cardboard upon the ground, directed the ray of an electric torch upon the spot uncovered.

"The footprints of Colonel Menendez!" he explained. "Here he turned from the tiled path. He advanced three paces in the direction of the sun-dial, you observe, then stood still, facing we may suppose, since this is the indication of the prints, in a southerly direction."

"Straight toward the Guest House," muttered Inspector Aylesbury.

"Roughly," corrected Holmes. "He was fronting in that direction, certainly, but his head may have been turned either to the right or to the left. You observe from the great depth of the toe-marks that on this spot he actually fell. Then, here" — he moved the light — "is the impression of his knee, and here again — "

He shone the white ray upon a discoloured patch of grass, and then returned the lamp to his pocket.

"I am going to make a hole in the turf," he continued, "directly between these two footprints, which seem to indicate that the Colonel was standing in the military position of attention at the moment that he met his death."

With the end of the ash stick, which was pointed, Holmes proceeded to do this.

"Colonel Menendez," he went on, "stood rather over six feet in his shoes. The stick which now stands upright in the turf measures six feet, from the chalk mark up to which I have buried it to the slot which I have cut in the top. Into this slot I now wedge my sheet of cardboard."

As he placed the sheet of cardboard in the slot he had indicated, I saw that a round hole was cut in it some six inches in diameter. We watched these proceedings in silence, then:

"If you will allow me to adjust the candle, gentlemen," said Holmes, "which has burned a little too low for my purpose, I shall proceed to the second part of this experiment."

He walked up to the yew tree and, by means of bending the nail upward, he raised the flame of the candle level with the base of the embedded bullet.

"By Heavens!" cried Lestrade, suddenly divining the object of these proceedings, "Mr. Holmes, this is genius!"

"Thank you, Lestrade," Sherlock Holmes replied, quietly, but nevertheless he was unable to hide his gratification. "You see my point?"

"Certainly."

"In ten minutes we shall know the truth."

"Oh, I see," muttered Inspector Aylesbury. "We shall know the truth, eh? If you ask me the truth, it's this: that we are a set of lunatics."

"My dear Inspector Aylesbury," said Holmes good humouredly, "surely you have grasped the lesson of experiment number one?"

"Well," admitted the other, "it's funny, certainly. I mean, it wants a lot of explaining, but I can't say I'm convinced."

"That's a pity," murmured Lestrade, "because I am."

"You see, Inspector," Sherlock Holmes continued, patiently, "the body of Colonel Menendez as it lay formed a straight line between the sun-dial and the hut in the garden of the Guest House. That is to say: a line drawn from the window of the hut to the sun-dial must have passed through the body. Very well. Such an imaginary line, if continued *beyond* the sun-dial, would have terminated near the base of the *seventh* *yew* tree. Accordingly, I naturally looked for the *bullet* there. It was not there. But I found it, as you know, in the ninth tree. Therefore, the shot could not possibly have been fired from the Guest House, because the spot in the ninth yew where the bullet had lodged is not visible from the Guest House."

Inspector Aylesbury removed his cap and scratched his head vigorously.

"In order that we may avoid waste of valuable time," said Holmes, finally, "let us take a hasty observation from here. As a matter of fact, I have done so already, as nearly as was possible, without employing this rough apparatus."

He knelt down beside the yew tree, lowering his head so that the candlelight shone upon the aquiline, eager face, and looked upward — over the top of the sun-dial and through the hole in the cardboard.

"Yes," he muttered, a note of rising excitement in his voice. "As I thought, as I thought. Come, gentlemen, let us hurry."

He walked rapidly out of the garden and up the steps, whilst we followed dumb with wonder — or such at any rate was the cause of my own silence.

In the hall, Pedro was standing, a bunch of keys in his hand, and evidently expecting Holmes.

"Will you take us by the shortest way to the tower stairs?" my friend directed.

"Yes, sir."

Doubting, wondering, scarcely knowing whether to be fearful or jubilant, I followed, along a carpeted corridor, and thence, a heavy, oaken door being unlocked, across a dusty and deserted apartment apparently intended for a drawing room. From this, through a second doorway we were led into a small, square, unfurnished room which I knew must be situated in the base of the tower. Yet a third door was unlocked, and:

"Here is the stair, sir," said Pedro.

In single file, we mounted to the first floor, to find ourselves in a second, identical room, also stripped of furniture and decorations. Holmes barely glanced out of the northern window, shook his head, and:

"Next floor, Pedro," he directed.

Up we went, our footsteps arousing a cloud of dust from the uncarpeted stairs, and the sound of our movements echoing in hollow fashion around the deserted rooms.

Gaining the next floor, Holmes, unable any longer to conceal his excitement, ran to the north window, looked out, and:

"Gentlemen," he said, "my experiment is complete!"

He turned, his back to the window, and faced us in the dusk of the room.

"Assuming the ash stick to represent the upright body of Colonel Menendez," Holmes continued, "and the sheet of cardboard to represent his head, the hole which I have cut in it corresponds fairly nearly to the position of his forehead. Further assuming the bullet to have illustrated Euclid's definition of a straight line, such a line, *followed back* from the yew tree to the spot where the rifle rested, would pass through the hole in the cardboard! In other words, there is only one place from which it is possible to see the flame of the candle *through the hole in the cardboard:* the place where the rifle rested! Stand here in the left-hand angle of the window and stoop down! Will you come first, Watson?"

I stepped across the room, bent down, and stared out of the window across the Tudor garden. Plainly I could see the sundial with the ash stick planted before it. I could see the piece of cardboard which surmounted it — and, through the hole cut in the cardboard, I could see the feeble flame of the candle nailed to the ninth yew tree!

I stood upright, knowing that I had grown very pale, and conscious of a moist sensation upon my forehead.

"Merciful God!" I said in a hollow voice. "It was from *this window* that the shot was fired which killed him!"

34.

THE CREEPING SICKNESS

From the ensuing consultation in the library we did not rise until close upon midnight. To the turbid intelligence of Inspector Aylesbury, the fact by this time had penetrated that Colin Camber was innocent, that he was the victim of a frame-up, and that Colonel Juan Menendez had been shot from a window of his own house.

By a process of lucid reasoning which must have convinced a junior schoolboy, Sherlock Holmes, there in the big library, with its garish bookcases and its Moorish ornaments, had eliminated every member of the household from the list of suspects. His concluding words, as I remember, were as follows:

"Of the known occupants of Cray's Folly on the night of the tragedy we now find ourselves reduced to four, anyone of whom, from the point of view of an impartial critic uninfluenced by personal character, question, or motive, or any consideration other than that of physical possibility, might have shot Colonel Menendez. They are, firstly: Myself.

"In order to believe me guilty, it would be necessary to discount the evidence of Watson, who saw me on the gravel path below at the time that the shot was fired from the tower window.

"Secondly: Watson; whose guilt, equally, could only be assumed by means of eliminating *my* evidence, since I saw him at the window of my room at the time that the shot was fired.

"Thirdly: Madame de Stämer. Regarding this suspect: in the first place, she could not have gained access to the tower room without assistance, and in the second place she was so passionately devoted to the late Colonel Menendez that Dr. Rolleston is of opinion that her reason may remain permanently impaired by the shock of his death. Fourthly and lastly: Miss Val Beverley."

Over my own feelings, as he had uttered the girl's name, I must pass in silence.

"Miss Val Beverley is the only one of the four suspects who is not in a position to establish a sound alibi so far as I can see at the moment; but in this case, entire absence of motive renders the suspicion absurd. Having dealt with the *known* occupants, I shall not touch upon the possibility that some stranger had gained access to the house. This opens up a province of speculation which we must explore at greater leisure, for it would be profitless to attempt such an exploration now."

Thus the gathering had broken up, Inspector Aylesbury returning to Market Hilton to make his report and to release Colin Camber and Ah Tsong, and leaving Lestrade to seek his quarters at the Lavender Arms.

I remember that, having seen them off, Holmes and I stood in the hall staring at one another in a very odd way, and so we stood when Val Beverley came quietly from Madame de Stämer's room and spoke to us.

"Pedro has told me what you have done, Mr. Holmes," she said in a low voice. "Oh, thank God you have cleared him. But what in Heaven's name does your new discovery mean?"

"You may well ask," Holmes answered, grimly. "If my first task was a hard one, that which remains before me looks more nearly hopeless than anything I have ever been called upon to attempt."

"It is horrible, *it is horrible !*" said the girl, shudderingly. "Oh, Dr. Watson," she turned to me, "I have felt all along that there was some stranger in the house — "

"You have told me so."

"Conundrums! *Conundrums !*" muttered Holmes, irritably. "Where am I to begin, upon what am I to erect any feasible theory?"

He turned abruptly to Val Beverley. "Does Madame de Stämer know?"

"Yes," she answered, nodding her head; "and hearing the others depart, she asked me to tell you that sleep is impossible until you have personally given her the details of your discovery."

"She wishes to see me?" asked Holmes, eagerly.

"She insists upon seeing you," replied the girl, "and also requests Dr. Watson to visit her." She paused, biting her lip. "Madame's manner is very, very odd. Dr. Rolleston cannot understand her at all. I expect he has told you? She has been sitting there for hours and hours, writing."

"Writing?" exclaimed Holmes. "Letters?"

"I don't know what she has been writing," confessed Val Beverley. "She declines to tell me, or to show me what she has written. But there is quite a little stack of manuscript upon the table beside her bed. Won't you come in?"

I could see that she was more troubled than she cared to confess, and I wondered if Dr. Rolleston's unpleasant suspicions might have solid foundation, and if the loss of her cousin had affected Madame de Stämer's brain.

Presently then, ushered by Val Beverley, I found myself once more in the violet-and-silver room in which on that great bed of state Madame reclined amid silken pillows. Her art never deserted her, not even in moments of ultimate stress, and that she had prepared herself for this interview was evident enough.

I had thought previously that one night of horror had added five years to her apparent age. I thought now that she looked radiantly beautiful. That expression in her eyes, which I knew I must forevermore associate with the memory of the dying tigress, had faded entirely. They remained still as of old, but to-night they were velvety soft. The lips were relaxed in a smile of tenderness. I observed, with surprise, that she wore much jewelery, and upon her white bosom gleamed the famous rope of pearls which I knew her to treasure above almost anything in her possession.

Again the fear touched me coldly that much sorrow had made her mad. But at her very first word of greeting, I was immediately reassured.

"Ah, my friend," she said, as I entered, a caressing note in her deep, vibrant voice, "you have great news, they tell me? Mr. Holmes, I was afraid that you had deserted me, sir. If you had done so, I should have been very angry with you. Set the two armchairs here on my right, Val, dear, and sit close beside me."

Then, as we seated ourselves:

"You are not smoking, my friends," she continued, "and I know that you are both so fond of a smoke."

Sherlock Holmes excused himself, but I accepted a cigarette which Val Beverley offered me from a silver box on the table, and presently:

"I am here, like a prisoner of the Bastille," declared Madame, shrugging her shoulders, "where only echoes reach me. Now, Mr. Holmes, tell me of this wonderful discovery of yours."

Holmes inclined his head gravely, and in that succinct fashion which he had at command acquainted Madame with the result of his two experiments. As he completed the account:

"Ah," she sighed, and lay back upon her pillows. "So tonight he is again a free man, the poor Colin Camber. And his wife is happy once more?"

"Thank God," I murmured. "Her sorrow was pathetic."

"Only the pure in heart can thank God," said Madame, strangely, "but I too am glad. I have written, here" — she pointed to a little heap of violet note-paper upon a table placed at the opposite side of the bed — "how glad I am."

Holmes and I stared vaguely across at the table. I saw Val Beverley glancing uneasily in the same direction. Save for the writing materials and little heap of manuscript, it held only a cup and saucer, a few sandwiches, and a medicine bottle containing the prescription which Dr. Rolleston had made up for the invalid.

"I am curious to know what you have written, Madame," declared Holmes.

"Yes, you are curious?" she said. "Very well, then, I will tell you, and afterward you may read if you wish." She turned to me. "You, my friend ... "she whispered, and reaching over she laid her jewelled hand upon my arm, "you have spoken with Ysola de Valera this afternoon, they tell me?"

"With Mrs. Camber?" I asked, startled. "Yes, that is true."

"Ah, Mrs. Camber," murmured Madame. "I knew her as Ysola de Valera. She is beautiful, in her golden doll way. You think so?"

Then, ere I had time to reply: "She told you, I suppose, eh?"

"She told me," I replied with a certain embarrassment, "that she had met you some years ago in Cuba."

"Ah, yes, although *I* told the fat Inspector it was not so. How we lie, we women! And of course she told you in what relation I stood to Juan Menendez?"

"She did not, Madame de Stämer."

"No-no? Well, it was nice of her. No matter. *I* will tell you. I was his mistress."

She spoke without bravado, but quite without shame, seeming to glory in the statement.

"I met him in Paris," she continued, half-closing her eyes. "I was staying at the house of my sister; and my sister, you understand, was married to Juan's cousin. That is how we met. I was married. Yes, it is true. But in France, our parents find our husbands and our lovers find our hearts. Yet sometimes these marriages are happy. To me, this good thing had not happened; and in the moment when Juan's hand touched mine, a living fire entered into my heart and it has been burning ever since; burning-burning, always till I die.

"Very well, I am a shameless woman, yes. But I have lived, and I have loved, and I am content. I went with him to Cuba, and from Cuba to another island where he had estates, and the name of which I shall not pronounce, because it hurts me so, even yet. There he set eyes upon Ysola de Valera, the daughter of his manager, and *pouf!*"

She shrugged and snapped her fingers.

"He was like that, you understand? I knew it well. They did not call him Devil Menendez for nothing. There was a scene, a dreadful scene, and after that another, and yet a third. I have pride. If I had seemed to forget it, still it was there. I left him and went back to France. I tried to forget. I entered upon works of charity for the soldiers at a time when others were becoming tired. I spent a great part of my fortune upon establishing a hospital, and this child" — she threw her arm around Val Beverley — "worked with me night and day. I think I wanted to die. Often I tried to die. Did I not, Dear?"

"You did, Madame," said the girl in a very low voice.

"Twice I was arrested in the French lines, where I had crept dressed like a *poilu*, from where I shot down many a Prussian. Is it not so?"

"It is true," answered the girl, nodding her head.

"They caught me and arrested me," said Madame, with a sort of triumph. "If it had been the British" — she raised her hand in that Bernhardt gesture — "with me it would have gone hard. But in France, a woman's smile goes farther than in England. I'd had my fun. They called me 'good comrade!' Perhaps I paid with a kiss. What does it matter? But they heard of me, those Prussian dogs. They knew and could not forgive. How often did they come over to bomb us, Val, dear?"

"Oh, many, many times," said the girl, shudderingly.

"And at last they succeeded," added Madame, bitterly. "God! The foul villains! Let me not think of it."

She clenched her hands and closed her eyes entirely, but presently resumed again:

"If they had killed me, I should have been glad; but they only made of me a cripple. Monsieur de Stämer had been killed a few weeks before this. I am sorry, I forgot to mention it. I was a widow. And when after this catastrophe I could be moved, I went to a little villa belonging to my husband at Nice, to gain strength, and this child came with me, like a ray of sunshine.

"Here, to wake the fire in my heart, came Juan — deserted, broken, wounded in soul, but most of all wounded in pride, in that evil pride which belongs to his race, which is so different from the pride of France, but for which all the same I could never hate him.

"Ysola de Valera had run away from his great house in Cuba. Yes! A woman had dared to leave him, the man who had left so many women. To me it was pathetic. I was sorry for him. He had been searching the world for her. He loved this little golden-haired girl as he had never loved me. But to me he came with his broken heart, and I ... " — her voice trembled — "I took him back. He still cared for me, you understand. Ah!" She laughed. "I am not a woman who is lightly forgotten. But the great passion that burned in his Spanish soul was revenge.

"He was a broken man not only in mind, but in body. Let me tell you. In that island which I have not named, there is a horrible disease called by the natives the Creeping Sickness. It is supposed to come from a poisonous place named the Black Belt, and a part of this Black Belt is near, too near, to the *haçienda* in which Juan sometimes lived."

Sherlock Holmes started and glanced at me significantly.

"They think, those simple natives, that it is witchcraft — Voodoo, the work of the Obeah man. It is of two kinds, rapid and slow. Those who suffer from the first kind just decline and decline and die in great agony. Others recover, or seem to do so. It is, I suppose, a matter of constitution. Juan had had this sickness and had recovered, or so the doctors said, but, ah!"

She lay back, shaking her finger characteristically.

"In one year, in two, in three, a swift pain comes, like a needle, you understand? Perhaps in the foot, in the hand, in the arm. It is exquisite, deathly, while it lasts; but it only lasts for a few moments. It is agony. And then it goes, leaving nothing to show what has caused it. But, my friends, it is a death warning!

"If it comes here" — she raised one delicate white hand — "you may have five years to live; if in the foot, ten or more. But" — she sank her voice dramatically — "the nearer it is to the heart, the less are the days that remain to you of life."

"You mean that it recurs?" asked Holmes.

"Perhaps in a week, perhaps not for another year, it comes again, that quick agony. This time in the shoulder, in the knee. It is the second warning. Three times it may come, four times, but at last ... " — she laid her hand upon her breast — "it comes here, in the heart, and all is finished."

She paused as if exhausted, closing her eyes again, whilst we three who listened looked at one another in an awestricken silence, until the vibrant voice resumed:

"There is only one man in Europe who understands this thing, this Creeping Sickness. He is a Frenchman who lives in Paris. To him Juan had been, and he had told him, this clever man, 'If you are very quiet and do not exert yourself, and only take as much exercise as is necessary for your general health, you have one year to live — ' "

"My God!" groaned Holmes.

"Yes, such was the verdict. And there is no cure. The poor sufferer must wait and wait, always wait, for that sudden pang, not knowing if it will come in his heart and be the finish. Yes. This living death, then — and revenge — were the things ruling Juan's life at the time of which I tell you. He had traced Ysola de Valera to England. A chance remark in a London hotel told him that a Chinaman had been seen in a Surrey village, and of course had caused much silly chatter. He enquired at once, and he found out that Colin Camber, the man who had taken Ysola from him, was living with her at the Guest House here on the hill. How shall I tell you the rest?"

"Merciful Heaven!" exclaimed Holmes, his glance set upon her, with a sort of horror in his gray eyes. "I think I can guess."

She turned to him rapidly.

"M. Holmes," she said, "you are a clever man. I believe you are a genius. And I have the strength to tell you because I am happy to-night. Because of his great wealth, Juan succeeded in buying Cray's Folly from Sir James Appleton to whom it belonged. He told everybody he leased it, but really he bought it. He paid him more than twice its value, and so obtained possession.

"But the plan was not yet complete, although it had taken form in that clever, wicked brain of his. Oh! I could tell you stories of the Menendez, and of the things they have done for love and revenge which even you, who know much of life, would doubt, I think. Yes, you would not believe. But to continue. Shall I tell you upon what terms he had returned to me, eh? I will. Once more, he would suffer that pang of death in life, for he had courage — ah, such great courage! — and then, when the waiting for the next grew more than even his fearless heart could bear, I who also had courage and who loved him, should — " She paused, "Do you understand?"

Holmes nodded dumbly, and suddenly I found Miss Val Beverley's little fingers twined about mine.

"I agreed," continued the woman's deep voice. "It was a boon which I, too, would have asked from one who loved me. But to die knowing another cherished the woman who had been torn from him was an impossibility for Juan Menendez. What he had schemed to do at first I never knew. But presently, because of our situation here, and because of that which he had asked of me, it came — the great plan.

"On the night he told me, a night I shall never forget, I drew back in horror from him — I, Marie de Stämer, who thought I knew the darkest that was in him. I shrank. And because of that scene, it came to him again in the early morning — the moment of agony, the needle pain, here, low down in his left breast.

"He pleaded with me to do the wicked thing that he had planned, and because I dared not refuse, knowing he might die at my feet, I consented. But, my friends, I had my own plan, too, of which he knew nothing. On the next day he went to Paris, and was told he had two months to live, with great, such great care, but perhaps only a week, a day, if he should permit his hot passions to inflame that threatened heart. Very well.

"I said yes, yes, to all that he suggested, and he began to lay the trail — the trail to lead to his enemy. It was his hobby, this vengeance. He was like a big, cruel boy. It was he, himself, Juan Menendez, who broke into Cray's Folly. It was he who nailed the bat wing to the door. It was he who bought two rifles of a kind of which so many millions were made during the war that anybody might possess one. And it was he who concealed the first of these, one cartridge discharged, under the floor of the hut in the garden of the Guest House. The other, which was to be used, he placed — "

"In the shutter-case of one of the tower rooms," continued Sherlock Holmes. "I know! I found it there to-night."

"What?" I asked, "you found it, Holmes?"

"I returned to look for it," he said. "At the present moment, it is upstairs in my room."

"Ah, Monsieur Holmes," exclaimed Madame, smiling at him radiantly, "I love your genius. Then it was," she continued, "that he thought himself ready, ready for revenge and ready for death. He summoned you, Monsieur Holmes, to be an expert witness. He placed with you evidence which could not fail to lead to the arrest of Monsieur Camber. Very well. I allowed him to do all this. His courage, *mon Dieu !* How I worshipped his courage!

"At night, when everyone slept, and he could drop the mask, I have seen what he suffered. I have begged him, begged him upon my knees, to allow me to end it then and there; to forget his dream of revenge, to die without this last stain upon his soul. But he, expecting at any hour, at any minute, to know again the agony which cannot be described, which is unlike any other suffered by the flesh — refused, *refused!* And I ..." she raised her eyes ecstatically "I have worshipped this courage of his, although it was evil — bad.

"The full moon gives the best light, and so he planned it for the night of the full moon. But on the night before, because of some scene which he had with you, Monsieur Holmes, I nearly thought his plans would come to nothing. Nearly I thought the last act of love which he asked of me would never be performed. He sat there, up in the little room which he liked best, the coldness upon him which always came before the pang, waiting, waiting, a deathly dew on his forehead, for the end; and I — I who loved him better than life — watched him. And, so Fate willed it, the pang never came."

"You watched him?" I whispered.

Holmes turned to me slowly.

"Don't you understand, Watson?" he said, in a voice curiously unlike his own.

"Ah, my friend," Madame de Stämer laid her hand upon my arm with that caressing gesture which I knew. "You do understand, don't you? The power to use my limbs returned to me during the last week that I lived in Nice."

She bent forward and raised her face, in an almost agonized appeal to Val Beverley.

"My dear, my dear," she said, "forgive me, forgive me! But I loved him so. One day, I think" — her glance sought my face — "you will know. Then you will forgive."

"Oh, Madame, Madame," whispered the girl, and began to sob silently.

"Is it enough?" asked Madame de Stämer, raising her head, and looking defiantly at Sherlock Holmes. "Last night you, Monsieur Holmes, who have genius, nearly brought it all to nothing. You passed the door in the shrubbery just when Juan was preparing to go out. I was watching from the window above. Then when you had gone, he came out — smoking his last cigarette.

"I went to my place, entering the tower room by the door from that corridor. I opened the window. It had been carefully oiled. It was soundless. I was cold as one already dead, but love made me strong. I had seen him suffer. I took the rifle from its hiding-place, the heavy rifle which so few women could use. It was no heavier than some which I had used before, and to good purpose."

Again she paused, and I saw her lips trembling. Before my mind's eye, the picture arose which I had seen from Holmes's window, the picture of Colonel Juan Menendez walking in the moonlight along the path to the sun-dial with halting steps, with clenched fists, but upright as a soldier on parade. Walking on, dauntlessly, to his execution. Out of a sort of haze, which seemed to obscure both sight and hearing, I heard Madame speaking again.

"He turned his head toward me. He threw me a kiss — and I fired. Did you think a woman lived who could perform such a deed, eh? If you did not think so, it is because you have never looked into the eyes of one who loved with her body, her mind, and with her soul. I think, yes, I think I went mad. The rifle — I remember I replaced it. But I remember no more. Ah!"

She sighed in a resigned, weary way, untwining her arm from about Val Beverley, and falling back upon her pillows.

"It is all written here," she said. "Every word of it, my friends, and signed at the bottom. I am a murderess, but it was a merciful deed. You see, I had a plan of which Juan knew nothing. This was my plan."

She pointed to the heap of manuscript.

"I would give him relief from his agonies, yes. For although he was an evil man, I loved him better than life. I would let him die happy, thinking his revenge complete. But others to suffer? No, no! A thousand times no! Ah, I am so tired."

She took up the little medicine bottle, poured its contents into the glass, and emptied it at a draught.

Sherlock Holmes, as though galvanized, sprang to his feet. "My God!" he cried, huskily, "Stop her, stop her!" Val Beverley, now desperately white, clutched at me with quivering fingers, her agonized glance set upon the smiling face of Madame de Stämer.

"No fuss, dear friends," said Madame, gently, "no trouble, no nasty stomach-pumps; for it is useless. I shall just fall asleep in a few moments now; and when I wake, Juan will be with me."

Her face was radiant. It became lighted up magically. I knew in that grim hour what a beautiful woman Madame de Stämer must have been. She rested her hand upon Val Beverley's head, and looked at me with her strange, still eyes.

"Be good to her, my friend," she whispered. "She is English, but not cold like some. She, too, can love."

She closed her eyes and dropped back upon her pillows for the last time.

34.

AN AFTERWORD

This shall be a brief afterword, for I have little else to say. As Madame had predicted, all antidotes and restoratives were of no avail. She had taken enough of some drug, which she had evidently had in her possession for this very purpose, to ensure that there should be no awakening; and although Dr. Rolleston was on the spot within half an hour, Madame de Stämer was already past human aid.

There are perhaps one or two details which may be of interest. For instance, as a result of the post-mortem examination of Colonel Menendez, no trace of disease was discovered in any of the organs, but from information supplied by his solicitors, Holmes succeeded in tracing the Paris specialist to whom Madame de Stämer had referred; and he confirmed her statement in every particular. The disease, to which he gave some name which I have forgotten, was untraceable, he declared, by any means thus far known to science.

As we had anticipated, the bulk of Colonel Don Juan's wealth he had bequeathed to Madame de Stämer, and she in turn had provided that all of which she might die possessed should be divided between certain charities and Val Beverley.

I thus found myself at the time when all these legal processes terminated, engaged to marry a girl less than half my age, as wealthy as she was beautiful. Therefore, except for the many grim memories which it had left with me, nothing but personal good fortune resulted from my sojourn at Cray's Folly, beneath the shadow of that Bat Wing which had had no existence outside the cunning imagination of Colonel Juan Menendez.

THE END

EDITOR'S NOTES

In the late 1800s and early 1900s, at the peak of Sherlock Holmes' popularity, a number of writers wrote their own mystery stories that were in many ways similar to Holmes. Many of Sax Rohmer's little-known stories read, but for the names and places, almost exactly like Arthur Conan Doyle's original Sherlock Holmes stories — in fact, much of the language is more like the original Holmes canon than most stories written by modern authors. Rohmer was also a much better writer than many of the other "Rivals of Sherlock Holmes" authors.

The editor of this volume has carefully edited some of Rohmer's best Chinatown tales into Sherlock Holmes pastiches. The stories are set during the time and after Holmes's retirement to keep bees on the Susex Downs.

Many modern authors have attempted to recapture the nostalgic mood of gaslit London and the mystique of Conan Doyle's adventures of Sherlock Holmes by writing "new" Holmes stories; yet these attempts frequently fail to capture the original flavor of the Conan Doyle tales because modern writers simply don't think or speak like Victorians.

In the late 1800s and early 1900s, at the peak of Sherlock Holmes' popularity, a number of mystery writers wrote stories of their own which were in many ways similar to Sherlock Holmes. Conan Doyle's contemporaries wrote characters of their own invention; nevertheless they sound more like Conan Doyle than do any writers today.

Many of Sax Rohmer's little-known stories read, but for the names and places, almost exactly like Arthur Conan Doyle's

Sherlock Holmes tales — in fact, much of the language is more like the original Holmes canon than stories written by any other author.

Unlike Sir Arthur's modern imitators, Sax Rohmer wrote stories at the time Conan Doyle was at the peak of his popularity; and there is a ring of authenticity in Rohmer's narratives that modern imitators are lacking. Sax Rohmer was also a much better writer than many of the other contemporary "Rivals of Sherlock Holmes" authors.

The editor of this volume has carefully revised some of Rohmer's best Chinatown tales into Sherlock Holmes pastiches. These stories are set after Holmes' return from his retirement to assist the British Government in the WWI era.

— Alan Lance Andersen

Pastiches

After the invention of the detective mystery format in 1841 by Edgar Allan Poe, there were a large number of Victorian and Edwardian writers in both England and America who began writing detective mystery stories — for this was the era when Arthur Conan Doyle was creating Sherlock Holmes tales on a regular basis in *Strand* Magazine. And detective stories were very profitable financially. Many of the "period" writers intentionally imitated Conan Doyle's characters and story formula.

Modern authors from John Dickson Carr to Nicholas Meyer and Steven Philip Jones have attempted to recapture the mood of gaslit London and the mystique of Conan Doyle's adventures of Sherlock Holmes by writing "new" Holmes novels and short stories; yet these attempts frequently fail to capture the original flavor of the Conan Doyle tales, because modern writers simply don't think or speak like Victorians.

On the other hand, Conan Doyle's contemporaries — such mystery authors as Robert Eustace, L.T. Meade, Clifford Halifax, Sax Rohmer, and Richard Harding Davis — were writing about characters of their own invention; nevertheless they sound more like Conan Doyle than do any of his deliberate modern imitators. One of the more successful of these "period" writers was Sax Rohmer, whose stories were as familiar to readers of *Colliers* Magazine as the Sherlock Holmes was to *Strand*.

Unlike Sir Arthur's modern imitators, Sax Rohmer wrote his stories at the time Conan Doyle was at the peak of his popularity; and there is a ring of authenticity in Rohmer's narratives that modern imitatorsare lacking. Originally, Rohmer's stories used different character names — due to Conan Doyle's copyright protection. But now in 2016, both Sax Rohmer's stories and the Sherlock Holmes canon are all in the public domain. Thus it is now possible to present ... Sax Rohmer's version of Sherlock Holmes. The editor of this volume has carefully edited some of Rohmer's best mystery tales into Sherlock Holmes pastiches.

Literary historian John Kennedy Melling, author of *Murder Done to Death: A Survey of Parody and Pastiche in Crime Fiction,* says of *The Affairs of Sherlock Holmes*:

"Writing pastiches successfully involves loving your subject and his life and knowing every detail of his world. The editor of this book has experience in radio, conjuring, and interactive theatre — which ensures that these stories will intrigue new readers without upsetting original Sherlock Holmes aficionados. In THE AFFAIRS OF SHERLOCK HOLMES, the adaptation of Sax Rohmer's larger-than-life characters and distinctive style to the Sherlock Holmes purview triumphantly fills the pages of this intriguing book."

— Alan Lance Andersen

SAX ROHMER

(Born: February 15, 1883 – Died: June 1, 1959).

Sax Rohmer was the pen name of Arthur Henry Sarsfield Ward He worked as a poet, songwriter, and comedy sketch writer in Music Halls before creating the Sax Rohmer persona and pursuing a career writing weird fiction.

In 1911, Rohmer's first "Fu Manchu" novel, *The Mystery of Dr. Fu-Manchu*, was published, along with magazine serialization from October 1912 to June 1913. It was an immediate success, with its fast-paced story of Denis Nayland Smith and Dr. Petrie facing the worldwide conspiracy of the 'Yellow Peril.'

The Fu Manchu stories — together with his more conventional detective series characters: Paul Harley, Gaston Max, Red Kerry, The Crime Magnet, and Morris Klaw (an occult detective) — made Rohmer one of the most successful and well-paid authors of the 1920s and 1930s.

Rohmer was friends with Harry Houdini and based his crime-solving magician Bazarada on the great escape artist. Rohmer included a fictionalized version of the infamous Aleister Crowley as the arch-villain in one Bazarada story.

Rohmer's meeting and romantic love affair with long-suffering Rose Elizabeth Knox, who became his wife after a year-long star-crossed love misadventure, would make a marvelous subject for motion pictures or novel.

Also from MX Publishing

MX Publishing is the world's largest specialist Sherlock Holmes publisher, with over two hundred titles and one hundred authors creating the latest in Sherlock Holmes fiction and non-fiction.

From traditional short stories and novels to travel guides and quiz books, MX Publishing cater for all Holmes fans.

The collection includes leading titles such as *Benedict Cumberbatch In Transition* and *The Norwood Author* which won the 2011 Howlett Award (Sherlock Holmes Book of the Year).

MX Publishing also has one of the largest communities of Holmes fans on Facebook with regular contributions from dozens of authors.

www.mxpublishing.com

Also from MX Publishing

The Missing Authors Series

Sherlock Holmes and The Adventure of The Grinning Cat
Sherlock Holmes and The Nautilus Adventure
Sherlock Holmes and The Round Table Adventure

"Joseph Svec, III is brilliant in entwining two endearing and enduring classics of literature, blending the factual with the fantastical; the playful with the pensive; and the mischievous with the mysterious. We shall, all of us young and old, benefit with a cup of tea, a tranquil afternoon, and a copy of Sherlock Holmes, The Adventure of the Grinning Cat."
Amador County Holmes Hounds Sherlockian Society

www.mxpublishing.com

www.ingramcontent.com/pod-product-compliance
Lightning Source LLC
Chambersburg PA
CBHW060813030726
47503CB00002B/469